SIX YEARS

Unfrozen Four Series
Book Four

Six Years
Copyright © 2023 Joelina Falk

All rights reserved. No part of this publication may be reproduced, distributed, or transmitted in any form without written permission of the publisher, except for brief passages by a reviewer for review purpose only.

This is a work of fiction. All names, characters, locations, and incidents are a product of the author's imagination and used fictitiously. Any resemblance to actual persons, events, or things—living or dead—is entirely coincidental.

Copy Editing: Kayla Morton

You can find me here:

http://www.joelinafalk.com/
https://www.instagram.com/authorjoelinafalk/

Content Warning

This book contains topics which may be triggering for some readers.

For a full list, please head over to:

https://www.joelinafalk.com/six-years-content-warnings

To those who ever felt like they didn't belong;
Fuck the norm and be whoever **you** *want to be.*

PLAYLIST

or click *here*.

Enchanted — Taylor Swift ♡

Parents — YUNGBLOOD ♡

A Sky Full Of Stars — Coldplay ♡

Stupid Feelings — 220 KID, LANY ♡

Contact — Jordan Fisher ♡

Summer Of Love — Shawn Mendes, Tainy ♡

You Need To Calm Down — Taylor Swift ♡

Beautiful Scars — Maximillian ♡

Almost Is Never Enough — Ariana Grande, Nathan Sykes ♡

Undrunk — FLETCHER ♡

Island Time — Dan + Shay ♡

A Million Dreams — P!NK ♡

Chapter 1

"what if I flipped our whole world upside down?"—Kesi – Remix by Camilo, Shawn Mendes

June 2022

He reached a hand into my pants, feeling my wet—

Nope.

I press the off button on my phone and look up toward the sea, wondering what the fuck I've just read.

It's dark outside and I haven't even noticed. My first day back in Malibu and I have fucked up already, just great.

My father celebrates his fiftieth birthday in a few days, hence why I am here. If I missed my father's birthday, he'd loathe me even more than he does now, though I guess missing our family dinner isn't any better.

To be honest, I think he'd be happier if I didn't show up *at all*.

I do love El Matador Beach though, so at least there's that. It's the only reason being here is bearable, and my sister's presence. Even as a kid I used to sneak out to the beach and just lay on the sand, watch the waves as they reached the shore, listen to the sounds, and tune out the world. Nothing would've happened to me unless I decided to get in the water, so my parents never cared much about me being out here. Even late at night, nothing would've happened. We have a private beach that came with the house.

Now that I am older, I no longer hang around our private beach. In fact, I am anywhere *but* in sight of our house.

As much as I love my family, I'd rather not be around them too long which is exactly why I am *so* glad I can leave and go back to New York in a month. Back to my friends. Back to the people who accept me for who I am. And back to playing ice hockey.

"Why'd you turn off your phone? It was just getting interesting." A deep voice speaks from right behind me. I flinch at the sudden appearance, but quickly shake off the shock before I lean my neck back to look up, finding a curly headed guy stare down at me.

"Do you always look at strangers' phones?"

The guy walks around me, taking a seat on the sand beside me. "Only those who I believe look lonely and could use a friend."

I huff unfazed. I've been called my fair share of words in my life before. Reaching from racist insults to homophobic slurs, anything but something that isn't an attack against *me* in general. Well, I guess insults are supposed to attack, but there's a difference between *insults* and being a racist and homophobic asshole. But my point is, I've been called *many* things before, none of those words were *lonely*.

I am not lonely, per se. I have *three* best friends, very great ones, too. One of whom I would give my life for if it saved his. And his daughter is pretty adorable as well, so that's his bonus. With those three guys in my life, there's not *one* single second I could ever feel lonely because there's always something happening.

In New York City.

Now that I am back in Malibu, back where I've got no one but my sister to talk to, perhaps curly head is right. I am lonely.

But that doesn't give him the right to look at my phone without my permission. Who even does that?

"I'm Luan," he says and holds out his hand for me to shake. I don't take it. "Okayyyy." He pulls back his hand slowly, awkwardly, yet still keeps a grin on his face. "So, are you from around here?"

"No." Technically, I am. I grew up here, but I don't live here anymore, so that's a no, right?

"You're on vacation then?" I nod. "Alone?"

"No."

Miles, my number one best friend, will be in Malibu next week. It's just for a few days and only because Emory—his wife—wants to see the beach art gallery but a win is a win. He'll fill in at least three days of my life without me having to exchange a single word with my family. I seriously can't wait for all three of them to show up here.

They won't stay with me, but as soon as they get a hotel room, I might just stay there with them. I'd do anything to get away from my father, even spend a few nights in a hotel room together with my best friend, his wife, and his daughter.

"So, why are you alone by the beach then?" Luan asks. I internally roll my eyes. "At night."

I don't have a problem with people, but I do like them to keep their distance from me. Eighteen-year-old Grey was different to twenty-one—almost twenty-two—year-old me. At the age of eighteen, I loved meeting people. I was more open to meeting them, hence why I somehow found three idiotic best friends. Now, I'm happy to stay as far away from everyone as humanly possible. That excludes Miles, Aaron, and Colin though.

People are cruel and I'd rather not go through more heartbreaks.

Once upon a time, I loved *Love*. It was a time where I used to jump *heart* first and not care about how deep I was falling.

Now I keep the people I have close, and the rest can fuck off.

"Enjoying the silence," I answer, side-eying Luan. "But someone's making it really hard to enjoy the silence while talking."

"Ah, well." He shrugs like he doesn't *care* about what I've insinuated. "What book were you reading?"

Book?

Oh. Right. *The* book I was reading which made Luan talk to me because I turned off my phone.

"A friend wrote it." I don't exactly consider Sofia a *friend*. She's Aaron's girlfriend and although she seems to be quite fun, I barely ever talked to her, and it's been almost six months since she's been around. Sure, we hang around each other a lot, and if she called me out of the blue and said she needed my help, I'd run to help her, but that's just being kind, isn't it? I am not actively trying to get to know my friend's girlfriend. Emory's a whole other story since we've lived in the same house for a few months.

"Well, they're freaky. What's the name of the book? I want to buy it."

"I don't know." I don't think Sofia even came up with a book title yet. Aaron asked me to read it so I could give honest feedback because Sofia believes Aaron would tell her it's great no matter what. She's right, of course, but he'd never admit that.

Luan hums, probably due to my lack of helpful answers. "My ex-boyfriend used to write poetry, but he was really bad at it. I'm not just bashing him because he cheated on me or something, he was genuinely so bad at it. He tried to rhyme "chaos" with "Laos," which, yes, kind of works, but the whole poem had *nothing* to do with Laos. He only used it because he couldn't think of anything else. I think he went something like: *the pain in my heart is in such chaos, now fly with me to Laos*."

I sigh heavily. He reminds me of my sister. Sun, too, talks a lot and doesn't know when to stop. It's kind of refreshing to find out there's not only this eighteen-year-old girl who shares the same DNA as me having this weird urge to fill silence with unnecessary conversation.

Nonetheless, I get up. Apparently I have two choices; stay and listen to some stranger whom I have no interest in or go back home and listen to my sister tell me all about whatever she wants to talk about. I choose the latter.

"Are you going to the beach party tomorrow?" Luan comes running after me. Can't he take a fucking hint? "You'll find it pretty easily." He points toward where people already start to build up a stage, probably for some live entertainment.

He's persistent, I can give Luan that much.

I stop in my tracks, now looking at Luan for the first time. *Really* looking at him. He's got bright eyes, so it looks, but I'm not sure. It's a little too dark to be able to tell. It could be green or blue, maybe a very light brown. But I'm certain his hair is a dark brown with a *lot* of curls. The hairs on his sides are shorter than the top of his head, like most guys wear it. He's got a fit body, defined muscles. His skin glows, the water drops reflecting from the moonlight. His nose is surprisingly small for someone his size, and his lips full. He's a whole lot of confusion at once.

He also seems to be around my age, maybe a little younger, maybe a year older, I can't tell. The choice of his tie-dye swimming trunks also doesn't give me an answer to that question.

Luan has a yellow shirt draped over one shoulder instead of wearing it, but since his skin is still covered in water drops, I suppose he had just gotten out of the water before he walked up to me.

How didn't I notice him?

"Maybe," I eventually answer. I don't have anything else to do, so I might as well stop by and check it out.

"I will be waiting for you, stranger." Luan winks and then *finally* takes the hint. He turns around and starts walking away.

I don't know what comes over me, but before I even know, words leave my mouth loud enough for him to hear. "I'm Grey."

Chapter 2

"you're more than a sunshine in my mind"—Sunroof by Nicky Youre, dazy

Luan

June 2022

GREY.

I keep looking around, trying to spot him somewhere. How is it so difficult to find a six-foot-four guy with black hair and tattoos around here?

"He never *confirmed* he would come," Dorothy-Jane, my best friend in the whole wide world, reminds me, laying her hand on my shoulder.

Doro is the only person who always stuck with me despite everything. Through middle school when kids called me names for no reason, she would always throw her lunch at them, then proceed to eat mine instead. Or in high school when I had my first boyfriend and he broke up with me, that blonde evil girl went behind my back and toilet-papered that guy's house because he broke my heart. And then in College, when my newest ex-boyfriend cheated on me, Doro went and slept with his new boyfriend just to get back at my ex.

She's the only one I trust a hundred percent with everything. Especially with making sure I don't humiliate myself. Before that happens, this woman would throw me into the ocean to drown.

"Do you know where he's staying? I can go there and do… something."

I almost laugh at that. "You can't beat him out of his own hotel room just so he'd meet me here. Plus, he said he wasn't alone in Malibu, so maybe he has a friend he travels with. A *girl*friend, even."

Doro hums for a whole second, thinking. "Nope. No guy would leave his girlfriend behind in a hotel to sit *alone* by the beach at night."

"How do you know that?"

She shrugs. "I don't, but if one does, he's not worth it." Doro wraps both of her hands around my arm, shaking me like I've just signed up for a carousel ride or something. "How do you even know he's gay?" She gasps, *loudly*. "What if he didn't understand you were trying to invite him on a date?"

"It's called the *gay-intuition*." Mine is never wrong. Okay, rarely. Mostly… Almost always. God, I am not good at this dating thing. I lean forward and hit my head on the wooden countertop of the bar. "Urgh. I've known him for a whole five minutes, Doro. What the hell am I doing?"

I lift my head only to let it drop down against the wood one more time. "I am so stupid."

"You're not stupid," a manly voice I've had yet to hear says. "Though, if you dent the wood, I will take that one back."

I look up, staring at the bartender across from me. "I asked out a guy without asking him out directly, not even knowing for sure if he's into guys. Plus, I had just met him five minutes prior and there was like *not a single sign* that could've told me he was into me. In fact, there were more signs that he *wasn't* into me than there were ones that said he was. I've been single for like two years, and I am finally allowing myself to get back into the ring and date, and I do *this*. Stupid." I let my head drop back down against the wood. "Stupid." Another hit. "Stupid."

When my forehead hits the counter once again, the bartender chuckles and slides a towel between my head and the wood. "I've heard fairytales of love at first sight, but I never actually heard it does happen in real life."

Six Years

I groan. "It wasn't *love* at first sight. It was... Jesus. He is so hot with his black hair and black clothes. And he looked so lonely. And he read a fucking porn book that his friend wrote. And he was so—Wow, I am so single." Or deprived of *normal* people in general.

"You want a drink?"

Before I even have the chance to react, I know Doro's already shaking her head. "He just got back from rehab, let's not tempt him."

I turn my head only to glare at her. My sobriety isn't something I am ashamed of. In fact, I think I should be proud of it. I managed something a huge chunk of people struggle with. It was a bumpy ride, but I did it. Kind of. I *will* continue to stay sober now that I am out of the clinic.

I mean, I suppose I do think a drink every once in a while won't hurt, but deep down, I know it will. Because I will tell myself it's just *one* drink once a month. And then it's twice a month, then once a week, twice a week, once a day... hourly. Been there before, and I'd rather not go back there.

I hold up my thumb to the bartender when he whistles with what I hope is respect. I don't know, don't care either. "What's your name anyway?" I ask and finally look up, having decided I can't kiss the countertop with my forehead forever.

"Josh."

"Of course it is."

"What's that supposed to mean?" He flashes me a cheeky smile, currently drying off a glass.

"Nothing bad. But you look like a Josh, so it doesn't surprise me." God, what do Joshes even look like? What's the plural of Josh? Joshes? Joshs? Joshi? More than one Josh? "Dark hair, some stubble, you know?"

"You've just described a bunch of men *without* the name Josh."

Perhaps I did.

"Leave him alone, Josh. Luan is heartbroken over his date,

who's not his date, not showing up, okay? How about you offer him some apple juice to drown his feelings in?"

Oh, apple juice. "I'd love that. Apple juice. It makes me happy."

"I know it does." My best friend smiles at me, then slaps her hand to my back. Hard.

I sit up in milliseconds, gasping in pain. "Are you fucking—" I turn in my seat, trying to get this pain to stop but it just so vanishes when I look up at the Li's house and find two someone's standing on the balcony toward their private beach. A very familiar looking someone being one of them.

Chapter 3

"but you gave the impression / that this was the inception / of something real"—The Way You Felt by Alec Benjamin

Grey

June 2022

"He was definitely asking you out," my sister repeats for the third time in the past twenty minutes.

I've been leaning against the railing of my balcony for at least double the time, staring toward the beach party. The tiki bar looks pretty crowded, and yet my eyes stay focused on that curly headed guy. They shouldn't be able to see me from up here. Well, not to the point where anyone could tell I'm *me*.

"He was not. That guy doesn't even know me." We talked for like five minutes. *He* talked. I ignored him as best as I could.

"Ever heard of blind dates?" Sun nudges me with her elbow.

"It's not a blind date if I know who I am dating."

My sister jerks around, looking at me. Her eyes narrowed, a sheepish grin on her lips. "So he *did* ask you out on a date!"

"No." He said he'll be waiting for me. That's not asking someone out, is it? Even if it was, why would Luan ask *me* out? I barely provided him with answers, let alone was kind to him. "Besides, Sun, I am not even interested in dating anyone at the moment. I'm playing for the pros now. It's off-season, but still, I am an NHL player now. Getting into any form of committed relationship right now is stupid." Who even said something about commitment?

"Each of your best friends are in one," she reminds me.

"Aaron and Sofia met when they were like three years old. They've been separated longer than every now and then during a hockey season, they'll survive. And Colin and Lily have been dating for almost a year now as well. They've had their time. If I started dating someone *now*, I'd have what? Two months to get to know them before I'm constantly on the road. Besides, I only have about a month in the year to come back to Malibu, so getting involved with some local here is the stupidest thing I could ever do." Not to mention, if I ever dated someone from Malibu, my father would officially disown me more than he will the second he'd learn I date a *man*.

As he would say it; I can do my *unholy business* far away from where he has to witness it. Malibu is his. New York mine. If I don't play by his rules in his territory, he'll get rid of me in all ways possible.

"That poor guy looks depressed," Sun says, ignoring my attempt to talk myself out of going down there. "He could use a midnight kiss."

I don't even want to get to know this guy. He seemed a little annoying if I'm being honest. A little too… happy. I'm not used to happiness, except for my sister's but I grew up with that girl. She sees rainbows on rainy days, and sometimes, even that's too much for me to handle. Imagine what my life would be like if I lived with another one of those kind of people.

Miles had his moments. He is a sunny person but has been put through too much to really let it show. Most of the time, he only gets all hyped when his daughter is near so she would only ever see the best of him. And I like that about him. He's broken like every other person, but he would never let his kid see that. That's the only reason I survived the past four years with him.

"That only works on New Year's."

"Nope. Midnight kisses are great. Ever tried it?"

Can't say I have. "I am not discussing any of this with you."

She's only eighteen. If I ever talk about lovers to her beyond the potentiality of dating, please shoot me in the head. Or better yet, make it painful and torturously long.

"I am just saying, Grey, kissing someone at midnight is a different kind of intimacy. It's rare. God, or a midnight kiss in the rain! Even better."

"Sun, if you—" I stop myself from continuing my sentence without even realizing.

Remember when I said the people from the beach couldn't see me well enough to know it's me? I was wrong. The same curly headed guy who managed to confuse me more than my best friend's four-year-old daughter when she asked me whether animals get frustrated when they make sounds to speak to us, but we don't understand them, is staring at me.

How can someone ask someone else out without asking them out?

Imagine I went down there expecting this to be… a date? And then it's just two strangers hanging out. Maybe we won't even talk. Maybe he didn't even want us to talk but just suggested I go to this party and make some friends because, apparently, I am lonely.

I'm usually really good at reading people, but this guy just hacked my entire system. Everything screams *error*.

What do I do?

I should call Miles; he'll know what to do. No, he'll say it's a date and then proceed to book the next flight here to witness my embarrassment.

"What would happen, Grey? So then it's not a date, big deal. You'll never see him again anyway. It's not like you're planning on coming back here for the next ten years."

She's right. The next big birthday is my father's sixtieth. My mother never celebrates, so I don't have to be there for her fiftieth. Which means my next *forced* reason for coming back to Malibu is ten years in the future. Even if I embarrass myself, I'll never have to see Luan whatever-his-last-name-is again.

"You're right." I nod, convinced I'll be able to make my way down to the beach. Walking back into my bedroom, I only faintly hear my sister following me. "I'll go there and down a few drinks, then come back and complain to you about how badly tonight went."

"Sounds like you."

I stop in my tracks, taking a deep breath. "It does, doesn't it?"

Don't get me wrong, I love my sister. Sun is the only reason my stay here is bearable. Without her, being in one room with my father at any hour of the day would be as awkward as spitting at someone while talking and they notice.

I tell her everything, mostly because she's the only one who knows what my life is like. The only person who understands me without me having to explain why I can't just rebel against my father. In the eyes of most people, I should tell my father to fuck off and let me live my life. But if I did that, I'd face consequences that I'm not sure are worth it.

If I had to choose between my family or my own happiness, I'd choose my family. If my father disowns me, I'll never see *either* of my siblings again. My mother will walk right out of my life like she never gave birth to me. I'd never exchange a single word with my cousins again, my aunts or uncles. They'll all be gone. So, yeah, if choosing to keep the people I love in my life kills my own happiness, I'll take it.

Miles wouldn't understand, which is why I don't tell him any of this. He grew up with a very loving father. And he himself would *always* accept Brooke the way she is. He'd want to help me, and as much as I love that about him, him trying to help me is only going to cause more problems.

"On another note, maybe he didn't ask you out because how would you even know he's into guys?" Sun queries, watching me switch my shirt over and over again.

What the fuck is wrong with me?

The last time I acted like this was *never*. I didn't even get nervous when my ex-boyfriend and I were in our getting-to-know-each-other phase, or when I started to crush on him big time. It was all calm. It was great.

So what the fuck is this?

"He said he had a boyfriend before." If I remember correctly, he said *ex*-boyfriend. Some bad poetry freak.

My sister frowns at me. "He just told you?"

I nod.

"Out of nowhere? He went, 'Oh, I have an ex-boyfriend, by the way'?"

"Not like that."

"Maybe he just tried it out, didn't like it, and now he's straight. Who knows?" Sun shrugs unapologetically.

I drop the shirt in my hands, staring blankly at my sister. "Can you stop fucking with my head?" What if she's right though? People experiment with their sexualities all the time. It is possible Luan only *tried it out*. It didn't work for him.

This isn't even a date, so why should I care?

I'm only going down there to get wasted. That's it.

Besides, you don't make assumptions about other people's sexualities, that's rude.

"Are you coming with me?" I ask, finally settling on a plain black t-shirt. All I ever wear is black, so I'm not sure why I even bothered to try on different colors. Why do I even *own* a red shirt?

Sun shakes her head, laughing. "And end up watching you make out with some guy? No thank you."

"There won't be any making-out because it's not a date."

"Still. I'll keep an eye out for Dad. Watch your phone, I'll text you when he goes outside."

I walk over to my sister and press a quick kiss to her cheek. "You're the best."

Chapter 4

"I'm known to go a little too fast"—Can We Dance By The Vamps

Luan

June 2022

"SHIT, LU." DORO STARES at the massive mansion a little up on the rocks. They have a whole ass private beach and everything. Granted, they have to go down some steps from the little hill first but if I lived there, I wouldn't mind it either.

El Matador Beach has a lot of rocks all over, and hills just before the beach starts, so it's not unusual to have a few houses built on them. Or a massive mansion. Though this one is the only actual *massive* one.

There are a few houses around, but none quite of that size. And none close to the Li's property.

"You said he wasn't local."

I bob my head slowly. "He said he wasn't." But then why in the ever-loving heaven would Grey chill at the Li's house? Nobody goes there. Nobody *dares* going there. Their property has a better security system than Disneyland.

But I suppose with the CEO of Li Co. living there, it's to be expected.

"Maybe he's befriended one of the kids," I say, being hopeful.

Doro laughs. "Mm-hmm. You know, their second born son's name is Grey right?"

I did, in fact, not know that.

I never cared much about that family, even if Ji-Hoon Li is my father's ultimate rival. They're both in the baby business, both producing unnecessarily expensive items like toys and clothes or pacifiers etcetera. Hayesland isn't as known as Li Co. is, even though Hayesland was founded years before Li Co., hence why my father despises Ji-Hoon Li.

Deep down, I believe my father still hopes I might take over one day, but I'm not interested. At all. I'd rather keep on coaching soccer to my girls. They're all doing so great this season, especially the U6. It's their first actual season playing games and such. Last year we didn't participate because I thought little four-year-olds shouldn't be getting all violent on the field. Neither should five-year-olds but whatever. U5 will forever be the *practice* year to me. Just fun games, no losses. Even the U6 don't have losses because there aren't any *big* games like the U16 have going. It's all just fun at that age.

My father respects it though, so it's not like he'd ever force me to take over.

Grey had gone inside about five minutes ago, and still I'm staring up at the balcony, waiting for him to come out again. Maybe he didn't see me, why would he? I probably look like an ant from down here.

The lights to the room connected to the balcony are still on, but I don't think Grey is still in there because my eyes catch a little movement down in their backyard, and then on the stairs to the beach.

Their entire beach part is fenced. The fence is tall enough to show little of what's happening on the other side. All I can see is some movement, shadows. And then the gate opens, and a tall Korean boy comes walking out of there.

Who the hell wears long pants to the beach? He wore something similar yesterday. Black cargo pants, a black shirt. His shoes are white though.

Grey has a powerful walk. I never thought that existed. He walks like he owns the entire world, like he could get anyone to die by just walking past them. Determined. Straight-forward. He doesn't look away or gets distracted. His eyes remain focused on me, knowing exactly where he's headed.

I wish I looked only half as powerful as he does right now.

"Jesus," I hear Doro mutter under her breath. "Now I understand what you meant with 'he was blasé.'"

Yeah. Blasé.

If he's the son of Ji-Hoon Li, of course he is used to random people approaching him. Of course he knows how not to show interest, how to stay a mystery.

Grey maybe-Li is intimidating. And yet, when he finally stands before me, all the intimidation leaves like it's just him and I again, by the beach, at night, me talking his ears off.

"Was about time you made it," I say and smile at the guy like I didn't just think about running for the hills. "You know, the last time someone almost stood me up, I… Actually, that never happened. You would've been a first."

He doesn't smile back at me or even gives me a sign he heard me. But he does take a seat next to me, so I'll call that a win.

"So, you are local then?" I try to get him to talk back. I'm not sure if he's seen me, but if he has, maybe that'll be an icebreaker.

It isn't.

"No," he answers.

"You just came out of the Li's house. Unless you're dating their only daughter or are related to them, I don't think you'd even make it inside." His family name might not be known to most people. Maybe the name is, but not the people behind the brand. However, around El Matador Beach, the Li's might as well be celebrities.

"How do you know they only have one daughter?" he asks, not looking at me. Hey, at least he's talking.

"There was never a mention of a second or even a third one." I should know. My father sent me to a school across the entire city just because the Li kids went to the one I was supposed to go to. If there's one family my dad would never allow me to get involved with, it would be them.

But since I never really cared, I only know they have two sons and a daughter. Their names don't exist in my brain, nor do their faces. Honestly, I am not even sure there ever *were* faces to the names online before.

Grey slowly lifts his head and meets my eyes. He's got dark eyes, but I already knew that from last night. Full lips. Black hair and a tattoo that goes down the front of his neck; Korean letters, I'd assume. I don't know what it means, but I won't ask either.

"So, I take it the big Grey Li doesn't like Malibu all that much, huh?" I grin, proud to have figured that one out. I hope.

"Davis," he corrects. "It's Grey Davis."

Huh? "Why?"

Instead of providing me with an answer, he turns to Josh and orders himself a drink. I do the same, only I don't order a whiskey but apple juice. God, I love apple juice.

I look next to me to find my best friend, but she's gone. How dare she leave me behind with a stranger? Granted, I wanted to be left alone with said stranger, but that was before he confused me.

Taking a deep breath, I turn back to look at Grey only to find him already staring at me.

"Do you play sports?" I try. Maybe asking fewer personal questions will be easier for him to answer. "You look like you play sports."

"Yup."

I hum, thinning my lips into a satisfied smile while bobbing my head. So personal questions are off the charts for now, but I can work with surface stuff. "NCAA?"

He nods but doesn't confirm with his voice.

So he's still in college then? "Are you a senior?"

"Graduated this year."

Aha, okay. Yeah, that makes more sense. He looks like he graduated. I don't know what having graduated college looks like, but if I had to guess, just like him. It doesn't make sense at all, but it does to me.

"So, what do you play?" I ask, taking a sip from my apple juice.

He hesitates to answer, but I suppose that's understandable. For someone who claims to not know him, and then knows he has two siblings, it doesn't exactly scream I'm someone he wants to get to know. But I will prove him wrong.

I am someone *everyone* wants to get to know.

So let's do this.

"Wait, no, don't tell me," I say. "I want to guess."

"Okay."

I take in his body. Underneath those baggy clothes, I think he might be pretty muscular, but that doesn't say anything about his sport. "American Football," I guess. I don't think he plays American Football, it would be too basic for him.

Grey shakes his head, seemingly unbothered but there's a slight hint of resentment on his face. At least now I know he does have feelings. Sports guys are easily offended when associated with any other sport but the one they play.

"Well it's definitely not soccer," I say. "You don't have a soccer body." What a soccer body is, I am yet to find out, but as long as my guesses draw out some reactions, I am good with it.

"What's a soccer body?" he asks in return, seeming genuinely interested.

I shrug. "You know, bruises, abrasions, scars everywhere." My description makes perfect sense, however, it fits a lot of sports.

There are only a few kinds of sports that don't leave scars. Ones where the players wear more protection than anything but even with those sports, injuries happen. Blood flows in every sport, even swimming.

"You can get abrasions playing football," he says. "Or field hockey, lacrosse, baseball. Possibly even golf if you trip."

I laugh. "Got me there."

"Keep on guessing," he challenges. So there is a fire inside of him somewhere. I'll find it, I'll just have to figure out how first.

But that's the thing with games, right? There's always a way to win, and those wins come almost as soon as you figure out how to play.

Chapter 5

***"I speak in grey to match the shade on the inside of my brain"*—Colours Of You by Baby Queen**

Grey

June 2022

HE'S SO EAGER, IT'S KIND OF ENTICING.

Something about Luan is mesmerizing. Unlike everyone else who ever found out who my parents are, Luan still talks to me and I'm not sure why that is. He still tries to get answers and reactions out of me despite barely getting any.

It's intriguing. A freshness I didn't know I'd need.

"Something that covers you up entirely," he speaks to himself, still thinking. "Or a water sport. Do you swim?"

Only ever when I'm here, which is rarely. But instead of giving him an actual answer, I shrug.

He plays soccer. Or played. Whichever it is. I know because his first thought went to soccer, like mine always immediately drifts over to ice hockey. It's a huge giveaway.

Okay, his initial guess was American Football, but that's such a basic answer. He just wanted to see if I'd react.

"Maybe like an indoor thing. Handball or something."

"You can get abrasions from falling on a gym floor." I know because I got tons back in high school during P.E. It's kind of embarrassing, I admit. It got so bad that I stopped showing up, I *failed* P.E. in ninth grade. *Me*, a guy who *loves* working out.

"Right." He nods, now tapping his fingers on the wooden

counter. Three times. "It's not lacrosse, I don't think." Maybe I should be offended by this. "Your face is too handsome for a baseball player."

I almost let a confused *what* leave my mouth. However, I know he's just playing, trying to see whether my eyes would twitch with anger or disgust, or if I'd eventually stop him.

Joke's on Luan though, he can talk all he wants because I am a patient guy with a lot of self-restraint. Also, his voice isn't all *that* annoying, so I'm okay with listening to him talk.

He snaps his fingers. "I know, you're secretly a make-up artist."

"Or a tattoo artist," the bartender adds. Can he stop talking? Luan's voice I can handle, but the bartender, whatever his name was, I can't.

Luan narrows his eyes at me, humming. "Nah. I think our beloved Grey Davis here would rather feel the pain than be the one to hurt others."

Is he painting me out to have some weird kink? That I love pain or something? I think he is, but that's okay because I don't care what he thinks I do in my free time. It's certainly not having others inflict pain on me, or me inflicting pain on others, but if he'd like to think that, sure.

"He looks pretty brutal to me."

"No, now turn back to your drink-making. I don't like your input in this conversation," Luan says, waving the bartender off three whole times. "I'd like to flirt with Grey Davis without you making it weird."

Flirt with me.

When Luan turns back to look at me, even though I still don't look back at him, he finally mentions another sport. "Ice hockey. I believe you're an ice hockey player. It's all protection and I don't know what else, but it seems safe."

"Not safe." Is any sport ever really safe? "But yes, I play hockey." He got there slower than I thought he would.

He taps himself on the back as if to congratulate himself for guessing correctly on what felt like the twentieth try. "Around here?" he tries again.

"No. I'm from New York." Which isn't true. I am *from* Malibu, but I now *live* in New York. And I sure as hell don't plan on coming back here unless I have to.

"So, what are you doing here then?" He asked that before.

"Vacation," I lie again. If anything, this trip is more torture than relaxation.

"And how's that going for you?"

"You ask a lot of questions," I note, staring at the drink in my hands.

"And I plan on getting answers to each and every single one of them."

Determined, I like that. "It's going great."

"Your face says otherwise." He pokes my cheek with his finger. I flinch at the contact, then swat his hand away. And he just laughs at that, like getting rejected from physical touch is the most hilarious thing in the world. "So, what's it about your last name?"

He tries to poke me again, but I swat his hand away once more, this time before his finger could even come in touch with my cheek.

Ignoring his question, I say, "Don't touch my face."

"Ouch." He shakes out his hand, the one I never touched. He smiles again when I look at him, and I have absolutely no idea why. Or how. "Grey Davis, not Li, but you're related. You're Ji-Hoon Li's son. So why don't you have his last name?"

My family's quite known around here. It's a curse, honestly. My mother doesn't work, she lives off of my dad's money because he asked her to. She can't say no. And my dad? He owns a toy company. Not like sex toys, thank god. Just toys and clothing for kids. And other essentials. I used to think he was Santa Claus, but he is not. Obviously.

However, that doesn't explain how he knows my father's first name.

We're a lot more known here in Malibu, so I give him that. And still. He knows too much, but I'm not sure how. Or why.

"Why is that a thing you're so hung up on?" I ask in return. Truth is, I've never had my father's last name. It was a safety precaution my father took. Not everyone knows us, a lot of people do, but not *every*one.

There are no pictures of either of us online, not from business shoots or paparazzi, anyway. Not a single family picture either. It's like Sun and I don't exist. Except that we were mentioned before.

He did this so we could have a normal school life. That we could go out without people trying to get information about our father's company out of us. Or use us. And to give us the chance to stay anonymous.

We could've decided to change our last name at the age of eighteen, publicly become a part of the family. Moon, my older brother whose pictures also show up online, did, but Sun and I refused.

I don't want to be associated with Li Ji-Hoon, that's the thing. He might be my father and, yes, thanks to him and this company, I was able to study wherever I wanted. The money I grew up with opened doors for me other people could never get close to even if they worked their whole lives.

I am grateful for what I have, how I grew up, but that doesn't mean I'd rather not make a name for myself.

I don't need people saying I only got to where I am because of my father, and I know that's what's going to happen. Every time Colin reads a comment or an article about how he's only a good ice hockey player because his father is a literal NHL coach, I see the self-doubt in his eyes. He doesn't want to show it, but I can see it anyway.

Nobody wants to be compared to their parents, especially not when it comes to their own successes. But what's worse than comparisons, is the people saying you've only gotten to where you are *because* you've had the *money* to get there.

Six Years

People say Colin only got onto the NYR team because his father is the coach, has connections to the team owner. And while that's true, if Colin wasn't a great player, even Coach Carter wouldn't be able to do a single thing about it.

During college, I've heard people say that Aaron was only good at ice hockey because he could afford skating lessons, more than average. Again, it's true. If he needed extra training, his father could afford to give him those. But I know it still sucks being told you're only any good because of the money your parents have.

Miles wasn't too talked about. The only rumors spreading about him were that he fucked ninety percent of the women on campus, which is bullshit. That guy fucked two at most. He likes to pretend he's all cocky and a manwhore, when in reality he was just trying to get people to think he's too much of a prick to have a child.

That backfired.

Anyway, nobody knew the real him. They knew his father had money, but the manwhore rumors trumped the ice hockey related ones, so none ever really made it big.

And with me, since nobody knows I am the son of Li Ji-Hoon, nobody could ever say anything about my ice performance in relation to money and the possibility to easily afford lessons, or only being there because I had a known father. And I plan on keeping it that way.

"I'm curious," Luan answers, still keeping that bright smile on his face. "But alright, I'll ask again tomorrow. Maybe then you'll provide me with an answer, Grey Davis."

"Who said we'd see each other tomorrow?"

Luan downs the rest of his apple juice like it's a shot, setting his glass down like one as well. "I did." His green eyes sparkle with challenge. "Can't two friends meet anymore these days?"

Friends. "Who said we were friends?"

He rolls his eyes all dramatically, then turns on his chair, averting his body right to mine. His knees brush my thigh, and while that's not a problem in general, it almost takes my breath away.

His kneecaps slightly pressing into my body feel like two balls of fire digging its way through my skin. Did you ever wonder what it would feel like if you held your hand into a flaming sparkler?

Would it prickle because that's what it looks like? Would it burn because it's fire?

I don't know the answer to it, but I know Luan's knees on my body feels just like it.

"I did," Luan answers. He spreads his legs for a moment, then with little to no strength turns me on my chair so I'd face him. And then his legs close again, trapping one of my legs between his, and one of his between mine. "Do you have a problem with that, Grey Davis?"

When I don't answer, still too mesmerized by our tangled legs situation, he laughs. Deep and raw. So real and sweet. It's the kind of laughter that you feel right in your bones. The one that shakes you. Puts you in a trance.

"Do you like apple juice?" he asks. "Because I plan to bring a whole bottle just for me, and if you want some, I'll have to bring two. I, for my part, love apple juice. It's the taste of childhood. Freedom and irresponsibility, don't you agree?"

Again, I don't answer but I don't have to either.

"When I was younger, my best friend and I used to pour apple juice into the kiddie pool because we thought it would make us smell good. It did nothing but turn us into sticky little kids, but it was worth a try. We even asked his mom to slice up some apples and throw them in there because we were convinced it would speed up the process of turning us into apple-monsters. His mom thought we peed into the pool so much that it turned that color."

The bartender snorts, shaking his head with what I believe is amusement yet disbelief. Why does he listen in on our conversation?

"You were a weird kid, Luan," he says, and sets down a new

glass of apple juice on the counter.

"Now, Joshi-looking-Josh, that's not very nice of you," Luan counters but gladly takes the apple juice. "Here I was thinking we could be best friends in a short time, but no, you just had to ruin it."

"I'm probably double your age, kid."

Luan gasps offendedly, holding a hand right over his heart. "Are you saying I cannot befriend older guys because I am 'too young'?"

"Yup."

"I'll have you know, most of my friends are either older than seventy, or minors."

Bartender-Josh blinks in shock, as so do I. What the fuck?

"I'm a soccer coach," Luan tells me to at least ease some of my concerns. "I coach girls. The younger ones are *really* nosy. But they're good company for an hour twice a week. The U18 ones are somehow even chattier than the little girls, and their problems consist of relationships and how Rebecca from science class didn't wear pink nail polish when they all agreed on doing just that."

I lean my arm onto the counter, bringing my hand up to press my index finger over my lips. Somehow, I don't think he minds the chattiness of said girls.

"Also," he adds, clearing his throat. "I go to a retirement home once a week, every Friday. Bingo-night is such a vibe. I'd much rather be there than attend some parties, I'm too old for those anyway."

"How old are you?" I ask, now curious.

He gasps out loud. "Was that a *personal question*, Grey Davis?"

"No." I take a sip from my whiskey. "It's useful information."

Luan narrows his eyes, trying so hard not to smile this time. "If you're in love with me, Grey Davis, you can just say it. That's fine. I get it. I am *very* likable and hot. I have cute dimples and a perfect smile. There's no need to be subtle."

And he's very… confident.

My eyebrows quip up, for the first time tonight showing an actual reaction other than resentment. "So, are you going to answer me?"

He hums while getting off his seat. Luan quickly downs the rest of his apple juice and then turns to me again. "Maybe on our second date. I'll see you tomorrow."

Shocked and a little surprised, I don't even stop him from walking away. That is until the bartender reminds me that Luan never said where I'm supposed to meet him, or when.

Once I realize what that means, I shoot up and almost run after Luan. It's a little more difficult in the sand but manageable.

"Wait," I say and lay my hand on his shoulder. Luan turns around, blinking in slow motion like this is a weird romantic comedy movie. "You never said where I should meet you."

He smiles, brings a hand to my jaw, and strokes his thumb over my cheek. Unlike the first time he touched my face, I don't swat his hand away. "If you want to see me again that badly, Grey Davis, you'll figure out a way to find me." With that he turns around once more and leaves me behind.

He didn't give me his number. Nor an address. Nor anything else that would allow me to find him.

Perhaps all this is just a game to him after all.

Chapter 6

"but just for this moment / let me live in my head"—
Made Up Story by Andi

Juan

July 2022

"NO, ZOEY! IT'S A *THROW-IN,* NOT A *CORNER KICK*!" Alice yells at her sister from outside of the pitch, groaning when Zoey doesn't hear.

Zoey is four years old, and I get the feeling she doesn't even like soccer that much. I believe she only plays because she tries to be just like her older sister who happens to *love* soccer.

"Well, aren't you going to do anything?" Alice looks up at me, her eyebrows dipped with anger.

I lay my hand down on Alice's shoulder, slowly shaking my head. "This isn't a match, Alice. They're playing for fun. You probably don't remember because it's been ages since you started, but when you first started playing, your Coach didn't have you play by the rules either."

She hangs her hands to her hips. "And how would you know that? You were still in diapers when I started to play."

"I don't think I wore diapers at the age of fourteen." But I did spend a lot of time on the field, watching my Coach because it was at least a little bit of a distraction. Even when I didn't have practice, I still showed up. I loved watching because I've always been more interested in the coaching aspect of soccer than I was interested in playing the game.

Plus I was a little too drunk at all times to play properly anyway.

Sure, I love playing, but coaching is far more fun to me. I can watch and I don't get injured. And I still feel the rush, the feeling of wanting to win, or losing a game. I just don't *participate* physically. Besides, if either one of the girls I coach makes it out there in the world, I can brag about having taught them all they know.

"You're old," Alice mutters under her breath, now crossing her arms over her chest.

I grin. "Nine isn't that much younger."

Alice's head shoots up, averting her eyes on me rather than the pitch. Offended. "You're like fifty but a young fifty."

"What's a young fifty?"

"You." She gestures to my body. "You're dressed like a grandpa, but your face looks young."

I nod, not even taking her description of me badly. I don't dress like a grandpa, only for practice because I'd like to keep my good clothes clean. Ash pitches do tend to get messy, especially with little girls that like to use you as a tree.

Alice groans when Zoey trips and instead of getting back up, she keeps lying on the ground making snow angels in the ash. "Can't you make them do Intersquad Scrimmages? You make us do them every time."

"They're four years old, Alice. They're here to have fun, not learn the technicalities of soccer."

"That's exactly what they are here for." She squats down, on the verge of giving up on me. "Have them kick the ball then. Learn how to fucking aim."

"Don't swear."

"Sorry."

"Good." I reach for my whistle and blow it to get the girls' attention, then walk right into the middle of the pitch. "Come here." I wave them all over and they come running, dropping everything they did before.

Once gathered around me, I wait for the usual group hug, and when it comes, my heart is overfilled with joy like every single time my girls do this.

"All of you did amazing," I tell them, and they start to cheer. Seeing them so proud of themselves for doing great is one of the best parts of this job. The older girls like Alice just don't understand why I can't make four-year-olds do the same practice tasks as I give them.

"We get a sticker?" one of the girls asks, and suddenly twenty of them shoot me the biggest puppy dog eyes known to humankind.

I grin at them and slowly pull out the sticker-roll from my pocket. "Line up," I say, and they do. For the next four or five minutes, I pull off stickers from the sticker-roll and stick one to each of my girls' forehead. They're star-shaped with little praises on them like "Good job" or "Well done".

They love them. I love them. Unfortunately my older girls are no longer as enthusiastic about the stickers. I make them get them anyway because I can.

"How was work?" Doro asks as I come back home and find my way into our living room. Our house smells like food, so I am praying she cooked, and dinner's ready for me to devour.

"The usual. Alice was all upset over Zoey's performance. The U15 had *a lot* to talk about. Mostly boys. And the U19 were flirty as ever."

"Why don't you ever just tell them you're not interested in a Coach-Player relationship with an eighteen-year-old?"

"Because, my dear,"—I plop down on the sofa right next to her—"I don't want to kill their spirit. Right now they're really enthusiastic about giving their all to impress me. So why would I be stupid enough to take that spirit away, huh?"

She laughs, shaking her head. "You're unbelievable."

I stand up again, being in desperate need of a shower. "Unbelievably smart, and not interested in women. So, they can try flirting with me all they want, nothing's going to come out of it."

"But I know someone whom you have an interest in." She follows me into my bedroom.

"Shut up. He didn't even try to find me all week." I take off my shirt and throw it onto my floor. I'll put that away after my shower.

"How would he?" Doro sighs, being done with me. "You do this all the time, Lu. You show interest in someone and then don't provide them with a possibility to get back to you."

"Charlie found a way."

"We were neighbors."

Yeah, alright... she's got a point.

Before the thoughts of Charlie can toss me right back to wanting-to-drink territory, I shake them all off and bring back my positivity. "Still. If Grey Davis wanted to find me, he would."

"This isn't a fairytale, Luan. People in our lifetime don't have magical powers to appear by your front door out of nowhere. They don't run around town and ask everyone if they've seen you or know you."

I shrug, then walk right into my bathroom. She follows.

"I know where he lives." I push down my pants and step out, letting them remain on the floor for now. "So it's not that difficult."

"Because you've seen him there. You know who he is. One quick google search and you'd find out his address even if you didn't know it yet."

Rolling my eyes, I now get rid of my socks. "One quick google search and he'd find out the same about me."

"No, he wouldn't. First of all, you didn't give him your last name. Second of all, he would show up at your parents' house and ask for you. If your father sees this guy and hears him ask for *you*, not only will Mike have a heart attack, but he will also cut off your precious dick for getting involved with the enemies' son."

Again, she has a point. "It's not like I fucked him. We didn't even kiss. We just talked."

"*You* talked."

God, I hate that I tell her everything.

"So? He showed interest." I cross my arms over my chest, our eyes now locked.

"Did he, or did you force that interest onto him?"

I hate her.

Chapter 7

***"it's enough to drive you crazy"—by Hopeless Romantic
by Sam Fischer***

Grey

July 2022

"How's my favorite hockey playing cousin?" Phoenix asks as a greeting, holding his arms open for a hug. I don't give him one.

"I'm your *only* cousin who plays hockey." I look at his girlfriend, nodding. "Hello, Vienna."

She smiles a little shyly. "Hi."

I still don't know how she of all people can love Phoenix. Vienna Storm is one of the most anxious people I have ever met. She barely goes outside, so the media says, and Phoenix doesn't tell me otherwise either. She's so different to my cousin, yet somehow they're so much alike. But I mean, as long as they're happy, right?

I have met her a couple of times before when we were younger, but the past four years, since I started college to be precise, I haven't seen either of them at all. Not even my cousins.

"Where's Kimia?" I ask, being sure Phoenix used to have a sister.

"Too annoyed to show herself to people until dinner is served," Vienna tells me. Ah, sounds like the Kimia I remember.

Just when I'm about to say the same thing aloud, Vienna's sister and her fiancé make it inside, approaching us.

Allie immediately swings her arms around me. "Ah, you're

so grown up now!" she says. We're around the same age.

"Hi to you too, Cheeseball."

She groans. "Don't call me that."

"I happen to think it's a great nickname," a deep voice from right behind me says. There's only one man this voice could ever belong to.

Wringing myself out of Allie's hug, I turn around to lock eyes with Atlas Storm, next to him, his wife and the other three kids.

He's one reason why tonight hopefully won't go the way our family dinners usually go.

That man has nothing to do with my family, other than the fact that his daughter is dating my cousin. But he doesn't have to be *here*. At my father's birthday dinner. They only came because I asked for their presence.

Storm doesn't like my father very much, nor does he like my uncle. He's investing in my father's company anyway, but I think it's only because Li Co. happens to make him tons of money, not because he has an interest in baby stuff.

But now that all of them are here at the same time, I might as well ask them for a little favor. "So, uhm, my best friend from New York is here with his wife and daughter. If it's possible, could you not ask them about Brooke's mother? It's a sore topic."

Dinner's going great so far, much to my surprise.

The Storms' presence does actually keep my father's wrath at bay. I think it's mostly Atlas Storm who keeps my father quiet. If that man terminates the contract with my father's company, sales will go down by millions, if it doesn't ruin the entire company, because once you're on the bad side of that man, nobody will want anything to do with you.

But I can't shake the feeling that something's about to happen. Today went too smoothly. It was too quiet to be true. If my father doesn't go off on me at least once a day, it isn't right.

Just yesterday he yelled at me because I came out of the bathroom shirtless, and my brother had a friend over.

I took a shower in *my* bathroom. My *en-suite* bathroom. As it seems, when my siblings have *male* friends over, I am not even allowed to take showers anymore or walk around in my room without a shirt on.

"Uncle Grey?" Brooke says and pulls on my hand to get my attention. She's sitting on the floor, playing memory games with Connor Storm.

I get up from my chair, not wanting that little girl to somehow annoy my father by talking too loudly or excitedly. For someone who owns a company focusing on babies and toddlers, he sure has a hatred for little children.

I kneel down to her and she immediately abandons playing games with Connor to launch herself into my arms. I love this little kid. She's the absolute sweetest girl and I'm not just saying this because she happens to be my best friend's daughter. It's the truth. Miles has done a great job raising her so far, and I don't know why he still struggles to see that sometimes.

"What's up, tiny princess?"

Brooke giggles and buries her face right into my chest. "You play the games with us?"

I sigh softly. "I can't right now, Brookie. Later, okay?" If I sat down on this floor right now, my father would have a stroke. Connor and Brooke aren't his kids, so he doesn't care about their presence on the floor. But if I sat down, he'd start yelling because no kid of his should let themselves down to that level. Floors are the lowest you can fall, apparently, and rich people don't sit on floors.

"Okay." At least she doesn't sound upset.

I plant a quick kiss to the top of her head and then get back up. Brooke immediately turns her attention back to Connor and the game.

Once I stand, I allow myself to look outside for a moment. It's a beautiful view from up here, but a sad one as well. The beach would be crowded or at least you'd still see a few people walking or sitting on the sand at this hour but that private beach of ours steals that sight. So it's just plain and empty out there.

It's a little windier today, the waves bigger than they were the days before. It would be a great evening to surf, but my father would murder me before I'd ever make it out there to do just that. It's a miracle he lets me play ice hockey.

We're businessmen, Grey, not adrenaline junkies, he used to say every time I wanted to pick up surfing. Can you believe it? I grew up next to the sea with perfect waves, and I never learned how to surf.

Looking out of another window, one that shows a little more than just our private beach, I catch a glimpse of dark curly hair. It could be anyone but…

I stare out for a little while longer, praying he'll turn around, but even if he did I wouldn't be able to tell if I know that guy or not. It's too dark.

This is just my mind playing tricks on me anyway. Why would he show up here almost a week after he left without giving me anything to reach him? Besides, I gave him exactly one sign of interest that night, why would he ever think I'd consider seeing him again?

I seat myself back down at the table, forcing myself into conversation with my cousin and his girlfriend while also still listening to the conversation between Miles, Emory, and Allie. She can be a lot to take in sometimes, and she's very curious but that's only because she likes knowing the people around her. It's a family thing, I'm pretty sure.

I spend a good time scrolling through my phone underneath the table, but mostly to check the security cameras. Maybe the cameras caught the guy outside better than I could with my eyes in the dark. I doubt it, but I am hopeful. Why is this bothering me so much anyway? It's not Luan out there, and even if it was, there's nothing I can do.

Even if it was Luan, going out there is a really bad idea. First of all, I wouldn't know what to say. We're not friends, and we certainly aren't dating. We met once. Twice. Both times didn't last very long. Both times I didn't really speak either.

Luan has me intrigued. He's piqued my interest with his tendency to babble and fill silence with conversation. Something about that guy is a mystery even though he seems to be an open book, and that entices me. He's a puzzle I want to solve, and it fucks with my head.

I'm good at reading people, knowing them before they get the chance to tell me as well. Body language speaks volume, and if you pay just a little more attention to the details of a person, what they say, how they act, you can figure them out so easily.

But Luan... he talks. He is confident and sure of himself. But there were moments he was the complete opposite. Like when I was standing on my balcony and watching him. He was more hunched over, lacking confidence. He didn't seem like the guy he presented himself to me, and I want to know why.

So I check the security cameras. Maybe the guy's still there.

He isn't. The spot he's stood at before is empty and nobody else is around.

I let out a deep breath, about to exit the security app when I notice some movement by the front gate. Someone's pacing around, walking from one end to the other. And then he stops and looks right at the camera like he knows someone's watching him.

My breathing stops, my brain not believing what I'm seeing, or who I'm seeing.

It's him.

Here.

In front of my house.

About to ask to come inside, I'm sure.

No.

Shit.

This can't happen. He can't come inside. If my dad sees him...

I turn toward Miles, about to ask him for advice when I notice his jaw a little tense. He's irritated by Allie, but I kind of already knew he would be eventually. "Bet you wish you didn't come," I whisper.

They had the choice to stay upstairs and not participate at the dinner, but both Emory and Miles decided to do the polite thing. They're staying with us for a few days because the hotels around here are crazily overbooked these days. I don't mind it—though I would've preferred spending a few days in a hotel with them— and neither does my family. My dad might be hateful toward me every now and then, but he welcomes my friends any time. Unless they're male.

Miles is a guy, obviously, but he has a wife and a kid, so my dad doesn't see him as a threat anymore. He used to when I was eighteen and just moved in with Miles, but I told my father about Brooke back then and that he had a girlfriend, so he didn't care anymore. Thank god he didn't because I don't think I would've been able to move out and leave Miles behind.

I don't give him the time to answer because I have to go out there and stop Luan from ringing that doorbell. Or buzzing that gate. Whatever.

"Cover me for ten minutes, okay? Luan's here and I need my dad to not see him." It's cruel of me to dump that onto him, but I have no other choice unless I want this dinner to turn into a crime scene.

"What?"

"Should somebody ask, just say I went to the restroom or something. Thanks."

Chapter 8

"looking at you got me thinking nonsense"*—*Nonsense* by *Sabrina Carpenter

Luan

July 2022

YOU CAN DO THIS, LUAN. It's just pressing a button and asking to speak to Grey, nothing bad.

I can't believe Doro convinced me to do this. Apparently it's my fault Grey didn't reach out to me, so I have to right the wrong. I think she's full of shit, if he wanted to find me, he would've… eventually.

Now I'm standing here in front of Ji-Hoon Li's house, trying to find the courage to ring the doorbell. It wouldn't be that much of a problem, if the guy who's known in all of Malibu wouldn't live in that house. I don't want to accidentally interrupt that man doing something important.

Just when I finally decide to lift my arm, the gate opens. I take a few steps back, afraid of who has noticed me standing here, but when my eyes meet the same dark ones from a couple of nights before, my nerves calm down just a little bit.

He's still wearing black cargo pants, a black shirt, and white sneakers but somehow he looks different. I don't know what is off, but something is.

"Are you stalking me?" he asks, not even saying hello first, but I wasn't expecting a greeting from him anyway.

"Stalking?" I shake my head. "I live here, Grey Davis."

The gate closes behind Grey, and he doesn't even flinch when the sound of metal hitting on metal sounds through the air. Even I flinch, and I saw it happen.

"You live here? On the street?"

"No, but around here… somewhere." It's the truth. I live on the same street as him, but where there are houses for the not-so-rich as well. Nothing with too much privacy, no private beach. I can even see the Li's house from my bedroom window. It looks a lot smaller, but I can see it.

"What are you doing here?"

I shrug. "I was hoping the stars look better from up here." I look up to the sky to check.

"Do they?" His voice comes closer, from right beside my ear, actually. As much as I want to look back down and turn to face Grey, I keep still and silently wish he doesn't move away again.

I'm not sure what it is about this man, but something keeps pulling me into his direction. It's not a crush or something deeper, that would be ridiculous. And yet that guy is like a magnetic field and I'm the magnet.

"Not really," I answer. "They used to be so much brighter when I was little. My friends and I used to climb up on trees just to be closer to the stars. It was stupid, and sometimes I fell off the trees and broke a few bones, but it was worth it every time."

"What are you really doing here, Luan?"

Can't he guess? "I'm twenty-three," I say instead of answering his question. Technically I am answering *a* question, just not the most recent one. "It's quite funny, actually, because my birthday is on valentine's day, but I never had someone to spend that day with. Not like one would, you know? Like the day's intended to. I did have a boyfriend though, but he was too busy writing stupid poems to remember it was my birthday, or valentine's day. But that's not a big deal. So, yeah, every year it's just me and my best friend, celebrating my birthday, with apple juice." At least *now* it's apple juice. It used to be stronger drinks, but I had those daily anyway.

Finally, I turn and look at Grey again. His eyes are softer than before, less bricked-up, more open to talk. God, his eyes display whole universes that I'm not sure he knows are in there.

"Give me your phone," he demands, holding out his hand to me.

My eyebrows dip a little in confusion, but I don't question him. Instead, I pull out my phone from my pocket and hand it over, telling him my passcode.

Grey types into my phone for a whole minute and just when I think he does more than just add his contact, his phone chimes at a rather suspicious timing before he hands me back my phone.

"What did you do?" I ask.

"Texted myself so I have a way to reach out to you should I ever be back here again."

Right.

Wait, but I thought he lived here. He said he didn't, but I thought that was a lie. I thought he was playing tricks on me.

"You *really* don't live here, do you?" New York…

Grey shakes his head. "I live in Manhattan." Okay… but that's just across the country, no biggie. "I'm only here for my father's birthday. I'll leave in two weeks, if not earlier."

Two weeks. That's like no time at all. How am I supposed to get to know that man when he's as open about himself as the mafia?

"Before I embarrass myself even more," I start, already knowing this question is going to be the most embarrassing thing I have uttered in Grey's presence, and I talk a lot. "You, uh, you are into men though, right? Because… otherwise I'll just make a fool of myself. Well, it's not like I planned on making a move on you or anything, but you know? Don't get me wrong, I totally would, but—"

The corner of his mouth tugs up just a tiny bit, it's almost nothing and not there for long, but I swear it happens.

"Did you forget? I'm in love with you and all," he says, the tiniest hint of amusement in his voice but not a lot. It's barely there. "You're *very* likable and hot. You have cute dimples and a perfect smile. There's no need for me to be subtle," he more-or-less repeats my own words back to me.

It's been days. How does he still know them word for word?

My smile breaks free, mostly because I'm glad he didn't reject me like I thought he would. Or feared he would.

I'm not good at this dating game. I don't know how people do it, or if there's one specific way to do it. When I saw Grey all alone by the beach, I just thought fuck it and went to talk to him. I wasn't giving myself hopes that he would be into me or that he'd be interested in getting to know me. I truly thought he could use a friend. I still think he does.

But it doesn't hurt knowing I don't have to reassure him I won't fall for a straight guy. And if I do flirt with him, which I know I will, he won't be disgusted. Hopefully.

"I am all of those and I do look pretty great," I confirm. "Well, then, Grey Davis, I'll see you around." I salute him with two fingers, and he just shakes his head at me like he cannot believe what he's gotten himself into.

Tough luck, my friend.

He'll love me. One day. As a friend or more, we'll see. And once he does, he'll never want to get rid of me ever again. In fact, Grey Davis will wonder how he used to live his life without my amazing presence in it.

Chapter 9

"and you call yourself a father"—Good Enough by Empire Cast, Jussie Smollett

Grey

July 2022

THE SECOND LUAN leaves, my stomach drops. The earlier feeling of something being off still isn't gone, instead it intensified.

When I walk up the porch to the house and my eyes land on my parent sitting on the Hollywood swing, I know what's about to come without even having to live through it yet.

I stop in my tracks and take a deep breath, waiting until my father gets up and stands in front of me.

His eyes are filled with fury and resentment, the vein on his neck so close to popping, someone should call an ambulance in advance.

He doesn't touch me, he wouldn't dare to. My father may be many things, but he'd never lay a hand on anyone, so at least I don't have to worry about that.

I look away from him, into the house where I find everyone still seated at the dinner table, chatting and being oblivious to what's about to happen out here.

Even though I know my father is going to yell at me now, I'm not too worried about anyone hearing it because the house is so damn soundproof, sounds from outside don't make it inside.

I'm a little surprised when he starts to talk and it's not what I thought he would say. "I see you got a new tattoo."

I've been living with this man for eighteen years. I might have not been home in four years, but I still know that this is a trap. He's not going to say it looks good, or even start a lecture. My dad is pointing out the new tattoo because he's about to disagree with it.

"I did." If he were anyone but my father, I would've said something like; "Looks like it, huh?" or "I don't know, does it look new?" Something stupid.

"On your neck."

"Had one there before." Somewhat behind my ear, I have a snowflake tattooed, the Korean word for it right underneath.

"*Jal doel geoyeyo*," he reads out loud, his voice spiteful.

The tattoo starts just above my Adam's apple, going downward. I wrote down the Korean letters myself to be sure the tattoo artist wouldn't accidentally mess up by adding a line where there's none. It happens. He still could've accidentally added a line, but thankfully, he didn't.

"Everything *would* be okay if only you didn't disgust me so much," he speaks. I thought he would start more nicely, to be honest. Something like "What the hell was that?" or "You can bring your gay-hoes to your own house, not mine." Any of the things he's said in the past, but not this.

I keep quiet. I always do.

Talking back to my father would be the equivalent to signing my own death certificate.

"You are a disgrace to this family, Grey."

To him. I am a disgrace to *him*, not the family. He's the only one not wanting to accept that I date whoever I want. I don't care about genders. If I like someone, I like them, but he just doesn't want to understand.

Or maybe he has a hard time understanding that I don't *want* to settle for any label. It would be easy to stamp "bi" onto my forehead, or "gay" or whatever the fuck he would prefer. "Straight," if it were up to him. But sometimes I think if I could at least tell him I'm into one group of people specifically, he would be more understanding.

Maybe not.

"You're not a kid anymore. It's time you put your silly activities aside."

"Silly—"

"I am talking." His voice raises an octave, not yet yelling but he's close. "What are you doing, *dating* other men? That's beyond you. It's unnatural. I let you do your thing during college because I thought you'd grow out of your shenanigans, but clearly, you do not learn. I should've sent you to military school when I had the chance."

Of course.

"The technicalities behind your doings are nothing like our bodies were made for."

It takes me a hot second to realize he's talking about sex. Always a pleasure talking to your parents about your sex life, I'd say.

I'd like to remind him that men have their g-spot in their ass, but if I did that, I'd be a guy without a family in about two seconds.

"You're supposed to build a family. With a *wife.* How do you expect to have kids of your own when you date *men*? How do you expect to expand this family in a proper way when the places you stick your dick are other men's asses rather than where they belong!"

Oh, okay. That's all sorts of wrong.

With all that was wrong with his statement, the outdated view on women my father has bugs me the most.

Even if I didn't date men or had sex with them, my dick still didn't belong inside a woman's pussy the way he makes it out to be. We're not in the 1790s anymore when women were useless without a man, when they had to do as they've been told and wouldn't dare talking back, when their bodies belonged to men.

Women have choices, *voices*. Even if some old white men think they have the rights over women's bodies. Why the fuck are we going back in time instead of evolving?

"ANSWER ME."

"What am I supposed to—"

"You will not see that guy again," my father says in a strict tone. It's not a question, it's a demand and if I don't stick to the rules, it'll end badly for me. I know that much. "I will set you up for a date with someone's daughter from my company."

"No." Shit, I've never said no to him in my entire life. Four years ago I would've nodded and agreed to a stupid date I didn't want to go on. In my head, I know I should've done the same right now, but my mouth just didn't want to form the word *okay*.

My father cocks his head, eyebrows rising, eyes filling with fire now. "No?"

"Yes, I said no. I will not go on some stupid date with someone I don't want to be with. Besides, he and I are *friends*." I don't say Luan's name for a reason. "Like Miles and I."

"Friends," he repeats, once more raising his voice. "That guy is trouble!" He points toward the gates, making it obvious he means Luan, not Miles. "I've watched you!"

Should've known he would.

"Are you dating him?" Father asks, giving me a solid 0.5 seconds to respond before he repeats the question, yelling this time.

"No." But I thought I answered that one before.

"Well, I don't believe you."

Aw, come on. What the fuck does he want me to do to prove it? I know something, but that's likely not going to happen.

I could go on that stupid date he wants to set up, date that woman but I just know I'd never feel anything for her. Okay, I might eventually, but I refuse to put someone through misery only for me to not get in trouble with my father.

And even if I didn't care, I simply don't want my father to set me up with someone. I want to be with whoever *I* decide to be with. It doesn't have to be Luan, that's most likely not going to happen anyway due to the distance between us.

Whether I end up with a woman or anyone else, it shouldn't matter to my father as long as I am happy. I really want to be happy and grow old with someone I truly love rather than being forced into loving.

"You should be with someone you were *meant* to be with, Grey."

What if I was meant to be with a guy? He wouldn't want to hear that question even if I voiced it.

"Are you even listening to me, boy!"

"I don't have any other choice, do I?" It's pretty impossible not to hear him when he stands right in front of me.

For the next several minutes, my father yells at me about how ungrateful I am, how he's given me everything, and how I can't even be a "normal" person. He yells at me about how I am a disgusting piece of shit just because I do things that are inhuman to *him*. He calls me the nastiest of words, says I'm not someone he could ever be proud of only because I am not straight.

It's one thing to have random people insult you because you're not part of the norm, it's another thing when your own family sees you as unnatural, someone they have to hide, someone they pretend doesn't exist because of it.

Moments like these make me wish I was a part of what people like my father call "normal". It makes me think something's wrong with me when I know I'm totally fine. It's okay to be someone like me. It's okay to not put a label on your sexuality or one that says anything but "straight". And still, it's easier to support than be part of the group because the hate you get sometimes doesn't seem worth it at all.

"When your friends leave in a few days, you can leave right with them. I don't want to see you anymore."

Chapter 10

"did you ever want me? was I ever good enough?"—
Boy's a Liar by PinkPantheress

Juan

July 2022

THE SOUND OF MY whistle catches the girls' attention, now jumping from squats to burpees.

Warm-ups are my least favorite part about this job. It's so boring watching the girls suffer. Well, it's great making them suffer when I'm in a bad mood, but that rarely happens anymore, so nowadays I just stand here, bored out of my mind.

"That's ten pushups for all of you!" I yell the second one of the girls starts talking to whoever else on the team. I prefer the U6 girls, their training is usually less strict and far more fun. But the U19 think they can do whatever they want because they're legal now.

Most of the time I let them talk during warm-up, but not today. I need them to have their heads in the game.

Just a few weeks ago I got an email saying the U19 team will be shut down because we don't have enough players. It's the truth, which is why I have been sending email after email to the sports club owner, begging him to let Coach Henderson and I merge the teams together. His guy team also lacks players, and neither of us understands why we can't just merge them together.

I mean, I understand the whole sexist aspect behind it; Boys play better than girls, and girls shouldn't be interested in soccer, blah blah. That's bullshit.

They also don't want to put boys and girls, especially boys and girls of age, in one locker room together for privacy reasons. That is one of the acceptable reasons, but we have more than *one* locker room. We have four. So even if they're playing home games, there's still enough space for two teams and separating the girls from the boys.

Mr. Harley finally agreed to allow the merge if my girls prove themselves mature enough. I'm convinced this is about them allegedly falling head over heels in love with the guys in seconds because that's what girls do. Again, bullshit, but better "proving themselves mature enough" than shutting down the team, right?

Thirty minutes later, I think I've put them through enough torture, so I blow my whistle once more and allow them to take a break.

While they go to get some water into their bodies, I allow myself a quick glance on my phone. There are no new notifications, at least none that I care about. After three days of absolute silence from Grey, I decided to shoot him a text last night. It's now four p.m. of the next day and he still hasn't responded.

All those past days I've wondered if I've done something wrong. Maybe I went too far with showing up at his house or asking him if he's into guys. Or maybe I'm just too much for him after all. His silence now doesn't exactly help the situation. He has read the text, so that's even worse.

Perhaps today *is* one of the fewer days I do like torturing my players on the pitch after all.

"Get back here, ladies!" I clap my hands together to get their attention. Keeping their bottles in their hands, all of them make their way over to me, standing in a circle.

"You're mighty grumpy today, Coach Hayes," Nora, one of the girls who always tend to flirt with me rather than see me as just their coach, says. I can accept the flirting as long as her performance keeps up because she thinks impressing me with doing good is beneficial in some ways. It's still kind of weird, but at least I know nothing will ever come from it.

"If I hear another word from one of you, that'll be an extra ten laps around the pitch. For *all* of you. I don't care who speaks, all of you will run." Punishing the whole team usually keeps them quiet because neither of them wants to be the asshole who got them into this mess. Especially when it's *ten* laps around the pitch. "Understood?"

They nod, not daring to use their voices.

"The guys will get here in ten minutes. If I catch any of you flirting with one of them, I will not stick up for your asses again." *Okay, Luan, a bit harsh there.*

Fuck it, man. How can some random guy ruin my mood this much? I love being happy, so why can't I be fucking happy?!

"Due to the lack of players on both teams, Coach Henderson and I decided it'd be in all of your interests to merge the boys U19 and you together. But there's one condition; professionality." I clap my hands together, once. "From both sides. Coach Henderson and I expect you, as well as the boys, to be on your best behavior and respect the others. There will be no flirting,"—I look at the small group of girls who tend to do just that all the time—"and no sexism. If Coach Henderson or I catch either of you saying something that could be remotely counted as sexist, you're benched at first. If it happens a second time, you'll be kicked off the team immediately. We're not pushing gender roles here. You're playing soccer because you like the sport, not because either gender is supposed to be better than the other; that's bullshit. You're either good because you practice, or you suck. It has nothing to do with what's in your pants."

I take a quick breath. "Speaking of your pants; they stay on. No funny business here. What you do in your free time is none of my concern, but the second you step foot on soccer ground, whoever you might date is no longer your partner who you can get nasty with. They're now your team member and you will respect natural boundaries. No touching. No kissing. No anything but being friendly. We had these rules when it was just you, and they'll stay the same with the guys around."

Damn, I'm shocked by my own rules here. I don't normally give a shit what they do during practice for as long as it stays PG13, and they still participate properly.

"Should you have a problem with someone, *any*one, I advise you to come speak to either me or Coach Henderson and we'll handle it. It's not kissing and telling, it's what the team needs if you want this to work out. All of you are aiming to play professionally someday, and while I'm sure there are still a lot of issues within the pro teams, being able to solve them rather than silently hate one another will get you far. So, start practicing now."

Just as I finish my little anger-filled speech, I can hear the chatter from the guys getting louder with every step they come closer.

Luan: There's a firework by the beach tomorrow evening, do you want to go?

Maybe it was my message that scared him off? Perhaps I should've sent a boring "Hi" or "How are you?" Anything like that.

It *is* tomorrow evening by now, and I am sitting here all by myself, every now and then looking up the Li-or-Davis' house to see if he might be standing back on that balcony. He doesn't have to be *here* to see the fireworks because I'm sure he can see them from his bedroom window, but I thought…

It doesn't matter what I thought, I thought wrong. Clearly.

I am pushing him, aren't I? I tend to do that a lot, push people. I like getting them out of their comfort zones and showing them there's a life beyond what's known and safe. And I guess

Six Years

sometimes I go too far with it.

I lift my head up, facing the stars. It's a beautiful night, a clear night sky. If I wasn't in such a bad mood, maybe I'd enjoy it a little more.

Stars are beautiful, they hold secrets. They're so far away yet shine so bright that we can see them.

I used to think every person who dies turns into a star, except bad people. The better people we were, the brighter our stars would shine. And when I thought about that just a year ago, I knew my star wouldn't shine at all. But these days, I'd like to think that even my star could shine. Maybe not the brightest, but a little bit would be enough.

"Are you Luan?" a female voice asks from right behind me.

I turn my head to see who's talking, my eyes then follow her when she seats herself right next to me on the sand.

She's got black hair and dark eyes like Grey. Her cheeks are a little puffier than his are, her jaw not as defined. Her features in general are more on the feminine side, but other than that they look the same.

"If I'm in trouble, then no, I'm not," I answer.

She laughs, such a sweet and innocent laughter. It makes me wonder what Grey's would sound like. "I'm Sun," she says. "Grey's sister."

I guessed that the second I laid my eyes on her. "He's not coming, is he?"

Sun shakes her head. "He had to go back to New York. I'm sure he would've come if he was here."

But why didn't he just tell me that? He could've sent me a text saying that he had to leave and not ignore it.

"Did he tell you to come find me to tell me that?" Because otherwise I don't quite know why his sister would be here with me right now.

"No, but, don't tell him I told you this, he showed me your message and freaked out."

"Your brother *freaked* out?" She nods. "Are you sure we're

talking about the same brother because the Grey I got to know doesn't strike me as one to *freak* out. He's more silent and grumpy. And he probably hates that I talk so much. I'm a great talker and I know it annoys people sometimes, but he never said it annoyed him. He seems like the kind of person who'd just stop me mid-sentence and say, 'Shut your stupid fucking, much-talking mouth, Luan.' But I probably wouldn't stop even if he told me to because I am petty like that, I'd just talk more. But then, he also smiled that one time we talked. Well, it wasn't a *smile*, it was like a lip-tug for a solid nanosecond, but I swear it was there. So maybe I wasn't annoying him with all the talking after all."

I'm doing it again. Talking. But from the looks of it, Sun is more amused than annoyed. She's still smiling. I am not used to people smiling back at me as much as I am smiling at them.

But then she shrugs. "He wasn't annoyed. He grew up with me, so Grey's used to listening a lot and having someone talk his ears off."

"You're a talker?"

Sun laughs. "My best friend once put headphones on in the middle of a slumber party because she wanted to sleep, and I wouldn't stop talking."

"So did mine!" Why this excites me so much, I don't know. Don't care either. I like Grey Davis's sister. "I live with her now, and she locks her bedroom door so I can't come inside to talk to her about random things. I hate it, so I sit down in front of her door and talk anyway. She ends up unlocking that door to throw a pillow at me and then closes the door again and locks it. She then puts on some music loud enough to deafen the entire city."

Chapter 11

***"boy, you make me make bad decisions"—Bad Decisions
by Ariana Grande***

Grey

September 2022

"LOOK AT THAT!" Colin says all excitedly, holding up a blue dinosaur onesie for newborns. "We should get it. What's Eden's size?"

Eden is Miles's son. He was born about three weeks ago. Ever since then, Aaron and Colin have been buying everything baby related they found remotely cute and gifted it to Miles and Emory. I mean, babies grow out of their clothes rather quickly, so I'm sure they're glad. They couldn't do this for Brooke because she was already a year old when we met Miles, so buying newborn clothes was off the charts. And to be fair, I don't think Miles would've put Brooke into a dinosaur onesie either.

But she gets a whole lot of toys now. Miles must hate it.

"Can't we just go back to the hotel?" We're in Pittsburgh right now for a game tomorrow, and while I just wanted to get some painkillers from the pharmacy, Aaron and Colin spotted a Hayesland store and figured we should check it out.

Across the street from the store is a Li Co. one, and I'm really glad my friends decided not to go in there yet because stepping foot in anything that's related to my father makes me mad these days.

I haven't talked to him since he threw me out back in July.

Sun kept me updated on the mood back at home though, and it wasn't good at all. I don't know how to fix this without losing myself in the run, without turning into someone I'm just not.

I'm yet to find out how to live my own life the way I want and still not lose everyone who means something to me in the run.

Also, I haven't talked to Luan since that day either. He's sent me a couple of texts, but I never answered any of them. He sent me a hockey meme just a week ago, but other than that he stopped texting altogether, and some part of me hopes it stays that way because I don't want him to keep on hoping there will ever be something between us, friends or more it doesn't matter. Another part of me wants him to reach out, give me the opportunity to find the courage and text back.

I don't even know what about Luan keeps me so intrigued. I met people at bars all the time, brought them home, had a quick fuck and that was it. I was never hung up on them.

Even with my ex-boyfriend, I wasn't all that interested in the chase or thought about him all too much.

But something about Luan just keeps my head occupied. I want to figure him out, want to listen to more of his babbling. And I mean it, I'm not thinking about him in the sense of wanting to *be* with him. He seems like a cool guy, someone you'd want in your life as a friend. Someone you can hang out with and know you'll have an effortlessly great time because he'll make sure of it.

And then there are the secrets he holds in his green eyes. Darkness he hides behind the happiness.

"He's doing it again," I hear Aaron say. "Dude, what's up with you? You've been more distant than usual since you got back from Malibu." He shakes me, forcing me out of my thoughts.

"Nothing, I'm fine."

"Did something happen?" Colin asks, concern now in his voice. Miles didn't tell them the part of the story he knows, and I never mentioned anything either. I didn't even tell Miles what *exactly* happened outside with my father. In fact, I didn't tell anyone anything.

"No?" I turn around to distract myself by looking at baby clothes now. If my father knew I'm buying stuff from the enemy, he'd not only not talk to me anymore, he'd actually disown me. Though, I'm not sure he didn't already. "I'm trying to focus on our game tomorrow. I needed painkillers, not baby clothes."

"What do you need painkillers for? Your twenty-second ice time didn't lead to any injuries yet."

Rookies have it tough. If you're unlucky, you might get to spend your whole first season benched. "At least I had twenty-seconds, unlike you. How long were you on the ice again, Colin?"

He scoffs, mutters something unintelligible under his breath. His father didn't give him a single second ice time so far, and he's pissed off to say the least. "Shut up. And we're getting this dino onesie."

"You know that thing looks more like a frog to me." It doesn't, but Colin drops the onesie immediately anyway. We're all a little traumatized by them to say the least.

"Oh, can we go check out Li Co.? They have better stuff." Aaron eyes a frog-themed pajama with disgust.

"They don't," I say, my mood now lower than low.

"How would you know?" Colin gasps, smirking now. "It's your guilty pleasure, isn't it? Walking around a Li Co. store and knowing their entire collection."

Something like that. "Shit, and here I thought I could hide that side of me for the rest of my life."

"Liar."

"Nosy ass."

"Sometimes I ask myself how I'm friends with you." Colin keeps a smile on his lips.

The corners of my mouth lift slightly. "Because you love me. And you three idiots need someone you can tell your relationship drama to, otherwise you might die of a cardiac arrest."

Colin usually calls me "Mama Grey" whenever he needs to talk about something that's been nagging at him. I don't know when this started, but I learned to accept it. According to my friends, I'm the least likely one of us to give stupid advice. The one who'd rather listen than talk back. Which is true, I do listen more than I talk.

Sometimes all people need is for someone to listen. They don't always want to be talked back to or need advice. Often times, giving them a shoulder to cry on, a safe space to lay their thoughts out in the open will be more helpful.

Back in my hotel room, I stare at my phone as though I'm waiting for something, but I'm not.

A text from my friends maybe, but that's unlikely because it's almost midnight and they probably went to bed already to be well rested for our game.

Maybe a text from Sun, giving me another update on the home situation. She's been back in New York for college for a while now, so she no longer hangs around the house in Malibu to know that much. But she calls our mother every evening, which means she should know *something*.

When's a great time to call my dad to apologize? Apologize for what, I'm not quite sure but I better figure it out. I won't apologize for having *talked* to a guy. I didn't give my father a single reason to believe I was seeing Luan in any other way but as friends. And even if I had, I'm not sorry.

Luan breathed a little life into my lungs, even if it was only for a few minutes, even if I didn't let him see he did that.

Just as I drop my phone onto my chest, ready to give up on hoping my sister might give me the heads-up to call my dad, my phone chimes.

In mere seconds do I have the phone lifted, the brightness of my screen burning my eyes for a second there.

Six Years

It's not Sun who texted. It's Luan. *Finally*.

No, not finally. This is bad. When I said I want him to give me the chance to respond, I didn't mean it. Well, I did, but he couldn't possibly have heard my thoughts. And giving me the opportunity to text him doesn't quite go with my wish to stay as far away as possible from him while still figuring him out so I can stop obsessing over it.

Luan: Hi.

I'm about to hit delete when there comes a follow-up text.

Luan: You know, the last time someone ignored me as long as you did, I was on a farm with my best friend's family. My mom told me they'd take me on a weekend-trip to Disneyland but instead of an amusement park with rollercoasters and waterslides, I got to see cows and chickens. One of those chickens starts picking at my shoe, to this day I wonder why that chicken preferred my shoes to anyone else's because mine weren't half as cool as the ones my best friend wore. He had cool Spiderman shoes, I just had some blue sneakers which I'm sure had a hole in them.

Luan: I lied. Nobody ever ignored me as long as you did. But the story is true.

I shake my head as I read his texts, not wanting to believe this guy even babbles when he *types*.

Luan: I figured it out though. The reason why you don't text back.

That's a trap. He's waiting for me to ask why, which then has me respond, breaking my silence. But I'm considering it.

Still considering it…

What would be so bad about me responding?

He's kept this up for a little over *two months*, with a short pause every now and then. Either way, he texts me, sends me ice hockey posts that I'm sure he doesn't understand.

Two months in which he texts, and I never respond. Two months he spent on trying to get me to talk to him and I don't understand why.

Anyone else would've given up after the first text, but not Luan. Sure, there were days he stayed quiet, but he made up for those by texting more the following days.

I'm *still* considering it…

Fuck it.

Grey: Well, are you going to tell me the reason or not?

I can picture Luan looking at his screen right now, smiling because he finally managed to pull a reaction out of me. Or maybe he doesn't care all too much.

That's the thing about him. I don't know how he'd react because people like Luan surprise me all the time. They're unpredictable and I hate this, but that's also why this guy still occupies my head, I bet.

Luan: Because you're in love with me, obviously.

Grey: Is that what it is?

Luan: Definitely. I mean, name one person on this planet who hates me.

Grey: Your future partner's parents, I'm sure.

Luan: Shit. What'd I do to your parents?

My parents.

I like that he doesn't ask why I've been ignoring him and just talks like I never did. But again, who does that?

If someone ignored me for two months, you best believe I'd ignore them for four.

Luan: Wait, let me guess...

Luan: I talked too much.

Some kind of chuckle slips from my throat, and I want to slap myself for it.

Grey: Probably.

Luan: Aw, well, sucks for your parents. I am awesome. Besides, I'd rather them hate me than you.

Grey: You suck, and I do hate you.

Luan: I mean, I could but why would we go to third base when we didn't even have our first real date yet?

Luan: So, what are you doing right now, Grey Davis? Isn't it like around midnight in New York?

Grey: I'm in Pittsburgh, actually.

The time's the same though.

Luan starts to type but then the bubble disappears. A moment later it reappears but disappears again just as quickly. When he stops typing for about a minute, I start to get a little worried. There's no way he would just ignore me no—

My phone starts to ring in my hands, Luan's name pops up on

the screen as well as my own reflection.

Do I pick up?

I rarely even call anyone on the phone, so why would I pick up a FaceTime call from a guy I barely know? But I haven't seen him in so long, I do wonder if something has changed in that time. Probably not, it's been two months, not two years.

Before I can overthink this I swipe right, accepting the call. A moment later, green eyes stare back at me, narrowed and not nearly as friendly looking as I remember. But then Luan starts to laugh, his eyes now crinkling, his features soften. Somehow, right at this moment, I no longer feel as though I'd stay awake the whole night with my head running marathons.

"I thought someone stole your phone when you replied, to be honest," Luan admits. "Glad to see it's actually you texting. Though, I should've known. Nobody but you would dare give me such short and vague answers as you do."

I don't doubt it.

"So, what are you doing in Pittsburgh?" Luan sets his phone down on a kitchen island, turning his phone for me to still see him even though I think he's just about to do some dishes.

"Hockey," I answer. I didn't tell him I play for the pros, I just thought he knew, or at least could've made that connection. I said I play hockey for the NCAA, but also mentioned I graduated, so I don't know.

"Right. You went pro then, huh?"

"Yeah."

"I could've gone pro, too. Not hockey, obviously. But I refused because I'd much rather coach than play. I'd like to keep my limbs where they are, thank you very much." He looks at the camera, smiling at me. He's got a clean smile. It's awfully symmetrical, and his eyes spark every time he smiles. It's a little unnerving because that smile could easily make it onto magazine covers, but it's also calming at the same time because Luan just has that effect on people. Or maybe that's just me. "What team do you play for?"

Six Years

"New York Rangers."

He nods. Three times. "Should've guessed that. I googled hockey teams in New York the other day. Turns out, there are three national ones, so I figured you'd play for one of them. I don't know where they're all based because, I'm sorry, Grey Davis, but ice hockey is really boring. However, I wanted to know the team names because, even though I wasn't sure you're actually playing for the pros, I still wanted to tune in on their games because maybe I'd find out, you know? So, thanks for sparing me from having to watch every single hockey game with either of the three NY teams just to find out which one you're on."

I cover my eyes with my hand, letting out a deep sigh that somehow turns into the faintest of chuckle. Just when I thought it was inaudible through the phone, I hear Luan gasp.

"Was that a *chuckle*, Grey Davis?"

When I remove my hand from my eyes, I find him so close to the camera, I almost flinch. At this point, I might as well see every single pore on his nose if the camera would be able to pick them up.

"No, I sneezed, obviously."

Luan takes a few steps back, enough for his backside to hit the island counter behind him. He leans against it, crossing his arms over his chest. He wears a bright yellow shirt paired with white shorts, I'm assuming. And somehow that's exactly him. He's the whole ass sun and I'm not quite convinced he really grasps that.

"I'm not sure what's happening here, Grey Davis. First you laugh, now you're being sarcastic. What's next? Are you gonna crack a joke?"

I think about it for a second. Do I even know any good jokes? The only one I know is the stupidest dad joke to ever exist. Sun used to think that one was funny when she was six years old. "What did the police officer say to the belly button?"

Luan cocks his head, his lips slightly parted. "I don't know.

What did he say?"

"You're under a vest."

He stares at me for a hot moment, I stare back. Neither of us speaks or moves, it's like the line went dead. At least until Luan hunches over, clutches his hands to his stomach, and his laughter fills my ears like music.

It wasn't even a good joke.

"That was awful," he confirms, still laughing.

"I know. But my best friend's daughter loves it."

Luan straightens his back, now taking a few steps toward his phone again, grasping his phone in his hands and bringing it right up to his face one more time. Thankfully not as close as before. "How old is she?"

"She just turned five two weeks ago." My phone vibrates at the same time as a message notification pops up on my screen. Miles sent a picture to our group chat. I can look at that later since it can't be that important. There's a high chance it's only about Eden or Brooke anyway. Or their pets. He sends those all the time, mostly because Colin keeps asking to see Eden in his new clothes.

"Now that's adorable. I wish I had a little sister around the same age. I could bring her to soccer with me and make her the best player ever. And also, I could take her shopping and just spoil her because that's what older brother's do, right?"

I shake my head. "Nah, they're just mean."

"You should know. *You're* the older brother." The light turns off, temporarily going so dark that I can barely even see Luan anymore. At least until he turns the lights back on, but he is now in a whole other room. "I don't have any siblings, but I always wished I did. It's kind of lonely as an only child, but at least I got everything I ever wanted. My parents never *not* gave me anything I asked for, so maybe I am a little spoiled myself. No, I definitely am. You know that one time back in—Why are you laughing again?"

I'm not even laughing, but I suppose that slim smile on my

lips now counts as just that. "Nothing."

"No, no, Grey Davis. Tell me why you're laughing otherwise I will continue to talk. I'm a great talker, I could talk all night long and not get bored. You, however, would get bored listening to what I have to say. Trust me, I can make up whole ass four-hour stories when one sentence would've been enough to make my point."

Ignoring his little wannabe threat, I ask, "Why do you keep calling me my full name?"

I watch as Luan seats himself on his bed, leaning against his headboard like I do. Once seated, he shrugs. "Because I like your name, Grey Davis." He's impossible. "Do you know your hockey schedule already? Whom you're competing against and where?"

Oh, talking hockey now, that I can do.

"I do, mostly." I don't know every date by heart, but I'll know them when I have to. Hard to miss when you play one game and the very same day the entire team rants about how we'll crush whoever we're up against next.

"Are you ever coming down here somewhere? I'd love to watch a game of yours in person."

Okay, think brain, think. We know this. "We should be in San Jose on November 19th, but I think an almost six-hour drive just to not witness me on the ice would be a waste of time. We play against the Kings in L.A. on November 22nd. Anaheim on November 23rd. That's all."

"I'd drive a whole week just to watch you sit on a bench and it'd be worth it."

Uh… Okay. Wow, well… I definitely prefer the hockey talk because what Luan just said has my system screaming error after error all over again.

"Do you need tickets for either of those games because I get VIP tickets for each one, I can give them to you." Miles and Emory wanted to watch the game in L.A. and Anaheim since they're already around anyway, but Colin or Aaron can get them in with their tickets, so that's not a problem.

"Can I come watch two games? And can I bring a friend?"

I nod. "Sure. I get up to two tickets per game. But I also have two best friends on the team who have two tickets each, so even if I had promised to give someone else tickets, I'd just make my friends give me theirs. Neither of us really uses them since our friends are NY based."

Luan watches me with wide eyes, lips slightly parted, and a smile tugging at the corners of his lips. "That was the longest I have ever heard you speak in one go."

"You're welcome." It's kind of scary how my will to speak completely changes every time it's about something I'm passionate about. I mean, I talk to my friends a lot, joke around with them and I don't pay much attention to what I say because I know neither of them would judge me for it. Though, to be fair, if I do happen to say something really stupid, they'd make fun of it for the rest of our lives.

But that's not the point.

I don't know why it takes me forever to warm up to people only to talk to them properly unless it's about ice hockey. I can listen to everyone babble about their days, their problems all day and night long, but you'd never catch me doing the same. The only person I truly open up to is my sister, and I'm trying to let Miles in. He knows me the best of all of my best friends, and I know I don't technically owe it to him to be more open, but I want to be. I want to be able to talk about my struggles to him because he does to me. I'm usually the first person he comes to when something goes wrong, and I want him to know that he's that person for me as well.

Even though I am yet to succeed, he's always the first person I want to go to but just can't yet. So I'm working on that.

"I'm not going to bring Doro, she's not really a hockey fan. Honestly, I think she'd fall asleep, and I do not want her to get in a fight with some hardcore hockey fan because she looked bored or was asleep," he says, still smiling. I aspire to be as happy as he is.

"You're not a hockey fan either."

"No, but I have a reason to be there. Plus, I want to meet your best friends, I'm sure they know more about you than I do, so I'm going to have to squeeze some embarrassing stuff about you out of them."

"Good luck." The worst bit, all three of them would hand out that information about me on a silver platter.

"I don't need luck, Grey Davis. You should know by now, I get everything I want." His grin widens, sure of himself.

I hum, slightly disagreeing until I realize he might be right about that. "Why'd you keep on messaging me despite me never replying?" I start the topic first, needing to know.

His smile doesn't fall, it stays as bright as ever. "Why'd you keep on reading them?"

Because his messages were the highlights of most of my days. His messages were something I looked forward to every day. They distracted me for a short while, even when most of his messages were about his days. He kept me updated on everything he did, whether it was about soccer, or him getting some food. You name it, he let me know. "Got the notification, so might as well."

"I figured if you keep on reading them, you'll respond eventually. I just didn't quite know what would make you cave yet, so I did *everything*. If you hadn't responded to my message earlier, I would've started texting you when I had to pee and all. Every single detail. Besides, the more you know about me, the closer friends we are, right? Also, I needed a boyfriend, and you're in desperate need for a friend, so why not kill two birds with one stone?"

Honestly, his reasons don't surprise me as much as I thought they would. It sounds exactly like him. "What do you need a boyfriend for?"

Luan shrugs, then sighs right after. It's the most defeated I've seen him yet. He looks away from the camera when he says, "I don't know. For stuff you do in a relationship. Talk about anything and everything without really boring the other because they just love listening to you. Have that special bond you don't have to anyone else. Cuddles. Dates. Inside jokes nobody else could ever understand. Just for the feeling, you know?" After a short moment of silence—a *very* short moment—Luan looks at me again, smiling. "I think the last few weeks were a great example as to how our relationship would go. I talk, and you ignore me as best as you can but because you love me so much, you still listen and love me in all secrecy. I like that. It's like I'm your dirty little secret."

"You shouldn't be someone's dirty little secret, Luan." If anything, he deserves to be with someone who puts in the effort to keep him. Despite barely knowing him, Luan seems like a really great person, someone you actually want to have around you. He's what brings light when everything seems dark. He's bringing joy when everything's in despair. He brings good into someone's bad. You don't hide Luan, you put him on a pedestal for everyone to see.

Which is exactly why he and I could never work out even if I wanted it to. I'd have to hide him from my family when all I'd really want to do is to introduce him to everyone. I'd have to pretend not to know him, pretend I wouldn't be head over heels in love with him and I couldn't do that. Ever.

It's one of the main reasons why my last relationship didn't work out. I told my friends it was about something that scratched on the surface of racism on Izan's part, which is only partially the truth.

Yes, Izan did say he can't believe I'm not in the mood for rice, but it wasn't what broke us up. I get the stereotypes, some of them are kind of funny, others not so much. He didn't mean it in a bad way, and I'm really sorry I painted it out to be that way to my best friends.

The real reason we broke up was because our relationship didn't go beyond our bedrooms, or occasional visits to a bar. But if we were seen together outside, we acted more like friends than lovers. We never held hands, never kissed unless we were both drunk. And that was on me, not him.

Izan wanted to meet my parents, but I shot him down every single time, never giving him a reason why. Eventually, he snapped and said he didn't want to be my boyfriend if I couldn't behave like one.

I never made my sexuality a secret, not since I figured out that I don't want to put a label on myself. But to me, it's one thing to be in a relationship with a guy I love and another having to introduce him to my father. I can love them in private, but not where my father sees it.

Thinking about doing what I did to Izan, to Luan, doesn't seem okay to me. Unless I can be sure I'd be there for anyone I date the way I should be there, I cannot do this. A relationship goes both ways.

"I like private relationships," Luan says, now lying down rather than sitting propped up and leaning against his headboard.

"Private and secretive are two whole different things though."

"So don't keep me a secret, Grey Davis. What's stopping you?"

My father. "We talked for like two hours in total. *You* talked. You don't know me at all, and although I do know a lot about your days, I don't know you either. And I am not moving back to Malibu, ever. I don't even go there, and I won't be anywhere near El Matador Beach—except for hockey games—for the next ten years. Even if we somehow decided to get into a relationship, we'd never see each other, Luan."

He grins, and for a moment there I don't understand how, or why. "Challenge accepted, Grey Davis."

Chapter 12

"in my dreams / you're with me"—Imagination by Shawn Mendes

Luan

November 2022

I DIDN'T KNOW so many people showed up to an ice hockey game.

I mean, sure, I didn't think there'd be five people in total, but I didn't think the arena would fill up like at a football game, or soccer game. Then again, I should've known since it's a *sports* event. People love watching sports.

The game starts in about twenty minutes, and I thought I was early but seeing that most of the arena is already filled up, I come to think I am late.

The VIP area looks great though, and only half as crowded as I thought it would be, it's a miracle I found it. I thought I'd have to squeeze in here, but that wouldn't be all too beneficial for a *VIP* area, now would it? There are five people in here, two of which are a baby and a toddler, and one is me.

But you know who I did not find yet? Grey. But of course it would be that way. My only reason for being here, is not here. Maybe he is present, I just can't get to him, that makes more sense.

"Daddy, is uncle Co-in be playing today? And uncle Ron?" the little girl asks, trying to look over the railing to see the ice.

"We don't know that, Brookie. We'll see," her father answers.

"And uncle Grey? Does he play?" She turns around, staring up at her father. "And why you not play, Daddy?"

Okay, let's weigh out the odds here. There's a guy inside of this VIP box area thingy, whatever the ice hockey people call it. He has a wife (I'm guessing) and two kids. That kid calls someone on the team her 'Uncle Grey'. I know a Grey who happens to have invited his best friend to this game, who has a daughter as far as I know.

Would it be embarrassing to ask if this guy happens to be the one I'm thinking of?

Nah. I've done way worse in my life.

What was his name… I'm sure Grey mentioned him the other day during one of our FaceTime calls. We've been on one every evening ever since he texted back a few weeks ago. I still can't believe he did, to be honest. Or that he keeps on picking up the phone when he should be asleep to be well rested for his games or practice.

I approach the guy before me, offering him a soft smile. "Hi, are you Miles?"

He has a little longer hair, wavy and blond. It fits the somewhat description I could squeeze out of Grey last night. I wanted to know who to look for, and although Grey didn't want to give me a description because he doesn't want me talking to this Miles guy, I still got it out of him. I don't know why I'm not supposed to talk to Miles, but I am guessing it's because best friends love talking about embarrassing stories for a good laugh. And I'd *love* to hear some about Grey.

Hey, don't blame me. The guy barely gives me anything, so asking his friends is all I can do. And I'll gladly do it.

"No, he's my daddy," the little girl answers before the blond guy could.

"Oh, I'm sorry," I say. "I should've known that." She nods.

"You're Luan, aren't you?" the guy asks in return, somewhat confirming he is, in fact, Miles. "I wanted to meet you back in Malibu last summer, but Grey refused to let us meet. Said I'd just embarrass him."

My smile widens. *He talked about me*. I don't know why hearing this makes my heart skip a beat, or why I get all giddy thinking about Grey mentioning me to his friends. I talk about him to my best friend all the time, so it shouldn't excite me so much. However, Grey doesn't strike me as the kind of person who talks to anyone really.

"Wow, you do smile a lot," Miles notes, chuckling a little.

"Is that a bad thing?" I ask, a little worried now. What if that's why Grey still hasn't warmed up to me yet? He lets me do most of the talking, so I usually ask a ton of hockey questions even though it doesn't interest me at all, but that's the only times he talks and talks. I'm sure he could go on and on about ice hockey for hours, and I'd gladly listen to every second of it, but he stops himself a lot, too.

"Not at all," Miles answers. "Please, take a seat. I'm beyond excited to finally meet you."

"He's just jealous," his wife tells me, slightly chuckling. "Miles never had to compete with anyone for Grey's friendship."

"Yes, but me, Memory," the little blonde girl shrieks, jumping up onto her lap. She then looks up at me. "Sometimes, I go over to Uncle Grey's house because Daddy says he's all lonely and needs my cuddles and so I cuddle with Uncle Grey until I get the ice cream and then I go back home."

Why does this warm something inside of my chest? The thought of Grey all alone at home, and then suddenly this little girl shows up just for some cuddles… But this is exactly the kind of information I was hoping to get. Something about *him*. Something real. What he's like when he's not being the grump or the loner. What he's like around his friends, the people who love him.

"Ignore them both," Miles says and shoots a look into his wife's direction. He then proceeds to introduce all three of them to me, shaking my hand. "So, Grey told me you're very persistent."

Persistent. That's one way to describe me. I guess I am.

I nod very faintly. "Yeah, I like annoying people. I mean, not like in a sense where I *annoy*-annoy them, you know? I like talking, and if I realize someone doesn't like that then I'll back off… eventually. Takes me a hot minute though."

"Well, good thing Grey listens more than he talks, huh?"

Indeed. Though I wish he talked more. I like his voice. That sounds ridiculous, I admit, but I really do. He has this deep voice that calms nerves in my body I didn't even know were begging to be tamed. And in the morning, just after waking up, he has a really adorable rasp in it. I only caught it once, ever since then he didn't pick up his phone in the morning. But I will keep on trying.

"You know hockey, right? So, speaking of Grey, is there *any* way I will be able to see him after the game? Or do the teams just give interviews and then run for the hills and never return?" I ask. It would be a shame if I didn't get to speak to him face to face tonight. Sure, I'm here to watch him play, *if* he gets some ice time, but I am hoping I can speak to him. I haven't seen him in so long, I forgot what he looks like.

That's not exactly true, but you get the point.

"It'll be almost impossible to get to the team while they're at the arena. They've got tons of security to get through first, unless security knows you're with one of them, or the player in question takes you back there themselves, of course. However, since the game tomorrow is around here, I can tell you the hotel they're staying at. You can try getting in."

"I'm sorry, but I can't let you in," the receptionist tells me. "Mr. Davis did not inform us that he was expecting visitors, and to ensure his safety, we cannot let anyone up."

I figured as much. It makes sense as I could be anyone, a fan, a stalker, a murderer. If they let everyone up to the players, there wouldn't be any space left for *any*one. "Can't you call him? He'll tell you it's okay." I hope. He should, we're friends.

"I'll try." He reaches for the phone and dials what I'm assuming is Grey's room number. It takes a bit, but he picks up eventually. "Mr. Davis? There's someone wanting to speak to you, and he insists he is your boyfriend."

Yeah, I had to lie there. I mean, I could've said I'm a friend, but I bet everyone who's trying to get in says that. Maybe a bunch of people also go for the partner lie, but not as many. I think. I don't know, honestly. I have never put too much thought into all this before.

"What's your name, sir?" the man asks me.

"Luan Hayes."

"Luan Hayes," he repeats, then gives Grey a brief description of me. My hair, eye color, stuff like that. He nods, then hangs up the phone. "Room 305."

I thank him quickly, then rush toward the elevator to get up there.

Is it weird that I'm nervous to see him again? To stand in front of him again? To be able to smell and feel him again?

Is it desperate that I want all those things more than my next breath, too?

Maybe a little… or a little more. But I don't care. I deserve this after months of even just getting him to text me back, okay? I deserve to see my friend.

When I reach his room, I take one or five encouraging breaths before I knock on his door three times. It takes a moment until the door opens, but when it does, my breath gets sucked right out of my lungs.

Grey stands before me, a towel wrapped around his hips, his hair wet, and water droplets dripping from the strands. I try not to, and yet my eyes wander over his torso, not to ogle him but to look at each of his tattoos. He has way more than I thought he did. They look so random, like most of them were drunk decisions, and still I wonder if they have any deeper meaning. If so, he won't tell me.

I don't know how much time passes until I get woken up from my trance when Grey snaps his fingers. "My eyes are up here, *boyfriend.*"

My eyes snap up at the last word, our gazes meeting. Grey looks a little bemused, the frown only half as deep as usual. There are no signs of a smile, or a smirk or anything remotely close to joy, the only way I know he's happy to see me is the softness of his voice and the only half-deep frown.

"If I said I was your friend, that guy wouldn't have even called you," I defend myself. "Besides, boyfriend has a better ring to it anyway, wouldn't you agree?"

Grey rolls his eyes, stepping aside to let me in. I didn't think he would. Yes, I did think he'd greet me at the door, but not that he'd allow me to enter his hotel room. I thought we'd have a quick talk and then he'll send me back home.

Technically speaking, I could've called Grey from my phone myself but I wanted my visit to be somewhat of a surprise.

"Let's just hope that guy doesn't sell this information to some news portals," Grey says as he walks away. I follow him.

"Right, sorry. I didn't think about that. Honestly, this whole you being a *pro* player is kind of unnerving. I never even talked to a professional soccer player before in my life, and now here I am, talking to *you,* Sir Superstar."

He ignores my attempt at an apology, but that was to be expected. "I'll just get dressed. If you need anything, take it. I don't pay for any of it, so even if you want the most expensive drink, just take it."

"I don't drink," I tell him, now getting more nervous than I did on the elevator ride up here.

My sobriety isn't a secret because I am very proud of it, but there are still some days I want to say fuck it and pick up that bottle again. Usually I have my best friend around to stop me before I can. If Grey hadn't told me there's some around here, I wouldn't have given it any thought, but now that I know and he's going to leave me all by myself...

"There's water, too, you know." His eyebrows fall. "I'm not sure about apple juice though."

"Okay."

Grey nods and walks away, leaving me behind in a hotel living room, right across from a cabinet that looks awfully a lot like a *liquor* cabinet.

I'd just have to walk over there, get me a glass, and fill it up, down it and that'd be it. It wouldn't hurt anyone.

No, yes it would. It would hurt me.

I slap my hands to my head, closing my eyes to concentrate.
You do not need alcohol to be brave.
You do not need alcohol to be brave.
You do not need alcohol to be brave.

I can do this. I can be alone in one room with all sorts of liquors and not feel the need to open one of the bottles. I can stand here and admire the modern interior of the hotel room, the expensive looking wooden floor, the white couches, the glass table… the white shelves and cabinets that look like they hold tons of great bottles.

My heartbeat increases, my eyes focusing on that cabinet before me. Just three steps separates me from it. Three steps and I could—No.

No, I can't. I promised myself I wouldn't. I promised to be a better version of myself. To stay strong.

But it's just one drink…

"Are you okay?" Grey asks and lays a hand right onto my shoulder. My head snaps into the direction his voice comes from.

Only when my eyes meet his dark ones do I realize my heavily rising chest, my shaking hands.

The moment before I answer Grey, I take a deep breath, closing my eyes to gather myself again. And then I nod.

"I've been sober for almost nine months," I tell him. Honestly I'm not sure from what day people normally count their sobriety, but I chose the day I went to rehab because that's when my journey began. "It's not usually a problem but sometimes it's still difficult especially when I know I'm alone in one room with alcohol, you know? It's fine though, I promise. I wasn't going to drink anything. Okay, I was thinking about it, but I stayed strong. Mostly."

"I'm glad you did." This time, there's the slimmest smile ever on his lips as he speaks. "You can be really proud of yourself, *boyfriend*."

I groan, tilting my head back in my neck. "I'm not your boyfriend until *at least* the fifth date." It's a lie, but he doesn't need to know.

I grin at Grey, watching the tug on his lips fall back into his usual frown.

Ah, there he is: the Grey I know.

"You're not planning on driving back to Malibu at eleven p.m., are you?" he asks, ignoring my somewhat plea for him to *finally* ask me out on a stupid date.

He doesn't have the time for one, I know, but he could ask anyway. Asking now or in a month won't make a big difference.

"Nah, I can stay another hour, it's fine." I follow Grey over to the couches, taking a seat *right* next to him. I think he hates it, but I don't care.

Our thighs touch slightly, and so I spread my legs just a little bit to increase the contact. He scowls at me but all I do is smile at him innocently.

"You could spend the night here, you know?" he says, shocking me there for a moment. Grey did not just ask me to spend the night in his hotel room, I wouldn't believe it even if I was dead. "Spares you three hours of driving."

My smile widens once more, and I know he can sense what I'm about to say without him having to say it. He rolls his eyes, then gestures for me to go on.

"If you're in love with me, Grey Davis, you can just say it."

Chapter 13

"I wish I could make myself stay"—Grace by Bebe Rexha

Grey

November 2022

I CAN'T REMEMBER a time when I spent a night with someone in the same hotel room without having sex. Miles is excluded here, he's *always* the exception.

The most surprising bit, Luan and I didn't even share a room. I mean, yes, technically we did, but I'm talking about bedrooms. Since I had two bedrooms, Luan slept in one and I took the other. I did give him some of my clothes though, just so he wouldn't have to sleep in his.

When he got here, Luan was all colorful. He wore a bright yellow shirt with some sort of affirmation. Somehow, that shirt hoodie is just *him*. He wore jeans and white shoes, something bright.

After I gave him some of my clothes, I really had to force myself not to laugh. The image of the bright shining Luan Hayes in black clothing… it was hilarious to say the least. It was not him at all, and still it looked good.

I'm just about to walk out of my bedroom when my phone rings. Not having a clue who would call at six in the morning, I immediately go to pick it up without checking the caller-ID first. "Hello?"

"What the fuck did you do," my father's voice comes through

the phone, harsh as always whenever he talks to me. But what did I do? I don't know.

"I played hockey? I don't know, Dad. You're gonna have to give me more information than that if you want a genuine answer." Should've let the call go to voicemail.

"You went against my wishes!" he yells, making me flinch.

"Against your…?" *Ah, Luan.*

That fucking receptionist. There's no way my father would know about any of this if there weren't currently some pretty interesting news going around about me.

I've been on the team for a couple of weeks only, so this has to be a record of some sort.

And still, I pretend like I have no idea what my father is talking about. "What wishes exactly? You have a bunch when it comes to me."

"Don't get disrespectful now, boy."

Inhale. Exhale.

Just because I talk doesn't mean I am being disrespectful. When will my father understand this? Chances are never.

"I'm sorry. Now, could you please tell me what exactly it is that I did?"

"The entire internet is filled with news about you dating that *boy*." There's a whole lot of disgust on the last word. "Pictures of him at your game and your hotel. I ask you not to be with that *guy*, and you go behind my back to be with him anyway. He is bad news, Grey. Now the whole world thinks you're…"

We all know the last word he can't, for the life of him, say out loud. I'm actually glad he can't say it as that prevents him from putting a label on me, even if that's what he does with unspoken words anyway.

"The whole world thinks I'm what, Dad?" I press, not because I want him to say it, but because for some unknown reasons, I can't stop myself from pushing him.

My whole body fills up with anger so quickly, it's a miracle I'm not steaming.

Six Years

"You know what I mean."

I ball my free hand into a fist, using every ounce of my willpower not to punch the nearest wall. "I'm not gay," I tell him for the millionth time.

"You better not be, Grey."

"But I do like *people*, other than just women."

He keeps quiet, except for that one faint growl that strongly disagrees with me.

The urge to scream is creeping up on me with every passing second. The urge to tell my father exactly how many fucks I give about what he thinks of me, about who he wants me to date, is so close to breaking free that my knuckles are turning white from the amount of pressure I put into my fist.

I'm so close to breaking that I can taste it on my tongue, but then there's the aftertaste. The hate. The loneliness I'll encounter when I let all of my thoughts run wild. The loss of my family… of everyone I love.

"Him and I aren't dating," I finally say, giving in. I take a seat on the bed, lifting my face to the ceiling, my eyes closing.

I'll never be able to live my life the way *I* want unless I figure out a way to talk to my dad without getting disowned.

As I fall back on the bed, ready to just die right here on the spot, there's a knock on my door.

"Is that him?" my father asks immediately. "Did you have him in *your* hotel room, Grey?!"

"No, it's just Miles," I lie at the same time as the door opens and Luan sticks his head into my room. "I have to go. Coach wants to see us." Without letting my father argue, I hang up the phone and throw it somewhere on the bed behind me.

"You kind of look like someone ran you over with a truck," Luan says as he comes walking inside without even asking if that's okay with me.

And I feel like it, too. "Are you saying I look dead in the morning?"

He nods, that signature smile of his slowly making its way

onto his face. It's six in the morning, how the fuck does he have the strength to *smile*?

Luan's still in my clothes. He fills them in surprisingly well.

I never noticed before, nor paid any attention to it in the first place, but Luan and I must be about the same size. I'm taller than he is, but he has more muscles than I do which makes my clothes the perfect size for him. The shirt isn't too loose or too wide, it just fits perfectly. So do my shorts.

"I have decided something," Luan announces, getting closer to me with every word. By the time he says the last word, he stands right in front of me, between my legs, his hands lying on my shoulders, our gazes locked.

"You love ice hockey?" It would be a miracle if he did.

Luan shakes his head. "No, but I'm going to watch every game of yours anyway. And if I'm at work while you play, I'll make sure I at least get some notifications about the score to be up to date."

I lay my hands on the back of his thighs, at first without even noticing, but then the heat of his body almost burns my palms. Every inch of his body that touches mine is awfully hot, kind of like they're burning themselves a way right into my memory.

"So what did you decide then?" I ask, my voice low, almost a whisper.

Luan slides his hands down, following my arms until his hands meet mine. He pulls them up until they rest somewhere between his hips and waist instead. And then his hands find my jaw, enveloping my face.

"I have decided," he speaks quietly, his voice lower than usual as well, "that I'm going to keep your clothes as a souvenir."

"Okay." I pull him in a little closer. "What do I get to keep?"

He smiles again, then strokes his thumb over my bottom lip. Luan doesn't move in to kiss me, he's just looking, touching me and somehow that's even worse than if he just pressed his lips to mine.

"What do you *want* to keep?"

Without thinking, I pull up his shirt enough to sneak my hands underneath, needing to feel his skin on mine. He doesn't stop me.

"What do you have to offer?"

His smile grows a little smug, still sweet and innocent though. Then he leans down, his mouth by my ear when he says, "It doesn't matter what I have to offer, Grey Davis. I'd give you anything. It's about what you're willing to take."

Luan Hayes

November 24th, 6:06 AM

I can't sleep

Like, not at all

Hello?

It's only three in the morning for me, Grey Davis. So it should be around six for you.

Please wake up.

Night, Luan.

Luan Hayes

December 3rd, 7:52 PM

I just got home from practice, and honestly, I thought I was going to freeze to death!

Well, I supposed fifty degrees is still warmer than whatever you have over there in NYC. Wait, aren't you like in Canada right now for a game? If so, yikes!

I'm definitely a summer guy. A beach guy. Snow is awful.

Actually, I don't know if snow is awful, I've never even seen snow in my entire life.

> Just go to Toronto for the winter, you'll see snow.

That's all you have to say?

> Yeah. I have to go.

Luan Hayes

December 25th, 6:03 AM

MERRY CHRISTMAS!

Have a lovely day with your family

Or friends, whoever you're with

Just have a great day, okay?

> Thanks, you, too.

Luan Hayes

December 25th, 4:22 PM

I wish you were here...

Luan Hayes

January 1st, 12:00 AM

Happy New Year!! xx

> Happy New Year.

I hope you had a great night

Luan Hayes

February 13th, 7:57 PM

Do you have any plans for Valentine's Day?

No.

I'm coaching tomorrow. I told the kids in relationships, like I do every year, if they show up, they'll be tortured for not being single.

Do you want to FaceTime? We haven't talked in ages.

Luan Hayes

February 13th, 9:21 PM

A no would've sufficed, you know...

Luan Hayes

February 14th, 12:00 AM

Happy Valentine's Day then, I guess

Luan Hayes

March 7th, 9:51 PM

That was a good game, I think? You did win...

Thanks

Grey, if you don't want to talk to me, can you just tell me, please? Because I would gladly spend another six years texting you daily and get vague answers, but I'd still like to know if all my efforts are even worth it.

Luan Hayes

March 8th, 12:01 AM

I guess that answers that

Chapter 1

"what the hell did I do?"—New by Days

Grey

June 2023

"I WAS THINKING, UNCLE GREY…" Brooke holds on to my hand a little tighter when we cross the street. "When I ask Daddy for the pink dress princess, maybe I also get the blue dress princess because I saw on the TV that they are friends and then I need both, right?"

Miles asked me to take Brooke in for the week as Eden's sick and he wants to try and reduce the chances of Brooke getting sick as well. I suppose having two sick kids is a whole lot more exhausting than one. I wouldn't know, I don't have kids.

Because I know Brooke would only ever run back to Miles if we stayed in my apartment, I decided to take Brooke on a little vacation. In Malibu.

I am not here to see my parents, though I am hoping to see my mother. But there's this little voice in the back of my head that says if I just walk around El Matador Beach, I might cross paths with a certain curly-headed guy. Yup, I have sunken that low.

He just won't get out of my head, and I am convinced if I see him one more time, I can finally put him in the past. By now, he should be mad with me, especially given how I've treated him the past couple of months. First I ask him to spend the night in my hotel, and then I barely even respond anymore like he's done something wrong.

It's not him, and if I could, I'd *love* to get to know him a little better, but I think that's also mainly because he's a mystery to me. Figuring people out has always been my favorite occupation, and me not being able to read him like a book annoys me.

"Well, Brookie, how about instead of us going to get some ice cream, we will go to the toy store, and I will buy you both princesses?" She'd get ice cream either way, and I love spoiling her.

Brooke gasps. "But what about Daddy? He said no more many Barbies."

He did say that. Brooke barely has any room left in her bedroom, however, as her uncle, it is my duty to make sure she gets all the things her father tells her she can't have. "Well, if you already have them, he can't say no anymore, can he?"

Brooke giggles, nodding. When she looks up to me as soon as we reach the other side of the street, her eyes fill with tears. "When we go back to the hotel, Uncle Grey, can we call Daddy?"

Brooke might be used to being away from Miles for the nights, but even when she lived with Miles's stepsister up until the beginning of our last year of college, he still showed up to see her every day. He drove from New City to Manhattan just to say good night to her every single day. There were times when he couldn't make it, but that was okay because Brooke was used to it. And now that she's been living with her father for almost two years, has him around her all day, every day, it's a little hard on Brooke not seeing Miles for a week. She's been on more phone calls with him in the last two days than she was asleep. She even refuses to take her usual naps only so she can FaceTime her father.

We're about to pass a Hayesland store when I pull out my phone, ready to call Miles right now. I would take Brooke into that store because it's closer to our hotel than a Li Co. store, but if my father happens to see me in there, I'll be dead.

"Do you want to call him now?" I ask, already passing Brooke my phone. She grabs it, clicking dial because she knows I opened

Miles's contact for her in advance.

Brooke then stops in her tracks, staring at the screen as she waits for Miles to pick up. And when his face finally pops up on the screen, Brooke smiles so widely, she might as well be ripping the corners of her mouth.

"DADDY!" Brooke shrieks, not caring about the heads of strangers passing us turning around to stare at her all judgmentally. "I miss you!"

I can't really see Miles because, first of all, I am a whole lot taller than this little five-year-old, and second of all, she has the phone so close to her face, even if I could see the screen from up here, I still wouldn't be able to see a lot.

"I miss you, too, little monkey."

Truthfully, I never really understood why Miles calls her that occasionally, that is until I now share a bed with her because she's too scared to sleep alone. Whenever she sleeps over at my apartment, Brooke isn't scared because she knows her father is across the hall. If something were to happen, he's there in the blink of an eye. Malibu, however, is different. Miles isn't near to protect her, and the entire city is unfamiliar to her. She's been here once, though with Miles and not for long either.

Anyway, now that she spends the nights in one bed with me, being frightened most of the time and missing her father, Brooke clings to me like a fucking monkey all night long. If I try to move, she'll groan all adorably and gets mad at me for waking her up, so I try my best not to move.

"Do you know that Uncle Grey and I had the Pizza for breakfast, Daddy!" she tells her father like it's the best thing ever. To her, it most definitely is.

I can't cook, okay? And since we slept in and missed breakfast from the hotel, I had to get creative. Brooke is really picky when it comes to food, and she tends to *puke* that shit out if she doesn't like it. I wanted to avoid that happening at all costs, and since she loves Pizza, it was all I could come up with for breakfast.

That kid might be the most spoiled child in the whole world, at least when it comes to food. I mean, her father does happen to own Rêverie, which is a five-star restaurant with a couple of them spread all around the U.S. He learned how to cook from his father, who built those restaurants and treated them like they're his kids. Miles's a damn great chef, so yes, that kid has standards when it comes to food.

Unless it's ice cream.

Also, I wasn't sure if I could take her to breakfast at the hotel anyway. They usually serve fruits as well, and Brooke is severely allergic to strawberries. I don't want to risk her smelling them by the buffet and then ending up in the hospital, or even worse.

"You did?" Brooke nods to which Miles chuckles. "Well, but you are eating vegetables though, right?"

Brooke looks up at me, furrowing her eyebrows like she doesn't know what to say. When she looks back at the phone, she ends up shaking her head. "Nope. Just the Pizza and ice cream. Oh, Daddy! Yesterday Uncle Grey and I go to the fruit market, and I ate the Dragon."

It wasn't a *fruit market*, it was a flea market that happened to sell all sorts of exotic fruits. When Brooke saw one of the dragon fruits, she begged me to try them. Naturally, because I am a great uncle, I bought two of them and we tried them back at the hotel. She never ate a dragon.

Whatever Miles responds, I don't hear because when I turn toward the Hayesland entry doors, I spot an only too familiar guy with the greenest eyes staring right at me. But he's not alone.

Chapter 2

"still a flicker of hope that you first gave to me"—
Flicker by Niall Horan

Luan

June 2023

WHAT THE HELL IS HE DOING HERE?

I've spent the last three months trying not to think about him, trying not to picture his handsome face and the tons of tattoos I know he has. I tried not to imagine what other kinds of tattoos he's hiding underneath those black pants of his, or what the Korean letters on his neck mean.

Just when I thought I finally managed to leave my fantasies behind, he's here. Standing maybe two feet away from me with this little blonde kid who I know is his best friend's daughter.

Truthfully, I was ready to wait a million years for him, not because I have some kind of obsession with him—I don't—but because I know a good person when I see them. He may not let it show that freely, but something tells me Grey Davis is nothing like the guy he pretends to be.

And still he ghosted you.

It's okay. I am a patient guy, knowing very well that I *always* get what I want. My mother used to say I tend to want to have everything my way because I'm an only child and was spoiled more than anyone could imagine. However, a decade later and we all know it's not being an only child that allows me to get everything I want.

"Daddy, you know what Uncle Grey said?" the little blonde girl speaks all high pitched and excitedly. She doesn't even give her father a second to respond before she continues. "He said, when we come back home, then he take Eden for a day so we can go to the playground together without him!"

That's nice... but why does Grey take his best friend's *daughter* across the country? Seems a little weird to me. If Doro had a kid, I wouldn't take them anywhere without her, at least nothing farther than a playground. Maybe another city for a daytrip, but definitely not out of the state, or even across the state. Anything that's farther away than an hour car ride would not happen.

There's a slight chance they moved here, but I doubt it.

Before I know it, the little girl hands over the phone to Grey, and while he's trying to pocket it, she grasps his free hand and tries pulling Grey into Hayesland. But he's not budging. It's like he's frozen in place, staring at me though his eyes aren't on mine.

He's taking in my body, and when I look down at myself, I realize why. I'm still wearing my soccer uniform. I don't play anymore, but all the Coaches promised our teams we'd play if the U19 won their game last week. They did, and so we clocked in our promise today.

And then his gaze falls to the stroller in front of me, to my hand that's firmly wrapped around the handle.

His eyes heat up a little, darken with something dangerous, but I wouldn't know why. Even if that baby in the stroller was my kid, Grey Davis has no right to be mad about it. He was the one to ghost me after all. And if he used his brain for a second, he would realize that it should be impossible to suddenly have a newborn in just three months.

I don't owe him any explanations, but when he finally shakes off his shock and allows his niece, I guess, to pull him right into the store and he passes me, my head just snaps.

"Grey," I say and even though I can tell he doesn't want to stop, the little girl does.

She looks up at Grey, then at me before she scrunches up her entire face with a smile. "Uncle Grey, look!" The little girl points at me. "Someone wants to talk to you."

Grey visibly exhales then turns to me. Before he even gets to utter a single word, the blonde kid cuts him off. "But no rude-talk, okay, Uncle Grey? Daddy says you have to be nice."

I almost want to laugh.

Deciding to listen to his best friend's daughter, he says, "It's great to see you again."

Is it? I mean, I am awesome and meeting me is always a pleasure, but I'm not sure he would agree right now. "That's not my kid," I blurt out without greeting him first. "He's the son of one of my co-coaches, I just offered to take him for a walk because he was getting restless."

Grey nods, his face stays unchanged, still almost robotic. "Cool."

The girl, I think her name is Brooke, but I'm not sure, kicks her tiny feet against Grey's. "Be nice, Uncle Grey. We practiced."

Grey looks down to her, a hint of a smile now tugging on his lips. "Did we?"

She nods. "Yesterday, remember? When we practice a smile?" She lets go of Grey's hand, then brings both of her index fingers to either side of her mouth, slightly pushing up the corners. "See, like this!"

Grey shakes his head, and the sound leaving him almost takes my breath away. He actually *chuckles*. Then he picks her up from the floor, holding her in his arms. "Are you going to tell your daddy that I was being rude, Brooke?"

See, Brooke. I knew it.

Brooke nods proudly. "Unless you be nice now, okay? Daddy always say you need more friends, Uncle Grey."

"I have plenty."

I doubt that. Sure, he has his teammates, but are those really considered friends? It's more of a forced friendliness they have to keep up, isn't it?

"Like who? And not say Daddy, or Uncle Ron, or Uncle Colin. Or Memory, and Lily, or Sofia. They don't count, Uncle Grey."

That's surprisingly a lot more people than I thought he'd genuinely accept in his life.

"I have you and Eden," Grey answers, then tickles Brooke's belly to make her giggle. "That's plenty of friends."

Brooke narrows her eyes at Grey, then seemingly shrugs off the entire conversation like it never mattered and turns to look at me. "Uncle Grey said we go ice skating later, do you want to come?"

"Ice skating? The rinks are closed, aren't they?"

Brooke shakes her head. "We always go to the arena when it's the summer too in New York. My uncles and Sofia and Lily and Daddy and me, we always skate when they don't play the ice hockey anymore. But Memory never skates with us because she has to watch my brother because he's very little so he can't skate yet. So the ice hockey arena is open, right, Uncle Grey?"

"An acquaintance on the LA Kings team pulled some strings so we could skate in their arena for a little while. If you want to come…" Grey doesn't voice the invitation all the way, but I'm a little moved anyway.

As much as I want to say yes, despite knowing I shouldn't, there's one problem. "I can't skate," I say, feeling weird having to admit I am *not* good at something. "I've never skated in my entire life. I am a beach guy with a love for summer temperatures, not a… cold-freak." I have never even seen snow before, not in real life.

"That's no problem. Uncle Grey can teach you." That kid is going to grow up being the wingman for everyone she knows, I'm calling it.

"Do you know how to inline skate?" Grey asks, to which I sort of nod.

"It's been a while." Like a *long* while. I think the last time I inline skated was when I was twelve or ten. Maybe eight, who even knows. Definitely sometime before my teenage years started.

"It's like riding a bike. Once you know how to do it, you don't unlearn it. You might be a little wobbly on your feet at first, but you'll get used to it. Ice skating is sort of like inline skating, it's why a whole lot of figure skaters inline skate and practice stunts even *outside* of the rink."

Where are all these words coming from? Grey Davis barely texted back more than three words at once *when* he was still replying.

Wait, never mind. When it comes to skating and ice hockey, he would talk a whole lot more last year as well. That minor information must've slipped my mind.

"To you it might be, but I can count on one hand how many times I *inline* skated, Grey Davis." I don't like showing my weaknesses in front of other people because showing a weakness leads to embarrassment, and embarrassment leads to being made fun of. Though, I am twenty-four years old, so maybe I should start seeing all of this a whole other way.

Grey shrugs. "It'll be fun."

To him. "Okay, I trust you on that." I wink at him, to which Grey rolls his eyes, already regretting inviting me on behalf of Brooke. As they're about to head right into the store, I blurt out some words just to hold up the conversation a tiny bit longer. "Do you always shop at the competition's stores?"

Grey looks right inside of the Hayesland store then back at me. "Sometimes."

How he still doesn't know that *I* am sort of the competition remains a mystery to me. Unlike Grey Davis, my face is plastered all over the internet if one googled Hayesland or my father. Then again, a whole lot of people have the same last name as me, and just because my last name is in the brand name, it doesn't mean I am associable with it. It's like saying anyone with the last name *Swift* is automatically related to Taylor Swift.

"I see. Got to keep an eye out for them, huh?"

Grey's eyes narrow at me just that tiny bit. "Always."

"We go now, okay—What's your name?" Brooke asks.

"Luan."

"Okay, Luan. We go now because I get two new Barbies, and then when we go ice skating we call you and Uncle Grey come pick you up with me, okay?"

Chapter 3

"light the room up without trying"—Piece Of You by Shawn Mendes

Grey

June 2023

"THEY'RE TOO LOOSE," I tell Luan when he tries to get up after attempting to put on his skates.

I almost laughed the second I stopped the car in front of him when I picked him up, seeing the skates he had draped over his shoulder. He must've bought them last minute because they look *very* new. However, as a now professional ice hockey player, I know my fair share about skates, and the ones he has might as well have cost twenty dollars.

I guess the price is okay for a beginner, especially when he might never use them again. However, I don't think he'll ever be able to skate in those as the ones he bought are speed skates. Sure, they're great for someone who skates frequently and professionally as a speed skater, but they're not for him.

Luan leans back against the locker behind him, groaning. "How should I know how to tie stupid skates?"

"You have the wrong skates, Luan," Brooke tells him, saying what I couldn't bring myself to do. She's already standing right beside me, her skates all tied up perfectly for a five-year-old. I'll have to tighten them a little, but that's about a ten-second work.

"There is something like '*the wrong skates*'?!"

I don't know if I despise or love his knowledge about skating.

It's kind of adorable, but on the contrary, who the fuck knows as little about all of it as he does?

Still, I nod, keeping a straight face. "You need hockey skates or figure skates, not speed skates."

Luan blinks at me a little lost. "Well, I don't have anything else."

"What's your size?" I never leave New York without at least two pairs of skates with me. You never know when you might need them.

"Ten?"

"Shoe size, right?" He nods. "So an 8.5." I'm not quite sure if this is normal, but I can translate shoe sizes into skate sizes in my sleep. "You can have mine if you want."

Luan shakes his head, though he grins at me as always. "I bet your skates cost about the same as my house, so no thank you. If I break them, I'll owe you both of my kidneys and my heart."

I only offer him a sort of disagreeing yet also acknowledging hum. My skates didn't cost that much, they were about eight hundred, I think. A thousand two hundred at most. That's almost nothing to me given the money I grew up with, and as an NHL hockey player, even in my second year only, I make enough money without having my trust fund to go back to if needed, so a thousand still isn't a lot to me.

"Uncle Grey!" Brooke shrieks a little madly this time. "Like we practiced!"

Oh this kid…

I love her, truly. I've known Brooke since she was about to turn one, now she's turning six this year and let me tell you, there has not been a single day in my life that she doesn't remind me to be nice. Granted, only *if* she's around me. But even if she's not, recently, she tends to call me a lot using Miles's phone and guess why, to tell me to smile a little more on TV next time.

I don't do smiles, especially not in public. That's gross.

But for her I gladly let a smile slip. Not right now though.

"Where did your smugness go anyway?" I ask Luan, only to

earn myself a slap from a certain five-year-old. *Rude.*

"Uncle Grey, if you don't be nice to Luan, I go tell Daddy."

Because he'd do anything about it. Miles is more likely to throw a party because I scared off some guy rather than tell me to be nice. Somehow, he's a little scared I'd replace him with another best friend. That won't happen, ever. Not only because we've gotten a fucking best friend tattoo together, but because Miles is just… Miles. I love that guy, even if I'd never say that to him without it being a hundred percent necessary. Or when I'm drunk. I get affectionate when I drink, especially with him.

I'm not *in love* with Miles. He's just my best friend, and I happen to think having a best friend is a whole lot like being in a relationship.

Best friends offer to fake date you in any situation *for fun*. They stick up for you like nobody else ever would. They call you out on stupid shit then dive right into that mess with you. They do all the things you'd do with someone if you were dating them, minus the whole sex thing, I guess. They're the ones you *always* choose over a partner unless there's a great reason why that's not what you should be doing.

Best friends are for-lifers.

"Do you want the skates or not?" He's definitely not going to be able to skate in the ones he has.

Luan smirks at me, his eyes follow down my figure before they travel back up to meet mine. "I think you only want me wearing something of yours."

Of course. I forgot how cocky he is. "Unless you threw away the clothes you stole from me last year, I'm sure you wear something of mine all the time." He probably doesn't, but if he gets to be smug, so do I.

Luan shrugs. "Picture me in them a lot, huh? I do look very good in your clothes, just saying. Though, I think yellow suits me a whole lot better than black."

Frankly, I think so too. I don't understand how *anyone* would want to wear a bright as fuck color like yellow, and depending on the shade of yellow, it's even pretty damn ugly too, but it suits Luan. Even right now, that stupid bright yellow jacket he decided to wear looks good on him, despite it burning through my eyes down to my soul.

Why's he even wearing a jacket in the first place? Yes, ice rinks are cold but it's not like he's going to fucking die in there. Or maybe he will, he really doesn't strike me as the kind of guy who appreciates the cold.

I love the heat, I grew up with it, but the cold is a million times better. You can't do anything about burning up, except for AC's maybe, or moving into a pool. But with the cold, you can put on layers of clothing until you're no longer freezing. It's a whole lot cozier on the dark side of things.

"Are you done being smug?"

"Nope."

"Great," I breathe out, feeling a little sorry for myself there, as I walk away from him to get the skates from my bag.

While I get the skates, I hear Brooke speak to Luan, but I can't make out her words. I'm just hoping she isn't talking about me, and knowing that little girl, she most definitely isn't. All she really talks about is princesses, Eden, her father, and Emory. Sometimes she throws school and Reece into the mix. Reece is Colin's younger brother who's around the same age as Brooke. They're basically best friends, though I know Miles is already suspicious of that guy. According to both Miles and Colin, Reece has a little crush on Brooke, but Brooke has no idea.

Kids seemingly in love is the cutest thing ever. Some of those little fellas are way more attentive to their crush than some my age are to their actual partner. And at twenty-two, one should know better than to treat their partner like a piece of garbage.

If little five-year-old Reece can pick up a fucking daisy and gift it to Brooke for no reason at all, a twenty-something-year-old should be able to even just *listen* to their partner, communicate, and have more braincells to know that cheating is stupid and you will get caught.

Six Years

Luan shakes his head, grinning. "Your enthusiasm for me is blowing me away, Grey Davis. Careful, or I might think you actually like me."

I let out a gruff in response, then without saying a word, help Luan out of his skates and exchange them with mine.

"You know, the last time someone went down on their knees for me to help me out with my *footwear,* I must've been eight years old because I still somehow put the left shoe on the right foot and the right shoe on the left," Luan tells me, chuckling a little at the memory.

"Daddy always do this for me too!" Brooke shrieks, and I just know she's currently grinning up at him so widely, it's sickening. But her grins are the only ones I can stand all day, every day, so that's alright.

"Oh, he does?"

"Yup." Brooke pops the *p* in the end. "Then he call me a duckling, but in our language so Memory don't understand, and she can't be mad then."

Luan gasps dramatically loud just as I start tying the first skate. "Really? So did you tell... Emory?"

"Yup!" Brooke kicks her legs around, almost hitting me. "And she laughs then. So I go tell Uncle Grey, and Uncle Grey always gets mad with Daddy. Also, when Daddy says no to a new Barbie, I tell Uncle Grey and he gets me a new one. Like today! I got *five* new princesses, Luan. *Five.*"

...What? She couldn't decide on just two, so I got her all five.

As her uncle of some sorts, I have a duty to spoil that kid, okay? I am supposed to be the single, rich uncle who spends his days on yachts after I retire in a few years because my limbs are stupidly unusable. And as said Uncle, I am obligated to buy my friend's kids anything their parents won't. It's the law.

I pull tightly on the skate laces, making Luan gasp one more time.

"Grey Davis, that's rudely tight. I feel like it's cutting off the blood circulation to my feet," he complains. I ignore him and move over to the other foot. "I get it. You want my feet to fall off so that you can make sure I cannot run after anyone else as you want me all to yourself." *Of course.* "It's adorable, really. I feel honored, and although I can admit, I'd love for you to be head over heels for me, I think we should take it a little slower. Maybe go on a date first, you feel me? You ghosted me for almost a year, so I think it's only fair you give me a second to weigh my options first. After I decide on you, you may cut off my feet."

Almost a year. It's been *three months.*

I look up to meet his eyes. My mouth opens but no words pass my lips, and so I close my mouth again.

This guy is definitely… something.

"So, I take it you can still feel your feet then?"

Luan nods. "A little." And so I pull the strings a little tighter. He wheezes in response. "A little tighter and I swear my feet will fall off. Should that happen, you can explain to my parents why their only child now no longer has feet because I sure won't tell them this story."

"You'll find a day to tell that story, don't worry."

"That wasn't my concern—"

I pull onto the strings once more. "Still feel your feet?"

"Nope."

"Perfect."

Chapter 4

"my devil is the devil that's inside"—Shadow Of Mine by Alec Benjamin

Inam

June 2023

"When I was six, my best friend's parents took us to a skate park because they believed me when I said I knew how to handle a skateboard. I couldn't, in fact, I barely knew how to *stand* on that board without falling right off. Anyway, fast forward a hot second and I stand on that ramp, ready to skate that thing down when Charlie yelled stop. He startled me so much that I *fell* down that ramp. Well, I slid down, kind of. I was lucky to not have broken a bone, though that would've been cool at least to six-year-old me."

Is this my long and bad way of saying that I am *not* ready to step on the ice? Yes.

Does Grey understand a single word of those I just uttered? I don't think so because that man doesn't even react. He steps on the ice like that's the most normal thing to him ever. It probably is.

But it's not for me.

During a normal summer day in Malibu, I fear slipping on the fucking pathway, so imagine my fear right now.

I only agreed to come here because… honestly, I don't know why. I was mad at Grey for ignoring my presence up until he stood there right in front of me. Somehow, the second our eyes locked, all of my madness left me with my breath. When he stood there in all his sexy glory, a perfectly fine reasoning to hold a grudge evaporated into thin air. Poof. Gone and left no crumbs.

So when he asked, sort of anyway, my brain couldn't think of a reason as to why I shouldn't go to a stupid ice rink with him, when I know for a fact that I cannot skate.

I am confident, more than what's good for me, but standing an inch away from slippery ice with a *toddler* skating like she's been a professional figure skater for fifty years has my goddamn ego crumbling bit by bit.

I will not be able to skate that effortlessly, let alone *stand* on this ice without almost slipping while Grey stands there, holding out his hand for me, knowing fully well that the slickness of the ice isn't an enemy to him and that he will not fall on his face and break his beautiful somewhat pointy nose.

I am just about to get my shit together and take his hand when Grey voices a question that has my entire body freeze to a more solid ice than the one beneath his feet. "So, where's Charlie now?"

Where's Charlie now… That's a very good question.

Instead of answering, I smirk at Grey. "Is that a personal question, Grey Davis?" If I recall correctly, I am not allowed to ask him personal questions. Well, I can ask, I just won't get an answer, and him showing interest in my life is about as rare as his text replies. Or any responses, really.

"It is," he confirms. "Though I believe it's a question about *him* and not you."

My smirk grows a little more smug. "No, I think you're meaning to ask whether he's my boyfriend now or if I'm still as single as the day we met."

"Or, I just want to know whether you have more than one friend or not."

Right, because he knows so much about me? He hasn't even met Doro, my only friend. Grey saw her once, but they didn't talk so that doesn't count as having met. Grey also knows that I coach soccer and that I—

"I have tons of friends," I answer, lifting my nose up a little higher. "You should know that."

"Elderlies from Bingo-night don't count."

AHA. So he does remember. That's quite interesting. If he still remembers a thing like this, something I have mentioned *once* and only vaguely, he's got to be at least a tiny bit interested in me. I think.

"Charlie is dead," I finally answer, spitting the words out fast and a little spitefully, like I blame my best friend for dying. I do in some ways, but I also know I can't do anything about it.

"I'm sorry to hear that." Although his apology sounds sincere, his face is still as unbothered as ever. There are no signs of sympathy, no signs of regret for having asked. Nothing. It's like he can't feel emotions at all, but I know he can.

"It's alright. He's been dead since we were twelve, so… I'm over it." Mostly.

"Are you ever going to step on the ice, or will you continue to stall?" He shakes off the topic like we never even started it. *Maybe he's not so interested after all.*

"I'm good right where I am, my shoes—"

"Skates," he corrects.

"Yes, yes, skates, they're probably way too loose now too. I'll trip and snap my ankles or something."

"You know what we call *players* like that?" *I don't.* "A bender."

I nod slowly. "Because…?"

"Benders are usually terrible at skating and tying their skates properly."

Crossing my arms over my chest, I narrow my eyes at Grey. "Wow, you hockey players really have a name for that?"

He nods. "We also have a name for players who only get ice time when the team is so far behind on goals, that even the worst player wouldn't be able to make it worse."

Now that seems fairly mean. Imagine you overhear someone

call you that name, or well, I guess you just know everyone's calling you that if you spend more time benched than playing.

I put one foot on the cold, slippery ice, already feeling my life slipping through my fingertips. This is how I will die, I just know it. I can *feel* it.

"How do you do this for a living?" I ask as I grip the railing with both of my hands as though it's the only thing that's keeping me up on my feet. *It is*.

Grey shrugs, then holds out his hand to me. "I love skating, and I love ice hockey."

I take his hand, but I swear to you, the two seconds I'm not holding that railing with both of my hands send me to hell and back to earth.

"Who decided to step on a death-trap like *ice* and make a sport out of it?!"

Grey pulls on my arm, forcing me to let my other hand go off the railing.

I squint my eyes shut, expecting to hit my ass on the ice but somehow I am not falling. When I decide to open my eyes again after a short while, I realize I'm not falling because Grey now has both of his hands on my body, holding me up right.

"You really never skated in your life before?"

I shake my head. "I grew up in Malibu, Grey Davis. You should know we don't do ice here." At least it's really rare if snow falls or it gets cold enough to have the streets freeze over a little. Though, I suppose it's more likely to happen here than in Florida.

"I chose ice hockey over surfing, so your excuse doesn't count. Besides, Malibu has hockey teams. Not playing for the NHL but they do have teams."

Is it too late to decide that I hate him?

"Uncle Grey, look!"

Both Grey and I look just in time to catch Brooke ace a spin on one fucking foot. I can't even stand without falling and this little five-year-old can do spins.

"When did you learn that, Brookie?" Grey asks as soon as Brooke comes to a halt right in front of us.

Brooke lifts her shoulders. "Sofia taught me." And she skates away again like it's the most effortless thing in the whole wide world. Though I suppose Brooke is growing up with her uncle being a professional hockey player, and whoever Sofia is, so of course she's learning how to skate from a young age.

Grey looks at me again. "Here, hold my hands," he says and takes my hands in his, so I don't have to move all too much.

I try not to scream when suddenly Grey starts to skate backwards while he pulls me after him.

Now he's just showing off. Nobody would want to skate backwards, right? That's a useless skill to have. Why would anyone want to be able to skate without seeing where they're skating toward? What if they end up hitting a wall or something?

"Are you never scared to hit one of the walls when—"

"Boards," he says.

My eyebrows dip in confusion. "I'm pretty sure there are no boards here."

"No, the *walls*, we call them boards."

I roll my eyes. "It's like you hockey players make up a whole new language."

Grey shrugs. "Like soccer doesn't have any weird slang nobody but players, coaches, and hardcore fans would understand."

"Touché."

Though I don't have to move much since Grey is pulling me after him, I can already feel my feet throbbing in pain. "Are you sure skates are supposed to be that tight?"

"Yes."

I doubt it wholeheartedly. He just wants to torture me. "Do you tie up little kids' skates that tight as well?"

"I don't know that I have ever tied kids' skates, but yes, I would."

I look toward Brooke then back at Grey and raise my

eyebrows. "You tightened hers." She did most of it on her own, which, frankly, I kind of envy.

"Today I did. It's usually her father, Colin, or Lily who tie the kids' skates." I'd love to ask who Colin and Lily are exactly, but even if I did, I doubt I'd receive an answer.

"So you don't help out at a rink when someone doesn't know how to tie their skates properly?"

"Considering that I don't usually go skating in my free time, no, I don't. My teammates obviously know how to deal with their skates, and the arena is closed during practice, there's never a reason for me to help strangers. But I would do it, and yes, I'd still tie them like I did yours."

"And here I thought I was someone special to you."

Grey lets out a gruff in disagreement and avoids talking by simply picking up the pace. I hold onto him a little tighter, almost squeezing his hands to death with the grip I keep on them. But, hey, at least I don't let out an embarrassing shriek.

That same evening, when Grey drops me off by the Hayesland store from earlier, I only barely make it into my mother's boutique without dying.

My limbs are hurting, every single muscle in my body is sore and throbbing. I will *never*, not even if it would save my life, set a single foot on stupid ice again. My feet are pretty much dead, and the only way I can tell they're still attached to my body is *because* of the pain. Grey's skates were definitely too small for me, I think, but what do I know?

Maybe skates are supposed to make your feet hurt like you've been walking on Lego for hours.

"How was your date, honey?" my mother asks when I finally make it over to the register where she stands. Her boutique is closed, but I suppose she still has some things to do.

"It wasn't a date." I lean over the countertop and reach a hand to the first drawer, opening it. I pull out a granola bar, forcing it down like I haven't eaten in years.

"It sounded like one when you called earlier." She looks up from her papers, lifting her eyebrows at me. "I take it your date didn't go well then?"

I scoff. My '*date*' did go well, I'd say. Grey talked more than he ever has before, though ninety-nine percent of his conversation was about ice hockey, and the other one percent was whenever his niece was talking to him.

However, I think Grey was on the edge of smiling a few times, even laughing if I dare say so. He was snorting at my awful skating skills, but with Grey, a laughter like that is better than none. And when he dropped me off, he said he had fun. Grey had *fun*, that has to count as something, right?

"We went ice skating," I say, still leaning over the counter like an old sack of potatoes.

My mother tsks. "Poor choice for a first date. Doesn't he know that not everyone knows how to skate? Especially around Malibu."

"Again, it wasn't a date, Ma. If it weren't for his niece, he would've never invited me."

"But wasn't he the guy from last summer?" Mom sets her pen down, now looking at me with confusion. "The guy you've been talking about so much."

I cringe internally. "I do *not* talk about him *that* much." At least I refuse to acknowledge it.

"Sure do, honey. But you know, I am proud of you for trying to go about this the non-obsessive way."

Non-obsessive... "Ma, if I am talking about Grey as much as you make it out, which I will keep on denying, this is *not* a non-obsessive way."

She waves me off. "You know what I mean. You're not..."

"The old me," I finish for her.

Mom nods. "You're showing interest in a healthy way."

Let's just hope it'll stay that way.

Luan Hayes

June 25th, 9:03 AM

> Daily check-in to let you know that you cannot get rid of me that easily, Grey Davis.

> Cool

> Bet you missed being in NYC, wherever nobody would annoy you

> Well, you're texting me so that didn't work

Luan Hayes

June 26th, 9:03 AM

> Daily check-in to let you know that you cannot get rid of me that easily, Grey Davis.

> Am I going to receive that message daily now?

> Eh, yes? Did you even read what I wrote?

> No

Luan Hayes

June 27th, 9:10 AM

> Are you okay?

Perfectly fine, Grey Davis. Why are you asking?

> Because you didn't send your daily check-in yet.

Miss me?

> No, but you not following through with whatever you said just didn't seem like you. Especially when you tried to send those messages at the exact same time.

So you've been thinking about me ;)

> And that's a goodbye.

I call this chickening out, Grey Davis

> And I call this not wanting to talk to you anymore, Luan. I got worried, is all. Don't read shit into this, please.

Harsh much

> We can't see each other again. I only invited you to go skating because of Brooke, so...

> Yeah, figured. I'll wait until you come around.

> I won't. And Luan, we can't talk anymore either.

> That's what you're saying now. I'll see you next year then!

Chapter 1

"'cause he made a little too much money to be 20 and sad"—I Lost a Friend by FINNEAS

Grey

February 2024

"ONE MORE!" COACH CARTER YELLS, being awfully upset with us for nothing. We've been doing warm-up drills for over an hour. Which generally would be fine, but not when it's always the *same* one—drill number two for level two—and yet Coach Carter doesn't seem to be okay with whatever we're doing.

By now, all of us should be able to do that drill in our sleep.

Apparently, when that very one came in handy, we messed up which is why we lost our last game. We've been doing so well this season, lost only about two games by *one* goal.

And then yesterday happened.

We didn't even get one goal, lost by five. Talk about humiliation.

The last time he was this pissed was when I was still in college. He made our team shoot pucks over and over again until we had at least ten goals each. The problem was, our goalies decided that day to be extra great ones.

Coach had taken a year away from the NHL because of his daughter dying, so instead he became a coach for the St. Trewery hockey team. Now we're here, playing for the NHL, him back coaching the pros.

"The fuck is wrong with your dad, dude!" Aaron pants,

purposefully skating right into the boards.

I've been standing here for a hot second, needing a short moment to breathe but clearly, Colin and Aaron had other plans for me.

"It's Eira's birthday," Colin answers, sighing while sliding down one of the boards to seat himself onto the ice in protest. We're one of the youngest members on the team and that makes us three stick together even more. We do have some younger guys, but they'd also rather hang around each other.

The older guys are chill and all, but the difference between them and us is visible. While most of them have families or at least their life together, all three of us are a year and a half out of college, still figuring life out.

They're mature, mostly, anyway, and take practice way too seriously while Aaron, Colin, and I still joke around every time we get the chance to. Correction, *they* joke around, and I listen.

I really miss Miles here. Playing without him sucks, but he's happier with his family around. Being away from home as much as we currently are definitely wouldn't have been any good for that guy. But still, I miss him around, on the ice with us.

Eira died in October 2021 due to cancer. Although Colin never speaks about Eira's death or that it's still very hard on him or his entire family, I know he struggles with his sister's death a lot. Always did. He may brush it off like it's nothing any day of the year, except the day Eira did die and her birthday, that's when even Colin Carter can't hold back tears anymore.

"She would've turned nineteen today." His voice breaks and he immediately looks up, blinking away the tears. He looks up at me like my presence brings him comfort. I don't know how, but at least he's no longer on the verge of tears.

"You can take five minutes," Coach yells, dismissing us for a short break. It's to go drink some water, but some of us are too exhausted to even skate over the ice to go get our bottles, including me.

"It's valentine's day tomorrow," Aaron says like he just

realized it. "Shit. Sofia's going to *kill* me!"

I nod at him. "What? Did you forget to buy a present?"

Aaron shakes his head, then keeps on hitting the back of his head against the board. "Worse. I forgot to book a table for two at the Rêverie. Sofia wanted to go there *without* me using the 'my best friend owns that restaurant' card."

Ah, yes. We love that card. Not even Miles can free a table for us most of the time, but we try every single time anyway. Sometimes it works. On days like tomorrow, it sure as fuck won't. The Rêverie will be booked to its last table. I bet the tables for the holidays are booked *years* in advance.

"Just fly her out for the day," Colin suggests. "It's what I do with Lily. We've got a whole three days just for us. No hockey. Not even practice. So, it's the closest we get to a vacation."

He's not wrong. Though, I will spend my three days off in my apartment, catching up on some TV shows. I would spend them with Miles and Emory, and I might still do that, but I'd rather not be a third wheel on *any* of my best friend's valentine's plans. Miles and Emory wouldn't care about keeping me around, simply because that gives them someone to watch the kids while they go off to do other business. There's a high chance they'll dump Brooke and Eden on me even if I don't third wheel them, but I gladly watch them. I mean, Miles keeps me alive. If it weren't for him, I'd have starved to death years ago, so watching two adorable little kids for a couple of hours is nothing.

"Or I just convince her that three days in our bedroom is worth more than an evening at the Rêverie, where she'd been a million times before already anyway."

"GREY!" Miles comes barging into my apartment without knocking. What if I had company? "I need a favor."

"I am not watching your kids tomorrow," I say, not meaning it. He doesn't have to ask me to take them. Miles could sit them on my couch and leave and I wouldn't question it one bit.

He halts, eyebrows draw together as he stares at me with surprise and confusion all at the same time. "I wasn't going to ask that. Em and I are taking them to Disneyland because Brooke wants to see the princesses. We're leaving in like two—"

"You can't," I interject. "What am I supposed to eat while you're gone without me? Takeout for three whole days?" Maybe I should learn how to cook. I can do the basic things like… bread. *Maybe* boil an egg and such. I think.

I never had to learn it. Back at home, we had a chef to do the cooking for us, and when I moved across the country, I had Miles to cook for me. Now that I live mostly on my own, I am screwed.

While we're on the road, the team goes out to eat at restaurants or we eat at the hotels, so again, no need for me to cook. And usually when I am home, I have Miles since he's my next-door neighbor. It's only a walk across the hall, very beneficial to me.

"Will you listen to the favor I have to ask after I told you that I prepared food for you? You'll just have to heat it up." Now that's the best friend I know. Of course he wouldn't let me starve… unless I pissed him off.

No, seriously. A couple of weeks ago, he kicked me out of his apartment because I didn't get him an autograph from some singer I met at a game, and then he refused to serve me dinner. I was *forced* to order in.

I get up from my couch and walk over to Miles. Reaching him, I plant a kiss right to his cheek, knowing he hates it when I do this. "You're the best, love."

"I know." He pulls up the sleeve of his shirt over his hand, wiping my kiss off his cheek. *Rude*. "Now, about my favor…"

"Just spit it out."

"I need you to get Sun far away from here, so she won't follow us to Florida."

Sun? Doesn't she have classes? "What happened?"

He groans. "She said she can't believe she's going to be single for *another* valentine's day, so she said she'll follow Em and me around. Knowing your sister, that's *exactly* what she's going to do. I don't mind her sticking around sometimes, and I wouldn't care if you came with us either, but have you met your sister?"

I grew up with my sister. "Not that I recall."

Miles cocks his head, every ounce of joy draining off his face. "Why don't you take her to Malibu and… I don't know, sort out your family issues."

I get the feeling that this has nothing to do with my sister at all.

My family issues…

I haven't talked to my father ever since he called me back in November two years ago, when the news about my boyfriend spread. The boyfriend who is in fact not my boyfriend.

The interview that evening after the game was interesting to say the least. Instead of asking about the game or hockey in general, most of the questions were about me and that *boyfriend* of mine. Some reporters don't know what privacy is, so they went all in with asking my teammates how they feel about having "a gay one on the team". None of their questions were answered, it's what PR told us was the best to do: ignoring all of those questions, denying wherever we can.

I believe if Colin and Aaron hadn't been there with me, I wouldn't have been able to stay as calm as I did, internally, anyway. I'm always sort of calm on the outside, not wanting people to be able to read me like I read them. But I could feel my nerves, I was scared during the interview, nervous. I didn't know what would happen next. It seemed like everything would stay the same, but it didn't.

The Team Manager was forced to throw out a statement because my teammates were harassed because of me, and I wish that was the worst that happened.

"If I wanted to, Miles, I could sort out my *family issues* on the phone." It'd only take a quick, *I'm getting married to a woman*, and my father would be the happiest man alive. "So what are you actually asking me to do?"

"Dude, you've been worse the past year-and-a-half than you've ever been. Just yesterday, Brooke asked me why you never smile anymore," he tells me, now taking a seat by my kitchen island while I make my way over to my fridge to get myself a bottle of water. It's the best I can think of doing to delay this conversation.

I've been trying to be more honest and open with Miles, so I know I should give into the conversation eventually… but as long as I find things to delay it, I'll take it.

"All you do recently is hide here or in your hotel rooms."

"That's because I don't like having my picture taken and *recently,* wherever I go, that seems to be the only thing on people's minds." It's more or less the truth. I know having my pictures taken comes with the job, and it's not like they *only* take pictures of me. Sometimes some people walk up to me as well and ask the most random questions, which wouldn't be a problem if a whole lot of those didn't include my dating history.

Sensing my best friend's disappointment, I turn to him and scowl. "It's been fifteen months, Miles," I state. "*Fifteen.* If it turned out someone else on the team was now committed to someone, nobody would give a shit for longer than a week, and I am *still* getting attacked. So, if that puts me in a bad mood, then fucking deal with it, okay?"

The NHL might try to be more open-minded, but there are still a whole lot of toxic masculinity standards as well as homophobia within the NHL *and* coming from fans. Being the odd one in this system puts you on a stage with tons of eyes staring at you, just watching, while others throw tomatoes and scream *boo!* from the top of their lungs. There's no support, even if individual teams claim to support their queer players. Sure, they have to throw out some statements because that's to be expected from the public and without those statements, the teams will be called out for their homophobia, but it's different behind closed doors.

Though, I do have to say, my team is very supportive of me. Most of them don't care about seeming rude publicly when someone tries to attack me, and they don't give a shit when PR tells me to keep quiet should reporters ask stupid questions about my private life. A bunch of the guys on my team call out the interviewers for false behavior and asking inappropriate questions. But even in my team, there are a few guys who won't get close to me, guys who eye me with disgust, guys who leave the shower room when I enter because they fear I'd jump them.

"Ever think that maybe they're still asking questions because *you* never gave a statement at all?"

"I shouldn't have to." What am I even supposed to say? Sure, I could let PR write a statement for me and I'll post it online or sit myself down in front of a camera and read it aloud, but what would it change? There's still going to be people sending fucking hate-mail to the arena in hopes I'll open it.

Every single time we're back there for either a game or practice, there are at least three packages for me, none of them include a sender name or address. The first couple of times, I opened the packages, thinking it might be something important, but the things I've seen...

The less bad packages included things like dildos or lube as a " useful gift", like I'd ever use either of them. But there were also the horrifying packages, ones where you could smell the contents of the package without having opened it.

"You're right, you shouldn't. But I am not talking about giving a statement about your sexuality, Grey. I am talking about clearing the air. People think you've been dating that Malibu guy for a year now, all because you never denied the rumors. Of course they're going to keep on asking if you never say you're not dating him. And if you were dating him, you could at least say you were and then that question would also disappear."

It wouldn't disappear. People would still keep on asking because there's always someone who doesn't know, but at least they could google an answer.

"Luan and I don't even talk anymore." Not ever since that ice rink date or whatever that was. Once again, I did my very best to push him away and I don't think there's ever going to be a way to get back from there. I didn't just ghost him once, but now twice... if there were any chances for him and I together, I ruined them.

And the last message he received from me was a clear cut as well. I straight up told him we couldn't talk anymore.

Telling him we could no longer *talk* hurt more than a stupid breakup.

"What about your father?" Miles asks, I shake my head. "If you don't want to talk to your father yet, that's fine, you know? But you should take a few days off to clear your head. Go somewhere fun, where you can be yourself."

Without saying so much as one word, I turn away from Miles and make my way over to my bedroom, locking the door so he can't follow me. He'll have to leave eventually to catch his flight, so until then, I suppose I am trapped in my own bedroom only to avoid a conversation I am not ready to have.

Chapter 2

"I'm sure you're busy now, why else would you ignore me?"—Break My Heart Again by FINNEAS

Luan

February 2024

"Five more!"

I don't think twenty-five extra squats will hurt the kids. Not today anyway. They're here to feel some pain. It's valentine's day, and all the kids in relationships did the right thing and listened to my warning—that I give them every year—about showing up today. Except for that one couple who gets hated on big time.

Anything they do, even just looking at each other, one of the guys comments something like, "I swear to god, one more of those looks and I'm gonna puke." or "Anyone interested in sleeping on the highway tonight?"

I am interested.

It's honestly quite rude of that couple to show up here today because hello? I don't have anyone looking at me like they're so deeply in love with me that some sixteen-year-old soccer player comments suicidal jokes. And I want that so badly.

"Okay, you can stop. Except for Dove and Elio. You may do another ten squats." Fair punishment for being in love if you ask me.

"Seriously?" Elio cocks his head in annoyance. "It's not my fault you're single, Coach."

"Well, no. But it is your fault all the others, including me, will have to watch you be all in love while we wanted to spend today wallowing in self-pity." Or at least that's what I wanted to do today. Along with eating a whole cake by myself because that's what I usually do on my birthday, minus the alcohol this year.

"Right," Nolan, the kid who keeps on commenting funny things whenever Elio so much as glances in Dove's direction, says. "I didn't sign up to feel my lunch come up every other second today."

Dove flips him off, kissing her middle finger to be extra provocative.

God, I love these kids.

I might find the toddlers easier to handle because they rarely talk back, and when they do, it's easy to quiet them. But these kids right here, they understand jokes. Instead of starting to cry, they insult right back—jokingly, of course. If I sense something having been serious, they're spending the entire hour either doing more exercises than necessary (the people involved only), or I'll turn it into a lecture like some teacher.

"Anyway, let's do penalty shootouts next." I blow into my whistle to signal the beginning of the next exercise. One can never do enough ball-kicking toward the goal, right? "All of you."

But neither of them jumps to action like they usually do. Each of their gazes stay fixated on whatever's behind me, so I turn around to see what has caught their attention.

When my eyes land on a guy with black hair, carrying more than one fucking balloon in his hands, I almost pinch myself to make sure I'm not just seeing things.

What is he doing here? It's been almost eight months since he told me to leave him alone because talking seems like a bad idea.

But more importantly, how the fuck did he find me? I never told Grey *where* I worked or what my work times were. He doesn't even know where I live exactly.

Bringing my hands to my hips, I stare at Grey like he's some alien that fell from the sky. And honestly, he might as well be. When he approaches me, I expect him to be all rude as always, but that's my favorite kind of Grey.

"I'm sorry," he apologizes instead of either keeping quiet or saying something slightly insulting.

I narrow my eyes at him, thinking about whether to accept his apology or not. Ah, who am I kidding? He could throw me out of a plane without a parachute and I'd be okay with it. Grey just needs a little time to warm up, I knew he wouldn't ignore me forever.

I have that kind of effect on people.

"Well, it's a surprise to see you on *Valentine's* day," I say, grinning again. He always makes me smile for some unknown reason. I swear, I don't usually smile as much when he's not around. I mean I do, but it's far more when Grey does happen to be near me.

Grey shakes his head. "It's your birthday." *He remembered, but why?* "So, happy birthday, Luan."

"Thank you."

Grey looks over my shoulder, probably counting all the teenagers standing there, ogling him. They're not watching *me*, that much I know.

The blame's on him for looking too stunning for his own good. My eyes feel blessed from some higher power above every time I get to look at that handsome face. Not even holy water could erase some of the thoughts running wild inside of my head when I look at a picture I find of him online.

"Shit, that's Grey Davis," one of the guys says a little excitedly.

"Who the fuck is Grey Davis?" another asks.

"That guy!"

"Not a very known soccer player then."

"He plays ice hockey, dude." Nolan scoffs. "Don't disrespect a legend like him ever again."

I just know Grey is agreeing with Nolan, even though he

keeps said agreement unheard or unseen.

Grey looks back at me, his frown deepens a little and fills with concern. "I didn't want to interrupt."

I wave my hand around to show him I don't give a flying fuck about that. "How'd you find me?"

For the first time, Grey smiles. An actual smile, not a lip-tug or a twitch. There is a whole ass smile on his face. "You once said if I really wanted to see you, I'd figure out a way to find you. So, here I am. I found you."

Ah shit. That's not fair. He can't just come here being all cute when I'm supposed to be mad at him for telling me to fuck off when we both knew he didn't mean it. Of course I knew he'd figure this out someday, but I didn't think he'd show up here without telling me first.

"I didn't have enough time to buy a present, so I got you a million balloons." His smile fades again, but I don't care at all. I've seen it now, and I don't think my brain will ever be able to forget that smile.

"Five," I correct. "They're five balloons."

"Like I said."

He shifts a little uncomfortably, and I bet it's because of the twenty other people right behind me, still staring. And so I turn around, looking at my team. "Didn't I say you're doing shootouts?" I clap my hands three times, then wave them off. "You've got one minute to start, or I'll make you run laps until all of you have emptied your guts on the pitch, and then you can clean it up yourself."

Just like that, they're running off.

"Coach did exactly that yesterday. With scrimmages," Grey tells. I didn't even have to ask. *Who is this guy?* "He made us perfectionate every move until we were so close to dying, his own son begged him to stop."

"I strive to become him."

Grey shakes his head. "Trust me, you don't. Unless you want to lose two kids and that's why you get so endlessly angry sometimes."

Oh, yeah, okay… I will pass on that. "So, what I'm hearing is you want to have kids with me, huh, Grey Davis?"

Grey's eyes roll as though he's currently regretting coming here. He isn't, we all know that. He missed me. And so I laugh, but not because this is hilarious, which it is, but because I'm glad to find out it wasn't just all in my head.

"I could see us having two kids." I look into the distance, thinking. "A boy and a girl. We'll name the boy Ash and the girl Sage."

"You're making fun of my name, aren't you?"

I nod, and proudly so. "I like your name though, but it'd sound better with my last name, just saying."

"Grey Hayes? I don't think so."

"You're saying that now..." I finally take the balloons from him, each after the other so I have some time to look at the shapes. Three of them are heart shaped, the other two are boring round balloons with *Happy Birthday* written all over them.

Maybe that's a coincidence because there's no way Grey picked up on that little tick I have. Everything being in three's. I clap three times, hit counters three times, knock; all of them and more three times. Buy decorations like candles or picture frames three times. I even wave someone goodbye three times, all because three is my lucky number.

I was tested for OCD when I was a kid, but as it turns out, I just like my stuff in threes.

"Hm, hearts, huh?" I grin up at him. He's a little taller than me, but I don't mind that at all.

"I swear, that store didn't have anything else. Everything's filled with hearts and love stuff."

"Yeah, *Valentine's day*." But I don't mind the hearts anymore. It used to be annoying when every single present of mine would be heart-shaped because of Valentine's day.

"Anyway, since I'm already here, I thought we could turn today's Valentine's day into one you won't forget. It's not quite spending it cuddling with a boyfriend but it's the best I can give you."

All those words. I think he keeps using more and more, the more often he sees me. And I absolutely love it. Maybe one day he will be the one who talks and I'm only listening… Nah.

"I mean, you can still cuddle me, you know?" I lift one eyebrow, smirking. "You don't have to be my boyfriend to cuddle me."

"I don't do cuddling." I knew he'd say that.

"We'll see about that, Grey Davis."

"Coach!" Elio calls out so I immediately turn around to see who's broken a leg this time. Nobody, thank god. "That'll be ten extra squats. You said so yourself. Today's practice is for the *single* people who want to wallow in self-pity."

Urgh, I did say that, didn't I?

Good thing I am single, at least in some ways.

Grey Davis doesn't know it yet, but he's my boyfriend. Or will be when he finally realizes that I'm worth more than whatever keeps him from committing to me.

Well, I would like to get to know him a little better first because that's what normal people do. And since I promised myself to get better, to *be* better… that's what I will do. Get to know Grey, let Grey get to know me. We'll take this step by step.

Plus, he *did* just ignore me for eight whole months.

"Yeah, Coach Hayes," Grey says, laying his hand on my shoulder this time. I think that stupid hand might just cause my knees to give in but whatever. "That'll be an extra ten squats."

"But why? I'm single, aren't I?"

He doesn't answer.

Chapter 3

"you're the sun to my moon"—you! by LANY

Grey

February 2024

LUAN SAID HE HAD AN idea of what we could do other than spend the rest of the day back at his house with his best friend. I was fine with that, to be completely honest here, but of course Luan would find a way for me to be outside.

And I don't like it one bit.

Especially right now when we're standing in front of a stupid *clothing store* with Luan's wish for us to get matching hoodies. I don't think I have ever hated an idea as much as I do this one.

Luan wears yellow, he wears colors, and I live my lonely black and gray life. There is absolutely no way that I will walk out of that store with a *yellow* hoodie in my hands. I think the last time I wore anything with color, I was around fourteen years old, maybe twelve.

Actual clothes, we're ignoring my hockey ones.

"It'll be fun," Luan encourages me to take a step toward that store. I shake my head, not being convinced of it at all. "Don't be such a grumpy cat, Grey Davis."

I scowl at Luan, now definitely regretting having listened to Miles. I should've stayed home, but after Miles finally left yesterday I had a long time to think about his words.

He was right, I need a break from everything. From responsibilities. From being lonely. From being *not* me. From hiding. I need a little sunshine in my life, a few days of being accepted for being me, without being judged by anyone. There was only one person who could manage to force me out of my comfort zone. Only one person who likes to talk more about his fun childhood memories than anyone I know. Only one person who, despite me constantly ignoring him every now and then, is still somehow happy to see me.

Even if that person apparently lives so close to my parents' that I can see my bedroom window from his bedroom. I can't confirm, I haven't been to his house yet, but I guess I'll find out soon enough.

"Okay, you have three choices," Luan says, grinning up at me with this devilish smile of his. That's not good at all. "One, we walk in there and buy matching hoodies. Or two, we stand here, and I'll talk all about why we should get them and how much you love me already. Or three, we go to your parents' house, and you introduce me to them."

I sigh a little defeated. The last one definitely isn't even an option for me to consider. The second option will turn into option one so… "Fine. Let's go in."

Luan reaches for my hand, ready to pull me after him but now that his hand is wrapped around my wrist, my ability to walk leaves me altogether.

My eyes fall to our hands. His thumb rests right on the butterfly tattoo. His grip on me is so gentle yet firm at the same time, I couldn't describe it if my life depended on it. The tips of his fingers are a little cold but that's great because I wholeheartedly believe I'd have burn wounds on my skin if they weren't.

Then, after a short while of me staring at our hands, Luan slides his hand down, interlacing his fingers with mine. When my eyes snap up to meet his, he's smiling so softly, I think that startles me more than his hand locked with mine.

Luan has smiled his fair share of times every single time we see each other, but none of them were as soft as this one. It's like he knows how I feel about our locked hands without me having to say a single word. His smile is so soft that I feel this weird urge to run a finger over it, *feel* that smile. And then the most unimaginable thing happens.

I smile right back at him.

He takes it in for a single second only, then his soft smile turns devilish all over again. "Well." *Oh, no.* "If you're in love with me, Grey Davis, you can just say it."

I look away from Luan, licking my bottom teeth while slowly nodding. Should've known this was coming.

"I'm not in love with you, Luan."

He shrugs. "That smile of yours said otherwise, but okay. I'll give you another chance in an hour." I don't doubt it.

That said, Luan pulls me across the street, forcing me to follow him.

Just when I thought this was any regular clothing store, I am proven wrong when Luan walks us up to the register. His smile brightens even more.

"LUAN!" the woman behind the register shrieks excitedly, then makes her way around the counter to greet him.

He lets go off my hand to hug her, and I'm not going to lie, the loss of his hand is like a knife to my heart. *What the fuck is happening?*

"Happy birthday, honey." It looks like her grip on him might as well be so tight, she's close to squeezing him to death.

"Thanks, Ma," Luan chuckles, patting a hand on *Ma's* back.

On. *Ma's*. Back.

That woman is his *mother*?!

I was prepared for literally anything today. Yes, even going shopping with Luan. What I wasn't prepared for was meeting his parents. I don't think I ever even thought about meeting his mother. And I mean *ever*. Parents don't like me.

When they pull away from the hug, Luan's mother looks at me with wide eyes but a smile on her face, nonetheless.

Luan doesn't have a lot of features in common with his

mother. She's got brown eyes, his are green. She has a rounder face, Luan's isn't. His features are more defined. Her skin is a little darker than his, her hair, too. But he got the curls from her.

"Now, who do we have here?" she asks, making her way over to me. Mrs. Hayes looks pleasantly surprised to see me, and not in a bad way at all. She smiles at me and looks at me all kindly. And if her son is anything like her, she might as well be a blink away from pulling me in for a hug.

"Remember that guy I told you about?" Luan says, looking at me now. "That's him."

His mother chuckles. "I see." She holds out her hand and I take it. "Grey, is it?" I nod. "God, it's nice to finally meet you. Luan has been talking about you nonstop. He calls home every day, and usually I listen to him talk about soccer or how his days went, but recently all he talks about is how amazing you are."

How he can picture me as being amazing, I do not know because I'm far from it. "It's nice to meet you, too, Mrs. Hayes."

"Armina, please."

Yeah, because that's not scary at all. I have never first named anyone's parents. Not even Miles's father when he was still alive, and Mr. Desrosiers did tell me to call him by his first name at least a million times.

"Yeah, you two can chat after we've gotten married, Ma. I need a favor."

Ah, after our *wedding*. Good to know we're getting married. I get the feeling Luan loves to decide things before asking me. Like us getting married someday. *Major* things that I should probably have a say in.

"So, you remember those hoodies you sold years ago? The yellow ones that said *Smile*?"

I don't like where this is going. At all.

Armina gasps and immediately shakes her head. "Luan. You cannot put this poor guy in a *yellow* shirt."

"Exactly." Maybe meeting his mother wasn't so bad after all. "Yellow isn't my color."

Luan waves us both off. "You're getting the other one," he tells me. "You can still print them, right? Also, you need to do me another favor…" He walks closer to his mother, pulling her away from me so they can talk without me hearing it. Now *that* I like even less than thinking about having to wear something… *yellow*.

It says *Frown*.

The hoodie I am forced to wear says *Frown* right on the front for everyone to see. At least the hoodie's dark gray, I guess.

Luan's wearing a matching one but in yellow and it says *Smile* instead. It suits him, actually, and it matches his shoes perfectly. They're also yellow. He even switched into white sweatpants just to match my black cargo pants a little better.

But that isn't even the worst bit yet.

Each side of our sleeves has an initial embroidered. G for me and L for Luan. That wouldn't be all too bad if mine didn't have the L on it and his the G. And a heart right next to the letter as well.

At this point, I'm far deeper into a relationship with Luan Hayes than I thought I am. Or consented to being. Maybe I skipped that part or something, I don't know.

"Okay, tell me the best pickup line you got," Luan demands, then bites into his burger, not caring a single bit about how everyone in this restaurant keeps staring at us.

Luan thinks they're staring because I'm famous, but that's not true because I'm not *that* famous. Hockey fans know me, normal people not so much. They're definitely staring because he keeps on talking so loudly and wears the color of the sun while sitting next to *me*.

Generally speaking, we don't fit together in *any* way. While he's the literal sun, I'm the moon. We all know the sun doesn't show up during the night.

"Grey Davis." He snaps his fingers to get my attention. I look at him, cocking my head. "Pickup line. Now."

"So demanding." I groan but since it's his birthday, I give him what he wants. I'm not sure why he wants it, but I learned to not question Luan. Taking a deep breath and leaning back in my seat, I say, "I don't use pickup lines because I don't want to pick you up; I want to pin you down."

"Oh, please do." He mutters a little dreamy right before his jaw drops when he realizes what exactly just left my, and then his mouth. "Well, you can pin me down anytime you want, Grey Davis." He winks. I didn't expect anything else from him.

I hum, not wanting to say *I won't* in words because I don't know what the future holds, but also not taking him for his offer. With Luan, I sometimes don't know what he means and what's a joke, I'm still trying to figure him out. That annoys me the most. Every other person, I would've been able to figure out in a few hours, a day max. But Luan… he still remains a mystery to me. And he's an open book.

"You say one," I say.

He grins, and from that grin alone I know whatever comes out of that pretty mouth of his next will not be any good. "I heard that the tongue is the strongest muscle, so… wanna fight?"

I'm considering it…

Still considering it…

Yes. "No."

"Hm, okay let me try another one then."

I nod for him to go ahead, it's not like I can run away from it or him anyway. No matter how hard I try to stay away, I always end up right back in his proximity.

While taking a sip of water seems great at this moment, it turns out to be the worst thing I could do.

"My favorite color might be yellow, but I can make you yell-oh."

I cover my mouth with my hand, but it's too late. Water just spurts out of me, and in my state of shock I don't even care that half of our table is now wet, or that my clothes, too, are wet now. Or that about the entire restaurant is staring at us more than they did before.

"What the—Luan!"

He hands me a paper towel, laughing. "Did it work?" he asks. "Are you going to kiss me now?"

I shake my head, wiping off the water from my face first, then my pants which doesn't work, and then move over to the table. "If someone wants to kiss you, you shouldn't have to ask them to do it."

"Yeah, but I might have to wait another year until you do, so I'm speeding up the process here."

"You've done nothing but *speed up the process* ever since we met." Is it a lie? He's been dropping things like this since day one, god knows why. Even if he saw a spark in me that day at the beach, nobody else would *ever* say the things he does so early on.

Luan liking me was never a secret, and I believe it never will be. Quite frankly, I'm not sure if that scares me.

It took me ages to find friends that I'm comfortable around. Friends who don't judge me for *any*thing. I could tell them I murdered someone and all three of them would help me hide the body. No questions asked.

It took Miles four-and-a-half years to get some answers out of me, to *really* get to know me deeper than the surface stuff.

And then there's Luan who somehow decided to like me in the first two minutes he met me. At the time I didn't talk to him at all, or very little.

I don't understand it.

Chapter 4

"and if my wishes came true / it would've been you"—
the 1 by Taylor Swift

Ivan

February 2024

My mom likes him. I know because she hasn't messaged me to tell me to get rid of him like she did with my ex-boyfriends. There was only ever one exception, and that exception was Charlie. He was never my *boyfriend*, but I don't talk about him that much either.

She always said nobody could ever measure up to him. I used to think she was right because, truthfully, nobody ever caught my attention like Charlie did before our forced *friendship* breakup happened and I ended up drinking away my feelings. But these days I start to realize that there might very well be someone who could potentially be even better than Charlie was.

I'm just praying she'll still like him when I eventually have to tell my parents whose son Grey is.

"Seriously, *another* song?!" Grey groans, letting his head drop against the backrest of the sofa.

I shrug. "The movie's called High School *Musical*, Grey Davis. Of course there's another bomb song in there." We're only halfway through the first movie and he's already had enough.

When he first told me he had never watched either of the High School Music movies, I didn't believe him. I always thought everyone had seen them before at least once in their life. As it turns out, I was wrong, and I'm never wrong. What kind of person has never seen *High School* fucking *Musical*?

While I know most of the choreography to the dances, and all the lyrics to the songs, plus make it a big deal that I do, Grey sits there on my sofa with a blank expression (as always), sometimes scowling, sometimes rolling his eyes, or sometimes groaning and huffing in annoyance.

I like catching glimpses of him every now and then when he's not looking, but I'm almost certain he always notices it. That's okay. I don't make enjoying to look at him a secret, he can know, and gladly so.

I mean, have you looked at that perfection of a human being? Grey's so… wow.

He has probably the blackest hair I've ever seen, the darkest eyes with so much depth in them that I cannot wait for the day he finally gives me a key to unlock all of his secrets. His jaw is defined, he might as well shred cheese with it. And the tattoos… God, the tattoos.

I never liked tattoos before, but now I can't even remember why.

Grey is the complete opposite of the guys I used to date, not only personality wise but appearance wise, too. Maybe that's also why I'm a little too interested in him sometimes.

It worries me though. That I will get too attached to him. That I will go too far one day because I know I tend to do just that. I worry that I am forcing feelings onto him but if I am, I can't tell. I don't know when I'm going too far, where teasing and jokes stop, and toxicity starts.

Should Grey ever start to like me, I want him to like me on his own accord and not because my toxic tendencies couldn't be stopped, and I somehow manipulated him into linking me.

I don't want to be that guy anymore. I've been trying to get rid of the old Luan, get rid of the guy who manipulates people into liking him because I didn't know how else to make friends.

I've been going to therapy, still do just so I can live a normal life without wondering if someone likes me for me or because I made them like me.

But it's hard sometimes. It's still difficult for me to see the difference.

Maybe that's exactly why I like Grey. He doesn't strike me as the kind of guy who'd allow me to manipulate him. I think he'd see right through me.

He figured out Doro is a really outgoing person within two minutes of meeting her. He knew she prefers ice cream over plain chocolate, and he never even asked her, he just straight up mentioned it to me like I didn't already know it.

So, no, I don't think Grey would let me trick him into liking me. Before that could ever happen, he'd probably tell me to piss off for the millionth time, meaning it this time.

When Grey yawns, I jump right back into reality, only then really noticing that I've zoned out.

I look at him, praying he won't get up to leave me just yet. I don't know for how long he'll be staying in Malibu, but I do know that I don't want him to leave yet.

"Are you leaving?" I ask when he stretches while the end credits roll, but I don't pay any attenti—

Hold up. *END CREDITS?!* How long was I zoned-out for?

"Yeah, I still have to find a hotel." Grey sets the popcorn bowl down onto the coffee table. "We can watch the rest tomorrow if that's okay with you."

"You'd do that?" My eyes widen with surprise. I don't think he even liked the first movie. Maybe he did, apparently I stopped paying attention halfway through.

"Well, I'll still be around tomorrow, so sure."

"That means we can hangout or will you be visiting your family? That'd be fine, of course but I'm just wondering." The more time I have with Grey, the happier I will be. I already barely see him as is, let alone talk to him whenever he decides to ignore me due to whatever episode he has going on.

"I'm not on talking terms with them, hence the hotel."

Not on talking terms? That's so sad. I couldn't imagine not calling my mother daily or visiting my parents at least once a week.

"You can stay here if you want. I don't have an extra bedroom, but I promise my bed is more comfortable than any guest bedroom one would be," I offer.

Please stay.
Please stay.
Please stay.

"I can sleep on the floor." Grey stands, stretching once more. This time his hoodie pulls up when he reaches his arms over his head, revealing a little bit of his skin underneath.

"You'd break the floor with your abs, and to avoid that from happening, you'll have to sleep in my bed, sorry." I've seen him half naked *once*, and I haven't been the same ever since. He is all muscles, tattoos, and perfection.

"I'd break the floor, huh?"

I stand, closing the gap between us. My chest is now pressed to his, but he doesn't step back, neither do I. "Together, we'd break more than the floor."

I think he's either processing my words, or considering my subtle offer because at some point, his eyes somehow turn a darker shade, and he licks his lips like he doesn't know what else to do.

"That's a poor-quality bed then," he ends up saying. I knew he would say anything but acknowledge my attempt to seduce him. Attempt number five-million-six-hundred-thousand-three-hundred-and-four. I don't even do one-night stands.

"Who said anything about a bed? I was talking about… hearts. Together, we're going to break a whole lot of hearts because everyone loves me, and when we're together, you're the only one I want to love me. And you'll be the only one I'll love. Hence, a whole lot of broken hearts."

He hums, knowing very well that I'm trying to bullshit him.

Six Years

"You know, back in high school, I had just came out as gay, not on my will but I suppose the news was out so therefore me too, anyway, the guys used to hate me and exclude me everywhere possible. Some even insisted I go change in the girls' locker room since they don't have dicks. I didn't tell them that's not how 'being gay' works, that I didn't crush on either of them, because they got *really* jealous when I hung around the girls all the time and neither of them so much as glanced their ways anymore. My point of this story is, I broke the guys' hearts without even realizing because one of those guys had a *major* crush on Doro, but she hated him because he hated me, so every attempt of his to flirt with her got rejected *big time*. It was kind of hilarious."

"Only you would find bullying hilarious." He takes a step back this time, but I step closer again.

"Oh, no, no, no. I didn't find the bullying hilarious. That traumatized me so much, I woke up each morning and started to cry because I didn't want to go to school. I had to see a therapist for years after still. But I found the way they acted when they realized what they've done hilarious. The regret. Even to this day some still try to reach out to me to apologize."

One even thought I'd turn his son into a star one day. He deadass came to my pitch, stood that little *two*-year-old in front of me and said, "*He wants to play soccer, can you make him a good one so he can play professionally one day?*"

First of all, it's not really in my hands whether someone is a good player or not. Sure, I coach them, but I can't predict the way they can comprehend everything, the way they learn or turn out. It's a matter of skills. Like drawing.

Yes, you can learn how to draw, it takes time and many nerves. Soccer does too. You're not magically good at any skill right from the start. But without the kids' willpower, nobody can do anything to better them. A teacher can only do so much.

Telling someone to turn a human being into something big is like visiting Sweden without being able to speak Swedish but expecting to understand and speak the language anyway.

"I'm sorry about that, Luan. You didn't deserve that." His features soften a little. If only he knew how much even the little moments of him putting down that hard exterior means to me.

"Well, you don't deserve what they're doing with you at the moment either." And it's mostly my fault. If I hadn't said I was Grey's boyfriend over a year ago, nobody would've suspected anything, I think.

"It's nothing I'm not used to already."

Before this could get any more depressing, I grasp Grey's hand in mine again, the tingles from earlier coming back even before our hands touch.

Pulling Grey after me, I lead him into my bedroom. His eyes instantly fall to my bedroom window, looking out.

"You really do have a great view of my bedroom," he says with the slightest of chuckle in his voice. You can't really see anything because we're too far away, but last year, when Grey was visiting his parents, I could see shadow-him walk around at night when the lights were on.

"Yeah, it's really disturbing. The amount of times I had to watch you fuck other people…" I roll my eyes with an exaggerated sigh. I have not once seen anything, which I'm thankful for.

"Is that so?" Grey turns to me, his eyebrows raised, a smug *smile* tugging on his lips.

I nod, closing my bedroom door to distract myself from the view. But when I turn back around I gasp because Grey just stands there. Close to me. Like *really* close to me. So close, I can feel his hot breath roll over my skin.

My back hits the door behind me, my eyes locked with his as he hovers over me. He doesn't move in to kiss me, and as much as I want to lift my face to his to do so instead, I don't.

Call this me making sure I'm not forcing anything. I don't care how long it'll take, if I have to wait six hours or six years, I will not make the first move. I will not kiss Grey unless *he* initiates it. Even if the thumping heart in my chest is begging me to do it.

"How often did you see anything?" he asks, his voice dangerously low. Not the usual low, it's deeper, raspier. Sexier.

One hand of his presses against the door right beside my head, the other lays down on my waist. I try to keep my hands to myself, but they're moving anyway, ending on Grey's body. My hands rest on his torso, faintly feeling the ripples of his abs press against the hoodie now that I'm flattening it against his body.

"Too many times," I answer.

"Jealous?" His head dips further down, his lips now *almost* brushing mine. Our noses touch, my breathing so shaky, I'm sure he can feel it.

"Furious."

I don't have to see it to know he's smiling right now. But then he pulls his face away, not even leaving a soft, innocent kiss on my lips. No, instead he brings his mouth to my ear and says, "I have never fucked anyone in that house."

"Great, I'll be the first then." I don't think he's ever going to take me there. If his father sees and recognizes me… I honestly don't want to imagine what would happen next. My father isn't the only one who wouldn't approve of our relationship, if there was one. Even being friends crosses a line.

Grey straightens his back, looking at my lips rather than my eyes. He then takes a step back, that little intimate moment between us vanishing as quickly as it came.

Turning away from me, Grey's now looking at my bed. "That's my shirt," he states. "Do you sleep in it?"

"Yup. But it doesn't smell like you anymore."

Without so much as saying a single word, Grey takes off the gray hoodie my mother made him, throwing it on my bed. A moment later, he also removes the t-shirt he wore underneath, now standing in the middle of my room without any shirt on.

The sight steals my breath for a moment there, until I realize that obsessing over a guy's torso isn't normal.

But that also doesn't last very long because Grey must sense the change in my emotions. He turns around in record time, taking in my state of trying to avoid looking at him, so naturally he makes it even harder for me by walking to stand right in front of me.

He reaches for my hand, and lays it down on his torso, right over his heart. I can feel it beating against my palm, a little faster than what I believe a heartbeat should feel like.

I stare at his lips, not because I want to kiss him—which I do—but because I like his lips. They're a soft pinkish kind of color, plump but not all too big, and they look so kissable that it almost makes me salivate. Then my gaze moves down his chin, to the tattoo on his neck.

"What does it mean?" I finally ask, running a finger over the tattoo, my other hand still firmly pressed to his chest.

Grey looks down like he doesn't know which tattoo I'm talking about, trying to see it on his very own neck, which is very much impossible, and of course he knows what tattoo I'm talking about even if my finger wasn't currently touching it.

"You're just going to assume I speak Korean?" His voice is so much softer than usual, filled with so much more depth.

"You don't strike me as the kind of guy who would tattoo words onto his body without knowing exactly what it says whether it was a drunken decision or not. I think you'd rather not have a tattoo than there being the potential that it either doesn't make sense at all, or it's some kind of insult. And I'm not assuming you're fluent in Korean, I asked what the tattoo means."

His lips curve up just that tiny bit. "Everything will be okay," he says. "That's what it means."

I nod. "Like you and me then." Grey slightly cocks his head but before he gets the chance to disagree, I slide my finger over to the side of his neck, right by his ear. "And this one? What does it say?"

I'm assuming it means snowflake, given that there's one right above the letters, but I want him to tell me anyway.

"Snowflake," he confirms. "Well, literally speaking it says snowflower, that sounds way cooler anyway. It's a combination of words but it ends up meaning snowflake."

"Why'd you get it?" His heart beats a little faster, or so it feels. Maybe I'm imagining things though.

"Because I like the meaning."

"Basic answer, Grey Davis," I say, now looking right into his eyes. "Tell me the meaning, tell me the deep reason *why* you got it, not the basic version of it." I know a lot of people get tattoos for the sake of getting them, but Grey doesn't, I don't think. He's more practical, more tactical. Whatever he does, he has a reason to do it, a reason to get it. "Use that pretty mouth of yours, Grey. You can talk, I know that."

I can feel him shudder beneath my palm, and it makes me smile but for once I don't let it show because I don't want him thinking I'm making fun of him.

"The characteristics of a snowflake in nature are unique, hence why the term snowflake is used in reference to individuals who deem themselves unique. Or, well, special, thinking they deserve to be treated like they are, too. But that's not why I got it. I was more set on the part that resonates with snowflakes being deserving of recognition, as well as the connotation of them being inherently fragile."

See, that's more like the Grey I've gotten to know; having deep meanings.

I want to keep on asking about each and every single one of his tattoos, but I think he has reached his maximum level of opening up for today, and that's okay.

Grey releases my hand, but before I can move away from him, he grasps the end up my hoodie in his hands, telling me to lift my arms then pulls it up over my head, leaving me as exposed to him as he is to me.

"You see yourself in them then, huh?" I cup his face with one hand, wanting to keep on looking into his eyes but I find the swamp of birds on his collarbones instead. *Freedom and perspective*. It doesn't stand there but it also doesn't take a genius to know what birds symbolize.

What the hell has happened to this guy?

Grey ignores me, as always when it gets too much, but that, too, is alright. "Tell me something you've never told anyone," he says. "You have such a big mouth all the time, so *use it*."

Oh, I'll use my *big mouth* sometime, but definitely not for talking.

He runs a finger down my torso, following every ripple of my muscles, forcing goosebumps to make its way onto my skin.

"I tell everyone who asks that I started drinking at the age of eighteen, at the frat parties, but I was twelve and very much not interested in parties." That may be a little too heavy for the kind of conversation we're having, but I've been dying to tell someone the truth about it for so long, it's ridiculous.

"You're still sober, right?"

I nod. "Two years now."

He smiles. "You can be proud of yourself, Luan. You *should* be proud of yourself."

"Are you proud of me?" Not that it should matter because he wasn't there at the peak of my alcohol addiction. He didn't see me suffer, didn't witness me force relationships and let them crumble again when I got bored. He wasn't there when I picked out a handful of people and decided to make my problems theirs.

"Anyone who isn't proud of you for it shouldn't be in your life," he answers. "I *am* proud of you, Luan."

I think he's aiming to make me smile, and it does make me smile, but it also makes me exhale so deeply, like that one single breath is the only thing keeping me from falling apart right now. Something heavy is stuck in my throat, keeping me from speaking, from telling him more about my problem. But as much as I love to talk, I hate talking about *that*.

Not him being proud of me, I very much like that part and I will have *millions* of fantasy conversations about just that in my head until I see him again.

He takes his t-shirt, scrunches it up and pulls it over my head, then waits until I have my arms in before he pulls it down my torso.

Chapter 5

"it's something like an anchor"—Anchor by Cailee Rae

Grey

February 2024

"YOU DON'T PLAN ON sleeping with your pants on, do you?" Luan leans back on his bed, looking me up and down the second I come walking out of his bathroom.

Without saying a word, I walk over to my bag to get something to wear for the night. It's not a big bag by any means since I didn't plan on staying longer than two days because of ice hockey, but it was definitely more filled than whatever I'm met with the second I unzip my bag.

Looking up, my eyes find Luan's immediately. I raise my eyebrows at him, waiting for him to tell me what he's done with half of my clothes, but of course there's never an explanation coming.

"Where are my clothes?" I then ask because, apparently, with this guy, looks aren't enough to make him say what I want to hear.

He shrugs. "I don't think you packed any to sleep in, clearly."

"Funny, I never said only clothes to sleep in were missing." Like every single one of my shirts and the two shorts I had in there. The only clothes left are my boxers and pants that I'd rather not sleep in. "You don't happen to be a mind reader, do you?"

Luan shakes his head, humming a no. "I'm pretty sure you mentioned you forgot to pack your bag properly before coming here. Yeah, that's definitely it." *I never did.* "But I do know this cool lifehack. What was it again?" He snaps his fingers three times. "Right, just sleep naked. I won't look. Promise with fingers crossed."

Mm-hmm, he won't look, all right. That guy really is something else.

"You do know you're not supposed to have your fingers crossed when making a promise, right?"

"Oh, well, ankles crossed then." He grins, satisfied with himself for, once again, pulling a reaction out of me. I think it's his new favorite hobby. Seeing what makes me react and what doesn't. I kind of like that game.

So without further ado, I unbutton my pants and let them fall right to the floor. But unlike Luan's fantasy wishes, I keep my boxers where they are.

Somewhere in our friendship, there's a line. I don't quite know where it is yet, haven't really found it, but I know there is one. And I think sleeping naked in one bed with your friend crosses that line.

Well, if you asked Luan, I don't think there is a line, and if there is, it's probably drawn in invisible ink.

Wait, am I the only one here having lines in friendships? Specifically in Luan and I's friendship? I know for a fact I would sleep naked in one bed with Miles and not give a fuck, so why am I trying to find lines around here somewhere? Who the fuck even walks around in my life drawing those lines because I can't remember doing so.

Ah, right. My dad. He draws the lines…

"Are you just going to keep on standing there letting me stare at your god-sent body or are you going to come over here?"

I'm considering sleeping on the floor for a hot second, but the bed seems far more comfortable and so I walk over there, crawling into bed with Luan.

While he turns off the light on his nightstand, I stare up at the ceiling. "Do you draw lines in your friendships?" I ask, now genuinely wondering if anyone else has them. What's allowed and what isn't? What's accepted and where does friendship stop?

"Like boundaries?"

"Yes."

"Of course. They're depending on the friend though. I have other boundaries for you than I have for my best friend. I would push her off me if she ever tried to lay my hand on her body, but you can gladly do that all over again." He sighs, then I hear him turn but I don't check if he's turned toward me or away from me now. "On a serious note, yes, I draw lines. I think everyone does, but it genuinely always depends on the friendship itself, how close you are. If someone I barely see or talk to, talked to me in a flirting way, I'd be… not grossed out but it'd be weird, you know? But if someone I'm close to does it, it's funny. If someone I see once every three months tried to talk about my trauma, then I'd tell them to fuck off. But if someone I trust talks to me about it, then that's okay."

I guess that makes sense, though I personally don't talk to anyone about anything really. Except for my sister but I don't see her as a friend. Even Miles had to wait a whole four years before I *slowly* started to open up to him, and still, he doesn't know half of what's going on in my life right now. I'm sure he has some ideas.

"Do you tell Doro everything?" I ask.

"Yup."

"Like *every*thing?"

Luan moves closer to me, so I turn on my side to look at him through the dark, only to get startled when he's closer to me than I thought.

His breath is rolling over my skin, his nose touching mine.

"I mean, there are things I don't tell her. Things about *you*, for instance. Stuff you tell me about yourself. But other than that, she's the first person I run to when something goes wrong." Then he sighs dramatically long. "I'd rather you be that person though."

I close my eyes for a second, needing to take a deep breath to stop my heart from doing stupid jumps.

We aren't playing basketball here, heart.

"Can you cuddle me?" Luan asks, laying his hand down on my jaw. "I don't know when I'll see you next, so it's only fair."

"I don't do cuddling," I remind him. And even if I did, I'm sure friends aren't supposed to do that, are they?

"Because clearly you have never been with someone you wanted to cuddle, so, let me show you how great that can feel." He takes my arm, draping it over his own body.

"Who says I want to cuddle *you*?" Luan's a bit narcissistic, I come to realize. I don't know if there's a good kind of narcissism, but if there is, I'm sure that's him.

He listens, doesn't distract himself by doing anything but showing interest, unlike some narcissists would do. And he does show genuine interest in me.

He's a little self-absorbed, but not to the point where everything always has to be about him. He talks about himself *a lot*, and still wants to know me, encourages me to tell him about myself.

I am yet to find out if the other points resonate with him, but even if they do, I honestly believe everyone's a bit narcissistic. It's about how much they lean into it until it gets toxic.

"If you don't want to, you can always turn around," he says, speaking in a low tone. "Or you can tell me to move."

I do neither. In fact, I turn over onto my back and pull Luan with me so his head now lies on my chest. He swings one leg over mine, as well as lays his palm flat to my chest. I reach both of my arms around his body, holding him tightly to me.

It's just for one night anyway. I'll leave tomorrow evening to get back to NYC, back to playing ice hockey, back to my life.

Luan is a fantasy, one I know can never happen even if we did everything in our power to make it work. So, what's left is that fantasy, and I'd rather keep that one up than lose him.

"You'll come visit again, right?" he mumbles after a short

while, already half asleep. His sleepy voice is even better than his usual one.

"If I find the time." I should be free for the summer, unless the team makes it to the Stanley Cup, but even then I'd still be free for most of the summer. "You could come to Manhattan, too, you know?"

He nods softly, mumbling something unintelligible, but if I had to guess, it was something about not being able to because of his soccer teams. It's the most logical thing to me anyway.

Without even thinking about it, I press my lips to the top of his head and gently trace my fingers up and down his bare back.

"If you're in love with me, Grey Davis…" He yawns, and never continues his sentence.

"I know, I know. I can just say it," I finish for him.

"Good."

"Good night, Luan," I chuckle.

"Good night, Grey Davis."

Chapter 6

"if you ever wanna be my one / I'll be waiting"—I'll Be Waiting by Cian Ducrot

Iuan

February 2024

FOR OUR LAST COUPLE of hours together, I suggested Grey and I go out to the beach, find a nice spot to hang around. We did find a nice spot… by a tiki bar. Again.

I love living by the El Matador Beach, truly. It's not all too crowded like the more popular beaches in Malibu, and therefore the beach parties are far better because the people are better. With an average sixty-five degrees in February it's not warm enough to go swimming, but warm enough to walk around or sit at a bar. So that's what we're doing.

I think Grey hates it, but I like being amongst people.

"No, just one plain water and a plain apple juice, that'll be it. No alcohol," I hear Grey finish off our order for the second time. Apparently the bartender doesn't quite understand that there are people out here hanging around bars without touching the alcoholic drinks.

"You can get a drink," I say. There's a chance that if I hadn't told him about my recovery from an alcohol addiction, he would order anything but water, and that thought makes me feel bad.

I never wanted people to stop drinking around me just because I can no longer do that. It's why I like hanging around bars. It's hard sometimes, of course, even after two years, but how could I

ever trust anyone if I can't even trust myself around my biggest weakness? Besides, I like watching people have fun and get more careless with every other drink. The bullshit that comes out of drunk people's mouths is the best part of it all. I never knew being the only sober friend is that hilarious. Scary, because sometimes you think your friends are about to die from all the shit they're doing with an alcohol induced brain, but funny.

That also always makes me wonder if Doro ever thought I was going to die when she cleaned up after me. Every. Single. Day.

"I don't want one," Grey answers flatly. "I'm about to hop on a plane and I'd rather be stone-cold sober for that. Also, I plan on using the gym at the apartment complex later tonight when I get back home and working out with alcohol in my blood really isn't that beneficial."

Yeah, okay, that I can agree on. I used to work out mostly drunk and it did nothing good for my stomach. Then again, I was drunk about eighty percent of the day, every day, so maybe that was also a great reason why my stomach couldn't deal with alcohol *and* working out. But at least I stayed in shape, or got into shape, rather.

But the thought of Grey leaving again doesn't do good things for my stomach right about now either.

I reach for his hand, needing to feel him close before I won't get to do that for the next god knows how many months. FaceTime and texts just aren't the same as having him here with me, being able to touch him, feel him, even smell him. All those things will be gone in a few hours for months, and I honestly dread having to say goodbye.

Grey doesn't pull his hand away, in fact, he is the one to interlace our fingers. I want to smile at that *so* badly but keep it lowkey. Mostly. Not enough to hide it, apparently.

"Just say it." Grey blows out a breath, ready to roll his eyes at the one sentence I throw at him all the time.

"Nah, I'm good." I look away from him, pretending to be

upset because he just took away all the fun from my favorite sentence.

"Allow me then." He clears his throat. I swing my head around, staring at him with wide eyes. "If you're in lo—"

I bring my free hand to his face, squeezing his cheeks together to stop him from finishing that sentence. I can feel his muscles stiffen, and if I wasn't so keen on not wanting to hear him say it aloud, I would much rather let loose and watch him embrace that perfect smile of his.

"Don't say that. It's *my* sentence." I loosen my hand just so he can talk back, but I swear if he attempts to finish his sentence, I will silence him another way.

"Scared you might actually say it if I give you the chance to?" He smirks, and holy fuck does that do things to me.

I shake my head. "I don't fall in love with people I don't date. Especially not the ones I haven't even kissed yet. So you can ask away, but you won't get an answer."

Kiss me.
Kiss me.
Kiss me.

Grey chuckles and doesn't make *any* attempts to kiss me at all. He doesn't even move closer or *looks* at my lips.

How fucking difficult could it be to get someone to kiss you, my god. And why can't he take a goddamn hint?

Nobody can tell me he's just not interested and that's why he hasn't kissed me yet, because what he did last night says anything but *not interested.*

Every single time I tried to move away from him because it got a little too hot, he held me a little tighter so leaving was no option anymore. The satisfied hums that left him every time I gave up and just laid my head back down on his chest also said differently.

And he says he doesn't do cuddling.

I have this theory that Grey just pretends. That he pretends not to like me. That he pretends he doesn't want me as much as

I want him. His mouth says he's as interested in me as he is in soccer, but then his actions say we're already married.

He ignores me every now and then, and I also have a theory as to why that is. I think Grey ignores me every single time he realizes I've never been just a friend to him. That whenever we met, he knew there was a deeper connection and he's just too afraid to embrace it. Not love at first sight, because he doesn't love me, I know that, and I don't love him. Sure, I might have this *teeeennnyyy tiiinnyyy* crush on the guy, but it's not *love*. And still, I think Grey Davis has a crush on me as much as I have one on him, but for whatever reasons, he's just too stubborn to give into it. He's too afraid to… to what I'm not sure but definitely too afraid to take that step from friends to lovers. Or even to take the step from friends to seeing each other more frequently, dating.

But that's alright. If he needs time, I'll give him that.

I'll do this the right way with him.

No manipulations, I know I can do it.

I can be normal. I can be patient and feel the joy of finally getting what I want without forcing it. I can be strong.

I have to be. For him. Because Grey Davis deserves to fall for me because he wants to, not because I made him do it. He deserves to realize his feelings all on his own and not have me spoil the surprise for him.

If I have to wait another year or two for him to realize, I can do it. I can give him that time.

"So, what are your plans for the year?" he asks me, squeezing my hand a little.

"Watch as many of your games as I possibly can while trying not to fall asleep watching them."

Grey nods *very* slowly while narrowing his eyes at me. He hates it when I bash ice hockey, which is exactly why I love doing it.

I don't have anything against the sport per se, I just don't understand it.

Six Years

What's so great about watching adult men constantly crash into one another and press the other up against the walls—er, boards? Why does ice hockey have to be so brutal?

The two times I watched it in person, I thought the players were going to kill each other. And that one time I watched Grey on TV and was forced to see him get tackled or whatever they call it, I was seconds away from buying a plane ticket to go wherever he was because that shit looked like it was painful, and I wanted to hold him in my arms.

"Do you actually watch every game or are you just saying that?"

I turn around in my seat, Grey does the same. And like I did the first time we were here, I mingle our knees so that one of mine is right between his legs and one of his is between mine. I don't know why I keep doing it, I think I just like the closeness, the physical contact. I like touching him, even if it's just our knees that touch, or legs, or he allows me to hold his hand. I wholeheartedly believe I'd be totally okay with being allowed to touch his earlobe only, but I take his other body parts as well.

"Every single one with you potentially in it," I confirm. "I don't understand what's happening, but I can read the scoreboards, I know when you're winning. I can listen to the sports moderator tell me who scored a goal and who assisted, and every time they mention your name, I do a little imaginary backflip for you to cheer you on."

"Even when we don't talk?"

I nod. "I watch every game."

I'm a hopeful person, a dreamy one with a broad fantasy, too. Once I make up my fairytale, I do everything to make that fairytale turn into reality. So if that means watching ice hockey to know where Grey's at, how his team is doing and all that, I will do it. If turning my fairytale into my actual life means showing interest in Grey beyond what he knows of, then that's exactly what I'm going to do.

And I'll do it the healthy way this time.

Chapter 7

"every second I look at you, I want another"—There's No Way by Lauv, Julia Michaels

Grey

February 2024

THE GOOD THING about having grown up right next to the beach is that I know my way of getting into and out of my childhood home and staying unnoticed. So when I had to use the restroom, I didn't have to use these unhygienic and disgusting public restrooms, I could just sneak into my parents' house and use one of the bathrooms there.

But when I come back to the bar and find some random guy sitting next to Luan being all touchy, I wish I would've used the stupid unhygienic mobile-like toilets.

I stand there a few feet away from them, barely hearing anything they say while watching and slowly feeling a weird pain start to form in my heart. My mood immediately worsens more than it does every time I think about having to catch a flight in a few hours and leaving Luan behind for however long.

Luan laughs at something the guy says, but unlike he does with me, he isn't laying his hand on the guys' thigh when he sighs extra long to calm himself from laughing too much.

I hold my breath against pursed lips, feeling my own hands turn into fists so tight, if they go any tighter, I might as well break my own bones.

Watching them talk and laugh together makes me want to

hurl. It makes me want to throw that blond guy across the beach and tell him to fuck off, tell him to leave Luan alone because he's not interested.

But what if he is?

Blond guy is *here*, and I'm an hour away from going back to NYC, going back to traveling for months on end. Luan could see blond guy all the time, whereas we don't have the chance to meet that often.

They could get into a happy relationship and do all the fun things I want to do with Luan. They could spend days in bed and watch TV or talk. Luan is a great talker, so I know they'll always have something to talk about. And maybe blond guy likes talking, too. He looks like it because he's the one who's talking and Luan's just laughing.

I don't make Luan laugh like that.

I'm just taking a step forward when I stop in my tracks again after hearing the guy's question.

"Can I get your number? Maybe we can meet for coffee some time."

My breath leaves me in one go, the ache in my heart now pinching. I shouldn't feel this way because Luan deserves to be happy. He deserves to be with someone who has time for him and can be around. And that isn't me, still, I want it to be me. It could never be me though, I know that much.

"No, I have a boyfriend," Luan answers, offering the guy a slim smile. It's not a genuine one.

"You could still get my number. When you break up you can reach out to me," the guy suggests.

Fuck off, dude. Luan isn't interested.

It makes me happy when I know it shouldn't. Not because Luan has, once again, referred to me as his boyfriend when I'm not, but because knowing he's still holding on to the thought of us when I never gave him a single reason to do so before last night gives me hope.

Hope is my worst enemy. My father would never accept Luan

and I's relationship, no matter what I'd do. So hope is only going to make me feel worse in the end when I have to accept that nothing will ever happen.

Luan shakes his head. "We won't break up, ever. Because, God, Grey's so amazing, you know? He's all sweet and adorable, and kind, and he came here for my birthday just to see me, even though he lives across the country. He's so perfect. I know we'll get married someday, therefore, I don't need your number."

"I don't see your 'perfect' boyfriend around here somewhere." Why can't he take a hint, what the fuck?

But thanks to the blond guy's rudeness, I finally get my brain cells back and step forward, approaching them. I wrap my arms around Luan's neck from behind, looking at that guy with fire burning in my eyes. "Now you do."

Without having to see Luan's face, I know he's *genuinely* smiling now. The thought of his smile alone allows my nerves to calm down.

"You're dating an ice hockey player?" the guy says in what sounds like disbelief, but I think it's more resentment. I mean, he knows me, clearly, so I believe it's just resentment toward *me*, not ice hockey. "And you still think you're getting married one day? That's stupid. Everyone knows guys like him can't keep a relationship to save their lives."

"Clearly you have never been with one." Luan gets off his chair, forcing me to let him go. He turns around and looks at me, smiling like I knew he would. Soft. Warm. Just Luan. "Are you ready to go, baby? We have places to be."

Baby. My heart does a little involuntary backflip. I am not allowed to feel this.

I nod, even though I know "places" means the airport, and the airport means having to say goodbye.

"Are you sure you don't want to get your bag first? You still have an hour left before check-in even opens. We can make it to my house and back here in time."

I want to say yes, go back to his place, and get my bag, but the only reason for me to say yes would be because on the off chance that we get into traffic, we wouldn't make it back to the airport in time which then results in me having to stay longer.

"I'm good. You can keep the clothes." I'm wearing the most important one anyway. Plus, I stole one of Luan's shirts this morning while he was in the shower. I'm just hoping he doesn't care about that shirt too much. If he does, that's not my problem.

"Good, because I wasn't planning on giving them back to you anyway." Of course he wasn't.

For the next hour, we're waiting together for check-in to open. The time passes faster than I'd like, especially with Luan telling me all about everything he can come up with. His stories vary from anything that happened in his childhood, to college stories, though most of those are more sad than great ones like mine are.

My college life was great. I had my best friends, an amazing hockey team. I was somewhat loved by random people, even though I never talked to any of them. I was always the silent one in the group, nobody ever saw me and still they knew me. The parties were great and overall, college was just amazing, if we ignored the constant studying and boring classes.

Luan's college life was filled with bad grades and alcohol, so he tells me. He says he can't remember most of the four years, that he had more near-death experiences than he'd ever like to admit. There were moments when he stole liquor bottles from stores because his parents refused to give him more money.

I don't know how this started, or why it did, but I do know that I am so goddamn proud of him for finding a way out. For *still* not wanting to go back there. I can't imagine how hard it must've been to find the courage of wanting to be helped or staying strong all day long.

The entire hour while we're sitting here, Luan's holding my hand. I'm not sure he notices it himself, but every now and then, his hand tightens, especially when he looks around and remembers we're not in his house anymore.

Maybe I'm the only one who pays so much attention to his hand in mine, but even then I don't care. His hand fits so perfectly in mine, I don't want to believe that I will have to let go of it in a little while.

A moment later, they announce that check-in for my flight is now open and that's when the same pinch from earlier reappears. Maybe coming here in the first place was a bad idea, but I don't regret it. I wish I didn't come, but at the same time, I wish I could stay longer.

It's kind of ironic. Five years ago I said I'd never set foot in Malibu ever again, and now here I am not wanting to leave. It's funny how one single person can change your whole perspective.

I once thought Malibu was the problem, that if I left Malibu, my problems would disappear, but that has never been the case. My problems stayed, they were just further away from me. And now I'm here and somehow, those problems are still as far away in the back of my head as they've been when I was in New York. The only difference is that the problem could see me any second here in Malibu and cause a scene, while in New York that's not the case.

We get up from our seats and Luan follows me to the check-in, but once we reach it and I look at him to say goodbye, my heart breaks a little at the sight of his reddened nose, his bloodshot eyes, the tears pooling in them. There's no smile on his face, and I think that's what gets me the most. Without Luan's smile, the world seems only half as warm. Without his smile, it's like the world has tilted off its axis.

I bring my hands to his face, wiping away his tears. "Don't cry, Luan," I say quietly, softly.

"I'm sorry." He sniffles. "It's just gotten real."

I nod, understanding more than ever before. The last time I left Malibu, there was no real goodbye. The time I left after that morning in L.A., I didn't care enough to realize that saying goodbye sucks.

"There might be something that could cheer you up though," I say, waiting for that smile of his to resurface but it never does.

"I don't think so…"

I run my thumb gently over his cheek just before I shove my fingers through his hair and pull his head closer, then dip mine down and press my lips right to his.

No more thinking. No more excuses as to why this is supposed to be wrong.

A delicate gasp slips from his lips just before his hands grasp my hoodie by my waist and he pulls me into his body.

Chapter 8

"I'd rather you walk all over me than walk away"—
Worst of You by Maisie Peters

Ivan

February 2024

I THINK I'M DREAMING, but if I am, I am praying to never wake up again.

Grey is kissing me. *He* is kissing *me*. He initiated it. Our first kiss.

I am still trying to figure out if this is actually happening even when he tugs on my hair ever so softly, it might as well be the wind that's definitely present inside of an airport. Or when his tongue slides over my bottom lip, asking me for access, which fuck yes, I grant him.

Barely a second after I part my lips just that tiny bit, Grey pushes his tongue right into my mouth, mingling with mine.

The loud noises of people talking tune out.

The sounds of suitcases sweeping over the floor mute.

The echoes of kids screaming and laughing are no longer audible. The dogs don't bark, announcements don't happen, planes don't take off or land.

Everything is as silent as it was last night when it was just Grey and me in my bed, cuddling.

I can smell him over the scent of coffee that lingers in the air, or the baked goods from the café just around the corner from us. All I can smell is the fresh note of his cologne, the equal parts of musk and something wooden, yet flowery. I never paid much attention to Grey's smell, but I can now with one hundred percent certainty say that he is my favorite scent of all time.

I can taste him on my tongue, so much of him and a little bit like apple juice because he took a sip from mine just a few minutes prior. My two favorite tastes now mixed together equal heaven on earth.

Bunching his shirt up in my hands more than ever, I hold onto him tightly, not caring about the wrinkles I am causing. I don't think he cares much about them either.

My heart is beating so rapidly inside my chest, I believe Grey can feel the *thump-thump* right against his. It's good if he can because then he knows what this kiss is doing to me.

Oh please don't let him kiss me just because he wants to cheer me up, that'd be so cruel. It's working, but at the same time I hate him a little for doing this to me.

Why couldn't he have kissed me yesterday? At a time where we had enough time to make out a little, shared more than just one kiss before he has to leave me for months. We could've spent the whole evening kissing and cuddling, watching movies, and kissing some more. But no, he chose *now* to kiss me. Now when I only have him for another minute.

When our lips part, Grey leans his forehead to mine, still keeping his eyes closed like he doesn't quite want to come back to reality yet. But if there's one thing I learned about fantasies, they always end eventually, and right now, I really hate that for us.

He's breathing a little heavily, but so am I. We're still trying to catch our breaths from a kiss so good, it almost makes me forget I ever kissed someone before him.

All I want to do is move in one more time, get one more taste of him just for the sake of it, but Grey then lifts his head from mine and looks past me for a second before his entire face pales. His eyes stay fixed on something or someone right behind me, but as I try to turn around to see what's caught his attention, he slides his hands from the back of my head down to my jaw, keeping me from moving.

"Grey?" I say quietly, carefully. If there's one thing I refuse to do, it's scare him away.

His eyes snap to mine, his face immediately finding color again. "Yes?"

"Can you promise me not to disappear this time?" I ask, worried he'll ghost me again. Worried that he'll ignore me all over again.

Now that I know what his kisses taste like, I don't think I'll ever be able to not yearn for them. But if this kiss means losing him, then I'll happily pretend it never happened.

"I'm not going anywhere this time, Luan. I promise."

I nod, quickly, letting out a shaky breath. "So, you're not going to freak out because you just kissed me, which then results in you ignoring me again? Because, Grey Davis, I can pretend this never happened for your sake, but please don't ignore me again."

He smiles, actually smiles. Soft and sweet, and so fucking beautifully. And then he leans down again, presses his lips to mine one more time like he's telling me he, too, won't be able to forget this happened. That he cannot and will not pretend he never kissed me.

"I'll find a way to make this right," Grey promises. What exactly, I don't know, but I'll trust his words.

After that, Grey sends another look over my shoulder, this time a heated one rather than something anxious. It's not for very long, but it's there.

"Does that mean I can flirt with you now?" I ask, smirking at him.

Grey furrows his eyebrows. "Then what the hell have you done the past year?"

"Kept flirting a little more… low-key."

He tilts his head sideways, his dark eyes piercing holes into my soul. "Well, I guess flirting is allowed. But only to a certain degree as we're not a couple, you still have to win me over, you know?"

Oh, the game's on. If there's something I'm good at, it's flirting.

Okay, actually, I'm bad at it, but because I am a funny-bad, it's good, you know? He'll wish he never allowed me to flirt.

Grinning, I nod my head at him once. "You're so going to regret this."

He chuckles and then pulls me into a tight hug, kissing the top of my head. "I already do."

"Are you sure you don't want something, honey?" Ma asks, holding up an extra plate.

"No, thank you." Eating is the last thing on my mind right now. Grey was supposed to land an hour ago and he said he'd text me when he does, so now I'm worried something might've happened.

"Oh, honey," my mother sighs deeply, putting the plate back into the cabinet. "What's wrong?" She takes my hand in hers, lovingly stroking her thumb over the back of my hand for some comfort.

"Grey left again," I tell her, already feeling the waterworks come up again. The last time I truly cried must've been during my time in rehab, when the alcohol just left my body, and I was desperate to get some back into me. The time I started to feel again, when I felt like I was going to die without an ounce of liquor in me. And before that, the only time I cried was after losing Charlie.

I don't count saying goodbye at the airport.

Dad comes walking into the kitchen, ready to eat dinner, when he stops in his tracks as soon as his eyes land on me. "What happened?"

"His boyfriend left the city again," Ma tells him.

"He's not even my boyfriend, Ma."

"Well, why not?" she asks, her eyebrows draw together. "He seemed nice."

A smile crosses over my face now, happy to know she actually does think Grey is nice. "He is," I confirm. "Maybe other people would disagree, but Ma, he's so amazing. And so kind when one gets to know him. And he's so handsome, like did you *look* at him!?" I lean over the kitchen counter, pressing my face right into the stone. "And he's such a great kisser, Ma."

I hear my father chuckle before the sounds of plates rubbing against one another mutes him. "So, you kissed him but he's not your boyfriend?"

I groan. "He kissed *me*, Dad. I didn't do anything." I pause for a moment there, then add, "For once." My parents know what I've done before, how I used to make people like me instead of allowing them to get to know me and like me because they just do, because I'm a great person or something like that. They weren't proud when they found out, but neither of my parents ever blamed me or saw me as a bad person after I told them.

All they ever did was support me, gave me a helping hand when I needed them the most. And I am so thankful for that, truly. Without them, I don't think I would've been able to keep my promises, that I'd go to rehab for my alcohol problem, that I'd stop manipulating people. Without their support, my life could look so much different right now.

"Are you sure?" Ma asks, and although that question stings a little, I understand where she's coming from.

Grey is the first person I allowed to get to know me after rehab. He's the first person I am trying to be normal with. Of course she's worried I might not even notice I'm manipulating him.

I look up, meeting her eyes. "I think so."

Dad walks around the kitchen island and lays a hand on my back. "Did you tell him about it?"

How could I? If I told Grey that all of my relationships—

friendships included—before were forced, I don't think he'd ever exchange a single word with me again. I wouldn't if I was him.

"Luan, your therapist said you'll have to be open about it. It's the only way whoever you're talking to knows not to fall for your charm."

I know. "But why would I walk up to a random stranger and be like, 'Hi, I'm Luan, I am a known manipulator with narcissistic tendencies, so there's a high chance I might make you like me because I like you, but don't worry, now you know so if you're lucky, maybe I won't do it after all because I am currently trying out not to do it anymore'?"

My dad sighs, taking a seat by the island next to me. "How about you just tell him you tend to manipulate people and ask him to stop you when he notices you're trying to do it?"

"It still sounds bad." I don't want Grey to read too much into me, and when I tell him, he's going to read every single thing I say differently. He's going to overthink my jokes, overthink my flirting, overthink *everything* I do and say because it might sound like I'm trying to make him like me.

"Well, boy, it's your decision to make."

Exactly. And so far, I think I am doing great at being a normal person.

"Dad?" I say, suddenly remembering what I've been meaning to ask for a while now. I always forget. "Why'd you always keep me away from the Li kids?" I doubt it's because my father can't stand Ji-Hoon Li only because they're in the same business. "I met their daughter the other day, and she seemed nice. So why was I never allowed near them?"

That's not exactly true. I met Sun, but that's over a year ago, she was nice though. However, if I told my father Grey is Ji-Hoon Li's son, I fear he'd try to turn my building relationship around faster than Grey and I started piecing it together.

"Because their dad is bad news."

What the hell is that supposed to mean? Everyone has a wicked side to them, I believe. "Bad news how?"

Six Years

My father straightens his back, rolling his eyes just thinking about whatever he's about to tell me. "That man gives interviews about his success, which is normal, but the things he says. I never understood how people could support his brand. How they could keep on buying stuff from a man who believes colors and clothes have a gender, so dressing a little boy in pink is wrong in his eyes. It's just a color. All the Li Co. stores have separate sections for boys and girls. It might've been okay-ish in the 90s, but nowadays it's not. Most of the clothes Li Co. creates for girls have a sexist touch to them, while the shirts for boys say things like 'I'm a superhero' or 'Future Boss', all the girl clothes are about their appearance. About how pretty they should look, having checklists printed on the front, saying stuff like shopping, doing makeup and more. It's just wrong. So, no, I didn't want you anywhere near his children."

So what he's saying is… "Mr. Li is homophobic."

My father nods. "Always been, and I can't imagine he taught his kids to be anything else. I don't want people like them near you, never did."

But Grey, he's not… he's not like that. He kissed me. I slept in his arms. But it would explain his indecisiveness.

Unless he knows who I am, knew it right from the start and is now helping his father take down mine.

Chapter 9

***"fix you, help you mend, when it gets tough"—Friends
by Ella Henderson***

Grey

February 2024

"IZAN AND I DIDN'T break up because of a comment he made," I blurt out the second I unlock the door to Miles's apartment and walk inside.

After seeing my father at the airport earlier, I realized two things. One; I do not give a shit what he thinks about me anymore.

He wants to disown me, so fucking be it. If my family actually loves me, they can still talk to me.

I have to stop living by my father's rules because I am my own person.

Kissing Luan felt right. And if something feels right, why should I give up on it?

The other thing I realized; I have to open up to Miles.

Miles is my best friend, and I want to have that deeper bond with him. I want to have someone in my life who knows me better than anyone else. And after almost six years of being best friends, I think it's time he actually gets to know *me*. Not the guy my father wanted me to be.

Miles and Emory are both in their kitchen, him cooking, her sitting on the counter and watching. It smells delicious, so I'll probably take some home with me when I leave. Then again, everything Miles cooks smells and tastes great.

"Pardon?" Miles looks at me, confusion written all over his features.

"He wanted to meet my family, but I couldn't let him do that with the kind of father I have. He got angry because of it, all the time. The last week we were together, we only ever yelled at each other because he said if I loved him, I'd introduce him to my family. When I tried explaining to him why that wasn't possible, I thought he understood, but then he gave me an ultimatum. Him or my family. I chose my family."

Emory hops off the counter, whispering something to Miles before she plants a kiss to his cheek and walks over to their bedroom. After she closes the door to give us more privacy, Miles turns off the stove and looks at me.

"I figured it wasn't about rice."

My pulse increases, my nerves shoot through the roof when I ramble on and on about all the things I wanted to say to Miles for years. All the problems I wanted to let him be part of, wanted his help with but couldn't ask for. And all Miles does is listen, nod his head every now and then, understanding.

When I start talking about all the feelings I've been bottling up ever since I was twelve years old, Miles gestures for me to walk over to the couch to take a seat. I do, but only because my knees feel like they're seconds away from giving in and dropping me to the floor.

As we sit, I continue to tell Miles about my childhood, how my father used to hide his own kids from the public which wasn't necessarily a bad thing, but it always made me feel like he was hiding us because he was embarrassed. I tell him about how, even though Sun is three years younger than me, she was always the one I was closest to because she understood me.

But then we get to the part I've never told anyone about, not even my own sister.

"I had my first kiss with a guy named Luke at the age of twelve," I say, taking a deep, encouraging breath. "I freaked out because my dad raised us to be *normal*. He always said people liking the same gender as them is wrong and how that is something to be ashamed of. When I was little, I believed him."

I pause, feeling my cheeks heat with embarrassment.

Embarrassment... Wow. I can't remember a single day I was ever embarrassed. "It was at school, and I had a panic attack after I realized what had just happened. My teacher called my parents and told them about it. Not the kiss part, I don't think she knew. Anyway, my dad picked me up and in the car I told him what I had done. I was crying and thought I was going to go to hell now. That Satan was out to get me and all that crap."

Miles looks at me with only little sympathy, so much different from what I thought he'd look at me if he ever knew more about me. And he keeps surprisingly quiet.

"My dad sent me to a church camp that same summer because when he asked if I regretted it, I said no. I told him it was exciting and that I thought I liked that guy. It scared me, but I didn't see anything wrong with it. Dad thought I was being pressured at school, that I was depressed and needed to reconnect with God, because god forbid his son might actually just like guys. That camp did nothing but make me realize that liking guys isn't so bad. Sure, they aimed to tell me differently, but I didn't give a fuck. Fast forward like two years, I had my first actual boyfriend and when I introduced him to my dad, he was all nice in the guy's presence. But when said guy was gone, Dad yelled at me for the first time. Called me names and said I was disgusting. From there, it only ever got worse."

For the next hour, I continue to tell him about my childhood, about everything that pops up in my mind, really. More stuff about how my father treats me, I just tell him *everything* there is to know about me.

I didn't know talking about what has been eating at me for years could make me feel so light all of a sudden. I didn't think I would feel different after opening up about it, that I would be able to feel the weight lift off my shoulders, off my heart.

And when I say my final sentence, I catch the slim smile that Miles has on his face just before he wraps his arms around my body like he's been meaning to do that for the longest time imaginable. Maybe he has.

"I am so sorry you had to go through that, Grey," he says, still holding me in his arms. "I should've raised you. I'm a great dad."

That he is, but despite it being impossible because Miles is about one-and-a-half years older than me only, I still appreciate his attempt in making a little light of the situation.

"Why, you want me to call you Daddy?" Miles slaps his hand to the middle of my spine, causing me to gasp out loud in pain. "You fucki—"

"We don't use those kinds of words in this family, son."

This guy, I am telling you.

I pull away from our hug, scowling at my best friend. However, when I see the soft expression on his face, my scowl just fades away.

"Thank you for telling me," he says, like dumping my trauma onto him was the best thing that could've happened to him. I know for a fact it wasn't because to Miles, Brooke, Eden, and Emory are the best things to ever happen to him, but whatever.

"Wait, there's more." Now that I'm already spilling my entire life out to him, I might as well mention my most recent thing that happened. "I kissed Luan. Today. At the airport."

"The soccer guy?"

"The soccer guy," I confirm. "I spent the night in his bed, and all we did was cuddle. Can you believe that?"

Miles's eyes widen drastically, already shaking his head before the *no* makes it past his lips. "You're meaning to tell me, you, Grey Davis, did *not* kiss Luan last night when you were sleeping all cuddled up to him in his bed?"

"Yup."

"Not even a little peck?"

"Nope."

"No fucking either?"

"No."

"You didn't even… I don't know, jerk off together or something?"

Can I take back telling him? I mean, this is what I expected would come out of him when I mention Luan and my night together. It's how all of my friends would've reacted, how I know they reacted to each and every single somewhat relationship announcement of theirs as well. It's how *I* reacted hearing about Aaron's relationship, internally anyway.

The questions that shouldn't actually be of interest but just are.

"I'm pretty sure Luan offered to fuck me like six times in two hours, but no." Honestly, I'm surprised I turned down the offers as well.

Miles blinks at me, swallowing, then blinks again a couple of times before he manages to speak. "You shock me, Grey."

I fall back on his couch, letting out a huff when my back hits the backrest. "Welcome to the club, love. I'm shocking myself."

"So are you like crushing on him? Already in love? Ready to put a ring on his finger?"

Hypothetically speaking, if I took Miles out on his balcony, then stumbled and accidentally made him fall off said balcony, does that count as murder? Because I am considering it right about now.

"If you asked Luan that question, I'm sure he'd say we're already married and ready to adopt a baby, or five."

Miles bobs his head, humming in agreement. "Yeah, he strikes me as the kind of guy who already has his life planned out with you."

Scarily, I don't think Miles is that wrong.

But shit, speaking of Luan, I promised to text him when I land. So in record time, I pull my phone out of my pocket to shoot him said text, together with a much-needed apology.

However, before that, there's *one* more thing Miles should probably know of. "You know the brand Brooke and Eden's clothes and toys are from? Most of them, anyway."

Miles nods, eyeing me with suspicion now. "Li Co. or something. I still don't know how you have that shit just lying around like sacks of potatoes. Their stuff is expensive as fuck."

"Yeah, about that." I scratch the back of my neck. "I get them for free because my father owns the company. And honestly, I wouldn't even give them to you because it's like free advertisement every time Brooke wears them outside and some part of me has always hoped that stupid company would go down in flames. But despite not being on good terms with my dad, the clothes and toys are pretty good quality wise. And I only ever give you the stuff that's actually *good*, not the whole sexist shit my dad approves of sometimes."

"Yeah I noticed that. The sexist stuff, not your dad owning that company. What in the rolling flipping chairs, Grey!"

Well, he took that better than I thought he would.

Chapter 10

"honey, life it just a classroom"—New Romantics by Taylor Swift

Iuan

March 2024

MY HEART STOPS beating the second Grey's face pops up on the screen, not because I am happy to see him, but because his hair is wet. Wet as in completely *drenched*, water still dripping down from the strands.

Before he gets one word out, I hear the water running in the background.

"ARE YOU IN THE SHOWER?!"

Grey smiles into the camera, then turns his head to look behind himself to check. "Yup."

My mouth stands wide open, but my jaw drops once more when he takes a few steps back, now standing right underneath the stream. The camera doesn't reach below his belly button, but the image in my head is building itself up without my permission anyway.

How dare he?

Honestly, how dare he pick up the phone when he's in the middle of showering? Standing there in all his naked glory and yet still not giving me a show.

That man knows very well how I feel about him, so doing this is plain rude.

It's just a shower. Everyone showers. You shower. Your best friend showers. Grey's best friends shower. Grey showers.

With you watching.
With me watching.

It's nothing I haven't already seen, and yet this right here seems far more intimate than we've been before, even when we're states apart.

"How was your day?" he asks, putting some shampoo on his hand before he massages it right into his scalp. All I do is watch and wish it was me who was rubbing shampoo into his hair, then sneak in a little kiss before rinsing it back out.

I clear my throat, blinking away the image of Grey and I showering together. "Great, actually. I took the U13 out for some McDonalds after their game. It was the first time they have won this season, so I thought some celebratory McDonalds wouldn't hurt. Hannah, the oldest of them, challenged me to an eating competition. Whoever ate less chicken nuggets in five minutes would pay for them. I won, but I ended up paying anyway because she's a kid, you know?"

"Sounds like fun."

"It was! Though my stomach would love to disagree. I swear, I ate like thirty Chicken McNuggets. Afterward, I downed about two bottles of apple juice because I felt like dying. In hindsight, the apple juice might've not been my best drink choice, but I love apple juice, so I'd never regret choosing that one over anything else."

After having rinsed out the shampoo, Grey turns around to grab a blue loofah before he's facing me again. He then pours some soap onto it, foaming it up. "Thirty nuggets in five minutes. That's quite impressive."

"You think?"

He looks directly at the camera. "Yeah. It's not every day you hear someone say they ate *thirty* nuggets in such a short time."

That might be true.

"Did you talk to your dad yet?" I ask, changing the topic. After I found out his father is pretty homophobic, I spent all of yesterday reading articles and interviews, seeing it for myself.

Six Years

And as it turns out, Dad was right. Ji-Hoon Li said his fair share of homophobic things in the past, and the stores really do separate boys from girls clothes more than other stores do. And the prints...

I didn't ask Grey whether he's helping his father take down mine and decided to go with my gut feeling. Grey isn't his father, and it's not his fault his dad is an asshole.

However, I did ask Grey why he's on no-talking basis with his parents and he told me his dad was mad at him, but he never said why. I have my assumptions though.

"No, but I do plan on visiting him as soon as I find some time for it. It's about time we have a talk."

"And that would be when exactly?" Grey going to visit his dad to talk means he'll be in Malibu, which then means I get to see him.

"Hockey season ends early April." He takes a step closer to the camera. Washing his body is no priority seeing as he's too busy talking to me. "If we don't make it to the playoffs for the Stanley Cup, I'd have time after that. But with our current points, it very much looks like we'll have a safe spot. If we compete for the Stanley Cup, then the Finale would be June 23rd, so sometime after that. I'll be off until preseason starts back up again in September."

"So, what I'm hearing is I'll get to see you from July to September?" Logical conclusion to draw here.

I lean back against my headboard, positioning myself a little more comfortably while I continue to watch Grey shower. Or stand there buck naked, staring at me.

"If I can make it work, yes."

An excited shriek leaves me. July is far too long in the future, but I waited months for Grey to reply to my messages. I can wait five-and-a-half months to see him again. "You're telling me I have to wait almost six months to kiss you again?"

"Who said I'll be kissing you again?" Grey steps back underneath the water stream, still keeps his eyes locked with mine. He takes the loofah and then starts washing himself, suspiciously slow and seductive if you asked me.

"You when you promised you wouldn't have sex with someone else."

He freezes, his hand stops moving mid stroke down his arm. "I don't recall having said that. Ever."

True, but I am hoping I'll get an answer to a question that's been bugging me for quite a while. We never said we were exclusive or anything. I don't even think we have a relationship going in the first place. But I'd like to know if he's being intimate with other people either way. *Though it's none of my business.*

It won't be good for my health when he does happen to have other people beside me right now, but if I don't ask, I'll always wonder about it, and that's going to ruin my moods.

"So you cheated on me?" That would be impossible since, again, we're not in a relationship.

Grey smiles a little, and I wonder how he manages to smile at *this* very moment. The guy who barely smiles apparently finds joy in my misery.

"Luan, I'm not fucking anybody at the moment. Except my right hand."

"Oh," I breathe, kind of relieved but also a little embarrassed now. I shouldn't care about it, that's the thing, and I have no business caring either. But I do anyway. "Me, too."

Grey nods, but I don't think he really cared about me with that. I'm not the type to have one-nights stands anyway, so I don't know to what degree I relate to Grey. From what I've read on his former university's gossip blog, the ice hockey team was *very* active, especially Grey's best friend Miles. Every other day they posted a new picture of one on the team getting caught hooking up in public. A couple of those pictures included Grey, and let me tell you, my stomach turned looking at them more than once.

It was then when I realized I probably shouldn't have stalked a university gossip blog just to gather some information about

Grey. What was I expecting? Surely a *gossip* site doesn't talk about normal things like new skates for the hockey team or new equipment for whatever other teams they had at this university. Of course I was going to find headlines such as; "God knows who on the ice hockey team caught kissing his fourth victim in just one night".

"What are you thinking about?" Grey asks. "You look a little green there."

I grin at him. "What I would do if I was in that shower with you."

Grey elevates his eyebrows, slightly cocking his head as he dares me to say my thoughts aloud. I know the *What would you do?* is right on his tongue, but he's not voicing it.

"First, I'd kiss you on your lips," I begin, already imagining the pressure of his mouth pressing against mine in a deep kiss. "Then I'd move over to your neck."

Even over the sounds of water running do I hear Grey's sharp intake of breath. He looks down at himself, closing his eyes for a second before lifting his face back up to the camera, staring right into my soul. "And then?" his voice comes out a little strangled, a little breathier than usual.

Now that's interesting.

"Then, I'd probably bite you a little, leave a hickey to mark you as mine."

"Of course."

I smile at the flat but amused *of course*. "And then, I'd have my hands all over you, feel your soft skin, discover every inch of your body. I'd kiss my way down your torso…"

"And then?"

My dick hardens at the thought of what I'd do next. "I'd go down on my knees, wrap my hand around your dick and…"

Grey reaches a hand down, but I can't see much because his arm cuts off on the screen just below his belly button. I do, however, catch the slight upstroke of his hand, a small movement that I know wasn't to jerk off, but to pinch the head to keep himself from doing something really stupid.

And still. "You know, if you're going to masturbate, you could at least lower your phone a little bit."

Grey scowls at me, as always. But then he takes three steps forward, his face now right in front of the camera as he *slowly* lowers his phone. It's not by a lot, but he did lower it.

When he steps back again, I can now see below his belly button. He has a great and really defined V-line pointing directly to where his hand is holding himself. Still, anything below his lower stomach is not visible to me. I kind of hate him for it, but the knowing smirk tells me he did this on purpose, let me think he was going to show me his dick on camera. I should've known better.

"You want to watch?" Grey's voice is filled with lust.

"What?" I swallow hard, blinking a couple of times to make sure I *didn't* hear him say what I think he did.

"Do you want to watch?" he repeats. "My phone is stuck in a speaker that I can stick wherever I want. So I can lower it however low I want as well. If you want to watch, say it."

I think my mouth is running dry even though at the same time, I'm kind of salivating. I don't know what the fuck is happening with my bodily functions.

"Do you mean that? Because, Grey Davis, I think you're playing with me, so if you are, you need to stop."

He shakes his head. "I'm not playing."

But this has to be some kind of test because the Grey I know wouldn't just offer to masturbate on camera and allow me to watch. Not like this. Not when we have shared a total of two kisses.

"No," I answer. "I don't want to watch." I really do though, and maybe if I wasn't trying to be a better version of myself, I would've said yes. "When we go there, Grey Davis, I want to be physically present, not just over the phone." *Lies*.

He smiles sweetly, neither of his hands touching himself at all. "I knew you'd say that."

He did? I wouldn't have said that if he were anyone else.

"Luan?"

"Hm?"

"I am proud of you, you know?"

Proud of me? What for? "For not wanting to watch you jerk off?"

"*Pretending* you don't, and just in general." It's like he knows something about me that I didn't tell him yet, but how would he?

Chapter 11

"tell me if it's wrong, if it's right, I don't care"—Cool for the Summer by Demi Lovato

Grey

March 2024

FOR ONCE IN A rather short while, I am praying this phone call ends *very* soon. I love chatting with Luan, mostly because he talks and I have someone to listen to, someone around so I don't have to feel all that alone.

But this theory does *not* apply to moments like this one. Moments when my dick is hard as a rock and my balls are aching.

Over the course of two minutes, I've been slowly turning the water colder and colder without Luan noticing. If he saw me do it, he'd know why and, okay, yes, he probably knows I *was* hard a moment ago, but he doesn't know I still *am*.

"So anyway, I, once again, told her it'd be a waste of time trying to teach toddlers the rules of soccer. They'll learn at some point, but at four years old, these kids just want to kick the ball or run away from it, not play by rules. They want to have fun, not get yelled at when they accidentally use their hands."

What is he even talking about? Soccer makes as much sense to me as that one time my physics teacher made me do a presentation about galaxies, *plural*, and then ended up asking me how I knew there is more than one galaxy in the universe. Mind you, the presentation before mine mentioned there being more than one, and that man said *nothing*.

"Uh-huh." I glance at my phone screen, not looking at Luan this time. I look at myself, making sure I'm not accidentally flashing him more than I should. If I'm being honest, I wouldn't mind, but he might. No, actually, I doubt that.

Either way, I look down at myself, internally groaning because I have no idea how I'm supposed to get rid of that stupid erection while Luan can see every single one of my movements.

"You're not even listening," he chuckles, and frankly, it doesn't sound like he's mad. When I look at him, his eyebrows are raised, and his lips pull up in a smirk.

"I am," I veto. "However, I think I'll finish this shower in private because you no longer deserve to look at me half-naked." Ready to hang up, I step toward my phone.

His smirk deepens. "Uh-huh. You tried to be sneaky by turning that water colder, Grey Davis, but I *noticed*. I notice everything about you."

"You do?" I doubt it.

He nods. "Anyway, call me back when you're done with 'showering', okay?"

"Seriously? I'm not going to do anything." At least not with him being sure of it. It's not good for his ego. The more I give in to him, the bigger it'll get. "I'm soft as a pillow."

"Really?"

"Yup." I can see him shrug, I think? It's a bit difficult to tell over the phone. "Well, goodb—"

"I'm hard as fuck, Grey Davis."

I swallow thickly, freezing on the spot. There's no way he just said what I think he did.

"And while you'll finish off your shower, I'll do *other things*, 'kay? So, talk to you in a bit, baby." He hangs up the phone before I get the chance to respond, react, *blink*.

My brain tells me not to do it, not to give in to what I know he's trying to do… and still, I tightly wrap my fist around my dick at the same time as I call him back.

I wait.

And wait.
And wait.
Until he *declines* the call.

Looking at my phone in disbelief, I give it another try, only to get declined *again.*

I rip my phone out of my speaker holder and open Luan's chat.

Grey: Pick up your fucking phone, Luan.

Luan: Can't. Jerking off, thinking about you.

Grey: Exactly.

While Luan's typing, I turn off my shower, speed-dry my body before I find myself lying in my bed, hand on my dick.

Luan: Want to watch?

Grey: Pick. Up.

He might've been able to say no, but I can't.

I call him again, and when his face pops up on my screen, his cheeks rosy and the shirt he wore a second ago gone, I give myself a tight squeeze before stroking my hand down the length of my cock.

"That was quick for *finishing up your shower,*" he says, though by the sound of his voice I know he definitely doesn't want to talk about my shower right now.

Knowing Luan, he wouldn't make the first move, so I do. Though, maybe a little too direct. "Show me your dick."

"What?" he chokes, laughing a little. He's contemplating it though.

Well then... I turn my camera around, and the second my cock's on the screen Luan gasps. That fucking sound travels right through my body to my balls. Shit, since when does my body react to *that*?

"Holy… Grey!"

I watch his eyes widen a little more through the screen when I stroke my hand down the length of my dick and back up, assuming he does the same a moment later because his eyes fill with heat and his features tighten with lust.

"I want your mouth on me so badly, Luan, you have no idea," I say when his lips part just that tiny bit from inhaling deeply to steady his breathing.

Luan lets out a quiet whimper, his eyes closing halfway. "Not as badly as I want my mouth on you."

"Is that so?" Fuck, I feel like I am dying.

He nods, then lets out a shaky breath that forces me to grip my erection a little tighter. When has anyone ever turned me on as easily as Luan Hayes? Never, I'm sure.

It takes Luan two words to make me a little hard, five to have my erection standing to its full capacity. And those words don't even have to be sexual, it's his voice that does it for me. I love hearing him talk, even if he probably thinks he annoys me with talking so much.

"*Fuck…* Grey…" The camera shakes with every other time he jerks himself, his eyes, however, they stay focused on the screen, watching me cup my balls to massage them.

I press my head into my pillow and let out a need-filled groan. "What are you thinking about?"

"Our kiss," he answers, his voice small and mostly a gasp. "I really liked that kiss."

"Me, too."

"I want to kiss you again," he says. "And I want to touch you, and—"

Shit, my dick throbs at the sound of yet another gasp that leaves him. Breathing hard through my nose, I pinch the head of my dick, then slide my hand down to continue to jerk myself off. Blood rushes downward, building a pressure inside of my balls that almost tips me over.

"I am dying here because you're not in my bed right now." I wouldn't give any fucks whether it was to fuck or cuddle. Either of them would be fine with me. Though right now, fucking Luan seems like the better idea, and then some cuddles.

I don't even like cuddling.

My head is pounding, every thought erases itself within a second every time my eyes fall onto any part of Luan's face.

"How close are you?" I ask. I want to come with him, but I get the sense that I am the only one fighting demons not to come this instant.

Luan's face is glowing, his lips still somewhat parted and it's a treat to see that, even though I wish he was here with me in *person*, and that we could hook up instead.

I've never had phone sex before, and I'm not sure what made me have it now, but I can't say I'm mad about it.

"'Bout to come."

"Come with me?" I pump myself a little faster, hissing through gritted teeth, sucking in sharp breaths, and rolling my hips like Luan was here with me and he was the one to give me a handjob. Unfortunately, it's just me and my hand tonight, with the guy of someone's dreams on the phone, watching me jerk off while he's doing the same.

Luan's camera is shaking more than before, and the complaint that's about to leave me because I want to see his cumface on the tip of my tongue, when I realize he clicked the button to turn the camera around.

I watch as he gives himself a couple more strokes before cum spurts out of him, the bits of muscles I see tense and he breathes heavily. I come at the sight and sounds of it all.

Luan Hayes

March 23rd, 4:48 AM

I miss your face

And your voice

And your lips

> You're so weird, you know that?

Tell me you don't want to kiss me right now

> I don't want to kiss you right now.

Liar

> Not lying

Yes you are. I'm a great kisser.

> I didn't say you weren't. I said I don't want to kiss you right now.

L-I-A-R

> What the hell are you doing awake at 5 AM anyway?

It's only two for me, but I'm thinking about kissing you. WBY?

> Of course...
>
> Practice starts at six

Can you kiss the mirror for me? Just so at least one of us gets to kiss you?

You're so weird.

I AM DYING HERE, GREY DAVIS!

Well, die a little quieter then. I'm sure you woke up all of Malibu with all your whining.

... rude

Luan Hayes

April 13th, 8:12 PM

OH I JUST READ THE NEWS

STANLEY CUP! YOU GUYS DID IT!!

Congratulations, baby! x

Thank you

And don't call me baby.

... You're welcome, baby xxx

Grey Davis

May 2nd, 1:42 PM

FaceTime later?

Aww, miss my face?

Never mind.

> NO
>
> WE'LL FACETIME LATER! I WANT TO SEE YOU!
>
> HELLO??
>
> GREY DAVIS??
>
> Care to reply to your boyfriend?

You're not my boyfriend

> But it made you respond, so I'll see it as a win.

Grey Davis

June 23rd, 9:30 PM

> I don't get it. Did you win the Stanley Cup now or not because I swear it looked like you did but then they said another team's name on TV???

They did?

> Yup. So, DID YOU WIN?!

Yeah

> AHHHHHHHHH
>
> CONGRATULATIONS, GREY DAVIS!!!

Thank you, baby

...

I think I might've just died a little right there

Grey Davis

August 19th, 10:19 AM

My friends are planning a vacation together, so I don't think I'll make it to Malibu anymore, I'm sorry

Oh, maybe after?

I thought you were off from July to September

Yeah, but they're planning a whole month-long trip through Europe, so we'll only be back by September 23rd and preseason starts on sept. 25th.

Oh, okay

Well, have fun!

Send me LOADS of pictures. Let me live vicariously through you!

Will do

We'll still FaceTime though, right?

I don't know if the time difference will allow it, but we'll try, okay?

Okay. If not, that's fine, too. I just want you to have a great trip

You could come with us

I would love to, but I promised my U18s an end-of-the-summer party for winning their last game, and it'd be rude if I called it off now

Oh, yeah...

Well, okay. If you change your mind, let me know. I'll gladly fly you out.

Luan Hayes

September 15th, 12:00 AM

HAPPY BIRTHDAY, GREY DAVIS!

Have the absolute most amazing day ever!

Wow, this is kind of weird because it's still 3 PM here, so definitely not the 15th yet.

Thank you <3

God, I wish you were here

Me, too

But hello??? Spending your birthday in Paris seems fun

> HA! I wish. I don't understand a single thing these people say, and they're SO rude for no reason whatsoever. If it weren't for Miles being fluent in French, I'd die here of starvation. Even little Brooke can order food all by herself and I'm here relying on my best friend.

Well, look on the bright side

You now have an actual reason not to speak to anyone!

> True
>
> Maybe it's not so bad after all

Seeeee

Luan Hayes

October 31st, 9:23 AM

People say if your hearts fit together, it's meant to be. But I'd rather see if other parts of us fit together

> Well, good morning there to you, too

Good morning!

Hey, do you remember that store I dragged you to?

> The one your mother owns?

Yup.

Their clothes are 50% off this week

But at my house, they're 100% off

> LUAN!

Luan Hayes

November 11th, 11:11 AM

It's 11:11, make a wish!

> Okay

What'd you wish for?

> Can't say, otherwise it won't come true

Right.

I wished for you to leave me alone

Grey Davis

January 1st, 12:00 AM

Happy New Year, Luan <3

> Happy New Year!! x

> Are you busy? Can we Facetime?

I'll call in a few minutes, I have to put Eden back to bed first, but Brooke's crying because my neighbors thought it's a great idea to throw a New Year's party on the rooftop.

It's already 3 AM and they're still going.

Anyway, as long as Brooke's awake, Eden won't sleep either.

AW YOU HAVE THE KIDS OVER?!

Yup. Miles and Emory are busy doing things

I, too, would like to be busy doing things with you. But you're so far away

...I regret having kissed you last February.

No you don't.

It's been almost a whole year. I fucking miss your lips. UGH

I'm sorry

I miss you more though

Come see me again!

I'll see what I can do

Grey Davis

February 14th, 2:12 AM

You fell asleep and somehow ended the call, but anyway, Good night <3

Have a great birthday, even without me

Grey Davis

March 12th, 3:29 PM

Are you okay???

Grey Davis

March 12th, 4:01 PM

Grey?

What happened? Is your phone dead or something?

Grey Davis

March 12th, 4:35 PM

Please don't ignore me again

Grey, please. I am begging you at this point and I know I shouldn't, but please...

Please don't ignore me

You promised you wouldn't do it this time...

Grey Davis

March 13th, 3:33 AM

I'm sorry, I was asleep.

You've been asleep since yesterday or what?

Yeah. I caught the flu or something. Probably from Miles's kids.

Oh

Get well soon, baby! <3

Feel hugged.

And cuddled.

And kissed.

And loved.

And everything else that would make you feel better.

Having you in my arms would be enough…

Chapter 1

"made it pretty far on the first try"—Stargazing by The Neighbourhood

Luan

March 2025

"ARE YOU SURE that's a good idea?" Doro asks with concern in her voice.

"Yup." I open another drawer, trying to find my passport. I swear, I have one I just don't know where. "Have you seen my passport?"

"No?" Shit. "But New York's in the US, Luan. Your driver's license will suffice."

"What if it doesn't?" I've never been on a plane before, the only reason I even have a passport is because Doro, Sarah, —she moved in with us last month, but Doro has known her for years—and I did plan a trip two years ago, I went to rehab instead. "What if I miss my flight just because they won't let me through without a passport, Doro?"

"Just don't fly over to NYC then? Grey's *sick*, not dead."

I look up at her, scowling for the very first time in my whole entire life... at her. I've never been upset with Doro. I mean, sure, the normal being annoyed with someone when you *live* with them, but never to the point where I was genuinely mad at her.

"Fuck off, honestly."

"Woah." Doro holds up both of her hands. "You do realize you're acting like a love-sick puppy, right?

"Shut. Up." I am *not* acting like a love-sick puppy. I haven't seen Grey in *over* a fucking year. I miss him endlessly and now that I have the chance to be there for him when he needs someone, I can do that.

My co-coach is taking over practice for the month because he needs more hours, more money. I don't need the money because I could have a great life living off of my trust fund alone. I only coach because I have to have something to do to distract myself from thinking about alcohol or Charlie. And now Grey, too. And because I like coaching.

"You're not even dating him, Luan," Sarah says and leans against the door frame.

I turn away from them both, going back to opening drawer after drawer.

"How are you even sure he's still somewhat interested in you? It's been a year, Lu. If he wanted to see you, he would've gotten on a plane to visit."

Grey had little time, and I understand that he wanted to use some of the time he did have off to travel with his *best friends*. He deserved a break after stressful months on the road and constantly having cameras shoved right into his beautiful face. I, too, would choose a trip through Europe with my best friends over seeing some guy.

"Weren't you the one who made that poor guy find you without so much as a last name because you thought if he wanted to find you, he would?"

I nod, though don't open my mouth. I don't want to talk to either of them because I fear they might convince me to stay home before I embarrass myself.

"He said he wants me in his arms, Doro. If he wasn't interested, he wouldn't say that."

She's worried about me, I know that, but even if Grey turns out to have been a waste of my time, then it's me who has to figure that out. It's me who he has to tell that he doesn't want to see again. It's me who'll have to feel the disappointment and the heartbreak, but I'd rather go through that than wonder if Grey and I would've ever worked out if we both just put a little more effort into it.

We'd have a long-distance relationship, they *need* work. Work neither Grey nor I have put into it yet. At some point, one of us will have to start, otherwise we'll always keep on going back and forth. It's scary to think about seeing my (potential) boyfriend once a year only, if at all. It's scary to think about how to make this work, and if it even does, but that's still better than wondering and never finding out.

"Fine," Doro sighs. "Your passport is in the back of your closet. You put it there after getting wasted the night before going to rehab." Her eyes fill with fear, concern. "Are you sure you know what you're doing?"

I nod, getting off the floor. "I really like him, Doro. Flying over to New York is all I can think about doing right now. I want to be there for him and take care *of* him. I want to hold him and wait this out together, make him feel better, you know?"

"You never wanted to do that before."

I chew on my bottom lip, bobbing my head. "It scares me a little..."

Maybe I didn't think this through after all.

New York City is a *whole* lot bigger than I thought it would be, and as it turns out, finding out where someone like Grey Davis lives is far more difficult. People here don't tell you shit, especially over their beloved ice hockey players. Either they have no idea because, again, big city and such, or they won't say a thing because you might want to sneak into their house and murder them.

I did, however, find out most of the players of the NYR are living in an apartment complex close to Madison Square Garden. I have no idea where that Garden thing is, or what it is, but

Google Maps tells me it's about a thirty-three-minute walk away from the airport I'm at. I can do that. Though, I will call an Uber because I am not walking around NYC all by myself.

Just as I open the Uber App on my phone, I hear loud shrieks coming from behind me. It's probably just another celebrity, they seem to be running in and out of the airports here in record time. I look up anyway only to see *who* it is. But when I find a certain hockey team making its way out, I have about two seconds to decide what to do next.

I could walk up there, find Grey's friends, which are probably all of them since they're on the same team, but I mean his *best* friends. They'll tell me where Grey lives, I hope.

Or I can just follow their bus? Someone's going to pick them up from the airport, right? Or maybe they will get picked up by loved ones now that they're back at home.

So the first option it is. Thank god I know their names, just not the faces of the names. Honestly, whenever I watch the games, I only ever pay attention to Grey, the rest doesn't interest me nearly as much.

Now I just have to find out how to get past the onslaught of security around them. Unless I don't have to because one of the guys walks up to *me* instead.

The guy has blond hair and a friendly face. At least he doesn't intimidate me nearly as much as the brunette guy right behind him does.

Both of the guys stop in front of me, creepily staring at me until they exchange a look of confusion.

"You are seeing the same guy as me right, Colin?" the blond guy asks, side-eyeing me.

Colin. Oh, my god.

Colin looks at me again, humming. "I should've paid more attention to the pictures Miles showed us."

Miles. That's the guy I already met a while back. Grey's *best*-best friend.

"You know Grey, right?" I ask, ignoring their little confusion.

Six Years

It's a stupid question, I realize, because, duh, of course they know Grey. He's on their team.

"Depends on which Grey you're talking about," Aaron, the blond one, says, narrowing his eyes at me.

I almost roll my eyes. "Grey Davis."

Colin nods. "Yeah, heard of him. Why?"

Seriously? "I'm Luan, which I am assuming you already guessed anyway since you walked up to me and were all confused as to where you know my face from. So anyway, I need your help."

"Grey's not with us," Aaron tells me.

"I know, he's sick."

Colin's mouth opens wide before he turns his shock into a grin. "Shit. It's so great to meet you. Aaron and I were convinced Grey was hiding you from us."

"He only ever talks to Miles about you because, apparently, Colin and I make his life harder by teasing him about you and all. But you have to know, Grey in love is like as rare as a blue gummy bear in a normal Haribo Goldbears package."

In love. Yeah, I doubt that's what Grey is, but I'm not here to crush his friends' fantasies yet. Or mine.

"Anyway, can you tell me where he lives because I don't know his address, and nobody here is telling me anything. I mean, I understand why, but it's annoying as fuck and I don't want to call Grey to ask because I think he might be asleep and sleep is good while he's sick, you know?"

"172 Madison Avenue," Colin answers. "We'd take you there, but we're heading right to the arena for practice."

"That's fine, I was just about to call an uber anyway."

"Do ask for Miles King though, because chances are Grey isn't in his apartment but in Miles's. Or well, he's asleep and then he won't even answer the call from the reception."

"Okay, thank you," I say and offer them both a genuine happy smile. They just saved my ass here.

"No, we have to thank *you*. You're bringing a little light into

213

Grey's life."
Yeah, I know that much by now.

Chapter 2

"my receipts be lookin' like phone numbers"—7 rings by Ariana Grande

Luan

March 2025

EVEN JUST STANDING outside of that apartment complex makes me feel poor, and I'm not. It's almost completely reflective, and the entrance doors…wow. It looks like walking into a *super* fancy Luis Vuitton store, and they're already as fancy as it gets.

Depending on which side his apartment is on, he should also have a pretty amazing view on the Empire State Building.

Living here must cost *millions*.

I almost don't dare walking in there, that's how cheap I feel wearing sweatpants and my yellow smile hoodie. It wouldn't surprise me if they throw me out for just wearing anything but an expensive suit. But for Grey, I do so anyway.

Looking around the lobby, my jaw is on the floor almost immediately, but thank fuck I can swallow down my astonishment on the outside.

Grey Davis lives *here*?! No wonder his shower looks like there's space for a whole soccer team. How can he be willing to leave this place for more days than he's here? If I lived here, I'd never step foot outside ever again.

Anyway, I walk up to the reception only to get stared at with a very questioning look. I get it, I look like a homeless guy in here, I looked at myself the same way when I passed one of the mirrors in here.

"Hi, how may I help you?" the woman asks, offering me a customer-tending smile.

What do I even say? *I'd like to visit Grey Davis.* That sounds wrong. Let's treat this like a hotel then, I think that's safer.

"Could you tell me the apartment number of Grey Davis?"

Her eyebrows quip up for a moment before she hides her surprise. "Are you on the visitor list?"

I don't think so. "Probably not?"

"May I have your name, sir?"

"Luan Hayes." Wait, I was supposed to say I want to see Miles, not Grey. Shit.

She clicks a few buttons on the iMac before her. Her eyes widen drastically when she reads something on that screen, I wonder what it says.

I swear if he blacklisted me…

"For safety reasons, I'm going to have to see your ID before letting you up." That sounds about right.

I pull out my wallet and hand over my ID, only for her to clear her throat as she tries not to show any reaction. *What is happening*?

"Grey Davis was it?"

I nod, again forgetting that I'm supposed to say Miles. Before I get the chance to correct myself, the woman reaches into a drawer and pulls out a key then slides it over the counter to me. "Apartment 26B, twenty-fifth floor. Mr. Davis asked us to give you a key should you ever show up."

What? Why would he do that?

Probably because he knew if I showed up, I wouldn't exactly tell him about it, and in case he wasn't home, I'd still get inside. That's the logical reason, right?

"Okay, thank you."

She hands me back my ID and points me to the elevators.

—

I check about twenty times whether I got the right apartment before I unlock the door and walk inside. The last thing I need right now is trying to unlock a door that does not, in fact, belong to Grey.

Thank god the door unlocks, and I can actually walk inside. But as soon as the door is opened, I stop in my tracks and chuckle. Of course he would have it super dark in here, even his flooring is black and gold marble.

I don't get much time to admire the fanciness of Grey's apartment before the door right across from Grey's opens and a little blonde girl comes running out.

I've seen her before, but she was a whole lot tinier then.

"You're not Uncle Grey," she says with a little attitude, furrowing her eyebrows while looking at me all madly.

She takes a few steps toward me, puffing out her chest when she stands in front of me. "Who are you?"

"I am Luan." I don't take it badly that she doesn't remember me.

She hums. "And why are you in my Uncle Grey's home?"

"Because I'm visiting him."

Brooke nods, keeping her eyes narrowed at me. Then suddenly, her features soften, and she waves me down to her. I kneel and wait for what she has to say next.

"Are you his boyfriend?" she whispers like it's a secret or something.

"No, I'm not," I chuckle to which I earn myself a sad expression from that little girl.

"Why not?"

"Ignore her, she's curious." I look up to find Miles standing in the door to his apartment, holding a pot in his hands. "Does Grey know you're here?"

"Nope. I thought he'd need someone right now, so I hopped on a plane, my very first flight *ever*, and came here. It was scary, like I thought I went on the wrong plane and would end up in Panama. And then the plane took off and I almost—I'm talking too much again, sorry."

Miles smiles at me softly and shakes his head. "It's fine. I have two kids, they, too, talk a lot so I'm used to it." Great, now I am being compared to kids. It's not the first time, but still.

"I don't even talk much, Daddy," Brooke disagrees, crossing her arms over her chest.

"Mm-hmm. You're worse than Eden, Brookie."

"Not true! Eden babbles all day long, and I don't. Plus, sometimes I don't even understand what he says!"

Miles chuckles. "Can you go tell Emory that I'll be back in two minutes?" he asks his daughter who's already running back inside before her father even finished his sentence. When she's gone, he nods for me to head into Grey's apartment. I do, and he follows me, closing the door behind him.

"Grey's super sick, which is mostly Brooke's fault but if we told her, she'd feel bad," Miles says and walks into the kitchen to set down the pot of what I assume is chicken soup. He opens one of the upper cabinets, takes out a bowl. "Do you want something as well? I made more than enough."

"No, thank you."

Miles takes a ladle to transfer soup into the bowl. "It's good you're here though. That means I don't have to care for three kids. Grey turns into a literal baby whenever he's sick. Well, not like a *literal* baby, but he might as well. I think it's because he grew up with tons of people who worked for his parents around him, making sure he was cared for, you know?"

"Probably."

"You're staying, right? Because it's fine if you want to leave again now that he's sick." Miles puts the lid back onto the pot, now turning around to look at me.

"That's the whole reason why I'm here."

"Well, great then." He holds the bowl out for me, I take it without a question. Miles opens a drawer and pulls out a spoon, handing it over to me as well. He then opens the refrigerator and takes out a bottle of water, setting it down on the kitchen counter. "Grey should be in his bedroom, it's uh"—he rounds the corner of the kitchen and points toward his bedroom door—"right there."

"Okay, thanks." I offer Miles a smile, watching as he walks toward the front door to leave. But the second he reaches the door, he stops and turns around again.

"If you need anything, either of you, I live right across the hall as you have probably figured out. Grey doesn't usually have meds at home, but I hid an emergency Advil bottle in the very back of his bathroom cabinet. I made him take antiviral drugs an hour ago, so there's a slight chance he might be completely knocked out for another few hours, or he'll wake up somewhat… hazy. He also probably doesn't have food at home, so if you're hungry, come over, Grey does."

"Okay. Thank you."

"Oh, and Luan? Have fun snooping around."

I grin in response. I wasn't thinking about snooping, but now I am.

But Grey comes first.

Chapter 3

"and if Heaven doesn't want us, would you go with me to Hell?"—nobody else by LANY

Grey

March 2025

"GREY?"

I don't even open my eyes and still reach for my phone, holding it to my ear. Every muscle in my body is sore, making it almost painful to pick up the phone.

"Hello?" I force out, feeling the soreness in my throat worse than before.

I hear the sounds of a lovely and very familiar chuckle, and if I could, I'd smile like crazy right now.

Hold on.

Did my phone ring? I don't remember hearing it, and I'm almost a hundred percent sure you can't hear someone talk *before* the phone even rings.

Slowly, I force my eyes open only to stare at a black screen. Wow, am I really that out of it that I'm now hallucinating? So infatuated from medication that I am imagining Luan's voice and his chuckles.

God, I love his voice. It's so cute and deep and sexy. I wish he was here.

"Grey?" his voice speaks again to which I groan and throw my phone to the foot of my bed. Traitor. That shit could've at least told me he called. He always calls me. At least once a day, sometimes twice or more. I like the calls, but I'd never tell him. It's the only time I ever get to hear his face and see his voice— Wait, no, that's not right. It's the only time I get to *see* his *face* and *hear* his *voice*. That's the right order, I believe.

Why do I care, nobody's hearing me say this out loud anyway.

"Baby?" Two hands now lay down on my jaw, my eyes rip open again because I swear if I am imagining someone touching me, I'll call an ambulance or an exorcist because that's not right.

Once my eyes are open, they meet the most beautiful green ones I have ever seen in my entire life. They're so dreamy, greener than grass, and beautifuller than the moon. Is beautifuller a word? It should be one.

"I believe it is, but it's not in the dictionary, nor does it get used that often." The voice to the green eyes chuckles, and so I blink a few times because Mr. Green Eyes is all blurry, but I already know who those eyes belong to anyway.

"Woah. What kind of pills am I on?" Miles gave me something, that I know. He wouldn't drug me, I don't think. Clearly he did though because there's no way my Luan is here right now. He lives in Malibu, he doesn't get on planes and fly out to see me. I think he's afraid of flying, but that's okay because I will fly with him when he moves here one day.

"Some antiviral drugs."

Ah. Don't know what they are, don't care either. So I'm high as a kite, I take it. I've never been high before. Drunk, yes, but high?

Does one get high from antiviral pills?

Isn't *any* pill technically a drug and should get you high? I guess it depends on the doses. I don't know, I'm no pharmacist.

"Are you real?" I ask, still blinking over and over and over again. "Or am I tripping?"

"Both, I think."

Huh? Imaginary Luan pulls me up to sit, but then I sit up myself if he is imaginary, right? I don't know. Maybe I've died and an angel is taking me to paradise right now. Or a demon is taking me to hell, like my father would say.

"If you're real, what's my name?"

He chuckles again, taking my hands in his now. His are warm and comfortable. I like Luan's hands. Even Demon/Angel-Luan's hands are great. "Grey Davis."

Huh, interesting. "What's my middle name?"

"I don't know." I don't think I ever told him either because I don't have one.

"It's Blue." It's not, I don't have a middle name.

"I think you're lying, Grey Davis."

"I am," I confirm. "And I think you're a demon who's about to show me the way to hell. Or an angel who's flying me up to heaven. Either way, I don't think you're my Luan. I think you're trying to play tricks on me. Because my Luan lives far away from me. Oh god, do you know that I miss him so much?"

"I know now, baby." He brings a hand to my forehead, most definitely to check if I'm hot. "Do you want some chicken soup?"

I ignore his question. "Are you actually here? Because if you're not, please tell me so I can go back to sleep and dream of you instead."

He takes a seat on the edge of my bed, and lays my hands down on his jaw. "I'm real, baby."

Without thinking, I wrap my arms around Luan, shedding tears when I can feel him. He's here. Like actually *here*. In my bedroom. In my arms.

"I've missed you so fucking much," I mumble, closing my eyes for a small moment as I enjoy his presence, his warmth, him. The familiar scent of something sweet and flowery hits my nostrils, causing me to smile more than ever.

I love his scent. It's comforting and could easily describe him because Luan just *is* all kinds of flowers. He's what I expect the sun to smell like, minus the fire.

When we pull apart, I almost move in to kiss him, but stop myself when I feel the soreness of my muscles again.

I'm sick. Right.

He shouldn't be here while I'm sick, I'm contagious and I sure as fuck don't want to get him sick, too.

"No, Grey Davis, kiss me. Please."

I shake my head, regretting it immediately. God, my head's pounding. Shouldn't antiviral pills make me feel better? I swear I felt better *before* taking them. "You're going to get sick."

Luan shrugs. "One more reason to stay with you for longer."

That year I hadn't seen him, it felt like an eternity. Every time I planned on leaving to fly over to Malibu, something got in my way. But he's here now. And I can't even kiss him.

"Are you going to brush off everything I say as me having said it because I'm on drugs?" I ask, watching his nod. "Great. So, I like you, Luan Hayes. And I want to cry right now because you're here and I can't kiss you. And I swear, I want to kiss you so badly right now, I feel like I'll die if I don't have my lips pressed to yours within the next five seconds."

Luan smiles widely at me, then pulls his bottom lip between his teeth. "Wow, I wish you got sick more often because you talk a whole lot more."

"Yeah. But that's okay because you can talk every day when I'm not sick, okay?" I love listening to him talk. He's always so joyful and sweet and funny and so enthusiastic. He's like the light in my life.

I'm the night and he's the day.

While he's the sun, I'm the moon.

And I wouldn't want to have it any other way.

"Can you cuddle me?" I blurt out when Luan gets back up from the bed. "It'll make me feel a whole lot better."

"I thought you don't do cuddles?" He's picking up my phone from the foot of the bed and putting it down on my nightstand.

"Yeah, but you're the exception. You're *always* the exception."

"Good to know."

I wish I could see him a little less blurry, and I wish I didn't feel like dying any second so I could enjoy having him here.

I do, however, notice the yellow hoodie he's wearing. I think it's my favorite hoodie of his, but only because I have a matching one.

When I look down at myself, I realize I am not wearing a shirt. That's too bad, I should've worn my frown-hoodie because then Luan and I would be matching again.

"I'm cold," I tell him, shuddering a little. I'm not really cold but I want his hoodie, so I hold out my hand for him to give it to me. But that stupid boyfriend—Ha, *boyfriend*. He's not my boyfriend yet—of mine apparently can't read my mind because he looks around my room instead. I think he's looking for my closet. I have a dressing room, but he won't find it that easily because my bedroom has way too many doors in here.

There are five in total. The bedroom door, en-suite bathroom door, doors to a mini room I made an extra closet for just hockey equipment—I think it was supposed to be the pantry or something—, and then doors for two walk-in closets. I don't know what I'd need two walk-in closets for, but I suppose single people usually can't afford millions of dollars' worth apartments. And if they can, I'm sure they'd choose a bigger one than mine.

I have two bedrooms. Mine and one for guests. Miles's apartment is much bigger, but he also has a wife and kids so that's good for him.

My apartment has three bathrooms, one en-suite for each bedroom and one half-bathroom right by the front door. Then obviously a kitchen and living room. That's it. A whole lot of rooms for it being just me.

But maybe one day Luan will move in here with me, and then he can have one of the walk-in closets and every room will be filled up a little more with his stuff.

"Will you move in with me?" I ask, clearly not caring about any consequences voicing this questions might have.

"Sure, but not any time soon, baby." He turns around to look at me with that cute confusion on his face. "Where are your clothes so I can get you a shirt?"

I refuse to tell him where my closet is. "I want your shirt."

Luan looks down at himself, then back up. I think his eyebrows are slightly raised, but I'm not sure. They're also dancing a little, and I am certain eyebrows don't actually do that. "You want my *yellow* shirt?"

I nod. "I want to have you *all* over me." Maybe if I dressed a little more like him I'd also be happier.

"Is that so?" He chuckles softly and makes his way over to me. When Luan stands before me, he pulls his hoodie over his head and all I do is watch him patiently.

"That is very much so."

Once the hoodie is off, he sends an adorable smile my way. "Can you lift your arms?"

I do, even if it hurts my muscles. Carefully, Luan pulls his hoodie over my arms and my head, and then a little deeper down until it covers up my entire torso. His scent is filling my heart with warmth, love, and comfort immediately.

"Would you actually move to New York for me?" I stare at his perfectly sculpted face, feeling the urge to cry just laying my eyes on this handsome mess.

Luan nods. "I'd move anywhere for you, Grey Davis."

"But you don't like the cold."

"I like you, so I kind of have to like the cold."

Chapter 4

"can we make it outside this dream?"—Romeo by Bryce Xavier

Luan

March 2025

WHAT DO YOU THINK, how much of a chance is there that Grey won't remember a single word he utters to me right now? Because I think the chances are *really* high. Still, I'm hoping they're super low because the Grey Davis I know would never ask me to move in with him. So maybe if he can remember he already did, he will do it again in a few years, perhaps even months.

I do have to say though, Grey definitely is *not* himself when he's sick and I kind of like it, but I also hate it. He's talking nonsense and says so many things he'd never utter if he wasn't sick, or pumped up with antiviral drugs. But right now, he's saying all the things I've wanted him to say for over a year.

I wanted to hear him say he can imagine a future with me, and yes, he may not have said it in those words, but you don't ask someone to move in with you if you didn't.

I wanted to hear him say he likes me, but the one coming from high-Grey doesn't come close to what I'd imagine it'd make me feel when he *truly* said it.

"Do you want your chicken soup now?" He's already seated, so why not try again.

"No. But you can come cuddle me now." Grey opens his

arms, waiting rather impatiently.

"You've got to eat something."

Of course he ignores me, guess there's still *some* Grey inside of him after all. "I want to sleep." He scoots a little over on the bed, patting the now free space next to him.

I do take a seat, crossing my legs and keeping Grey from cuddling up to me. He gets frustrated with that, starts whining a little but that's okay.

"Let's make a deal," I start and take the bowl with chicken soup from the nightstand. "You eat just a little bit and then we can cuddle for hours until you feel better."

"I'd already feel better if you just hugged me."

If only the flu would leave that easily. "Grey Davis, you have two choices. Eating and cuddling afterward. Or no eating and I'll go back home."

Even if he didn't eat, I wouldn't have it in me to leave him again so soon. Only God knows when I'd see him next.

"Fine," he mumbles, somewhat sitting up straight. He was already half-sitting but not enough to eat in that position.

Because I fear he'd accidentally pour the whole hot bowl of soup over himself, I keep on holding it, slowly feeding him spoonfuls of soup. His face scrunches up every now and then when he swallows, and it breaks my heart every single time. I don't like seeing Grey in pain, but I also have no idea what would help against a sore throat.

If I had to guess, it took us about twenty minutes for Grey to have eaten ten spoons of soup, but ten spoons in twenty minutes is better than none at all. Plus, it's good to go slow, it won't affect his stomach all too heavily that way.

Another five minutes later, I put the bowl away because I believe Grey is seconds away from falling asleep and the last thing I want is him to fall asleep sitting up.

"You can lie down now," I tell him, and he does so immediately. I barely have the chance to lie down myself before Grey has his arm draped over my body and his head resting on my torso. I'm just glad his bedroom is warm since I am no longer wearing a shirt and I wholeheartedly believe that I will not get to move for the next few hours. Freezing to death was not on the top of my to-do list for today.

"I like you here with me," Grey whispers before I can feel him press his lips to my chest.

"Go to sleep, Grey Davis." I can't possibly tell him that I like being around him as well. I could, but it feels wrong telling him when he might not even remember it in the morning.

"Okay, baby."

My head falls deeper into the most comfortable pillow I have ever laid on, my eyes staring at the ceiling as I let that one single word sink in.

It's just a pet name, nothing big, and he's called me that before. Still, my stomach flutters, a smile as soft yet wide as ever making its way onto my face as that one word repeats itself in my head over and over again.

Right in this very moment, I realize that if someone came walking in here and shot Grey, I'd die right with him without the bullet ever touching me. It's a scary realization. For the longest time in my life, I thought I'd never need anyone again. I used to think that I was meant to be alone because of all the people in my life, the only ones who stayed were my best friend and my parents.

Doro only stayed because she's known me *before* I fucked up my life. She has known me before I went crazy because of Charlie. And my parents stayed because they gave me life.

All this time I made people like me because I thought if I was being myself, nobody would ever care about me. That nobody would need me, and nobody needing me meant I didn't need anybody either.

I was on my own, and I was okay with it. But now... thinking about having to be alone scares me more than the flutter in my heart does every time I look at the guy who's currently in my arms. But there is one thing that scares me *even* more than the thought of dying alone.

That would be not being with Grey.

I can wait for months for his reply, I would wait a lifetime for a stupid text back because admitting my fantasy was never real is something I am not willing to do. I know that, should Grey and I never speak again from this day forth, I'd still be waiting for a text or call in sixty years all because just having him in my life as a thought is better than not having him there at all.

And if that isn't scary, I don't know what else ever could be.

I plant a kiss to the top of Grey's head, lingering there for a short moment only so I can breathe him in for a while longer.

Chapter 5

"just a little more than just friend"—Just Friends by Ally Barron

Grey

March 2025

"How are you feeling?" Luan asks the second I come walking out of my bedroom, still rubbing one eye to make sure that I've woken up.

I swear, if I hadn't woken up *still* wearing a yellow hoodie, I would've been convinced I was hallucinating the past couple of days.

"You're actually here." He's currently sitting by my kitchen island, drinking a coffee. I don't think he likes coffee that much because his face scrunches up in disgust every time he takes a sip.

"Yup. Like I told you about twenty times in three days." Luan smiles up at me, so wide and enthusiastically, I don't even want to believe he is a real human being. It has got to be seven in the morning, who the hell is so *joyful* at this time?

Don't get me wrong, I am a morning person. I wake up early every day, but I do *not* feel joy after waking up.

"So, back to my question, Grey Davis. How are you feeling?"

I walk over to my refrigerator, opening it. "Sick, but better." At least I can walk around and not just spend my days in bed anymore. It's day six of being sick, so it was about time I got to feel a little better, right?

After taking out not one, but two bottles of water, I close the refrigerator door and slide one of the bottles over the island counter to Luan. "Sorry I don't have apple juice here."

"It's alright, you didn't know I was coming anyway."

That I did not. I'm just glad Miles tidied up my apartment a day before. He was bored while looking out for me, and since I was sleeping he thought why not clean up a little bit? I never really learned how to clean up after myself thanks to the housekeepers I grew up with, but I'd like to think that I'm doing an okay job now. Tidying up annoys me, but at least I clean up anything I might spill immediately. Like drinks or food.

Either way, I go back to my refrigerator and take out a bottle of some drink Sofia brought with her when she came back from Germany the other day. Turning toward Luan again, I hold up the drink. "I may not have apple juice, but I have some German version of it."

His eyes light up, which makes me believe he didn't exactly look around my entire apartment yet, otherwise he would already know this.

"Is it not the same?"

I shake my head. My biggest mistake in life was to believe Sofia when she said that stuff was good. Perhaps not my biggest mistake, but it's a close third. "It's carbonated apple juice. She told me the actual name of it, but it slipped my mind." I don't have the heart to tell Sofia that it tastes like ass, so I kept it here in my fridge to rot, occasionally slipping one or two bottles into Miles's fridge.

Luan gasps. "*Apfelschorle*?!" Sounds about right. "I've always wanted to try it."

I hand the bottle over to Luan. "If you like it, you can have it. I'll pay you to keep it."

He laughs and immediately opens the bottle to try it. From the looks of it, he likes it. Don't ask me how or why. But I guess I'm getting rid of that shit after all.

"See, this drink alone makes coming here worth it." He takes another huge sip. "And seeing you, of course." His voice gets quieter with every word, and I'm unsure why.

"I'm glad you're here," I say in all honesty. I hate that we barely see each other.

Luan nods a little absently. Something's on his mind and it's only a matter of time before he tells me exactly what it is.

Shit, did I say something weird? *Please don't tell me I professed my undying love for him.*

"Did you expect me to show up eventually?" he asks, fidgeting with his fingers.

I was hoping he would, but I did think he'd ask me for my address fir— "You didn't even know my address, Luan. How did you find me?"

He chuckles, once again grinning at me. "I wanted to see you, so I found you."

I walk over to the island, standing on the opposite side of him and lean forward, resting my arms on the countertop. The closer I get to him, the more nervous Luan gets. It's kind of adorable, but I don't think he's nervous about being so close to me. "You're freaking out because of the key, aren't you?"

"No," he lies, his nervous and awkward chuckle being the only giveaway that he, in fact, is freaking out because of it. "Yes. Kind of."

"It's just a key." It was just in case anyway. I didn't think he'd ever show up here for the first time unannounced, especially without knowing my direct address. I did, however, know if he ever showed up after knowing where I lived, he wouldn't tell me beforehand, and since the odds are higher for me *not* being at home, he would've had to wait for god knows how long before he was granted access to my apartment. The only logical thing to do was ask the front desk to give him a key should he show up. "I do want you to keep it though."

Luan shakes his head immediately. "Why? I live across the country, Grey Davis. It's not like I ever think 'Oh, might just give my dear old friend a visit' all of a sudden. Well, I do think that a lot, but I can't so…"

"Dear old friend?" I repeat, a slight tremor in my voice.

"Am I supposed to think I'm more than that to you?"

That little shit. I walk around the island, and he turns on his chair to follow my every move, which is good because as soon as I round the island, I stand myself right between his knees and lift his face up for his eyes to lock with mine. "You know you're more than that."

Luan lays his hands on my hips, pulling me that tiny bit closer. "Like a really good friend, huh?" He smirks, fisting my, or rather his, shirt in his hands.

"Or like a—"

"UNCLE GREY!"

My head snaps toward my front door, waiting for Brooke to manage sticking the key into the keyhole. Ever since she learned how to do it, she insists on opening doors by herself, so even when I hear her already, I'm not opening the door for her like I usually would.

When she finally manages it, Brooke comes marching inside like she lives here with me. I mean, I do happen to have a whole lot of her toys here, so she might as well. "Hello!" she shrieks and comes running over to me, but she stops in her tracks the second she notices Luan. "You again."

"Hello," Luan says a little awkwardly, gently pushing me off of him. Aw, he's so adorable.

Brooke scrunches up her nose with a bright smile, then waves me down to her. Instantly, I kneel because I know if I don't, this little kid will tell her dad I was being mean, and then I will have to listen to Miles lecture me on how not to be mean to a seven-year-old.

For a split second, Brooke looks up at Luan and then back at me. "Is he your friend, Uncle Grey?" Brooke asks, whispering so he wouldn't hear. I bet he still can. "Or is he your *boy*friend?"

"What makes you think he's my boyfriend?"

Brooke leans into me a little more, keeping her eyes strictly on Luan like she's making sure he's not listening. "Because he's funny."

I don't exactly know when she got the chance to witness Luan being funny, but I'm not questioning her anymore at this point. I don't think she remembers the ice rink with him.

"He is, huh?" I smile a little just thinking about it.

"Like Daddy, but funnier."

"You think so?" Brooke nods. "But don't tell your daddy you said that, Brookie. He'll be heartbroken." Knowing Miles, he would make a whole fuss about it. He might also force us to come over for Taco Sunday and make us take a poll on who's funnier; him or Luan. Our friends would vote for Luan simply to annoy Miles.

"Does he make you happy, Uncle Grey? Like Memory makes Daddy happy?" Brooke asks, now laying her hands on my knees.

Knowing fully well that Luan can hear every single word we speak, I want to say no. I want to lie, but Brooke would look right through me and then she'd throw a fit. "He does."

Her eyes narrow, her fingers play the piano on my knees. "So he is your boyfriend then?"

I shake my head. "No, we're just friends." For another few minutes.

Brooke's eyebrows draw together as she looks from me to Luan and back. "But does he make your heart *thump-thump* when you look at him?" She brings one hand to my chest, showing me what *thump-thump* is supposed to mean.

"Why?" I ask, now narrowing my eyes at her. "Does yours do that when you see Reece?" Reece is Colin's younger brother. He's about the same age as Brooke and they're best friends. Now that Brooke's a little older, she has a few more friends than whenever she was four years old, but back then, he was the only friend she had. They still meet up at least three times a week.

Brooke's cheeks redden but she's quick to shake her head, denying everything. "Don't tell Daddy. He doesn't allow me a boyfriend yet, okay? It's our secret. And then I don't tell Daddy you love Luan."

I don't love Luan. I mean, I do, but as of now, not the way she thinks I do. I love him as a friend, and I do want him to be more than just a friend, but that's not quite the love she's talking about. Though, to her, there probably isn't much of a difference.

"You're okay with that?"

Instantly, Brooke nods. "Sure. But if he hurts you, Uncle Grey, you tell me, okay?" She looks up at Luan again, sending him an adorable little death glare. It's not that threatening coming from her. "If he does, I'll ask Daddy if I can talk to Luan with all the bad words I know."

Which shouldn't be a lot, I hope.

Still, I laugh and pull Brooke in for a tight hug, planting a kiss to the top of her head. "You'd do that for me?"

"Of course," she chirps. "But Daddy might not let me. Then you have to say the bad words for me, okay?"

Miles definitely wouldn't let her use any of those *bad* words. Just a few weeks ago, Brooke called Eden a *doodoo-head* because he took Brooke's Barbie. Miles almost had a heart attack.

Getting up from the floor, I pick Brooke up and sit her down on one of the bar stools next to Luan, winking at him when our eyes lock. He looks a bit pale with nerves.

"Now, tell me, what brought you here?" I ask Brooke. When I'm home, she usually stops by a couple of times a day just to say hello, never with a reason. Though it's maybe seven-thirty in the morning, I don't think she's here for no reason at all.

"Daddy told me to tell you he'll bring breakfast here in a bit." Interesting. Miles calls me to come over every morning as soon as breakfast is done. "For you both."

"Well, thank you for telling me."

"You're welcome." Brooke scrunches up her nose once again, but then her face falls and she gasps in excitement. "Oh, Uncle Grey! Yesterday, Daddy and I were playing catch and then I fell. It didn't even hurt, so I'm all good. But when I got up, do you know what happened?"

"What happened?"

"I lost *two* teeth! So when I woke up this morning, the tooth fairy got me *two* presents!!"

"Really? Wow."

Brooke turns to Luan, carefully tapping her finger against his arm to get his attention. When he looks at her, Brooke smiles all sweetly and says, "Do you want to see my new toys? I got two Barbies, one is a princess with a very beautiful purple dress. The other one is the prince, but I don't like the princes that much, they always have weird hair."

Right, Brooke shows *everyone* her Barbie princesses collection. She's a little obsessed with everything that has to do with princesses, except for the princes, I guess. The male Barbie dolls do have weird hair though, I admit.

"Sure, I'd love that," Luan answers to which Brooke jumps off the bar stool and runs toward the door to leave.

"Okay! I'll go back home and then I'll show you at breakfast." With her hand already on the doorknob, Brooke turns around and looks at me one last time. "I love you, Uncle Grey."

"I love you, too, Brookie." That being said, Brooke is out the door.

"She's adorable," Luan says as soon as the door is closed.

"Right?" Brooke's the only little girl I don't feel even a hint of resentment toward. Kimia, my cousin, I disliked her right after she was born already. I couldn't tell you why, but I just did. It hasn't changed much now that she's older, around sixteen maybe? She could be eighteen, I'm honestly not sure. My point is, from the second Miles introduced me to Brooke, I liked her. She was only a year old then. "She wouldn't actually use bad words when talking to you, by the way. Miles wouldn't let her."

"Yeah, I gathered that." Luan chuckles, taking my hand in his. "But it's cute how protective she is of you. How old is she?"

"Seven," I answer. "She turns eight this September." Why's almost everyone's birthday in September though? Mine is,

Emory's is, Brooke's is, Eden was also born in September. People *love* careless fucks in December, I suppose.

"Enough about Brooke," I say and stand myself between Luan's thighs again, praying Miles isn't going to come barge in here like his daughter did before. Taking an encouraging breath, I just blurt it out. "Will you go on a date with me? An *actual* date."

Luan licks his lips, a smile tugs right onto the corners of his mouth. "I would, but you're on bed rest and you've been standing for *way* too long already."

I hate him. No, really, I do.

"Fine. We'll have our first date in my bed then. I'll light up candles and make the owner of the Rêverie hand deliver us amazing food so it's a candlelight dinner but homemade."

"The owner of the Rêverie?" Luan scoffs, not believing that I happen to have *great* connections to said owner.

The Rêverie is a very popular five-star restaurant chain. The best of all the five restaurants throughout the USA is in New York, as is the owner of said restaurants.

I shrug like it's nothing. "You'll also be eating breakfast prepared by him, so…"

Luan's eyes widen, his mouth opens in shock. "You're kidding me."

"Nope."

"You get to eat Rêverie food *every* day like it's nothing?" I nod, though that's not exactly true. When I'm on the road, I live off of takeout. But, hey, at least I order salads with the burgers and stuff. "You're so lucky, I swear."

I wouldn't be so sure about that. "I'd be luckier if you finally agreed to go on a date with me."

Luan sighs heavily. "If you're in love with me, Grey Davis, you can just say it."

"I will, but for now,…?"

He smiles again, bringing both of his hands to my jaw. "Okay. One date and then you're going to have to ask me to be your boyfriend because otherwise I won't say yes to a second date."

"Is that blackmail I sense here?"

Luan nods with confidence at first, but then all of that vanishes at once. "Grey…?" His hands leave my face, fear fills his eyes as though he realized something that might scare me away as soon as he opens his mouth again. I think I already know what he's about to tell me.

"Just say it," I try to encourage when he starts to avoid looking at me.

"I'm a manipulator," he says, his voice breaks when he says it. "I don't know if you're being nice to me because I made you like me, or because you just do. And before one day you realize what I've done, I want you to know that. If you think I somehow manipulated you into liking me, then tell me and I'll leave before I can hurt us both any more than I already have."

"Luan—"

"No, let me talk." I don't know what else he thinks he has to say, but alright. "I've been trying my hardest not to do it anymore, but manipulating someone into liking me has been all I did for years so it's really difficult for me to just stop it, you know? You're the first person I wanted to not do this with because I really like you, Grey, and to think that I am doing to you what I did to a bunch of other people makes me want to punch myself. I should've told you this right from the start, so you knew what to look out for or something, but I was scared you'd overthink everything I say. I still am scared you'll do that now that you know, but you deserve to know. You *should* know what you're getting yourself into before you get yourself into it."

I cup his face with my hands, gently stroking my thumbs over his cheeks. "Baby, I know." It was one of the only things I could tell from the very beginning. The signs were right there, but I could also tell he was trying his hardest not to fuck up.

"You know?" His face pales a little, so I offer him a comforting smile like it would help him regain his strength.

"I knew all along, but thank you for telling me." He always

switches from confident to terrified in seconds, it's what told me he was trying his best. "I grew up with a narcissistic father, Luan. I see the signs before anyone even shows them. From the few minutes we talked on that beach, I knew you had narcissistic tendencies. I had no idea how far they went, but I knew they were there. The game you tried to play with me, saying I should come find you, I knew it was to engulf me, make you seem more interesting. I admit, I would've tried finding you because it did work. But it didn't work because you tried to make me like you this instant, it worked because you were a mystery to me. It worked because I needed to figure you out, find out why you switched from the most confident person to seeing your death right in front of you." I pause for a second, watching as his eyes soften little by little. "Luan, I like you because you interest me, because despite everything, you *are* a great person, and you shake every goddamn nerve in my body like no one ever has before. And all that *not* because you're making me like you."

God, I just want to lean forward and kiss him, show him how much I like him, and I'd do so if I wasn't still sick. I'm not sure I'm still contagious, but I'm assuming so. Would it even make a difference? I'm pretty sure Luan slept in my bed all these nights because I roughly remember begging him for cuddles on more than one occasion.

"Do you mean that?"

"I promise, Luan. I would never let you coax me into something I don't want."

His head bobs about three times while letting my words sink in. "So why did you ignore me in the past?"

Yeah... I should've guessed we'd come to that question eventually. Now, I could pull the *I'm sick* card and get out of this conversation for now, but I don't think it'd change much because we will get back to it one day. And I guess it's better he'll find out now than later, when he's asking to meet my parents and I have to turn him down over and over again, right?

"I ignored you because I am not allowed to be with you, Luan.

Your presence in my life is the cause why I haven't talked to my family in three years. I know how to fix this because it's what I've done all throughout college, pretend like I'm not also into guys. My dad knows, but he won't accept it so unless I can tell him I'm magically no longer attracted to men, he won't exchange a single word with me. I didn't want to lose my family, so I ignored you because I thought I could just tell my dad I wasn't seeing you anymore. But every time I was about to hit call, I couldn't." Somewhere between the end of college and now, I realized what I should've known years ago. That if my family truly wanted to see me, they would. If they wanted to talk to me, they would, despite my father not being okay with who I date.

Phoenix calls me after every of my games to tell me it was a good one or say he's sorry for our loss. He doesn't give a flying fuck about my father saying my family isn't supposed to talk to me anymore. Sun and I still talk every day and she, too, doesn't care that my father wishes she wouldn't.

So maybe giving up my family only meant giving up the people who don't give a shit about me, and I'm okay with that. I no longer rely on my parents anyway. They're not financing me anymore, I make plenty of money from hockey to live well. The only thing that's keeping me from officially cutting the ties is that little voice in the back of my mind that is hoping my father will come around. He won't.

Luan nods, taking a deep breath. "Yeah, I read the interviews he gave years ago. Made me want to puke." *Me too.* "I stand corrected, by the way. *This* is the longest I have ever heard you talk in one go."

"Blame it on me being sick."

Luan's hands lay on my neck, sliding up until the tips of his fingers push right into my hair. Once he's got a good grip on me, he pulls me down until our lips *almost* touch. "I'm sorry your dad is like that. I couldn't imagine not having my father's support."

"It's alright."

Luan shakes his head, then presses his lips right to the corner of my mouth. "It's not alright, Grey. *Buuttt*, once I broke the news to my father that I am now officially dating the son of the man he hates the most, you'll find yourself a whole new family."

Oh, yeah, I cannot wait. His mother is nice though, so I'm somewhat praying his father won't take the news too badly. "Does your mom know who I am?"

"Nope," he laughs. "Just like I did, everyone thinks your last name would have to be Li, so…"

Right. I'm glad Li's not my last name.

"When are you going to tell them?" I ask, sliding my hands down his body to rest them on his waist.

Luan shrugs. "I'll probably wait another few weeks, months, or years, maybe until my mom finishes up that scratch book she's making about us. You know, for when we get married."

"We have photos together?" I don't recall taking some. I mean, I guess there are the paparazzi shots, but I doubt anyone would ever use those in a photobook unless they're really cute or something.

"No, but she photoshopped some. They look horrible, but I like her enthusiasm. Honestly, my mom might be my biggest supporter ever."

That's sweet. "How'd she know we'd end up together anyway?"

Luan winks at me, then pulls me down to him one more time, his lips brushing mine when he says, "I always get what I want, Grey Davis."

Chapter 6

"as long as I'm with you / I've got a smile on my face"—
Here With Me by d4vd

Ivan

March 2025

I KNEW ANY DATE with Grey would turn out great, but I honestly didn't think staying in his apartment for our first official date would turn out to be the best date I've ever been on. But I think that's mainly because it's a date with Grey.

Halfway through dinner, Grey got a little tired, and I swear he looked *so* cute when he tried to force himself to stay awake because he didn't want to ruin our date. He couldn't have ruined it even if he would've ended up draped over the toilet and emptying his guts. I knew he wasn't completely alright yet, so it was only a matter of time until he got super tired; it's a miracle he lasted as long as he did.

I happen to think it's because of me, that I make him feel a whole lot better than he actually is, but maybe that's a bit too narcissistic to believe, so I'm not going to voice it to Grey.

He's been asleep for almost two hours now, his head lying on my chest. Even when he's fast asleep, Grey has this death-grip on me that tightens the second I move because God forbid I get up and leave him for just a nanosecond. It's cute, though he would probably hate me for saying this.

"Take it off," Grey mumbles out of the blue, but I ignore him, believing he's sleep talking. I've heard him do it before, it's been mostly unintelligible, but I suppose there's always going to be words to be understood when someone sleep-talks.

He groans when I don't react. "Take it off," he says again, this time a little louder.

"Take what off?" I ask, this time being sure Grey woke up and is genuinely talking to me.

Without voicing an answer, Grey pushes one hand underneath my t-shirt, pressing his palm flat to my abs. I'm just going to guess he wants me to take off my shirt.

"Baby, I can't take off my shirt when you're lying on top of me."

Grey sits up in record time, looking at me with deep brown eyes that let me know he's *wide* awake, not half-asleep. His hand slides from my stomach to just a tad below my lower stomach, and for whatever torturous reasons he keeps it there. If I sit up, his hand is going to slide even lower and I'm not sure I'd survive that.

So instead I ask, "Why am I supposed to take off my shirt anyway?" He's still wearing my yellow hoodie, I like seeing him in it. It's unusual since everyone knows Grey *is* the color black. Seeing yellow on him is definitely something.

I washed the hoodie yesterday because it was needed, though Grey tried arguing against it.

"I'm heating up," he answers, and in the very same moment, I can see his eyes gleaming with something dangerous.

"That's a *you*-problem, baby. If you're hot, you'll have to take off *your* shirt. Mine won't change much." Though, right now, I'm pretty sure it will change a whole lot down south on me if I see him half naked.

Grey nods faintly, pulls on the hood of his shirt, then removes the hoodie entirely, throwing it somewhere on the floor behind him. "Your turn... to make it equal."

"Nah, I'm good. Actually, I'm a little cold so I'll keep it on if you don't mind."

I think he's about to accept it when he moves his hand that

tiny bit farther down, most definitely involuntarily, and still the gasp that leaves me catches his attention.

His eyes follow from my eyes down my body until they settle on the slowly growing bulge in my pants.

A little embarrassed, I quickly look around the room so we wouldn't lock eyes again, only looking around seems to be just as bad of an idea. The candles Grey lit up about four hours ago are still burning, and thanks to it being dark outside by now, they're the only light source lighting up this room.

Candles already make everything seem so much more romantic, and now add the guy of your dreams being right there in bed with you into the mix. It's quite literally a teenage dream from a whole lot of people.

"How long are you going to stay here?" Grey now removes his hand from my crotch to give me some space to breathe again.

"I don't know. How long are you off for?" I'm staring out the huge window rather than looking at Grey. If I looked at him again right now, I know I'll never get rid of that stupid boner, and it *has* to leave.

"They want me back on the ice as soon as possible so basically the second I am able to walk around without feeling like dying, but the team doctor suggested for me to stay home and rest for the rest of the month. And depending on how long you plan on staying…"

My head snaps toward Grey immediately. Eyes wide and filled with shock, I'm sure. "You'd take off hockey to be with me?"

He nods. "I would. I could either go back out there in a few days and risk causing bad injuries due to only being half-fit, or I stay home for another two weeks with you, rest… among other things."

"Among other things, huh?" I smirk. "What's that supposed to be?"

Grey brings a hand to my chin, lays his thumb down on my lips, and slowly strokes the pad of it along the seams of my bottom one. He doesn't say his thoughts out loud, but I can hear them anyway.

Finally sitting up, my face is so close to Grey's that I can feel his breath on my skin. "You won't even kiss me, Grey Davis. So I doubt 'other things' would happen." Technically, that's wrong because one can still have sex and not kiss, but I don't do that. "Plus, you didn't even ask me to be your boyfriend yet and I don't have sex outside of relationships." He doesn't have to ask anymore, I'm pretty sure he's my boyfriend at this point.

"Ever?" His eyes might as well be popping right out of his head.

"Nope. One-night stands aren't my thing. I get attached easily." Which, frankly, kind of defeats the whole being a narcissist thing. Ever since I knew what a narcissist is, I thought they couldn't grow attached to someone. I thought all they felt was nothing at all, until I found out it's quite common for narcissists to get attached but they just don't love. Any relationship they're in is about fulfilling needs, but I want to learn how to love.

"What about our FaceTime… thing?"

I shrug. "It happened, and I probably only enjoyed it because it was *you*." I'd definitely think differently about it if Grey ignored me again after it happened.

"So you've been celibate for… three years?"

"Four," I correct. "My last relationship was in my last year of college, and I graduated a year before you." I'm a year older. "I take it you've been having one-night stands on the regular then, huh?"

It's not any of my business, and still I'd love to turn every single person's head who was with Grey before me.

When he doesn't answer me, I know that's a yes. I already knew that anyway. The internet, especially gossip pages, are filled with these kinds of information, even if most of them are assumptions due to pictures that were taken by fans. "How many since we've been talking?"

Six Years

Grey takes my face in his hands, gently stroking his thumbs over my cheeks. "You don't want to know the answer to that, baby."

Oh, well, that's reassuring for sure.

"More than twenty?" Grey shakes his head, a muscle in his jaw twitching. "More than ten?"

"Luan…" He sighs and leans his forehead against mine. "Would it help you if I told you that I haven't seen *anyone* ever since your birthday last year?"

"Kind of." I smile. "Fell in love with me then, huh? Our first kiss swept you off your feet so badly, you couldn't even fuck a puck bunny anymore."

"Well, I see, you picked up *some* hockey lingo."

"A little bit, but when I hear these game moderators on TV, I just look at the screen and don't understand a single word. Like, what the fuck is a *Barn Burner*? Since when were you in a barn and who the fuck put it on fire? And why do all the websites say you're a beautician? What even *is* that? And why do all hockey players love biscuits so much? Wherever you go, one of you is always asking for biscuits."

Grey *laughs*, toppling over by my incapability to understand hockey slang. It's not that funny. I bet if I spoke to Grey using soccer terms, he wouldn't understand a word either.

"Okay, first of all. A lot of players refer to the rink slash arena as a barn. And a Barn Burner is used to describe a high scoring game that's fast paced and exciting to watch."

"That's stupid. Just say '*the players are killing it*' or something." At least that could be understood.

He waves me off, dismissing my great idea. "They call me a beautician because, apparently, I'm good on the ice and off. You know, people like me. I don't see how or why, but there are worse things in life, I guess. It also means that I'm great at wheeling ladies off the ice, which, I suppose you can guess what it means."

Yeah, I don't want to think about that one. "You can wheel me off the ice anytime you want."

"Gladly." He presses his lips to my cheek. "Lastly, we refer to the puck as a biscuit." Grey pushes my cheeks together, puckering up my lips. "Can I kiss you?"

"Baby, you don't have to ask."

"I do. I don't want to get you sick without your permission."

If I could, I'd eat him up like a cookie, but unfortunately that counts as cannibalism, and I'd really like to see Grey alive sooo… "If I get sick, I'll stick around for another week or two."

Grey chuckles. "But I won't be home for that time. Only every other day or two."

I shrug. "Who cares? This building is *awesome*. It's like a hotel, but cooler. I mean, it'd be way better with you here, but that'd give me two extra weeks of snooping."

With the softest of chuckle ever leaving Grey, he presses his lips to mine. Gentle at first, then a little rougher. His tongue pushes into my mouth without any heads-up, but I don't care.

I bring both of my hands into his hair, messing it up because I can, while Grey's hands slide down my body, to my hips to pull me onto his lap. Once I'm seated, he tries to push my shirt up without me noticing, but of course I do. Still, I don't stop him.

I also don't stop him when the shirt is off my body and now lying somewhere on the floor, nor when he slightly lifts me up to lie me down on my back, hovering over me and kissing down my body.

But there is a point when I do stop him.

"Grey." I gasp when his lips lay below my belly button. "We can't. You're supposed to rest."

"I feel great," he tells me.

"Now you do." I grasp his face in my hands, carefully pulling him up until his eyes are on the same level as mine. "You should savor your energy and not exhaust yourself for one quick fuck."

"It would be worth it." He lowers his hips, pressing his erection against my body. If I can feel his, I don't doubt he can feel mine.

I shake my head. "You say that now, and in a few moments

when you feel like you're dying, you'll regret it. I don't want you to regret our first time together."

"Okay." He presses his lips back to mine, sweeter this time, softer. He does grind against me though, so I'm not sure his *okay* is to be taken seriously.

"Grey," I groan and wrap my arms around his neck to pull him closer. "You didn't ask me to be your boyfriend yet."

I can feel him smile against my lips. I love smiley-Grey, happiness is a great look on him, but I love the frowny-Grey even more.

"What if I want you to ask me?"

No way. "You'd reject me for the sole purpose of playing with me. My ego wouldn't survive that."

His lips brush mine once again, his hips still moving, causing me to get harder and harder. "I think your ego would survive just about anything, baby."

I. Hate. Him. So much.

"Fine," I grit out, reaching a hand between our bodies to lay it onto his dick just to stop him from moving. He sucks in a sharp breath. "Will you be my boyfriend, Grey Davis?" Do people even still ask this question? Is it outdated now, and people get together all magically?

"No, but thank you for asking."

I squeeze his balls almost hard enough to make him yelp. With my lips brushing his, I say, "If you don't say yes right now, I will squeeze again and harder this time."

For a split second I think he's contemplating it. Trying to figure out whether I'm lying or not. I'm not lying. I'll cut off his entire dick if I have to.

"I mean, okay, I guess. I can be your boyfriend."

I know he's not being serious when he's acting all unbothered, but it does hurt a little anyway. Maybe it's the part in my brain thinking he doesn't like me nearly as much as I want him to, the part in my brain that now tells me to say *anything* that would make him fall for me harder, but I bite my tongue.

I will *not* ruin this.
I will *not* ruin this.
I will *not* ruin *us*.

Us. Jesus. We're an *us*. Grey and me.

The thought breaks free my smile, so wide it makes my *boyfriend* roll his eyes at me.

I press my lips to Grey's again, over and over again and while I'm kissing him, I push my hand into his pants and wrap it around his thick, hard cock.

Fuck it, right? A handjob is okay. It won't exhaust him too much, and if it does, he can sleep it off.

Having made up my mind about this, I give him one long stroke, watching as Grey closes his eyes and opens his mouth, silently moaning a little.

"It's only going to be a handjob, you're not getting anything else," I warn. Though is it a warning?

"Okay," he breathes out, now leaning his forehead down to mine. "Do I get to return the favor?"

"If you still feel like it."

Chapter 7

"and you won't find no one that's better / 'cause I'm right for you"—Die For You by The Weeknd

Grey

March 2025

IF I STILL FEEL LIKE IT? I am *dying* to get my mouth on him.

I'm not used to celibacy, but I couldn't have changed it even if I wanted to. There were a few occasions over the past year in which I was so close to taking someone to a hotel with me, but each time I pictured Luan's face in front of me, staring at me with tear-filled eyes rather than a cute little smile on his face. It stopped me to say the least. It's as though that kiss from last year confirmed a relationship my heart agreed to, but my head didn't quite get the message yet.

Okay, there was also this one time I did take someone to a hotel last November, but I couldn't get hard. However, every time I so much as thought about Luan in the past year, I had an instant boner. It's a curse, I am telling you. And I honestly wouldn't put it past Luan to have casted it on me.

Planting a couple more kisses to my boyfriend's lips, I finally move off him and take off my shorts as well as my boxers, tossing them over to where my—or Luan's—hoodie lies on the floor.

I'm very comfortable in my own body, most of the time anyway, so being naked in front of other people doesn't bother me at all. And sometimes I forget other people might feel differently.

When I look over to Luan, I find him as speechless as I had yet to witness. His eyes are fixed on my dick which was to be expected but I didn't think he'd *stare*. Like straight up, blinking with his mouth agape fixating his gaze to my cock like it's the first time he's seeing one. I know for sure it isn't, even if he didn't have one himself.

"You okay?" I ask, turning his head to mine.

"I don't think that's going to fit in my ass."

Oh. Okay, well… that answers another question. "It will. But good thing you only allow me a handjob tonight." It's kind of rude, actually. If it weren't for Luan Hayes, I would've never gone over to celibacy and therefore wouldn't be as horny as a fucking teenager right now.

It's my first day of feeling relatively okay-ish in a few days. Imagine my surprise when I woke up this morning finding out the guy who won't get out of my head is here in my home because I'm sick. Of course my dick's going to think he can lead the way now.

"You hid that from me for *years*." Luan groans and reaches his hand over to grasp my dick back into his hand. His thumb brushes over my cockhead, spreading the bits of precum around.

"Not really. We've jerked off together before," I remind him.

"Hmm… but that was too long ago for me to remember."

My muscles tense when Luan slides his hand down my cock very slowly and back up, pinching my head a tiny bit once he reaches the top again.

I might as well be dying a *very* painful and slow death here. Only that it doesn't actually hurt but feels too damn great for my own good.

Luan's gaze is fixed on his hand on my dick while mine stays right on his face, taking in every slight reaction to the sounds that rush out of me.

He opens his hand and skids it down to my balls, cupping them. His thumb moves over my skin, and my throat constricts.

My right hand reaches over to his thigh, holding him tightly. I don't even aim to sneak my hand into his pants, although I'd love to do that, I just need something to hold on to.

When his hand moves back up, wrapping around the length of me, he starts to pump me a little faster than before. Up. Down. Up. Down. Like we're on a trampoline only with every thrust my hand holds harder on to him, my cock throbs, and my balls tighten.

My eyes travel down his bare chest. It's smooth and clean, so damn touchable. His skin glows from the light of the candles, illuminating his abs to seem more defined. All I want to do is run a hand over his body, find some way to mark him as mine.

He jerks me faster, squeezing my cock with every upstroke. I bring my free hand down to cup my balls, adding some pressure.

My head falls back against the headboard but not for long because Luan turns my head to face him, his lips attach to mine like that's where they are supposed to be for the rest of our lives. And frankly, I wouldn't mind.

His tongue pushes past my lips, hungry and eager. My balls instantly tingle with the need to come. Fucking hell, it's embarrassing how fast he makes me feel this way.

My heart beats faster and faster with every stroke, my lungs breathing heavier.

"Fuck, Luan... I—"

He shuts me up with another kiss.

I love his mouth. His kisses. I love the taste of him, the sound he makes when I tilt my head to deepen our kiss. I love his hand on my cock, fitting so perfectly around the length of me.

A husky groan leaves me when my climax hits me and cum spurts out of me, making a mess on Luan's hand and parts of my stomach. He jerks me through my orgasm, watching me with lust-filled eyes while I'm gasping for air, panting, and wheezing.

"That was fast," he teases, swiping his thumb over my cockhead one more time to remove the last bits of cum. It's a little useless since I'm covered in it.

"Shut up."

He kisses me, smiling. "It's okay to not last long, baby. Even the big Grey Davis is going to have flaws."

If I hadn't been celibate for over a year, this could've gone on for *way* longer.

I hum against his mouth, then go to kneel. "Let's see how long you'll last, shall we?" But I am not going to use *only* my hands. I wouldn't regret tonight even if it'd add another week of lying in bed to my life. It'd only be an extra week I get to spend with my boyfriend around.

Ah, shit. My *boyfriend*. The last time I had one of those it ended in a disaster so let's hope this one won't because I *really* want this to work out.

I pull Luan slightly forward on the bed then push him to lie down before hooking my fingers into his shorts and underwear, yanking them both down. He lifts his ass to make it a little easier.

When my eyes lay on his dick, my mouth waters with the temptation of going straight for it, with the temptation to wrap my lips around it and suck the life right out of him. But I'm going to take it slow and make it good for him.

As I lie down on my stomach between Luan's legs, wrapping a hand around the length of him, Luan's eyes fill with worry instead of desire, and that definitely worries *me*.

"Are you okay?" I ask. "I can stop if you want me to, Luan."

He shakes his head. "Just… promise me I won't be a one-night stand, Grey. Say you won't break up with me right after."

I crawl up his body until our faces are at the same height. I then kiss him, deep and passionate yet not quite as hungry as before. "I promise, baby. I am *not* going to break up with you." Ever.

Who would've thought that was what made Luan insecure? Being broken up with after sex, that's very specific, too. Who would've thought sex even intimidates him in the first place? He's all sure of himself and thrives on confidence yet lacks each of them when he's naked.

"Okay."

I kiss my way back down his body, keeping my eyes locked with his. The lower I go, the shakier his exhales become. Once I'm positioned between his legs again, Luan smiles at me softly. It's not lust-filled or generally hungry, it's just soft and sweet.

"Grey Davis?" he says when I wrap my hand back around his thick cock and slide my thumb over the head when he leaks some precum.

"Yes?"

"I really like you."

Now it's my turn to smile at him, wondering how that's even possible. How could someone like Luan Hayes start to like someone like *me*? I'm not as special as he is. All I do most of the time is scowl and appear annoyed. And still, somehow, he's seeing something in me that I'm not even sure is there.

"I really like you, too." Just a few years ago, I would've ignored him and not said a single word after his admission, but now not saying anything but the truth seems completely wrong.

I like him. I don't know how that happened or when, but if someone gave me the ability to travel back in time, I'd look for that very moment and yell at myself to give in already and not let us both suffer unnecessarily long.

Pressing my lips to his tip, Luan gasps, followed by a soft groan. His hips buck up, but I push them back down.

"We said *hand*job," he tries to complain.

"No, *you* said *I'm* getting a handjob. I asked if I could return the favor, but I never said I'd give you a handjob in return." That said, I lick his slit, then take the head into my mouth, sucking gently at first.

"Oh, fuck," he breathes out and reaches a hand into my hair, pulling on the strands.

Releasing him with a quiet pop, I dart my tongue out and lick up the length of him, then take his cock in my hand to give him a long stroke. My other hand cups his balls, adding some gentle pressure.

His cock pulses in my hand and I groan at the feeling, knowing it's *me* who pulls this reaction out of him.

I take him back into my mouth, this time taking as much of him as possible. Every bit that doesn't fit when I start to move, I pump with my hand. Slow at first, then picking up the pace by a notch at a time.

Luan shifts under me, moaning, panting. His fingers tighten in my hair, his other hand now gripping the sheets beside him. "Fuck, Grey…"

I knead his balls, not too much or too hard, just enough to hear him hum with satisfaction.

Sucking on his tip, Luan tips his head back and he lets out a sexy as fuck whimper that'll haunt me for the rest of my life.

His muscles flex, tensing and going slick with each bob of my head. And just when I think he's about to come, his phone rings on my nightstand.

I release his cock, looking up. Luan and I both look at his phone with annoyance, but when he's about to mute his phone, I reach for it, look at the screen long enough to read the contact name before picking up.

"This is Grey speaking." I slowly continue to stroke Luan with my hand, shutting him up before his complaints can make it past his beautiful lips.

"Grey?" The man's voice comes out with surprise. "Luan told us you were sick, how are you doing?"

"Oh, I'm just fine, Sir."

My eyes meet Luan's and although he's too busy trying not to come all over my face when his father's on the other end of the line, his eyes still display hatred for me at this very moment. He should know this only makes me admire him even more.

"That's good. Are you guys busy? I can call at a later time."

Busy? Maybe a little bit. "Hang on, please." I mute the call, checking twice to be sure. And when I'm convinced Mr. Hayes cannot hear a single thing, I wrap my lips around the tip of Luan's cock and suck, sliding my tongue over the slit.

He moans out loud, then slaps a hand over his mouth to tone it down. "Are you crazy!" His balls flex, telling me just how close he is to coming.

"A little."

I push all of him into my mouth, gagging a little when his tip touches the back of my throat. Squeezing his balls, Luan cries out an onslaught of *fuckfuckfuck*'s when he comes and shakes with release.

Cum spurts out and down my throat, and I swallow every bit of the salty drops.

Releasing him, I press a kiss to his balls and then right to the tip of his dick before I take the phone again and unmute Mr. Hayes. "Sorry, your son just came," I halt for a hot second, short enough for it to not sound suspicious, "back. I can give him the phone?"

I don't think Luan would be able to release any words, not with the way his chest is rising and falling from the aftershocks.

Mr. Hayes chuckles. "Ah, no, it's alright. You kids use all the time you have together. I just wanted to know when he's coming back home anyway, so nothing important."

"In about two to three weeks," I answer. "I'd keep him here longer, but I'll have to go back to work eventually." I wouldn't consider playing hockey *work* seeing as it's my hobby, but it does happen to be my occupation.

"Yeah, you keep him, Grey. Knowing my son, he wouldn't mind if you kidnapped him and held him hostage."

"I wouldn't be surprised, though I think Luan would disagree." He wouldn't, I honestly think Luan would thank me for keeping him hostage as long as he'll be around *me* this whole time.

"Well," Mr. Hayes laughs, "you come introduce yourself sometime, okay, boy?"

"I will the second my schedule allows it." I don't think Mr. Hayes will like me very much when he finds out who my father is, but why tell him now, right?

"Good. Now, you better go back to Luan or else he'll get mad."

"Good point." I say goodbye and then hang up the phone, setting it back down on the nightstand. Though when I look at Luan again, he's scowling at me. My little Luan is *scowling*. It's cute. "You should be happy, you know."

"You told my *dad* I *came*."

"Back," I add. "I said you came *back*." With a pause but I did say that.

Either way, I sit up, having to blink a couple of times because for some unknown reason, my head's spinning. Like actually *spinning*, with seeing spots and everything.

"Are you okay?" Luan sits up immediately, taking my face in his hands. "Baby?"

When I don't react, Luan jumps off the bed and hoists me up, draping my arm over his shoulder. He slowly leads me into my bathroom, seating me down on the floor of my shower. He turns on the shower, letting the cold water splash all over me.

"Fuck," I hiss, shuddering but I stay seated.

Luan kneels down to me, worry written on his face. There might even be tears in his eyes, or maybe that's just a water drop from the shower raining down on us. "I told you this was a bad idea!"

"It was worth it." Though my body would definitely like to disagree. My head's still spinning, but the cold water is slowly regulating my circulation.

"Sex is not worth your health, Grey." He squeezes my cheeks with one hand, then leans his forehead against mine, exhaling deeply. "Your fever might be gone, but you're not good yet. I should've stopped you, dammit."

I wrap my arms around him, pulling him closer into my body for two reasons. One, I'm hoping the heat of his body will make the water seem less icy—it doesn't. And two, I really want to hold him in my arms right now.

"The flu kills so many people a year, and I don't want you to be one of them, do you hear me, Grey Davis?" He kisses me, soft and sweet like it's the last time he'll ever get to do it. "For the next two weeks, you'll do nothing but lie in bed and let me take care of you, okay? *Without* any form of sex. You're not allowed to lay a hand on me."

I swallow hard. Why does Luan getting so upset over my health make me emotional? "Not even for cuddles?"

"I'll allow cuddles and kisses, but only because I think I might die if I don't get them either. No hardcore making out though." How am I going to survive the next couple of months without this guy by my side? Correction, *physically* by my side. He'll support me from afar, I know that, but he won't be there in person.

"Okay. I promise. Just lying in bed and cuddling with you for two whole weeks."

Chapter 8

"I'd spend every hour, of every day / keeping you safe"—You Are The Reason by Calum Scott

Iuan

March 2025

GREY KEPT HIS PROMISE.

He got up a few times a day to walk around for a little while, or to pee and shower, eat and all that stuff. But other than that, we've spent the past two weeks in his bed, watching movies and TV shows, talking—though I talked more than he did. And we cuddled a *whole lot*. I don't think there was a moment I wasn't in his arms when we were in his bed together.

Though, there was this one time when he got a little mad at me because I offered to help Miles do the dishes after one of their Taco Sundays and send Grey back to bed alone. I was a guest, of course I was going to help do the dishes even when everyone insisted I didn't have to. It was the polite thing to do.

I did, however, feel a little out of place that Sunday. They're all very nice people, and they've been trying to talk to me as much as they could, but their relationships go so deep that I cannot compete. Grey is a whole other person when he's with his friends. He laughs a lot more, he's calmer and far more relaxed. They talked about stuff I didn't understand, and even when they tried to explain inside jokes to me, I still didn't fit in with them because no matter how good they'd explain it, I wasn't there to experience it with them.

I know it shouldn't upset me, but it does. Having been there and experiencing the whole family dynamic all seven of them have, it made me upset because I don't think I'll ever be part of that. Not because Grey wouldn't let me get close to his friends, but because I'm not cut out for huge friend groups. There's always someone who won't like me, and then I'll try to make them like me and when someone else finds out, the whole friend group will go against me, which then means Grey will go against me.

I already know that losing Grey won't do anything good to me.

"What's wrong?" Grey asks, holding his hand out for me to take. When I lay mine in his, he pulls me into his body and wraps his strong arms around my neck.

"I don't want to leave," I tell him. My plane is scheduled to take off around six in the morning because Grey has to be at the airport around the same time. He's cleared to go back to playing ice hockey, the happiness on his face when he got the news even made me happy, but I hate having to leave him even more.

I don't know when I'll see him again. It could be a few days, weeks, but also months or even years.

"My offer still stands," he says now pressing his lips to my temple. "Move in with me, Luan."

"As much as I'd like to do that right this instance, I'd still have so much to handle first. I'd have to find a job around here somewhere, register my car and transfer my driver's license, and I bet there's so much more I'm not thinking of right now. And I need more than a few hours to say goodbye to my family and best friend, and I definitely owe my kids a better goodbye, too." Let's be honest, I have planned a goodbye party for months now because I knew I'd eventually have to move to New York City. Grey wouldn't move for me, and I'm not mad about it. His whole life is here, his *career* is here. He has far more to lose than I do, and I'd gladly make the sacrifice for him.

Coming home to Grey would be one of the many fairy tales

in my head come true. But it'd also bring a whole lot of new challenges. Yes, he'd be on the road a lot so it's not like we'd be with each other twenty-four hours a day every day, but it'd still be a huge change in both of our lives. Neither of us is used to sharing their space as much, sharing their *bed*. When we need space, we're far apart to get said space, but when we live together, we'll have to find space without making possible arguments more than what they are.

"How long?" he asks.

"Maybe next year or the year after?" Next year sounds far too long, but I think it's the most realistic. We'll get to know each other a little better, even if we'll be miles apart, and I'll have enough time to say goodbye. Grey will have enough time to make space for me, too. "The year will pass in the blink of an eye."

"It better."

"In the meantime, we can FaceTime and I can come to your games in California, even fly out if I miss you way too much to handle. And when you've got a day or two to spare, you can come visit me if you feel like it. We got this, okay?"

"Okay."

I hold him a little tighter, praying to every single God out there to make this easy for us. Both of us have enough things to worry about with our families, there's no need to make distance that much of a problem in our relationship as well.

"And you're off this summer, right? No trips planned?" I ask carefully. Grey wanted to come see me last summer already but that was filled with a last-minute trip through Europe.

"Not yet. But if we come up with some, I'll go on my knees and beg you to come with us." He wouldn't. Grey Davis on his knees when he's completely healthy? I'd like to see that.

I think the hockey season ends in just a few days anyway, but it looks like they made it to the playoffs for the Stanley Cup, that much I picked up last year. Grey's team will definitely make it, though with less points than last year. I believe they fucked up in the time Grey wasn't on the ice with them, if Grey was there, they would've been first, I'm sure.

My head is pressed right into the front of his shoulder when I mumble, "I think I might die, that's how much I miss you already."

"You better not," he responds, but it's definitely not said in a sweet way. "The next time I see you, there's nothing that could stop me from fucking you, except maybe your death because necrophilia is not my thing. And a no. But other than that, nothing."

I laugh, my chest rumbling. Only Grey would know how to make me laugh when all I want to do is cry. "You're always thinking with your dick."

"And you made me a monk, so let me at least *think* about sex with my boyfriend, thank you."

He's not wrong. I did make sure he was *resting* the past two weeks, meaning no sexual intercourse at *all*. No handjobs, blowjobs or any other possible jobs. He wasn't even allowed to jerk off, even when he was doing a million times better. And let's just say I didn't exactly make that one easy for him.

Hey, it's not my fault he's attracted to me and happens to find my naked presence arousing enough to sport a boner.

"Well, look at you though, you survived. Cleansed your soul and such." I look up at him, grinning widely. Grey rolls his eyes, but I still see the faintest of smiles tugging on the corners of his mouth before he leans down and presses his lips to mine.

"If my soul's cleansed, does that mean I get to spend an hour in the gym today?" He's been asking for some workout time for days and said he'd get out of shape if he spends another day lying in bed.

"Fine, but no heavy lifting. You're supposed to take it easy." Even his doctor said Grey should go back to his normal routine one step at a time as the flu has sucked a whole lot of energy out of him. He bounced back like he was never sick, but I still worry about him.

It was just a *flu*, I know that much, it's not like he lost both of his arms and got them sewn back onto his body and now he has to be *extremely* careful. So maybe I'm overreacting, but when it comes to Grey, I'd rather overreact than underreact because this man hides pain as good as chameleons in the wild when they sense danger.

Chapter 9

"before you go home / I should let you know / I'm so glad that you came"—Look Up At The Stars by Shawn Mendes

Iwan

March 2025

ABOUT FORTY MINUTES into his workout, Grey is hunched over, his hands on his knees being the only thing keeping him up. "I hate you," he repeats completely out of breath, inhaling deeply, exhaling twice as long.

I hand Grey his water bottle, smirking. "You asked if I dare to make you sweat, I did." As a coach who mainly tortures little kids with workouts, I know how to make people sweat in no time. Especially eager jocks who believe nothing and nobody could break them. It only takes a few repetitions of a very intense practice and they'll be panting in no time.

Guys like Grey think they can do anything, so if you challenge them to do more than what they think "anything" is, it's getting quite funny. When you know they can do fifty push-ups with no problems, make them do twice as many, once they start to struggle just that tiny bit, that's when you've already cracked them open a little. They start to get vulnerable because they cannot believe they're struggling, like how dare their body do this to them? And then you push them further. You say, "I bet you can't do one-hundred-and-fifty," and knowing jocks, they'll be up to prove you wrong only to fail.

If they don't fail yet, go up another fifty. Eventually they *will* break, and all you have left is a guy like Grey who says he hates you when he doesn't. A guy whose ego you just bruised.

"You love me."

He straightens his back, downing the entire bottle in seconds. At least he's staying hydrated. "I don't love you."

"It's like you're screaming it. Wow. Careful, Grey Davis, you wouldn't want the entire city to hear you are in love with me." I hold a hand to my heart, looking up at the ceiling ever so dramatically. "What would your fans say when they find out you're already married."

"We're not married, and right now, I'm wondering if dating you was a good decision in the first place." He puts his hands on my waist and pulls me right into his sweating body. I gag jokingly, but he knows I don't care. Then he kisses me.

"Mm-hmm, that sounds exactly like something someone who's deeply in love would say." This time, I kiss him. "But alright, you may hide your love from me for little while longer, Grey Davis. It's not like I don't already know you've been in love with me from the second we met."

Grey covers my face with one hand, pushing me off him. I laugh. God, I love teasing him.

"You're full of shit, Hayes."

"No, you are, Grey Davis." I take a seat on the floor, crossing my legs. I'm about to add something when my phone chimes from across the room. Grey and I are the only ones in the gym, much to my surprise, so we keep our stuff everywhere.

Without me having to ask, Grey walks over to the bench where I put my phone and gets it for me. When he hands it over to me, he says, "It's your mom."

"I guessed that." My mom always texts me at least once a day to make sure I'm doing alright. She's scared I might've fallen back into old habits and cracked open a liquor bottle. I haven't in three whole years. And can you believe that I can be in one room with alcohol and *not* even *want* to drink any? I can look at the bottles and not give them a second thought.

Sure, sometimes it's still tempting, but saying no is far easier now than it was three years ago.

Mom: How is Grey, sweetie?

I stare at the message, wondering if I'm seeing things. I rub my eyes just to make sure my mother did, in fact, ask about Grey and not me.

Giving my phone a second glance, I gasp in shock. How dare my own mother ask about my boyfriend's health instead of mine?

"My mother has officially adopted you as her new son," I say, still staring at the message in disbelief. "She asked me how you are. She only ever asks how *I* am."

Grey takes a seat opposite of me on the floor. He has a towel draped over his shoulder, his breathing still heavy. "Can she un-adopt me? I'd rather not fuck my brother."

"Grey!" I groan then laugh because only Grey would turn a rather sweet thing into something sexual. "God, you're like completely sex deprived or something."

"I am." I don't doubt it. Two weeks of *nothing* has got to be torture for him, at least according to the internet and most of his own words. I think he's just exaggerating a whole lot. "Tell your mom you're torturing me."

"I'm *not* going to tell my mother that I'm torturing you. She'll call the police on me." I wouldn't take it badly either. If someone like me talked about torture, everything might be possible. But I'm learning, and I'm really proud of my accomplishments so far.

"Right…" He nods his head slowly, letting out a sigh. "I'm sorry."

"Not your fault, baby. You could make that joke with anyone else. Just not me."

Grey smiles at me, his eyes full of admiration. It's hard for me to believe anyone could ever think Grey was anything but the sweetest person to ever exist. Yes, he's quiet most of the time, and yes he scowls and ignores me a lot, but he, too, is learning. He's learning to speak, to open up. I think he's been genuinely hurt in the past, mostly by his father, I'm guessing, which then silenced him down. He's been waiting for someone to bring him back out of that hole of darkness.

Good thing I manage to light up the darkest places, huh?

"Well, then tell her I am upset with you because you… you refuse to let me have fun."

"Fun?"

"Yup. Fun. Sex is fun." With the right person for sure.

"Uh-huh." I pull my bottom lip between my teeth to keep myself from smiling, but it's not working. "I'll just tell my mom you're doing fine."

He's about to veto when I snap a picture of him all frowny and with the deepest scowl ever, then send it to my mother, captioning it, *As you can see, he's frowning, so everything's fine.*

My mother sends a thumbs-up emoji in return.

"You're boring," Grey says and rolls his eyes.

"Now I'm also boring? What else am I?" The fun police, the guy who turned Grey into a monk, the guy who forbids Grey to work out to his full capacity, then the guy who almost kills him with a workout, boring, that's a whole lot of things I am. He didn't even mention how great I look, or how deeply in love he is.

Grey untangles my legs to pull me closer, so when our bodies meet, I do the most logical thing; wrap my legs, as well as my arms, around his body like a koala bear. His clothes are drenched in sweat but I couldn't give any more fucks.

"Nosy," he says, pressing a kiss to my neck. "And you seek compliments all the time."

"Wow, you're really going there." I'm not sure if that should offend me. If I was a normal person, maybe it would.

"It's the truth, isn't it?"

"Yeah."

Grey nibbles on my neck, his teeth grazing my skin ever so

slightly yet firm enough to draw out a shaky breath from me. Oh, I know what he's doing…

"Grey," I warn, though I don't stop him when he pulls me closer to him until I can feel his dick press against the inside of my thigh.

"Tell me to stop."

I can't because I want this as much as he does, I'm just scared. "There are cameras in this gym," I try. I don't actually know that, but it looks fancy enough. I think this entire building has cameras *every*where. It would be better for them. Imagine someone broke in…

"It's just a free porno for whoever watches the tapes, it's fine. They're most likely going to skip it. Then I'll get a warning letter and that's it. Totally worth it."

"They could sell it for millions of dollars. And then our sex tape would be all over the internet."

He bites my neck and I moan, then I push my fingers into his sweaty hair. "Confirming a relationship with a sex tape sounds like fun."

"Yeah, because your future kids would *love* that," a deep voice from somewhere behind me chuckles, making me flinch. I try getting away from Grey, but he won't let me.

"That's a good point." Grey sighs, leaning his chin right onto my shoulder as he looks at whoever's here with us now. "But I think I can live with that."

The guy laughs. "You're impossible, Grey. What, you're not getting enough sex in your *new* relationship?"

Hello? They do see me here, right? I mean, I don't see their faces and they can't see mine, but they should still be able to see me.

"Wouldn't you like to know, love?"

There's only one person Grey calls *love*, and that's Miles.

Finally managing to wriggle myself out of Grey's arms, I turn around and my boyfriend immediately pulls me back into his arms, my back pressed flush to his chest. Well, at least I can look at Miles now, it doesn't make anything better, but alright.

"It's so weird actually seeing you in a relationship again," Miles says, then smiles at me kindly. "I thought he only ever gets affectionate when he's drunk."

So I read online. That gossip girl at his university did an amazing job, not sparing *any* details. Some of those, I'd like to unread and unsee.

"Miles," Grey warns, probably shooting his best friend one of the many mad scowls he has to offer. I'm not sure why he'd warn him off though, Miles didn't say anything wrong. Okay talking about ex-partners is always a little… weird, but I don't really mind it. I mean, I don't want to hear about Grey's sexual partners, although I did technically ask about them before, but ex-partners are different to sex-only.

"If Grey needed alcohol to be affectionate, then he wasn't with the right person," I say.

"You're not wrong," Miles mutters but I don't ask about it. If he wanted me to react, he would've said it much clearer.

Grey must've had enough of this conversation because he gets up, then helps me up as well. "I've got to take a shower."

And just like that, Grey and I are leaving Miles all alone in the gym.

Back in Grey's apartment, he ushers right into the bathroom, but I follow because something is off with him. I know he's cold sometimes and doesn't know how to show his emotions, but *this* is a whole new side of cold to him. It's more than just avoiding my questions, it's avoiding *me*.

"Grey?"

He closes the door before I get the chance to slip inside the bathroom with him. And when I hear the lock, I know there's no way for me to get inside without busting down that door, so instead I turn around and sit down, leaning my back against it.

I think this is about Grey's ex, it'd be the only logical explanation for his sudden change in mood. As much as I'd like to ask about it, I think it's better if I start with a whole other topic at first, just to get him to answer me.

"I think your friends don't like me very much," I say loud enough so he'd hear, even after he turns on the shower.

He stays quiet. I was expecting him to say it's not true, but alright.

"I know they tried their best to include me the other day, but I believe that was pure kindness and not because they want me around," I try again. "I get it though. I'm kind of like an intruder, messing up your whole family dynamic with my presence. You're this one big happy family, and have known each other for ages and then suddenly I show up and ruin it all, threatening to take you away from them."

I sigh, letting my head fall against the black wooden door. "I'm not trying to take you away though, just saying, but I get the feeling they think I want to. Especially Miles. He's nice and all, but every time he looks at me and thinks I don't see it, his face says that he doesn't want me around. Again, I get that. I don't know if you told him about me, or rather about me loving to manipulate people, but if you have, I think that's why he can't stand me. If you haven't, I still think he knows and hates me for it."

Grey keeps quiet, again.

Seriously? Nothing?

"I thought about it, you know?" My hand starts to shake just thinking about admitting this to Grey. "I thought about making him like me because I think you value his opinion a lot, and I fear that if he tells you I'm no good, you'll believe him and then leave me. So, yeah, I thought about telling him a story that'd make him pity me and then empathize with me, and then… like me. I thought about doing that to all of your friends, actually. But I didn't. I didn't because your trust in me is worth more than making some people like me. And Grey? I trust you enough to believe you wouldn't break my heart just because your friend tells you I'm not good enough for you. I'm not, so he'd be right with that, but sti—"

The door swings open without any warning—I didn't hear him unlock it—causing me to fall back and lie on the ground, now staring up at Grey from *way* below. He's already taller than me, but damn, he looks like a giant from down here.

Grey's still wearing all of his clothes, so I take it he preferred listening to me over taking his shower.

He looks at me with a hint of tears in his eyes, a look I've never seen on him. Then he kneels down at the same time as I sit up and turn around to face him.

Grey takes my hands in his, eyes locked with mine when he says, "Don't say that."

Don't say what exactly? I've said a whole lot in the past couple of minutes.

"You're more than good enough for me, Luan." He puts his hands on my neck, keeping his thumbs on my jaw. "They like you, trust me. But you're right, they're a little cautious with you because you're *new*. It was just the seven of us for years, actually, it used to be four of us for years before that, but that's not the point. You're barely around due to distance reasons, so you have to give them time to adjust to you. They don't know you, Luan. And for some god-awful reason, Colin, Aaron, and Miles like to have an extra eye on me than they do with each other. You'll be fine, and they'll welcome you with open arms the second you'll be around a whole lot more often."

I think it's great his friends have an extra eye on Grey. From what I've gathered, he may be the most stubborn and grumpy one of them, but he's also the likeliest to be broken.

"And Luan? I am so proud of you for not doing it," he says. He's talking about me trying to manipulate his friends, I'm sure.

I fall right into his arms to hug him, wrap my arms tightly around him to feel him that tiny bit closer. Also because I know this is going to be one of our last hugs for a while.

Hearing Grey say he's proud of me tops every single other "I'm proud of you" from *anyone* else, even the ones from my parents. And it's not even the first time he's said it.

Am I going to ruin the moment by asking about why he shut me out just a few minutes ago? I really want to know, but I also don't want to start an argument the day before I have to leave.

But I mean, if he's still in love with his ex, I should know, right? I don't want to be with someone who's still hung up on their ex-partner. But Grey also doesn't strike me as the man who'd be hung up on *any*one.

"Just ask," Grey speaks softly, apparently being able to read my mind. "You barely know how to keep your mouth shut, Luan. Don't start now."

It makes me smile but I don't know why. "Why does the topic of your ex upset you so much?"

If we started talking about my ex-boyfriend, I'd laugh about it because I know I deserved way better than a wannabe poet who rhymes chaos with Laos in a poem about music, and then cheats on me.

"It's not my ex who upsets me, but the reason we broke up, because I don't want *us* to end the same way."

"Why'd you break up?" I pull away from the hug to look him in the eyes.

He hesitates to answer, which then tells me this can't be any good. And it's not. "Because he wanted to meet my parents and as you know, that's pretty much impossible. Then he made me choose between him and my family."

"You chose family like anybody else would."

Grey nods. "I couldn't give him the relationship he wanted. We always kept it on the downlow because of me and he hated that. I couldn't love him openly, so yeah, the only times I was affectionate in *public* was whenever I was drunk. I told my friends he didn't want the whole PDA stuff, which was bullshit. And I just don't want that to happen to us, you know?"

My smile widens, mostly because Grey basically told me he doesn't want to keep me a secret, that he doesn't want us to breakup even in the future. I mean, I guess you don't start a relationship thinking about how and when you'll breakup, but still, it makes me happy to hear he doesn't want us to go separate ways.

"I told you, Grey Davis, I like secrets. And I don't mind being one."

He groans, like he did the first time I said this. "I don't want you to be a secret, Luan. You're my boyfriend, and I'm going to treat you like one. If I could, I'd introduce you to my parents but since that's impossible, I'll introduce you to my sister instead, once we find a day for all three of us to meet. And yes, I know you've met her before, but that was without me. I also don't want to hide you from the public just because I'm afraid of what they'll say, or hide you only because I know my father will see the pictures of us together."

He pauses, and I can see on his face that he's just realizing something, so I don't speak.

"You know what? The next time I'm in Malibu, I *will* take you to meet my mother. She'd be happy for me but she can't say it because of my dad. And if my dad's there, hell, I'll introduce you. He won't like you, but I don't give a shit."

My features soften so much, I can feel it happening. "You'd do that for me, Grey Davis?"

"I'd do just about anything for you."

Chapter 10

"I know that you're the feeling I'm missing"—If I Can't Have You by Shawn Mendes

Grey

October 2025

I ENTER THE LOCKER ROOM in time to hear my best friends talk about Miles, what exactly they're saying, I have no idea, but I did hear Miles's name leave Aaron's mouth.

We've been stuck in Michigan for a few days now thanks to a snowstorm. No planes are landing or taking off, so we have been forced to stay. And the team decided it would be a great idea to organize a charity skate for kids. As in we're supposed to teach kids up to the age of thirteen how to skate and play ice hockey. I am not a good coach, I don't think, how am I supposed to teach a kid anything?

But I do have to say, this whole thing is great publicity, and it does make the team look better.

"Miles?" I say when I finally decide to walk inside the locker room. I set my bag down on one of the benches and turn my attention to Aaron and Colin. "I don't think anyone could get close to Miles."

Aaron snorts but agrees. I still don't know what exactly we're talking about. At least until Aaron tells me. "Our princess asked my sister to marry him."

My eyes widen drastically, my jaw now on the floor. *Definitely not coming close to Miles.* "You did not!"

I know Aaron and Sofia got married sometime before March this year, they just refuse to tell anyone yet, God knows why. They're not exactly hiding it, both of them wear a ring, but neither of them have said a word about it.

But hearing yet another of my best friends' is getting *married*... Wow.

"I have," Colin says, scratching the back of his neck. "We're getting married tomorrow. Nothing big or fancy. Just family and closest friends."

That's a little last-minute, I'd say.

"You're twenty-five years old," Aaron says. "Don't you think that's a little... early?"

Early? I look at Aaron with confusion, as does Colin. Miles got married just before turning twenty-two. And Aaron got married *before* he turned twenty-five. In fact, he just turned twenty-five today.

Colin ends up shaking his head, not letting Aaron know that we do, in fact, know he's already married. "I wanted to marry her an hour after I met her."

I don't doubt it. I knew something was off with Colin the second he said he *needed* to find Lily because she forgot her notebook in the ice hockey arena at St. Trewery.

"We're talking about starting a family sometime in the future. We're not getting any younger, and Lily wants at least two children before the age of thirty. So, no, I don't think it's early," he adds.

She does? The last time someone mentioned kids, Lily said she didn't want any because she feared they might inherit her depression. But if they decided they do want some now, that's also great.

And still, somehow Colin talking about kids irks me a little. I take a seat right across from him, sliding a hand down my face. "You're at the peak of your career, Carter." I could never imagine giving up hockey to start a family. Not yet.

"And that means I can't have a wife and start a family?" He

looks at Aaron, asking, "What if Sofia told you she wanted to get married, would you tell her no?"

Clearly not.

Aaron lets out a deep breath, but he doesn't answer. If he said he would tell her no, he'd be lying.

But then Aaron points a finger at Colin, his eyes narrowed. I've never seen him so mad at Colin, but I suppose hearing your best friend is getting married to your twin sister does that. "Fuck her over and I'll come for you," he says, his voice low and threatening.

"Fuck her over what?" Colin asks, smirking like the asshole he is. "An open fire? Sounds dangerous."

Aaron scrunches up his face in disgust to which Colin starts to laugh. "Well, congratulations on your engagement, Fairy Godmother." Aaron slaps a hand to Colin's back.

I can't believe he's still calling him that. I stopped doing it about two years ago. Colin got that nickname after he was punished for skipping practice to be with Lily in our senior year of college. He had to wear a tutu and a cropped top that Aaron got from Lily, and costume wings.

It was hilarious.

I smile, nodding my head at Colin, just about to congratulate him when I realize, "Did you propose to her on the *phone*?"

If he asked Lily to marry him weeks ago, he would've told us then. So when he's only telling us now, that means... Shit. That guy.

"It was a last-minute decision, okay?" He defends himself. "We were on the phone, talking, and then I just blurted it out. We got our marriage license months ago anyway because we said when we got married, it was supposed to be spontaneous. And that it is."

Certainly. "Congratulations, Colin."

"Thanks."

How dare I be the last one of us to not be married? I always thought if one of us *ever* got married, it would be me, not either of them.

Colin never even so much as looked for love in his life. He was happy with ice hockey. Aaron preferred to whore around, as it turned out, because the love of his life was too far away, but they found each other. And Miles? He never wanted to find anyone after the mother of Brooke presumably died.

At least I'm not single anymore.

"Do you think Luan could make it to the wedding? We'd love to have him there," Colin says, toying with his skates like he's nervous to even admit that.

See, I told Luan they'd like him.

"It's a five-hour flight, so that won't be the problem. It's more about how spontaneous he can leave, but I'll ask."

As I take out my phone to shoot Luan a text, the locker room doors swing open and the rest of the team, including Coach Carter and Coach Brenner—our vice coach—come storming inside.

All of us gathered together in the locker room when there's no game means bad news.

They all stand in a semi-good half circle around Aaron, Colin, and me, but their eyes stay locked on me. The fuck did I do?

Luan and I have not made our relationship public, although his comments under my social media posts leave *little* to people's imagination. I don't mind it as much as I thought I would.

Plus, after years of being harassed by homophobes, the insults have finally died down and I only receive about a hate-package a month. I'm pretty sure they'll come right back the second I confirm a relationship, but I'm prepared this time.

"Davis," Coach Carter says in his usual snappy and grumpy tone, telling me little about what the fuck I have done.

"Coach?"

Coach Carter looks at Nolan May, our team captain, nods at him as if to give him the go to speak.

Nolan clears his throat and looks right at me, but while he looks at me, I turn my head to see if either of my best friends have *any* clue what this is about. I find them suppressing smiles.

"The team has decided something," Nolan begins, his voice monotonous, not giving anything away. "As you may know, this is my last season."

Yeah, he's retiring next year.

I nod, still a little unsure of why he's talking to *me* like I didn't know that.

"A couple of days ago, I asked each member of this team who they think would make a great new captain. Someone who'd be willing to go the extra mile, but not just that. I wanted my follow-up to be someone the team can go to, who'd be supportive and still make sure to kick their asses if needed. I wanted someone who *deserves* to be captain of this team not just because he's great on the ice, but because he's a great person."

I don't want to assume where this is going because imagine it's not going where I think this is going. But it does sound like it, doesn't it? It's far too early to decide on a new captain. Nolan still has a whole year left, the season just started.

"Davis," Nolan says, his voice now a whole lot friendlier. "I'd like to ask you, in the name of *everyone*, to become the next captain of the New York Rangers. I'll still finish the season, but as soon as the season ends, we *all* would like to have you take over the title."

Oh, my god. I think my heart just stopped beating. Am I still alive? I don't think I am.

Colin wanted to be the new captain, he's great at being one, too. I know because he's been the captain of our college team since our sophomore year. I, on the contrary, have no idea what captains do. Do they even do anything really?

Shit.

Wow. I… Wow.

I look at Colin, then back at Nolan just blinking and barely understanding what the hell is happening. This has got to be a mistake, like an error in the matrix because there is no way I was asked to be captain.

"Davis?" Nolan waves a hand right in front of my eyes, making sure I am still alive. But am I really?

"Captain?"

"Unless you don't want to."

"What?! No, yes, of course!" Freaking Captain.

"Well, then Davis…"

Before anyone can talk to me any further, I get up from the bench and excuse myself. I'm sure Colin and Aaron are cracking jokes about me leaving to cry, and honestly, I might, but I'm actually leaving to call Luan.

I stand in front of the empty ice, blinking away a few tears that I blame on missing my boyfriend, for sure. Pulling out my phone, I instantly dial Luan's number and wait until he picks up.

I know he's at soccer practice right now, but I'm still hoping he won't let my call go to voicemail.

Come on, baby, pick up.

Just when I think I'll get sent to voicemail, Luan does pick up the phone. "Now, Grey Davis, if you missed me so much that you call me while you know very well I'm busy, you could've at least FaceTimed me."

He's right. "Colin is getting married," I say, starting off with anything but the news about me.

"He is?" I can hear the surprise in his voice. "Wow, that's amazing. Congratulations to your friend."

"Will you be my date?"

Luan's silent on the other end of the phone, now making me worried. Why wouldn't he say yes right away? I mean, this is Luan we're talking about. He says yes to anything I suggest even before I voice it.

"When?"

"Tomorrow. I know it's last minute, but he just told me. And Lily and Colin said they'd *love* to have you there. Not that this is the only reason you should come, but we'd get to see each other again. And then I get to hold you in my arms and kiss you, and I can tell you awesome other news." Telling him about being the new captain starting next season is definitely a thing I can tell him in person. I know he won't be as excited as I am, but maybe he'll still be happy for me.

"You had me at 'Will you…,' but kisses sound great. I'll be there."

"Good." I smile to myself, now even more excited because God, I miss this tiny curly-headed monster. He's not that tiny, but we're going to ignore that because he *is* a curly-headed monster. He is *my* tiny curly-headed monster. "I should be home around eleven p.m. tonight. We're still stuck in Detroit for a few hours and our plane leaves at nine. So depending on when you'll get on the next flight, you might be home alone for a few hours."

It's only two p.m. here, so around twelve for Luan. If he manages to get the flight in let's say three hours, he'll be in New York in eight and therefore he'll be home earlier than me.

"That's fine. I got your keys." That he does. "But depending on when I land, I might just wait for you at the airport to get that kiss I've been promised a little faster."

"I miss you so much." It's a miracle I manage to sleep at night. In just the two weeks Luan had been with me back in March, I've gotten so used to sleeping with him in my bed. And now all there is is emptiness whenever I'm at home. No Luan. But we'll change that in a few months. He asked me to give him at least a year, a year will be over in five months.

Luan laughs, but I know he feels the same way. Even if it wasn't for the million texts in the middle of the night, when I'm supposed to be sleeping, saying he misses me, I'd still know. "If you're in love with me, Grey Davis, you can just say it."

"Not over the phone." We haven't said it yet, either of us. We've been officially dating for over half a year, and trust me, saying I love you has been on the tip of my tongue for quite some time now, but I'm not going to do that on a stupid phone call. When I say it, I want to see him react and then kiss him right after.

Luan gasps and I bet he's grinning like always. "My, my,

Grey Davis, that sounds like a love-confession in my ears."

I snort. "Yeah, me ignoring you for months also sounded like one to you, so don't get your hopes up, baby."

Luan knows I love him like I know he loves me. I don't need to tell him for him to know, and still I know he's desperately waiting for it. For some reason, Luan doesn't make the first move. He was waiting for me to kiss him for the first time, he was waiting for me to ask him to be my boyfriend, and I know he's waiting for me to initiate anything more intimate, as well as he's waiting for me to say I love you first.

He wouldn't admit it, I don't think, but I believe it's because he's scared if he does either of those first, he'd be forcing all of those things to happen. It's bullshit, I think we all know that by now, but I get where he's coming from.

"I'll see you tonight then?" Luan's voice jumps an octave at his excitement. "I'm already checking flights. The next one leaves in two hours, and they have two seats left. If I leave right now, I could make it. But I won't have any clothes or *anything* with me."

"Good thing you have a boyfriend with two whole closets full of clothes that fit you, huh?" It's truly a blessing *and* a curse at the same time.

"Indeed."

Chapter 11

"if she gives you her heart / don't you break it"—If You Love Her by Forest Blakk

Luan

October 2025

I DIDN'T WAIT AT THE airport because their flight got delayed by an hour which then would've had me waiting for three whole hours. I preferred being somewhere warm and cozy than where it's noisy, cold, and uncomfortable.

It's just before twelve a.m. when I hear the door open. In seconds I jump off the sofa, run toward the door, and launch myself into my boyfriend's arms like I haven't seen him in years. Not years, but I haven't seen him in months.

Grey wraps his arms around me so tightly, I think I might suffocate. It would be worth it.

"I love you," Grey whispers, then presses his lips to mine right after.

I melt into his kiss like I never have before, feeling my heart hammer inside of my ribcage. Putting my hands on his jaw and slightly tilting my head, I deepen our kiss. A tear drops onto my cheek but honestly, I'm not sure if it's mine or Grey's, and I don't care either.

"You just said it," I say slightly out of breath when we pull apart to get some air.

"You kept on telling me to." Grey closes his eyes like he realizes what he said might sound wrong in my head. "Not like that, Luan."

"I know." I smile, he smiles back. The door is still open, Grey's suitcase stands in the hallway, and I swear I can hear a little boy giggling. But I don't care. "I love you, too."

Grey kisses me again, deeper, with more passion, hotter.

We take a step, the door closes, we take another step, and another, and another. I don't know how many more steps we take before Grey and I are in his bedroom, or how many kisses we exchange before his shirt comes off, then mine. I also have no idea how many gasps or soft moans leave either of us until all of our remaining clothes are off; his pants, then mine, his socks, then mine, his underwear, then mine, until we're lying here on his bed, buck naked.

Grey lies beside me, his lips attached to mine like they're sewn together. I wouldn't mind it one bit if they were.

His lips are so soft and tender, not one kiss ever gets a little rough, not even when he grinds his hips against mine and I can feel his hard cock against my stomach.

Grey slides a hand down my side, then brings it to my ass, giving it a squeeze hard enough to make me yelp, but not to the point where it hurts.

As he brings that hand between our bodies, about to fist either his own cock or mine, I lay a hand on his chest to stop him.

"I'm not very good at this whole sex thing," I admit. I've had a total of two boyfriends, three with Grey. In one of said relationships—excluding Grey—, I had sex. Not a lot either. I swear you can count the times off on one hand alone. It's one of the main reasons why my ex cheated on me.

Grey smiles at me warmly, strokes my cheek with his thumb. "That's okay, baby."

"Sex scares me a little," I admit. Because it's too intimate for someone like me, for someone who gets attached too easily to people he… loves.

There has only ever been one person I allowed myself to get that attached to *without* sex, and that ended up with me as an alcoholic. I can't say I'd like to repeat that.

"Do you want to stop?"

I shake my head immediately. "But I can't promise it'll be any good for you."

"I can promise that." He presses a soft kiss to my lips. "Just remember that I love you, okay? And I'm not going to leave you. And that at whatever point, if you want us to stop, we'll stop."

"Okay."

"Just a question in advance, do you want me to use a condom?" Well, it's not like I can get pregnant, right? "I'm clean, I promise. But we'll go with whatever you prefer."

Right. STIs. "Did you ever... not use one?"

Grey shakes his head. "Never."

"Then we'll go with no condom." Yes, yes, I am selfish like that. I'll take as many of Grey's first as I possibly can.

"Of course."

Grey reaches between us again, taking both, his and my dick in his hand and strokes them together, slowly.

I kiss Grey deeper, exhaling heavily when he strokes down all the way to the base of our cocks and back up to the tips, squeezing them lightly.

His thumb runs over my slit, spreading some of the precum around the tip.

My heart quakes with love when I look at him. His eyes are all soft and loving even though I know he's nearly drowning in lust. No one's ever looked at me the way Grey does.

Most of the time, Grey looks at me with this scowl on his face, and still there's always a certain softness in his eyes. When we do things together, anything that doesn't require him to continue to pretend like he's an asshole, Grey's eyes fill with joy. I almost die every single time I see that extra spark.

He also looks at me when he thinks I wouldn't notice, and I believe these cautious, secretive looks are my favorite ones. It's like he's saying he can't take his eyes off of me. I know I can't take mine off him either.

Grey suddenly hovers over me. He erases the distance between our lips one more time.

I love his kisses. I love his touch. I love his voice and every sound that leaves him. In fact, I love everything about this man.

Truthfully, I didn't really think we'd ever get here. A future of Grey and I together was my fantasy, and yet here we are. He loves me, and I love him… God, he better put a stupid ring on my finger one day because I know for damn sure that I will not let him walk away from me.

My balls tighten when Grey's cock rubs against mine as he rolls his hips into me.

While Grey reaches over to his nightstand, I run my fingers over his back muscles, and lower them until my hands are right there on his ass. I give it a firm squeeze, earning myself a moaned gasp from my boyfriend.

"Do you usually top?" I ask, only because he seems like the guy to be on top, but Grey Davis has already surprised me on multiple occasions, so who even knows?

His face is back over mine when he answers, "Most of the time, yes."

"Good," I breathe out. "I don't like it."

"You don't?" He chuckles though not in a way that's mockingly.

I shake my head. "Broke my dick that one time I tried it, so no, I don't like it. After that, I never had the desire to try again."

"Oh, God." He's laughing now, leaning his forehead against mine.

I slide my arms up for a hug, wondering if this is what sex with someone you truly love is supposed to be like. Do you laugh during it? Is that normal? Are you supposed to feel calm and not worry about what the person you're sleeping with might think about you this instant? Is it genuinely supposed to be *fun*?

"Maybe I just haven't been with the right guy yet," I say, shrugging a little.

"Well, you are now." Grey lifts his head off mine, then kisses me deeply.

"You'd let me try?" I won't want to because I'm deeply traumatized.

His nod comes immediately. "Of course."

"I love you," I mumble into our next kiss, and I can feel Grey smile.

"Yeah?" He rolls off me again, though still faces me. He lifts one of my legs over his body, grinding against me while I lie one hand on his jaw, tracing my fingers over his features, admiring his beautiful face.

"So much, Grey Davis." I slide my hand down his neck, over his chest where I take a moment to play with his nipples. He groans into my mouth when I pinch one of them between two fingers before letting my hand travel further south. I trace along every ripple of his abs.

Before I get the chance to touch his dick, Grey hands me the bottle of lube and I help him put some on his fingers. I close the lid, then put the bottle somewhere above our heads, and finally go to wrap my hand around my boyfriend's cock to stroke him.

He hisses out a curse, his breath coming out shakier.

"I love you, too," he finally says, then brings his lips to mine but for tactical reasons this time. To mute me. Mute me because he now has a finger on my hole, spreading the lube around and slightly massaging me from the outside.

"Fuckfuckfuck." I don't remember that feeling so good. He hasn't even entered me yet and I can already feel my orgasm ready to shoot. What the fuck? This is kind of embarrassing, I admit.

My hand on his cock stills, though at least I still keep it in my hand while Grey slowly, *very* slowly inches the tip of his finger inside of me.

My breathing stills entirely, all the words I know are no longer in my brain to formulate sentences.

With my free hand, I press my fingers into his back, moaning out loud when Grey starts to pull his finger out again, then pushes it back in.

"Are you okay?" he asks, kissing me softly as if to say it's okay if I want to stop. I don't want to stop, I want him to keep on going, let me fuck his finger at first and then move on to his cock.

"Mm-hmm," I hum, then gasp a *yes* when Grey starts pumping his finger in and out of me a little faster. I let go of his dick, not wanting to accidentally squeeze him too tightly just because I couldn't control my own body anymore.

I grind against my boyfriend, seeking him out. My eyes close and I can feel the heat on my cheeks.

Don't come yet.

Don't come yet.

Don't you dare fucking come yet.

Grey adds another finger, he moves slow at first and then faster, stretching me, and I can feel my thighs quiver.

"Grey," I gasp and press the tips of my fingers deeper into his skin when my balls tighten with the urge to come. "You have to… *fuck*." I pant, fighting for my life when he adds a third fucking finger. "I'm going to come if you don't—"

He kisses me to shut me up.

Well then…

His dick rubs against mine with every thrust of his hips, his fingers still penetrating me. My entire body tenses, my balls tingling as my orgasm swoops up my spine and crashes behind my eyes covering my vision with black splotches. Cum shoots out of me, landing on our stomachs.

So much for great sex with him.

I barely even touched him, and now I've ruined it completely.

Only that Grey doesn't seem to feel the same way because that man smiles at me mischievously when I open my eyes again. Yes, mischievously.

"Grey…" I say in an apologetic way, but he pulls his fingers out of me and rolls me over onto my back, then reaches for the lube. "I won't come again, let alone get another boner." At least I've never experienced *that* before.

He positions himself between my thighs, having his eyes locked with mine when he dripples some of the lube onto his dick before putting the bottle away. Grey fists his cock, spreading the lube while also giving himself a couple of strokes.

"You will." He grins at me as he nudges his tip against my hole, not quite entering me but adding a little pressure anyway.

I look down at myself, internally rolling my eyes when I see my half-soft dick. *Half*-soft. What the heck? I mean, I guess it takes a hot second before the erection leaves even *after* ejaculation, but this has never happened before.

"Breathe, baby." He rests one hand on my stomach, bucking forward. "Relax for me."

I take a deep breath, relaxing my body as I exhale.

Grey enters me carefully, taking his time so it wouldn't hurt me all too much. It's burning a little, but the new rising lust inside of me totally turns the burning sensation into a *good* sensation. It's a mind-numbing pleasure that threatens to swallow me whole with each push forward and ever so slight pull.

"Fuck," I choke out, "that feels so good." Who would've thought it's actually supposed to feel good and not just hurt? Or, well, hurt, then feel okay and then hurt again.

"Oh… God." His eyebrows dip together, heat displaying in his eyes when he leans forward and covers my torso with his.

"You need to move. Please," I beg, and before he can argue with me, because I know he will, I wrap my legs around him and push him that tiny bit deeper all at once. We both gasp, and then our lips meet, our tongues tangling.

He moves, fucking me slowly, letting me adapt before he increases his movements. Every time he thrusts into me, I moan and so does he. Every time he pulls back, I feel my dick harden more and more until I cannot take it anymore and sneak a hand between our bodies, fisting my cock.

Grey's beautiful face is flushed with desire, rosy cheeks and sweat on his forehead, and yet he's never looked better. This face right there is just for me, the half-lidded eyes, the hungry and still loving gaze, the hot and rosy cheeks. Only I get to see him like this.

My heart squeezes at the thought. God, I love him so much. There are billions of words one could use, over seven thousand languages, and still not a single combination of either words in either language, even mixed, could describe how important this man is to me, how much he means to me.

Grey kisses me one more time before he gets back up on his knees, changing the angle. My mouth opens with a cry of pleasure, my free hand gripping the sheets while I at least try to jerk myself. He must sense my struggle because Grey covers my fist with his own, helping me out.

He plunges inside me deeply, hitting that one very pleasurable spot over and over again. All this feels far too good to be real.

A knot of pleasure coils tight inside of my balls. Hot cum spurts out of me and onto my stomach, again and again, it just won't stop.

Grey keeps on fucking me, chasing his own orgasm. His features tighten, tensing the closer he gets, then he pulls his dick out of me, giving himself another pump before his cum spills out of him and right onto me.

He tips over, his head resting right next to mine as we're both panting, trying to regain our strength after a bliss like this one.

I don't know how much time passes until Grey gets off me, but I kind of wish he'd just keep on lying there and let me hug him.

Grey holds out a hand for me the second he's off the bed. "Let's take a shower."

It's the logical thing to do, the thing I should be wanting to do given that there's probably more cum on my body than inside of me right now. Or maybe not, but you get the point. The problem is, I just don't want to get up. And so I shake my head. "You've killed me."

"Corpses don't talk." He heaves me up and I wonder where the fuck he gets that strength from. I'm not weak, physically, but even so I don't have any strength left inside of me, and I didn't do anything.

"This corpse does." I point at myself when I stand on my feet, Grey still holding me up.

"You're being dramatic."

"And you're a fucking sex god, anyone ever tell you that?" He chuckles but doesn't answer me. You see, he could've said no, and I would've believed him, but chuckling and ignoring my question means yes, and I hate that it's a yes even though it's true. "I kind of want to put all of the people into one bus and then have them fall off a cliff."

Grey leads us both into his bathroom. "You'd need more than one bus."

Urgh. "Two then." He's quiet, again. My eyes widen, my mouth slightly opens in shock. "Are you kidding me? More than *two* busses?"

"I didn't count, but probably."

"I hate you just a little bit for that." Not because he's experienced. Honestly, I love that he is because wow. And still, fuck him for that.

"For not counting or sleeping with them in the first place?"

"Yes."

Grey leaves me standing in the middle of the bathroom while he goes to turn on the shower, making sure the water won't be freezing cold, I hope.

"How did you manage to do that anyway?"

He shrugs. "College. People are horny. Most of them were puck bunnies anyway, so quite easy, plus drunk hookups from bars or at parties. And then I started playing for the NHL, giving me another bunch of puck bunnies to choose from." Grey turns around to look at me, slightly tilting his head because he knows I did, in fact, not want to know any of this. But at least he's giving me answers, right?

"I hate you."

He comes walking over to me, laying his hands on my ass to

pull me into his body. "You love me."

"Not anymore."

He hums, knowing fully well that's bullshit. "If it's any help, I never loved any of the people I slept with. Or talked to them, really."

"Your ex-boyfriend?" My eyebrows rise.

"I liked him, but it wasn't love."

Now that I love to hear. "Sooo, I'm the first guy you ever loved?"

"No," he answers. "I love Miles, but it's different from the way I love you. You're the first person I'm *in* love with."

"Okay, I can accept that." When we step inside the shower, the warm water dripping down on me first, I remember something. "You had news to share with me." Or he said he did, I think?

Grey's face lights up, nodding. Without him having to say a word, I know that whatever he is about to say, he's really happy about and proud of . Just looking at the pride on his face makes me proud of him already.

"The team voted me as the next Team Captain after Nolan retires," he tells me.

My jaw drops with a huge smile for him. In seconds, I'm in his arms for a tight as fuck hug, not caring that we're in a shower or completely naked. "They did?!"

"They did," he confirms and closes his arms around me.

"You deserve that, Grey Davis!" I press my lips to his neck. "I'm so endlessly proud of you."

I don't exactly know if him being, or becoming, team captain means that he'll have even less time for me, but even so, I don't care. Ice Hockey is his whole life. It's his passion, one flame in his life that kept lit at all times. He deserves this more than anyone else. He fought so hard to be where he's at now, and I just want to cry from all the happiness I feel for him.

That's my man right there, people. Soon-to-be Team Captain of the New York Rangers.

Chapter 12

"I'm overwhelmed and insecure, give me something / I could take to ease my mind, slowly"—In My Blood by Shawn Mendes

Grey

October 2025

WHEN COLIN SAID the wedding was going to be small, I underestimated his meaning of the word.

Honestly, I was expecting *small* to mean big but still on the roof of our apartment building only. It's super fancy, and I cannot believe Emory and Miles managed to create this in just a day.

Everything's white with tons of fairy lights hung up everywhere. I swear, it looks like someone's dream come true. But personally, I think there's one aspect about Colin and Lily's wedding that just tops it all. Emory made sure there are two free seats reserved for Colin's deceased siblings.

The guys and I got here earlier to make sure everything's alright up here, and when Colin saw the seats, he started to cry. I can't imagine how hard it must be on a day like this, a day he'd definitely want his siblings around. *All* of them, not just one.

An hour after we've been up here, Colin remembers the rings he most definitely needs in a bit, but because Lily is in their apartment, he doesn't want to go there for traditional reasons. They slept in one bed last night, so I'm not sure how logical this is, but whatever. I go anyway.

The door stands wide open when I reach their apartment, and that wouldn't surprise me as much on a day like this if I didn't know that Sofia and Emory spent a whole hour this morning texting in our group chat to tell us to stay away from the apartment because they want Lily's dress to be a surprise to Colin. Apparently, Aaron would describe it to Colin in detail and ruin it. Sofia wasn't wrong with that, Aaron would do it.

However, since Aaron and Sofia live right across from Colin and Lily, the door should be closed in case either Colin or Aaron walk past it.

Walking inside the apartment, I already hear little whimpers that sound like someone's crying. Tears aren't too unusual at weddings, right? But when I walk deeper into the living room and find Lily crunched up on their sofa, sobbing, I don't waste another second to be by her side.

I'm not the right guy to talk someone like Lily into… into what? Feeling better? I listen, I don't *talk*. I can give advice but that's all. But I know that whatever is wrong with Lily, she'll need Colin or Aaron to make it okay, not me. Sofia, Miles, or Emory would be a better help as well. Fuck, even *Luan* would know more than me.

"Are you okay?" I ask and kneel down in front of her.

Stupid question, I realize. Clearly she is not.

"Yup," she hiccups, pulling her knees even closer to her chest.

"I, uh… Where's Sofia?" She was supposed to be here. Lily shrugs. "Emory?" Another shrug. Well then. "I'll go get Colin, okay?"

I'm just about to get up when Lily wraps her hand around my wrist, stopping me. "Don't," she begs, her voice trembling. "Colin…" She inhales a shaky breath, then sniffles. "He'll worry and call off the wedding. And then it was all for nothing."

Call off the wedding? I don't think Colin would *ever* call off this wedding. No matter what. There could be a snowstorm out there heavy enough to create snow tornadoes or something, and he'd still go through with it.

Though, there might be one thing that could make even Colin call of this wedding, but I don't want to entertain that idea.

"Lily, what's wrong?" I pull her up to sit, and she immediately crosses her trembling legs. At least she's not pulling them to her chest again, right?

"It feels like I'm dying," she cries and clutches her hand around her knees, only then do I realize that Lily is not even wearing her wedding dress yet. She's sitting here in panties and a…oh… lacy bra that is mostly see-through. Well that's not awkward at all.

She's avoiding my eyes, staring past me. To change that, I force her to look at me by laying my hands on her face and turning her face into my direction. "Why do you feel like that?"

Lily shakes her head, her nose reddening with every second. Jesus.

"It hurts, Grey." I know she's trying to take a deep breath but instead she's taking small and quick ones like she's having a… panic attack.

I know she gets them sometimes, but I was never there to experience it. The fuck am I supposed to do now?

"Everyone out there is going to look at me and think I'm ugly!"

"That's not true." I have met my fair share of women before, and none of them came close to Lily. That woman is effortlessly beautiful. Her brother not so much.

"I'm not good enough for Colin," she cries, her fingers press deeper into her flesh. Either she's about to poke right through her skin with her freshly done nails, or they're on the brick to break off. So to avoid both, I grasp Lily's hands in mine.

"Colin loves you, Lil." I have quite literally never seen any guy as obsessed with their girlfriend as Colin is with Lily. If she asked him to jump off this building, he would. It's sickening. "You're more than good enough for him."

She bobs her head like she's understanding but I'm not sure she's even listening. "Why does he want to get me so badly,

Grey? I'm trying my best to get rid of him and he's still here!"

"Who?" There's no way she's about Colin.

She swallows thickly, looking up at the ceiling. "The motherfucking Devil. He wants me dead. Fuck, I want me dead."

"Lily... Are you sure you don't want Colin here?" I'm really not cut out to talk her out of wanting to die. Lily and I don't have that kind of relationship. Sure, I love her because she's my best friend's girlfriend, fiancée, wife in a few moments, any of those. And she's cool and all, but we're not *close*.

Lily shakes her head. "No Colin."

"Aaron then?" At least I know where he's at unlike Sofia and Emory. Again Lily shakes her head. I sigh heavily.

Okay, I can do this. I can... calm her down somehow.

Think, Grey, thi—

"It's okay," she tells herself, trying to take deep breaths. "Itsokayitsokayitsokay."

Well, if there's one thing I know for sure, it's telling yourself that everything will be okay does absolutely nothing.

"You know, your brain doesn't technically understand languages." *Yes, talk science, that'll help her.* "It understands behavior. You can tell yourself it's okay over and over again, but unless you act like it actually is okay, your brain won't understand that you're alright."

"What?" Her hands are shaking, her voice breaking.

"Yeah, like with social anxiety. You're actively avoiding crowds and therefore tell your brain that people are dangerous, that being outside with strangers is dangerous. You can tell your brain it's not dangerous all you want, but it won't understand. So in order to work against that anxiety, you will have to behave as though it's not dangerous, go out despite the feeling in the pit of your stomach that's telling you to stay home."

"Grey...I—" Lily draws in a quick breath, more of a gasp than an actual breath.

"Right, not helping."

Okay, think... I can do this.

Colin talks to her when she's having a panic attack, I know that much. He holds her, but I can't do that because I am not Colin, and my touch might do the exact opposite to her.

Encouragement. I know how to be encouraging.

"Lily, listen..." She locks her eyes with mine, all tears and pain. "I'm not Colin, so my words may do nothing for you, but; if you truly believe the Devil is out to catch you, then there's something so fucking valuable inside of you. Thieves don't break into empty houses. You're worth so much more than you let yourself believe. And I promise you, every single person up there on the roof *loves* you. You're never going to be alone again, you'll always have someone by your side."

"Even you?" Her eyes soften a little, her breathing still shaky but it's calming, I think?

"Even me, Lily." I admit, I haven't really made it easy for her, or anyone, but Lily especially.

After Colin had told me Lily wanted to die and that it was the only reason she was around him, I was worried about Colin. I worried what it'd do to him if she died. I love Colin. I did four years ago, and I do now. And four years ago, I didn't think it was that good of an idea for Colin to stick around someone who wanted to die and not even want the help to stay alive. He was the one who tried keeping her breathing, and I didn't like it one bit.

Back then, I hated Lily for what she was doing to Colin. In my mind, there was no way she didn't know that he liked her, and for her to allow Colin to go through this seemed selfish to me. Not the fact that she was struggling and wanted to die, committing is *not* selfish. People who commit suicide die from an illness. It's not them who pull the trigger, it's the sick part in their brain that does. So Lily wanting to die was never my problem, but for her to allow someone else to get attached to her just before she *knew* she was going to die, *that* was selfish to me.

Thank god that didn't happen.

Now I'm glad Lily is still around, or rather that she *is* around.

Lily squeezes my hands, tears still run down her cheeks, but she also has a very small smile tugging on her lips. She opens her mouth but doesn't get to speak when someone cuts her off.

"Mi sol." Colin is on the sofa next to her in mere seconds, holding her tightly to his body. Lily starts to sob harder and presses her face into his chest.

"I'm sorry… I—"

Colin cuts her off one more time. "It's okay, sweetheart. Everything's going to be okay."

"I'm ruining everything," she cries. "I shouldn't be here, Colin. I shouldn't still be alive."

I thought she was doing a whole lot better than four years ago. She's always laughing, always the first to comfort others.

"You're not ruining anything."

"Everyone hates me."

"Nobody hates you, Lilybug. In fact, every single person up there would rather sit with you for days straight and listen to your story than tell it."

I feel like I shouldn't be here for this. I'm no good at comforting people. I might've studied psychology in college, but I still never bothered to care for anyone but myself. I know how to listen, give advice, but anything else is beyond me.

I get up and leave the apartment like I've never been there in the first place.

I never understood the bond Lily and Colin have because to me it always seemed strange. To have bonded during a time when she was one foot in the grave and he was about to lose his sister to cancer. Up until a year into their relationship, I was making bets with myself that they'd break up any day. I loved that they were happy, and after a year I slowly started to understand. Though it wasn't until I let Luan in that I finally realized why they work as good as they do.

They're each other's anchor. They hold each other in place. Whatever one lacks, the other fills in, levels it out.

On my way back up to the roof my own words keep playing

in my head like I didn't even mean to say them to Lily but to myself.

Thieves don't break into empty houses.

I don't get it. It didn't even fit Lily's problem, did it? But it doesn't fit mine either. Or does it?

My problem is my father and the fact that he'd never accept my relationship with Luan, that he'll disown me once he finds out Luan and I are actually dating.

It's not that my dad is trying to steal from me… unless he is. Because threatening me to disown me if I love who I want to love, if I let him decide over me like that, he's stealing my life away from me. I wouldn't be living my life, I'd be living the one he wants me to live.

But if there's nothing left he can take from me, when I just stop giving any fucks about what he thinks, how he'd react, he can't steal my life from me anymore.

I don't live off his money any longer. I stopped using my trust fund years ago.

The roof over my head is no longer his, and I pay for it myself, too.

I am slowly regaining my happiness ever since he cut me off three years ago.

Now that I no longer give him the chance to control me, he can't steal from me any longer.

Wow, and it took Lily's panic attack for me to figure that shit out? I used to think I was smart, apparently not.

"Is everything okay down there?" Aaron asks when I reach the rooftop. "Sofia said something's up with Lily. I swear, Grey, if you don't tell me—"

"She's fine. Colin's with her."

"Yes, I know. But *I* should be there. That's my sister."

I roll my eyes. Aaron cares about Lily, clearly, and I do believe he's glad she's with someone like Colin, and yet he still has to learn that Aaron isn't the person she wants to talk to when she's upset. I'll throw a party the day he realizes it.

"Your sister is with her *fiancé*, Aaron. Her *very* soon-to-be husband. He's who she needs right now, not you." I look over Aaron's shoulder, seeing Luan standing off to the side with Miles, Sofia, and Emory, laughing. I like that they're getting along. "She had a panic attack. If that happened to Sofia, you'd want to be with her and not share that vulnerable moment with her brother, so give Lily some time with the guy she loves before you storm down there to check on her."

Aaron turns his head, now looking at Sofia. The second his eyes lay on her, he smiles and his face lights up a little with all the love he has for her. "We got married, you know?"

I lay my hand on his shoulder. "Oh, *we* know. You guys aren't very secretive about it. And now, if I hear you say that to *anyone* else today, I will murder you for Lily and Colin because it's rude to make such an announcement on their special day. Okay, Marsh?"

Aaron holds up three fingers. "Scouts honor."

I don't think he's ever even been a scout.

Walking away from Aaron, I make my way over to my boyfriend, and when I reach him, the first thing I do is wrap my arms around his neck from behind and plant a kiss right to his neck.

Emory groans at that. "Grey in love is so disgusting."

I flip her off, but Luan slaps my hand as if to tell me to stop. I don't. "Imagine what I felt like having to watch you and Miles make out while I was on the couch with the both of you."

Emory shudders at the thought. They barely paid attention to me, but I stuck around because it was hilarious whenever they were all grinding up on one another, forgetting I was there and then at some point I just started talking and both of them flinched.

It used to be the highlight of my days, now my highlight of the day is picking up my phone to talk to Luan. It's crazy how much I anticipate those calls when we're miles apart.

I both hate and love that we barely get to spend time together in person. I hate it because, well, we're so far away from one another, that it'd take us at least six hours to get to the other's home, and on top of that all the waiting for a *plane* and finding time to spare a few days far away from home. But I also love it because every night, I get to listen to Luan tell me all about his day in so much detail just because he wants me to feel like I was there with him. I don't think he'd do that anymore when we live together, not in such detail as he does now.

Still, I'd take coming home to Luan over his detailed day descriptions.

"That still happens," Miles says.

"I'm sure that'll stop once I move in with him." Luan chuckles, saying it so easily that it gives me a heart attack. I mean, fuck yes, he's moving in with me. In a few months, hopefully. I'd take him moving in about yesterday, but I suppose in a few months is fine.

"You're moving in together?!" Sofia shrieks, a huge smile plastering onto her face.

"Sometime in the next year, probably," I confirm. It could be January, or December, or any month in-between. We have no exact date set, it all comes down to Luan because *he's* the one actually moving across the country. It's a huge step, so I won't rush him even if I want to.

"FUCK YES!" Sofia jumps right into Luan's arms, ignoring *me* there. Well, technically I am not in my boyfriend's arms but he's in mine, so what the fuck? "Oh, my God. I cannot *wait* to have you with us *every* Taco Sunday. Colin is still trying to convince Miles to buy a karaoke machine to add some extra fun. Imagine all the fun we can have when the two of us team up against Aaron and Grey, and then we make them weep!"

Ah, yeah… the karaoke machine only Colin wants, and Sofia, apparently. Oh, and Brooke loves the idea of making grown ass men sing Barbie songs. I'm all in for that.

"Language, Sofia!" Brooke yells from across the rooftop, and when all of us turn to look at Brooke, she's pointing at her three-year-old brother sound asleep on one of the chairs. Oh to be a careless kid again.

"Yes, language, Sofia." Miles taps his hand on her back before he dismisses himself to go over to his kid because Reece must be standing a little too close to our precious little princess again. They're both barely eight years old, and yet Reece keeps trying to kiss Brooke because he's oh so in love with her.

Of course Miles won't let this happen. He'd rather die than let anyone kiss Brooke. Though, I suppose I get it at that age.

But that reminds me. "Did Aaron ever try to kiss you when you were like six years old?" I ask Sofia. Knowing Aaron now, it wouldn't surprise me. He was obsessed with her then, and he is now.

Sofia laughs. "All the time. But I never let it happen because of Lily. I thought she'd hate me if I fell in love with Aaron. But you know *kids*, it wasn't *love* the way it is now. It was just curiosity and maybe a little crush."

"Nuh-uh," Aaron disagrees when he just so shows up beside her. "I knew we'd be together when I was three years old, so don't go on saying it was just a crush. I was in love with you from the second I saw you."

"You threw a candy cane at me when you 'first saw me'." Sounds like something Aaron would do.

"A candy cane of *love*, Icicle. I thought you were hungry." Aaron puts an arm around her waist, pulling her right into his body. "I also threw a croissant, so…"

Only Aaron, I'm telling you.

"That croissant was probably a week old. It was hard as fuck."

Aaron shrugs. "I never cleared out my hockey bag." I bet because he was well, three years old.

"You started hockey at *three* years old?" Luan asks. "I barely even liked walking at that age." *But I bet he loved talking.*

"Yeah, it was a toddler skating course. We didn't play hockey much, just learned how to skate until we were like almost five and could start playing. I was in one skating group with my sister and that thing next to me."

Six Years

Sofia rolls her eyes, and I bet she's ready to throw her husband off the building.

Luan Hayes

November 6th, 8:23 PM

I like carbonara, but your white sauce tastes better

> Oh, Jesus…
>
> Here we go again

I don't know Ronaldo, but we can get Messi

> Luan, we're already dating. You can stop these pickup lines…

Why would I?

I LOVE them.

> Alright then, use less sexual ones

Why?

> Because I'm like five states away from you

Luan Hayes

December 24th, 8:23 PM

They canceled my flight

> Are you serious?!

Yup…

> I WANTED TO SEE THE FUCKING SNOW!

That's all?

> Pretty much, yeah
>
> OH
>
> I ALSO WANTED TO LEARN HOW TO SKATE SO I CAN IMPRESS FINE AS FUCK HOCKEY PLAYERS

...

Honestly, valid.

> On a more serious note, baby
>
> I'm mad as fuck.
>
> I wanted to see your cute little face

I do not have a "cute little" face.

> Oh, yes you do, Ma'am

MA'AM?!

> Typo
>
> It was supposed to say "Wife"

...I'm breaking up with you

> You wish
>
> You love me too much to do it

> Oh, shut your cute ass mouth.

Luan Hayes

January 12th, 3:02 AM

> Are you awake?????

>> Luan, it's three in the goddamn morning

>> But yes, I'm always awake for you

> Good because I need you to call me

>> Okay. Why?

> Because I miss you

> And I love you

>> Give me a second to find some clothes

> No, no. Naked is fine…

>> Oh, dammit. You're lucky I don't share a hotel room with anyone

Chapter 1

"baby, you can rest assured / I'll always be there for you"—Little Bit More by Suriel Hess

Grey

February 2026

"Is Luan not home?" I ask when Dorothy opens the door for me. He could very well be home and still not have opened the door. Luan didn't know I was coming. It's his birthday tomorrow, and I thought we could spend it together. I do have a game tonight, but I asked to be off because I didn't feel very good. It was a lie, and honestly, probably not something I should be doing when I become the captain this September, but I had to.

This will be Luan and I's first Valentine's Day as a couple, *plus* his birthday. I wanted to be here.

"He is, but I think he's still asleep." She steps aside to let me in, not even questioning my presence. "He could be awake though. Luan barely comes out of his room these days, I'm not sure why."

My eyes narrow. "*You* don't know why?" Luan tells her everything. When he's upset, she knows about it.

"He won't talk. He's been quiet for like a whole week."

What the fuck?

I walk past her, ready to storm into Luan's room to find out what the hell is wrong with him. He's texted me like usual, so nothing changed there.

"Grey," Doro stops me, her eyes hold something apologetic

in them . "Maybe let him sleep it off?"

Sleep it off? "When my boyfriend has been sulking in his room for a week, I will *not* let him *sleep it off*. I will go in there and ask what's wrong."

So that's what I do. I mean, this is Luan we're talking about. Luan's barely ever upset, and he would definitely *never* lock himself in his room for a whole ass week.

Why didn't he mention anything?

I open his bedroom door and allow myself inside without knocking, which turns out to be a good thing because Luan's lying in his bed still fast asleep. Before I inspect his room to find anything that might seem odd, I close the door again to stop Doro and possibly Sarah from peeking inside.

When I look around, everything looks just like last time I was here. It's all tidied up, no crockery lying around, or empty water bottles. It's clean. It doesn't smell weird like he hasn't opened his window at all, it's all… normal, fresh. There is nothing odd.

So, I kick off my shoes, because I forgot to do that at the door, and walk over to his bed. Carefully lifting the covers, I sneak inside Luan's bed, hoping it doesn't wake him up.

Once I lie next to my boyfriend, I drape my arm over his body and pull him into mine. He makes a few soft sleepy noises, but then he's all silent again. But I think he woke up because his breathing isn't as deep anymore.

Then suddenly, he lifts my arm as if he's trying to find out why there's an extra arm on his body that doesn't belong to him. In mere seconds Luan turns around, staring at me with wide eyes.

"Hi there, ba—"

He presses his lips to mine, laying his hand on my face. His tongue pushes right into my mouth and I groan a little at the contact.

We haven't even been separated for as long as we usually are, and still it felt like way longer this time.

"You're here," he says like he can't believe it. "I mean, of course I knew you'd be here. I'm awesome and you probably missed my funny jokes." His voice is clogged with tears as he speaks.

"That, and I missed *you* to death, Luan." I think the more often we see each other and then have to part again, the harder it gets. I know I will spend the next two nights all cuddled up to him, and then I leave and all we're left with are phone calls and texts for the next couple of months.

Luan wraps his arms and legs around my body, clinging to me like some kind of monkey. "Did you read the TMZ article about you?"

There's a new article about me? "No."

"They said fans have been seeing you with a different woman each night for weeks. I know it's not true, but wow, reading that really kicked me right in the balls."

Oh. We still haven't made our relationship official yet, not publicly at least. My team knows, PR knows, and my management knows just in case the news gets out before Luan and I can do it ourselves. They'd release a flat and genuinely blunt statement about our relationship. I hate this because none of my teammates have to do it, but it's better than the alternative.

I don't want to receive another million packages filled with shit and god knows what else. I believe it'll still come that way whenever I do, but maybe having PR and my management handle the news is better than throwing an Instagram post out there, boringly confirming that Luan and I are, in fact, a couple.

We haven't said anything yet because we both enjoy the quiet and we know once we confirm it publicly, it will be anything but peace and quiet.

"Is that why you've been hiding in your room for a week?" I ask, stroking a hand up and down his bare back.

"No, I just missed you." I can feel Luan's tears wet my shirt, but I couldn't care less right now. "I can't do anything all fucking day but think about you. And then I read all those articles about you, making the whole missing-you thing worse. Now add the bad articles basically saying you're cheating on me when I know damn well you'd never do that, it doesn't exactly put me in a better mood."

"Oh, Luan…" I hold him tighter, hoping it'll make him feel a little better. It won't, and if it does, it'll only last for the next two days.

Though, while I'm holding him, I look over his shoulder and right out of the window. My eyes immediately land on the mansion in the distance. The same mansion I grew up in. My parents should be at home because it's a Monday and my dad doesn't work on Mondays. I haven't talked to either of them in so long, I don't even remember their voices.

"Do you want to meet my mom?" I ask without even thinking about what I'm suggesting. I know I told Luan I'd introduce him, but I always thought I'd have a whole plan for when I did. Guess my plan is to wing it after all.

"Today?"

"Yeah, we can go over there right now if you want." I need to see my mom anyway, even if it's going to be the last time. On my dad's birthday four years ago, I didn't get to say goodbye. I didn't think it'd be the last time I ever talked to her.

Sun keeps telling me Mom misses me, which I don't doubt because Mom always did. She never cared about who I loved but with a father like mine as her husband, she doesn't have many choices in her life. I hate that so much more than my father not wanting to accept I am not straight.

"My sister should be home, too." Sun graduated from College last summer. Maybe she'd live in NYC now if she hadn't transferred from St. Trewery to a Uni in Malibu in her Junior year because she had no one left in New York, let alone New City. Sure, she had me and Emory, her best friend, but without either of us actually close by, it was harder on her than any of us had anticipated.

Her sorority house *hated* my sister.

"And your brother?" Luan asks, mumbling a little against my chest.

"I don't know." Moon probably moved out by now. He's three years older than me, making him twenty-eight going on twenty-nine this year. If he still lived at home, I'd be worried. "Maybe he's visiting."

"Okay. But only if you'll show me your bedroom, too." Luan forces himself out of my arms, sniffling a little before he stands. He takes a deep breath and then walks over to his closet. "Should I dress up all nicely? Like… do I need a suit or—"

"I'm sure any pants and a shirt will be fine," I chuckle. "Anything but your naked ass." I lean against the headboard, bringing my hands behind my head as I let my eyes linger on my boyfriend's ass for a while longer.

Luan looks back at me over his shoulder, winking when he notices where my eyes lie. "If your dad doesn't kill me, you can have me all the ways you like when we're back."

Well… now I'm praying my parents aren't at home so we can get back here a little faster.

"Are we not using the front door?" Luan asks while I clearly lead him in from the backyard. But we're also not using the backdoor. We're using the climbing-through-Sun's-bedroom-window "door".

Sure, I could use my key and get us inside the normal way, but I want to see my mom, and if I come across my dad right by the door, that won't happen.

I texted Sun to ask if she was at home and she said yes, so going with her bedroom window is the best we can do. Or, of course, we could use my fifteen-year-old-me way. The one that had me climb up the side of the house to get on my balcony. It's a whole lot more dangerous though, and I'd rather not visit my boyfriend in the hospital.

Once we reach Sun's room, I knock three times like always, so she knows it's me. When she opens the window, I let Luan climb in first, pushing him up just because. He would've managed to do it all on his own, but with my help, I could have my hands on his ass.

Before I even make it inside, I can hear Sun talk to Luan as though she's known him all her life. They met *once* years ago.

"You're turning twenty-*seven*?" I hear my sister ask all surprised. "How are you older than Grey? You look *younger*."

"I don't know." Luan chuckles. "It's got to be your brother's scowls that make him look eighty."

I don't look like I'm eighty years old. Right? No. I don't have gray hairs or wrinkles, and I'm in great shape, thank you very much.

"Enough of that," I say and turn to my sister. "Clearly, I don't have to introduce either of you." I take my boyfriend's hand in mine, then pull him right toward my sister's bedroom door to leave. "Say goodbye, Sunshine."

"Goodbye." Sun waves after us like we're leaving to go to war. "It was nice meeting you!"

"I like her," Luan says as soon as the door closes behind us. "Woah. I knew it was going to be fancy in here, but what the fuck is this!" He waves a hand around, causing me to look around the hallway like I didn't grow up here.

When I was younger, I didn't know that the way I grew up was extraordinary. I didn't know that most people don't live in houses as big as the one I lived in. Sure, I knew houses looked different, but then I used to think there was only ever one family living in an entire apartment complex and I got so jealous because they must've had so many floors. All because I grew up with a silver spoon in my mouth and nobody ever taught me how to be humble or to be thankful for what we have.

The older I got, the more I understood. I understood that there are people out there who are homeless and have absolutely *nothing*. But since I was never taught how to be grateful for what I have, I didn't care until I started college. I didn't care about any of this until I watched other students struggle and worry about how they're going to pay their tuition. On more than one occasion, I anonymously sent people at St. Trewery envelopes filled with the money they needed to pay their tuition, housing, or simply afford food.

Still, whenever I'm inside the house I grew up in, it's like all of my knowledge on how poor some people are vanishes. When I look around and see Lux Touch tiles, pure gold picture frames, statues, and paintings that cost more than a heart on the black market, for whatever reasons, poverty doesn't exist in my brain.

I don't understand how some people can have *this* whereas others have nothing. And so when I'm here, it's like I think the whole world is rich, even though I know it's not like that. I don't see why this house would shock anyone, because to me, this has always been my *normal*.

But right now, watching Luan look around with huge eyes that are about to pop out, even though he grew up rich himself, I no longer see this as normal.

Instead of having bought the hundredth far too expensive painting, my father could've used those hundreds of thousands to donate to homeless shelters or any charity that would help poorer people. He could've chosen to help people in need, but instead he poured, and is still pouring, all that money into useless shit that nobody needs.

"Let's just go find my mother, okay?" I lead him down the hall and into the entrance hall where my parents usually host huge dinners like my father's fiftieth birthday. We have a dining room, but it's on the smaller end, meant for only a small family and not twenty people all at once. I think I've had more dinners in an *entry* hall than I had in our actual dining room.

Getting to the other side of the mansion, I lead Luan upstairs to where the bedrooms are. Sun's room is on the other side of the house because she's a girl. It was my father's way of saying my brother and I shouldn't get too close to our sister because her privacy should be valued.

It's a great thing at first, but when you consider that my father happens to be very sexist, it's not that great anymore.

When we reach my bedroom, I hesitate to open the door for a moment. Inside of that room is everything that shaped me into the person I am today. This room hides secrets that I never thought I'd ever share with anyone.

It's where I watched my first hockey game on TV and fell in love with the sport at such a young age. It's where I spent hours crying in my bed because I thought something was wrong with me. It's where I sat at my desk and wrote letters to my future self, asking if the pain ever ends, if I'll be normal again.

This room holds so many memories that I never think about anymore, not until I open that door and let Luan inside.

There is hockey equipment all over my room, neatly put aside thanks to one of the housekeepers, but it's around anyway. Most of those sticks and pucks that lay and stand around are ten years old or even older. There are sports magazines on my desk, mostly ones I cut my favorite ice hockey players out of to pin them onto a bulletin board. That board was a vision board to me; the one goal I wanted to reach in my life.

Luan walks over to my desk, looking at the picture frame. It's the only one I owned back then. "That's cute. How old were you in that picture?"

"Fourteen." It's a picture of Sun and I together. It was my first hockey game as team captain. We won, and Sun ran onto the ice to congratulate me afterward. She wasn't allowed to do that, and although everyone was trying to get her off the ice, my mother used a moment to take a picture of my sister in my arms. We were smiling at the camera. She smiled because she was proud of me, I smiled because I felt alive again in that moment.

"Oh, what I would do to see just *one* picture of you with no tattoos." Luan sighs dramatically long, turning around to look at me. "Do you have one?"

I narrow my eyes at him, ready to say no, but he gives me puppy dog eyes that I cannot say no to. So instead I nod toward my desk. "Last drawer on the left."

Luan grins at me, then turns around and kneels, opening the drawer. There are a million pictures of my siblings and I when we were kids, or me at hockey camp, school photos, all in order. My mother put that book together before I left for college. She even wrote down the dates from when the photos were taken. Luan's going to love that.

He takes out the photo book, then looks around himself as if to find a cozy spot to put it down and enjoy digging deeper into my childhood.

"Baby, you can go on the bed," I say with a little amusement in my voice. "No one's going to murder you because of it."

He jumps up onto the bed in seconds, lying down on his stomach with the book right in front of him. "I hope you know I will scream when I open this book and the first photo is you smiling."

Of course that would make him scream. "No, the first photo is me five seconds after being born."

Luan opens the photo book in seconds, scrunching up his nose. "Ew. You were all gooey."

"No shit."

"Aww, look at that cute little nose!" He looks up from the picture. "Yup, still the same one."

Why do I even like this guy?

Luan turns the page, and another one, and another one. The more pages he turns, the brighter his smile gets. Until it vanishes altogether. The second he stops smiling, I know which pictures he's reached without even having to see them myself.

"Where'd that smile go?" he asks, running a finger over the picture of twelve-year-old me. He freezes when said finger reaches a camp sign. That's when his head snaps up. "You went to church camp?"

I nod.

"I didn't know you were religious."

"I'm not." Not anymore. I used to be, and then my father tried to pray away the gay and that was the moment I decided I don't give a shit anymore. So then I'll end up in hell, at least I had a fun time on earth fucking whoever I wanted.

"Grey, please tell me this isn't some… I don't know, some camp to…" He can't even put it into words, and I don't blame him because neither can I.

"You know what's funny? Those nuns tried to make us '*normal*' again, but they forgot something. All of our parents sent us there because we were interested in boys, clearly. It was a *boys* camp though. I shared a room with three other guys. I kissed two of them."

Luan nods slowly. "Well, I always thought those camps were stupid."

They are. You can't just send your kids to church camp and expect them to come back suddenly no longer interested in the same gender as them after six weeks of trauma. The only logical reason for one of those kids to no longer want to date whoever they want would be because they've been completely traumatized. If they caught us kissing, we'd get beatings for thirty minutes straight, and then we had to seek out forgiveness from God. We had to confess what we had done and apologize over and over again, then go through another round of beatings.

It's sickening to even think that those camps *still* exist.

"I'm sorry you had to go through that, Grey…"

I wave him off. "It's fine. I actually had fun there when we weren't told how bad liking guys was or how it's a sin. I made it my personal mission to kiss that one guy anywhere I could without getting caught. And we used to pull pranks on the nuns all the time. We were a hopeless case."

"Well I'm glad you were. But it's still not okay that you had to go through it." Luan looks at me with tears in his eyes, but before I even get the chance to tell him that I don't want him to cry because of me going through that, he's already speaking again. "I don't get why parents do that. Aren't they supposed to love their kids no matter what? Like, if you cannot accept your kid for who they are or who they turn out to be, why even have some? Don't get me wrong, I'm glad you're here, but I still think your dad shouldn't have had kids if he can't love you the way you are."

I couldn't agree more.

Luan gets off the bed, making his way over to me. When he stands in front of me with his hands on my face, my heart does a little backflip.

"Fear not, Grey Davis, you've got me now. And I will love every single part of you for the rest of my life," he says, slowly stroking his thumbs over my skin.

"Even if I killed someone?"

He nods. "I'd help you kill them. We'll be like Bonnie and Clyde."

"They got caught and died."

Luan rolls his eyes. "Fine. We'll be like Romeo and Juliet. They're not allowed to be together, neither are we."

I chuckle. "They, uh… they committed suicide."

Luan groans, leaning himself back to the point where he'd fall to the floor if I didn't have my arms around his body to keep him standing. "You just had to ruin it, didn't you?" He lifts his head again. "Hadrian and Antinous!"

"Antinous dies."

"Cleopatra and Antony?"

"They die together."

"Are there *any* historical, fictional, or non-fictional couples that make it out alive!?"

Technically, all of them died at some point. "Honestly, I don't think so?"

Luan leans in a little closer, his lips brush mine when he says, "We'll just write our own story then, but with a happy ending. We don't die."

"We will at some point in life," I point out only to see Luan's annoyed face again. He's so cute when he's trying to look mad.

"No, we won't. We will live forever. Together. Even if it's just in a book."

Chapter 2

"I need you in my life, you're my necessity"—All I Ever Need by Austin Mahone

Iván

February 2026

I FINISH LOOKING through the scratch book, closing it quietly so Grey wouldn't notice I'm done here. He's sitting by his desk, either looking out of the window or at anything that might interest him. I think he's stuck in his head, worried about what's to come, and I wish I could tell him everything will be alright, but I suppose we all know that after today, nothing will be the same as it was. For Grey.

Wanting to give Grey another few minutes to himself, I allow myself to look around his room. Genuinely *look*, take every inch in like a stupid bedroom is as valuable as a museum. But in some ways, it is. This is where Grey grew up, where he spent most of his days at. This room is personal and gives so much away while also only bringing up more questions.

His walls are plain, there's only one bulletin board on *one* wall with a couple of pictures, all ice hockey related. The only other very unlike-this-house kind of things are his hockey sticks leaning against a wall and the pucks lying on his dresser. Other than that, it's all very *plain* in here. His apartment in New York doesn't look much different, though back there, there is at least *some* character. This room is just… blank.

"Grey Davis?" I sit up, stretching. "Did you ever consider

painting these walls… I don't know, black? I think you would've liked black in here. Honestly, I kind of expected it to be all black, like your apartment, but nope, it's so…*white*. So totally not you."

He spins around on his chair, slightly cocking his head while offering me a somewhat confused, yet also mad frown. "First you complain about my life being too dark, and now this room is too light?"

"I've *never* complained about your life being *too dark*," I say as a matter of fact. "I happen to like your darkness, actually. It allows me to brighten up those dark corners you never show anyone, then I can tell people that I know so much more about you and that they'll never figure you out because, boy, it took me *ages* to even find those nasty little dark as fuck corners."

Grey slowly lifts his head in a nod. "Yeah? Which ones did you find already?"

Probably none, really. Maybe the one about church camp and his father, but I think that's about it. Grey Davis would never make it easy for me to find them. "Like…" I look around myself, taking in this room one last time. Then suddenly something Grey has told me a while ago makes it back to me. My head snaps toward my boyfriend, and I grin. "Like that you have never had sex with anyone in this bedroom."

"That's not a secret," he argues.

"But it is, Grey Davis." My grin widens. "Name one person, other than me and you, who knows this."

"Doesn't make it a secret. I'm not actively trying to *hide* that information from people. It just happens to be something nobody asks about because it's weird. I don't go around asking Miles if he fucked someone in his childhood bedroom, which, he most definitely did because he's been dating Em—doesn't matter, actually. It's not something people usually *ask* about, let alone want to know of."

Alright, he might have a point there. To make my loss forgotten, I change the topic. "Why did your parents name you Grey? I mean, with your siblings' names, they should've thought of something that would've *fit* with theirs." Technically, they should've just given Sun a different name to miss-match it as well, since she's the youngest.

Grey rolls his eyes. "Grey's a whole lot better than the alternative. Imagine they named me Star or Cloud or anything like that."

"Milky Way has a nice ring to it." I shrug.

He snorts and gets up, making his way over to me. "What else *has a nice ring* to it?" Grey lifts my face up to his with just two fingers, forcing us to lock our gazes. I don't mind, I would die a happy death looking at him.

"Rain," I answer. "They'd have Moon, Rain, and Sun. Everything they need to build an ecosystem, I guess?" I honestly don't know if that's true, I didn't really pay much attention in biology.

"I don't think Moon, Rain, and Sun make an *ecosystem*, they do make for some weather changes though, which are somewhat essential, so I'll give you a D for effort."

"A D?!" I cross my arms over my chest. "That's rude, Grey Davis."

"I might know of a way that you can up your grade, if you're interested." He smirks, and holy shit that smirk... I've seen him smirk before, but none of them come close to the sight of lust-filled eyes and a somewhat smile on Grey's face.

Grey leans down until his lips are only a breath away from mine. "But I don't think you're that kind of student, are you?"

So we're talking about a whole other D, all right.

Oh, for him I'll be *any*thing. "Good thing I'm not a student anymore at all, huh?" I close the gap between our lips, only stealing a quick kiss from my boyfriend. "So, tell me, Grey Davis," I reach my hands to his pants, unbuttoning his oh so beloved black cargo pants. I still don't know who's crazy enough to wear cargo pants near a beach, but I love this idiot either way. He's lucky it's February, so not all *that* warm. "What does it take for me to get an A in biology?"

His breath comes out a little shakier this time, fanning over my skin. "You're off to a good start."

"Am I?" I glide my palm over his growing erection outside of his pants, then slide my hand up and sneak it underneath his shirt to feel his abs. Why does he have to have such great abs? I mean, I'm not bad off myself, but I like his more.

Grey kisses me while I discover his torso with both of my hands, burning every inch of his body into my memory like I'm not already all too familiar with it.

He groans into my mouth when I rest my hands on his ass, giving it a firm squeeze as I pull him closer to me. I then run my hands over the back of his thighs as his mouth tentatively moves against mine.

To think that the guy who's standing between my legs is all mine is still very much surreal to me. The Luan from a few years ago who was sure he'd end up with Grey Davis, yet still didn't know if it was just a fantasy or would ever be reality, would be crying with joy right now. I still might.

I honestly can't tell you what comes over me, but my next words even shock me a little. "I want to be the only one you've ever fucked in this room, Grey Davis."

Grey chuckles and moves to kiss me again, slow at first, but in a blink of an eye, our kiss turns lustful, wanting. He pushes his tongue into my mouth, deepens our kiss more than I expected him to. And then he pulls away to look at me like he's only now realizing what I've said.

I know this guy was sexually active, like *really* active, and I feel bad enough that he doesn't get as much sex as he's used to when I'm not around, and still not nearly as much even when we're together, but even so, he hasn't once complained to me about it. Not in a *serious* way. We FaceTime a lot, daily, and almost every other day we end up jerking off together, but it's not the same.

I've never asked him for sex either because, while it might be something Grey loves, sex and I have never been really good with each other. Sure, I *love* sex with *Grey* but it's not like I need it. I'm happy without it, he knows that, which is why his reaction doesn't really surprise me.

"You sure? Because I think you just want to slide into a slot of my life that hasn't been given away yet, and if that's the case, Luan, we shouldn't do this. I don't want to feed some part of you that we both know should be starved instead."

My narcissism, got it. "While I do find comfort and a little ping of victory in the fact that I'd be the first and only one, it's not about that," I say. "I'm horny, man. My boyfriend has been gone for months and, believe it or not, I do *really* want you to fuck me. I wouldn't care if we're in my bedroom, yours, a hotel, or the fucking sea, I want you, Grey Davis. Right fucking now."

"Okay." He brings his hands to the bottom of my shirt, tugging it up. I lift my arms and he pulls it over my head, leaving my torso exposed.

"You should probably lock the door though…" The last thing we need is his father walking in here—why he ever would—and catch his son balls deep inside of me. Though, that would definitely be *a* way of breaking the news to his homophobic father.

"I did the second we got here." Grey removes his own shirt, tossing both of our shirts over to his desk chair.

I get off the bed, laying my hands on my boyfriend's hips and pull him right into mine, attaching my lips to his as if that's exactly where they belong. Maybe it is.

Pushing my tongue into his mouth, tasting him with long, slow strokes as I take my time savoring each kiss we share. He might be in control of our kisses most of the time, but not right now. Right now, I'm going to drag this out as long as I possibly can, even though I probably shouldn't.

Every attempt of Grey's to touch me is denied by me swatting his hands away each time he tries to lay them on me. At some point, he lets out the softest fucking whimper I have *ever* heard.

My hands slide down his smooth, naked torso and I allow

myself to enjoy the feeling of every ripple like I've never touched Grey before in my life.

Once my hands reach the hem of his pants, I push them down his legs and he steps out of them, kicking them into some corner but I don't think he cares much. I turn us around, then start kissing his neck, sucking on his skin ever so lightly but I don't leave any marks, though I wish I could.

Grey lets out yet another whimper when he tries to lay his hands onto my stomach to touch me and I swat his hand away.

"Let me touch you," he groans madly, frustrated.

I shake my head. "Not yet."

I kiss over his collarbones, down his chest as I aim to go even lower, but I make a quick detour and suck one of his nipples into my mouth.

The lower I go, kissing every inch of his gorgeous muscles, the shakier his exhales become. When I push him to sit on the edge of his bed and I kneel between his knees, he might as well be barely breathing.

Grey lifts his hips as I hook my fingers into his boxers and tug on the fabric. I slide them down his legs, throwing the boxers somewhere behind me.

Once he sits naked before me, I allow myself a moment to admire him. My eyes travel from his handsome face, down his neck, his pecs. And after they find that perfectly defined V, pointing right to where I know he wants my mouth, my eyes land on his hard cock.

"I was going to suck you off, but now I no longer think that's necessary," I say and take in his heavy, full balls.

"Try me."

I smirk up at him through my lashes. "You just want my mouth on your dick."

Grey nods, then reaches a hand into my hair to guide me right toward his thick, hard cock. "I do, but I want to be inside you about twice as bad."

With a chuckle rolling off my tongue, I lean forward and lick the head of his cock, then wrap my hand around the length of him. Grey hisses in response, the hand in my hair tightens right away.

I wish I could enjoy this a little more, tease him for quite some time, but we have a timer hanging over our heads, and I'd rather not have either of Grey's family members interrupt us. Still, we definitely have time for a *little* teasing.

I close my lips around the head of his dick, swiping my tongue over the slit. When I suck, Grey bucks his hips, trying to force himself deeper into my mouth but that's when I pull my head away.

Our eyes meet; his are filled with lust, a kind of fire that only ever ignites when we're together. He never even gives me that bad case of horny eyes when we're jerking off together over the phone.

His breathing comes out ragged, whimpery when I blow some air onto his warm tip before taking his dick deeper into my mouth, licking along his length.

"Luan…" Grey pulls onto my hair, once again shifting his hips to push himself deeper into my mouth. This time, I let him.

His cock hits the very back of my throat causing my eyes to fill with water. I just want to suck him dry, but if I do that, this will be over, and I really don't want this to be over yet.

So I allow myself a couple more seconds, a few more strokes and licks, a few more seconds of listening to Grey moan and tremble beneath my touch, a few more moments of him fucking my mouth as though it's the only thing that's keeping him alive right now.

I cup his balls, add the slightest amount of pressure as I gently massage them, earning myself a raspy "*Fuck*."

When I feel his balls tighten in my hand, I remove my mouth from his dick and stand. My own cock throbs with the need to come.

"I hate you," Grey grits out, groaning at the loss of my mouth around him.

I grin at my boyfriend while I shuck off my pants as well as my underwear. "You absolutely love me."

Grey shakes his head, but he stops complaining when our lips lock and I push my tongue right back into his mouth. Nothing feels as right as having my mouth pressed to his.

I sit on his lap, thread my hands into his hair while I try not to come with his hands on my ass. It's rude, really. It takes ages to get Grey off, and I didn't even allow him to touch me and I'm still so close to coming, it's embarrassing.

Only when Grey circles a finger around my hole do I realize something. "We don't have lube." I know it's technically possible to do it without lube, but I'd rather not.

Grey chuckles into our next kiss, then lifts me up like I weigh nothing at all before he lies me down on his bed. Hovering over me, Grey kisses my neck, my jaw, then my lips again.

He reaches toward his bedside table, opening the drawer.

"Grey, whatever you have in there, I'm sure it's been expired for *years*." Especially since he moved out at the age of eighteen.

"Nah, I asked Sun to put some there earlier."

"WHAT?!" I rip my eyes wide open, feeling my own cheeks flush with embarrassment. There is *no* way Grey asked his sister to put lube into his bedside drawer.

He laughs and pulls out a small bottle of lube. "Don't worry, I bought it and put it here myself. Took a quick detour home when I came to visit the last time."

Oh… okay. That's at least a little better.

"Hm, so you planned to fuck me here, huh?" I smirk and wrap my arms around his neck, his chest now pressed flush to mine. "I'm glad I can help you make a dream come true."

"Oh, shut up."

"Or else?"

He grinds his cock against mine, rubbing up against me as he guides his lips back to mine to kiss me long and deep. It's almost long enough to make me forget I asked because all I can focus on is the way his dick feels rubbing against mine, so lazily yet just right. The way his tongue feels when it slides against mine, tasting me.

When we come up for some air, Grey sits back and slicks his fingers up with some lube. "Spread your legs for me, baby." I do, and he brings his hand down to run his fingers along my crease until he reaches my hole. The cold gel makes me gasp, but not quite as much as the feeling when Grey adds pressure to enter me.

I welcome the burn, but the stroke on my cock Grey uses to distract me from it even more.

Grey pushes his finger in and out of me, slowly at first, then a little faster, adding another finger to stretch me to where he needs me.

When he teases my prostate, a loud moan spills out of me to which Grey, once again, presses his lips to mine in order to silence me.

"You've got to keep quiet, baby," he whispers. "Can you do that for me?"

I nod, though I'm honestly not so sure about that. I'd do *anything* for Grey Davis, but it's about whether I can physically do it, not mentally.

Once he adds a third finger, my mouth stands open with a silent, needy cry. My exhales leave me short and shaky, my dick aching with need.

"Please…" My balls are so tight with the urge to come that it hurts. "I need you, Grey Davis…"

Grey reaches for the lube once more, covering his dick with it before he moves back over me. He starts to push inside me, slow, then all at once. His hips meet my ass and I gasp, followed by a moan that Grey tones down by kissing me. Again. But who am I to complain about his kisses?

I wrap my legs around his waist to pull him down to me, forcing his torso to collide with mine. His shallow, heavy breaths fan over my skin, his nose brushes mine, our foreheads touch.

"You're so tight." He thrusts a bit deeper inside of me. "So fucking tight."

I never know if that is a good or bad thing, but I think he likes it because he pounds into me a little harder, then reaches between our bodies and wraps his hand around my cock, jerking me off.

With each thrust, each time he teases my prostate and the friction on my dick, he's edging me closer to an orgasm I'm not quite sure I'm ready for just yet, but at the same time am longing for.

Our eyes lock, then he smiles at me and that's it.

I come so hard I see stars, cum spurts out of me without an ending in sight and covers my abs.

I'm so high up in the clouds that I only half realize when Grey collapses on top of me, coming inside of me. I do, however, close my arms around his neck and hold him.

He breathes heavily, trying to calm himself down. A soft sigh leaves him, though I'm not sure he even notices it. Then I can feel him leave a kiss right behind my ear, melting even the last bits of my body that were still solid.

Fuck, I love him so much and he has absolutely no clue. Yes, he knows I love him, but he could never imagine what I'm willing to do to keep him in my life forever.

"We should take a shower before…"

Grey groans. "You think my father would have a stroke if he knew I just fucked you in his house?"

"Probably."

"I kind of want to see how that'd play out."

Honestly, me too. "Get your ass up, Grey Davis, and show me where your shower is because there is *no* way I will meet your mother smelling like sex."

Grey does get off the bed, and while he's turned with his back toward me, I make a discovery that I'm surprised I haven't made before.

"What does MDK stand for?"

"Miles Desrosiers-King." Grey faces me. He then draws my attention to a tattoo just above the inside of his left arm. It's a child-like stick figure drawing of two guys, I assume. "Miles and I were a little drunk when we got them. The stick figures are cute, Brooke drew them when she was three. I don't know why we thought getting the other's initials tattooed on our assess would be a good idea, though. I don't mind it too much because I can't even see it."

"I knew you were close, but I had no idea you were *this* close." I wish I never asked. Do you think they had dated once upon a time? Should I be worried!?

Grey wraps an arm around my shoulders and leads me into his bathroom.

"Nothing ever happened between Miles and I. We did dumb stuff together, things that almost got us arrested, or, well, got a stupid tattoo when we were wasted. I promise you, there's nothing to worry about."

Chapter 3

"you've spent a lifetime stuck in silence / afraid you'll say something wrong"—Read All About It, pt. III by Emeli Sandé

Juan

February 2026

GREY AND I ENTER THEIR LIBRARY. A fucking *library*. He's not talking much as we walk through the house, he answers when I ask questions, but that's usually how our conversations go.

"Did you read a lot as a kid?" Surely if your parents own a whole ass library, you spend a good time being forced to read those books. Or maybe not, who knows?

Grey nods. "If I had the time. I spent most of my days at the arena even if I didn't have to be there. And if I wasn't there, I got a book and went down to the beach and read."

My heart is breaking for that little boy who just wanted to know why he was feeling the way he did. Unfortunately, he had the kind of father figure who wasn't even trying to help him, trying to comfort him. Instead, that father figure was beating him down for something Grey could never have influenced.

Nobody wakes up one day and is like "Welp, I guess I *want* to like boys now". You don't decide on who you fall in love with, it just happens. Love doesn't have a gender.

"Is your mother's last name the same as your dad's?" I don't want to accidentally call her the wrong name.

Grey shakes his head. "It's Han. She kept her last name,

which is not that unusual. Moon, Sun, and I would've taken my dad's last name, but like I told you, my dad wanted us kids to not be associated with Li Co. unless we wanted to. And since people know our mother thanks to Dad, we had to get a whole new name."

"Okay." We walk through one of the rows of bookshelves. Yes, one of the rows. It truly looks like a library in here. With rows and rows of shelves filled with older books but also newer ones.

Grey suddenly stops in his tracks, causing me to bump into him. He turns around and clears his throat. "If you plan on using my dad's full name, you have to say the last name first," he tells me. "You always go Ji-Hoon Li, but it's supposed to be Li Ji-Hoon. I never corrected you because I never thought you'd meet him anyway, so I didn't bother with it. But now that you might meet him, if you say it in the wrong order, Dad's going to throw you out faster than he will when I tell him we're a couple."

Oh, well… that does absolutely nothing to ease my nerves. I mean, I wasn't planning on using Li's first name in front of him, but that's good to know anyway. "What about your mom?"

"Han Eun."

I nod slowly.

"So every time I say your name in what is the correct order for me, it's wrong?" I note. "I'm supposed to say Davis Grey?"

"Technically, but nobody does that. And I happen to think Grey Davis sounds a whole lot better than the other way around. Also, I didn't really grow up with my own culture. I lived here my whole life and Dad always kept us as far away from our roots as humanly possible. He believed that the more 'Korean' we were, the more we would've gotten hated on. It's bullshit, like a whole lot that leaves this guy's mouth."

It really is bullshit. Even if Grey grew up feeling more connected to his culture, that wouldn't have mattered. As long as he doesn't look like the average American, there are still going to be people who hate on him for looking Asian. Getting to know the culture behind his genes wouldn't have changed a damn thing.

"You speak Korean though, right?" I think I sort of hinted at that question before, but I'm not sure. No, I did. When I asked about his tattoos, but he never confirmed if he actually spoke the language.

"I do."

That's at least something. "My mom never taught me Arabic," I tell him. I know Grey hates when we only ever talk about him, and I fear he will shut down very soon. "But she also doesn't speak Arabic sooooo,... I guess that's why. She understands it, but she doesn't speak it, if you know what I mean? I don't have any connections to Morocco except that my mom was born there and that my great grandparents lived there. My grandparents, however, moved from Morocco to Malibu after my mom was born, and then sometime later my mom met my dad and then there was me. The best human on earth."

Grey snorts a laugh, disagreeing with me. "I don't think there's something such as *the best human*."

"Uh, yes. You're looking at him?" I point at myself with both of my index fingers. "You're my boyfriend, Grey Davis. You're supposed to feel like I am the best human on earth, especially when I am blessing your life with my presence."

He shoves me away, a hint of a laughter bubbling in his throat, I can see it. I love making Grey laugh, even if he tries to suppress it every single time.

"I think a week of isolation made you even cockier."

Huh. "Cocky or narcissistic?" I ask, genuinely wanting to know which one it is.

Grey sighs. We both know the answer even without him saying it.

Shit. Shit. Shit.

Why do I keep on doing this? I don't want to be like this, dammit. I'll be twenty-seven years old tomorrow, I should be able to say things without making me out to be... the best person alive.

"Luan," Grey says and lifts my face to his. "It's okay. You've been doing so great, one setback isn't going to ruin everything."

Have I though? Grey's not around a lot, how could he be so sure about me doing great? I tried showing him the best side of me from the very first second. I have been trying to be on my best behavior around him from the day we met.

But I did stop myself from seeking out the validation of Grey's friends before. It might've been a small step in a long time, but it was a step.

"Are you sure meeting my dad is a good idea?" His eyes filling with concern. "I can promise you, he isn't going to like you, and I know how badly you'll want him to."

"Yes," I answer. "I don't care if he likes me because I don't like him. I love you, Grey Davis, and that's more than enough. I don't need to be liked by a man who would rather put his own son through hell, than accept him the way he is." I mean, my parents love me through all I've done. They loved me even when they found out that I was a manipulator.

If my parents could do that, Grey's father should be able to love Grey even when he's not *straight*. And trust me, being a fucked-up person is far worse than falling in love with *people* rather than a gender.

"Okay," he breathes out heavily. I'm not sure if he's more nervous for me to meet his parents, or if I am. From the looks of it, it's him.

Grey pulls out his phone from his pocket, ready to call his parents, I guess?

"You're *calling* them? I thought I was going to meet them in person."

He nods. "I'm calling my mom, asking her to come here. I'm not going to let you meet them at the same time because if that happens, my mother won't have an opinion."

That's... a whole lot of fucked up. If my father tried to silence my mother, she would slap him and put him in his place.

"Mom," Grey says, his voice filled with nerves. "If Dad's with you right now, pretend I'm not calling, okay? If he asks, say I'm Moon."

What? Now that's even more fucked up.

"I'm in the library. Can you come here?" He pauses for a second, then adds, "Without Dad." Shortly after, he hangs up the phone. "I hope he's going to let her leave."

"I hope you all know that *this* is so wrong. Your mother shouldn't fear your dad." Maybe I shouldn't have said this. Their family problems aren't my problems. I'm in no position to judge them and how they choose to live their lives.

"She doesn't fear him," Grey speaks quietly, and bobs his head softly. I'm not sure this nod is to agree with me anyway or tells me to fuck off. Probably a tad of both.

Then we can hear the doors open as a voice about an octave deeper than Sun's says, "Grey?"

Grey grasps my hand, pulls me back down that aisle before we round the corner. And there she stands, Grey's mother. She has the same black hair as he does, the same eyes. Sun has the *exact* same face. She's a lot smaller than Grey is, but most mothers are smaller than their sons. Mrs. Han wears a long sage green dress, it looks like it's satin but I'm not sure. The short arms of the dress are poofy.

Who wears a formal dress like this when they're at home?

But what's more shocking to me, Mrs. Han looks like she's maybe thirty, but she's not, that I know. I want to look that young in my late forties.

Grey lets go of my hand, then closes the gap between his mother and him, pulling her into his embrace. I hear them speak, but I don't understand a single word.

When they pull apart, Grey turns to face me again. He inhales deeply, then leads his mother that tiny bit closer to me before he says, "Mom, this is Luan. My boyfriend."

Mrs. Han smiles at me and holds out her hand. I take it.

"Mrs. Han," I say but she shakes her head immediately,

confusing me. I swear Grey told me that's her last name.

"Call me Eun."

Oh. Okay, yeah I did not expect that to happen.

I look at Grey to find him smiling. And when Eun sees it, she gasps and covers her mouth with one hand.

"You're smiling." Eun brings a hand to her son's face, drawing her thumb over the smile-lines by his mouth as if to make sure she's not seeing things. Is this the first time she sees him smile in a *long* time?

She then looks at me. "You're making him smile?"

"Yeah, I happen to think I'm the funniest person on earth, Grey disagrees though. But, still he smiles and laughs a whole lot more these days," I answer. "At least once a day."

"Laughs?" She says it like that's something Grey is incapable of doing. When she looks back at Grey, she says something in Korean. I think it's a question because Grey nods in response.

"Yes, Mom," he confirms, "Luan makes me happy."

I make him happy.

I, as in me, Luan Hayes, makes Grey Davis *happy*.

I noticed that he smiles more often, or that he talks more than when we first met. But I didn't think that was *because* of me. I thought he's just showing me the side he's been showing his friends for years.

Eun is smiling, until she isn't and her face pales. "You're not here to tell your father, are you?"

Grey was wrong. There *is* fear in his mother. Fear of her husband and what he'll do to Grey when this man finds out about me.

When Grey doesn't respond, his mother shakes her head. "Grey, you can't. He's going to..." she looks at me then back at Grey, continuing her sentence in Korean so I wouldn't understand.

"I know. That's why I wanted to see you before we told him," Grey says. I'm just going to assume this is about Grey's dad disowning his own son. "I'll never see or speak to you again, I know that. But Mom, I choose my happiness this time. I can't let Dad continue to control my life, and I won't let him decide over who I get to love. It shouldn't have to be this way but leaving my own family behind is my *only* chance of being happy."

A tear slips from Eun's eyes, but she looks proud of him. "I understand." She gives me a slim smile. "You look out for him, okay?"

"I will. I promise."

I wish I could say that Grey shouldn't have to do this. I wish I could say that he should've never told his parents about me because then he'd at least still have the potential of them in his life. If we break up one day, which I doubt, he could always go back but he won't be able to after today.

But the reason why I can't say either of those is because even if it wasn't for me right now, Grey still had to do this for himself. He'll never be happy if he keeps his father in his life, lets that man control him. Even if this wasn't for and about me, as fucked up as it is, Grey *had* to make that cut.

No kid should ever have to do this.

Chapter 4

"I guess that I forgot I had a choice"—Roar by Katy Perry

Grey

February 2026

I KNEW MY MOTHER would like Luan, there was never a doubt in my mind about that one. Mom just wants to see me happy, and as long as I am, so is she, which is why I know she really understands that I have to cut off my family. Or at least the ones who will leave once my father cuts *me* off.

Even if I didn't have Luan in my life right now and I'd been doing this for him, this is exactly what should happen; cutting off the people in my life who'll always hold me back.

As much as I'd wish it was different, my father will forever be keeping me from being happy. He'll always make me feel bad for who I am.

According to my mother, Dad's in his office so that's where we're headed now. I told my mom she doesn't have to be there, but she keeps insisting to come with us, not quite sure why. The second my dad sees Luan, he's going to be a breath away from getting verbally abusive with me and it'll only be a matter of time for him to insult me, my mother's presence won't change much.

By the time we reach my father's office, I'm not sure how I'm still breathing. I'm not nervous, and still my hands are shaking. I think it's fear that's causing my nerves to go nuts, fear that's pushing adrenaline through my veins.

"We can leave, you know?" Luan says and squeezes my hand for comfort. "If you're not ready, it's okay. You don't have to introduce me to him."

I shake my head. "I have to do this, Luan. It's not about introducing you, this is about taking back control over my own life." He could leave if he wanted to, but even if I suggested it, Luan wouldn't go. He would stay right here with me.

Luan lifts our hands to his mouth and presses a kiss to my knuckles. It's cute, really, and still I have this urge to laugh because I know he only did it because my mother is here with us, watching us. If she wasn't here, he would've kissed me instead.

So I lean down and press a quick kiss right to his lips. "I love you."

Luan smiles up at me. "More than ice hockey?"

I let go of his hand immediately and take a step back. "Now, let's not get ridiculous here." I do love him more than ice hockey, but if I said that, it wouldn't do any good for his ego, let alone the baby narcissist inside of him.

"It was worth a try." Luan sighs. "I love you, too."

My mother chuckles and when I look at her, I see nothing but happiness on that face.

I take another few encouraging breaths before I finally knock on my father's office door.

"Come in," he snaps from inside the room. The tone of his voice makes me want to back off and leave, but I can't. I'm doing this for myself, and it's about goddamn time I do it.

So I open the door, not yet stepping inside.

My father looks up from his laptop screen, then down but back up in seconds like he's taking a second look to make sure he's seeing *me*. "I didn't know you were coming home."

"I didn't know I would either."

"Well, come on in."

I don't want to, but I do so anyway. With one quick glance at Luan, I step inside, pulling him after me. Once my dad sees Luan, his features turn to ice. He sends a more than disgusted look into

Luan's direction, fire burning in his eyes, and I swear if looks could kill, my father just burned my boyfriend alive.

"Jesus," I hear Luan mutter under his breath, quiet enough so my father wouldn't hear. He squeezes my hand, only then making me realize I am even holding his.

However, I shake off my fear, clear my throat and say, "Dad, this is my *boy*friend." Again, I leave out Luan's name for a reason. The second my father learns his name, he will try to drag it through mud, and I'd rather not have him do that. I'm not sure my father knows who Luan is, that he's the son of the CEO of his rival company, but on the off chance that he doesn't, why give my father more fuel to light this whole world up in flames?

He scoffs, nodding slowly. "Boyfriend," he repeats back to me with venom. He knows my relationship with Luan is serious because I have never *seriously* introduced anyone to my father, hence why he doesn't pretend to be okay with this. He won't yell at me *after* Luan leaves like he did with every other guy I've ever brought home, he won't pretend to be a nice man.

"You're twenty-six, Grey!" he yells. *I'm twenty-five, as of now*. "Your stupid little gay-phase was supposed to end with *College!*"

"It was—"

"I am talking, Grey!" *Of course*. "When I talk, you listen."

Yeah, how dare I speak?

He waits… like I'm supposed to say something now. "Oh, am I—"

"SHUT YOUR MOUTH!"

Well, okay then.

From the corner of my eye, I can see Luan turning his head to look at me, but I don't have a death wish, so I don't look back just yet. Who knows, if I do, my father might as well throw a knife at me. I do, however, squeeze Luan's hand to let him know I'm okay.

I expected this. The yelling. The insults that surprisingly haven't come yet. Getting disowned.

"You have a career, Grey." My father looks at Luan but back at me a second later. It's like he can't even look at my boyfriend without having to throw up. I'm sure he feels the same way about me. "What is the NFL going to say?"

"N*H*L," I correct. "I play ice hockey, not football." Moon used to play football when he was in high school, but never beyond that.

He waves a hand around. "So? Excuse me for being such an awful father just because I can't get one abbreviation correctly. But of course that makes me the bad guy. You're the good one, you don't make mistakes. You're perfect." *I want to punch him.* "What do you think is going to happen when the N*H*L finds out that they have a gay guy amongst them? In a team filled with other men!"

I pinch the bridge of my nose. "I am not gay," I tell him for probably the millionth time in twelve years. I don't know why I keep on trying to make him understand because I know it's useless. No matter how often I tell him that I don't just like men, that I don't put a fucking label on myself, to him, unless I am straight, I am gay.

"But you have a boyfriend," he says with disgust. "So you're gay. You're such a disgrace, a disgusting piece of shit. What do they call people like you… a fa—?"

Before he gets the chance to finish that word, I allow myself to cut him off. "Is that the only word you know that's offensive toward *people like me*? You can't insult me any other way, do you really have to revert back to degrading my sexuality just because you don't see eye-to-eye with me?" In order to keep myself from jumping over that table and punching my own father, I take a deep breath and ball my hands into fists.

He ignores me, but of course he would. He got the reaction from me that he wanted, made me feel degraded, so that ends the conversation. My father looks from me to Luan, rolling his eyes. "You made my son gay," he accuses.

Oh, okay, so now that he's done with me, he moves over to

Luan.

Luan cocks his head and as it seems, he's about to explode more than I thought he would. "With all due respect, sir,"—he points at himself—"I didn't do that." He looks at me again, then back at my father. "Nobody can make anyone gay, that's not how this works. But how would you know?"

Luan lets go of my hand, and for a second there, I panic, even more when he takes a step closer to my father. It feels like there's no oxygen making it to my brain, like my blood is pumping through my veins a little faster yet at the same time it's running cold and freezes.

"Take another step and—"

"And what?" Luan laughs. "If you lay a hand on me, or even just try to threaten me, you'll end up in jail. You might have tons of lawyers supporting your ass, but so do I. And your wannabe charming ways won't do much this time, want to know why?"

Uh oh.

This was a bad idea. Not finally taking control over my own life but bringing Luan. I should've known this would happen. You can't put two people with narcissistic tendencies in one room together and expect it to go smoothly. Especially when one of them hates you and the other one somehow loves you.

"You can pretend to be the victim here, but I can do it a million times better." Luan chuckles at the more-or-less stunned expression from my father. Said expression quickly vanishes when he realizes. "What? You're not used to people talking back, huh? Especially someone younger than you. Oh, the disrespect on my part. Not only am I gay and very much venomous as I have apparently infected your son with my gayness, but I also talk. How dare I?"

"I don't want you here," my father spits out, now clutching his hands around the edge of his desk.

"Aw, but I was just getting comfortable." Luan takes a seat on the chair on the opposite side of my father, humming like all of this is a game to him. He leans back, makes himself comfortable. "What's that? Fake or real leather?" Luan runs a finger over the material of the chair. "Judging you, probably real leather, but I think you'd rather skin your *'gay' son* than animals, am I right?"

My father straight up *growls* at Luan, to which my boyfriend, once again, laughs.

"Wow, we're a real animal lover then, I see."

I lay my hands on Luan's shoulders to get his attention. Some part of me fears he's too far gone in his head that he won't even care, but he surprises me when he leans his head back to look up at me. Luan's eyes are soft, and he offers me one of his signature smiles, the sweet ones. That's the only sign he gives me to let me know that he's fine, that he *knows* what he's doing and didn't just fall back into an old habit.

"We can go," I suggest. There's no use in arguing any further anyway. My dad now knows I am in a relationship with Luan, he'll want me out of his life and that's alright because I don't want him in mine either.

"It's just getting interesting."

Yeah, which is why we should definitely leave. I don't want to trigger Luan's manipulative side any more than it already has. I trust Luan that he won't fall back there, but why push his luck?

"Baby…"

"Be gay outside of my house!" my father yells, hitting a hand to the surface of his desk.

I lift my head, my eyes meet my father's for a moment. I smirk, dip my head back down, and press a kiss to my boyfriend's lips. I can feel the corners of Luan's mouth tug up against mine.

Both of our smiles widen when we can hear my father gag.

As soon as we pull apart and I straighten my back, I find my father staring past me and toward the door. When his eyes darken by a whole shade, I know he found my mother.

"And you are okay with this, Eun?"

She doesn't respond at first, so I'm assuming she's shaking

her head. I don't turn around to get confirmation because I know my mother doesn't care whether I date a woman or a man, but seeing her say no just because she knows that's what my father wants would hurt me more than I'd like to admit.

"Yes," she says, which then does cause me to whip my whole body around, my eyes colliding with hers.

"What?" I choke on the word. My mother smiles.

"I don't think you're okay with your son dating another *man*, Eun," my father forces out through gritted teeth.

"It's none of my business, but even if it was, I am," she answers, averting her eyes from me to my dad. The smile that was on her lips just a second ago is now gone. "I am, Ji-Hoon, because unlike you, I don't care who Grey loves, nor is it any of my business. He's my son and I will love him no matter what."

She takes a few steps toward my father. My eyes follow her, but my head is somewhere I don't even know. *I* was supposed to "rebel" against my father, not my mother.

Luan gets up from the chair, standing beside me in seconds.

"Grey is no less of a human just because he has a boyfriend rather than a girlfriend. And I don't know what is wrong in your head, Ji-Hoon, to even think for *one* second that only because you don't want to believe your son could ever love another man, that he wouldn't."

"Mom…" Why would she do this? She's been silent about all of this for almost fourteen years, has never stood up to my father whether it was about me, my siblings, or herself. So why start now?

My mother holds up her hand, stopping me from talking.

"Maybe you—"

"How dare you?" my father interrupts. "How—"

My mother slaps her hand to his desk, leaning forward. In a dangerously low voice, she says, "I am talking, Ji-Hoon. When I talk, you listen."

"I don't li—"

My mother takes my father's laptop, then throws it against the wall behind him.

If I was capable of moving, my jaw would be on the floor right now, but it's as though I'm frozen in place. I didn't know my mother had a side like this to her. But I suppose it's good to know that my tendencies to throw stuff around when I get mad, I inherited from her.

"You will listen, or the next thing I will ruin is your company." She straightens her back, wiping off her hands like she was brushing off dust.

"You wouldn't dare."

"Try me, Ji-Hoon. Interrupt me one more time and find out if I dare." Right now, I wouldn't put it past her to have some kind of evidence against him that could potentially ruin his image and Li Co.

Luan moves closer to me, so close that our shoulders brush. "What is happening?" he whispers, carefully sneaking his hand into mine.

"I honestly don't know."

I came here to tell my dad that I have a boyfriend, I did that. And I was ready to fight for my life, but as it seems, my mother is taking that battle for me.

My mother never raised her voice before, at least not that I know of it. She never stuck up to my father, always allowed him to treat her however he wanted.

"May I proceed then?" She waits a moment for my father to stop her. He doesn't. "Alright then. Have you ever considered seeking out help, Ji-Hoon? Though, I don't think anyone could ever help you. You think you're oh so powerful, that you own the world, and yet the thought of people loving *whoever they want* frightens you. It's such a small thing, don't you think? When I married you, I never would've thought *love* would be your downfall. That *love* would be what would eventually end our marriage."

End their—WHAT?

"Eun—" He stops talking when my mother cocks her head. I

don't see her face, but honestly, I'm glad I can't because just standing here in this room, hearing her voice being as icy as ever, gives me goosebumps

"You pretend to be such a great and tough man, and I think you're honestly good at *pretending*, at manipulating people into thinking you truly are. And since nobody would ever tell you this, allow me." She lays her hands back down onto my father's desk, leaning forward one more time. "You are a whiny little *boy*, Ji-Hoon. You are a disgrace to humankind. You *disgust* me. For the life of me, I cannot understand how there are people out there *liking* you, because you have got to be the worst human I have *ever* met. People like you are the reason why others feel like they will never be good enough, that something is wrong with them. People like you are the reason why others *kill* themselves because they cannot take the constant hatred anymore. I don't know how you can be proud of yourself, how you can look in the mirror and be okay with what you see, how you can be okay with the person you are. I don't know how you wake up every day and think you're such a great guy. You're not, nor will you ever be."

My father opens his mouth as if to speak but once again, my mother goes first. "Last drawer." She nods toward his desk. "Sign the papers. Now."

The... *papers*? She tried divorcing him before?! Why am I only hearing of it now?

"Eun, think about—"

"I have," she cuts him off. "I've asked you to sign them four years ago. I gave you *more* than enough time to sort your shit out. I am done waiting. And I am done letting you walk all over my children. I should've packed our bags and left you the moment you *discussed* sending Grey off to some stupid camp ages ago. I should've had enough strength to stick up for him back then. Unfortunately you made that impossible for me, and it broke my heart every time I looked at Grey, every day that sweet and innocent smile of his faded more and more. While you were too grossed out to look at him, I was crying for him. I didn't have the opportunity, let alone the capacity to leave you and raise three children on my own. But I prayed with every single passing day that something would happen to you so all three of them were free of you." She clears her throat and wipes away her tears like they're not continuing to roll down cheeks anyway. "Sign the damn papers, Ji-Hoon."

"I am not going to sign those papers."

"You are. Otherwise I will get the police involved, and I'm not sure physically abusing your wife will look great in your records."

Physically... WHAT?! I knew my father was mentally abusing all four of us, but I didn't know he laid his hands on my mother even once.

"Nobody will believe you," he spits out, leaning back in his chair with a smug smile on his ugly face like he believes he won this fight.

My mother smiles, but it's not a soft or gentle smile, it's devious. It's the kind of smile I have never seen on my mother before, revengeful, dangerous. "No? You don't think the pictures of my bruises, the security footage of you beating me, and the voice notes of your threats will be enough proof? Let alone Sun having witnessed most of it all?"

Sun has? Why the fuck didn't she say anything? I could've helped. I would've gotten her out of here, made Mom move to New York with me.

"I could also throw out some statements, give an interview and tell them the truth about you. Plus, your beloved investor, Atlas Storm, remember him? He's just waiting for the day I reach out to him so he can take you down."

I fucking hope she does that even when he signs those papers.

The muscle in my father's jaw twitches before he bends over and opens his drawer, takes out a bunch of papers then lays them out on his desk. He grabs a pen, signs page after page. The second he sets down the pen, I walk over to my father's desk and take the papers from him.

I'm about to walk away, but there's *one* more thing that I cannot stop myself from doing.

Without even realizing it, I launch my fist right into his face. It stings in my hand, but I welcome the pain. Fuck, I think I wanted to punch my dad ever since he sent me off to that stupid church camp, and now I finally did it.

"If you so much as try and reach out to Mom again, find out what happens." He may have tons of lawyers on his side, but as it seems, my mother has a much more powerful guy on hers, one who's apparently been waiting for the day he gets to take my father down.

Not looking back once, my father not trying to hold us back either, we leave the office, setting an end to a story that should've been stopped the moment the first letter was written.

There are a million more things I'd love to say to my father, a million things that wouldn't even come close to the way he made me feel throughout my entire life. But even those million things wouldn't change much. I could ask him why he can't like me, can't accept me, but all it would do is to drag me further down. I could call him so many names, drag his name through mud like he did mine, but I am better than that. I deserve to put this past me, live in the present rather than the potential future he wanted to create, or my past.

I can decide to hold a grudge, be angry at my father for the rest of my life, or I let it go, accept all of this, and live the rest of my life the way *I* want to.

Frankly, the latter seems a whole lot calmer, more peaceful.

Once the door to my father's office is closed, I turn to my mother. I lay my hands on her shoulders, making her look at me. "He *beat* you?"

She doesn't confirm with her voice, but she doesn't have to either. Mom lets out a shaky breath before a sob breaks free and she falls right into my arms. "I'm sorry."

"Mom…" All this time, I knew my mother wasn't living the happy life she deserved. I knew she was battling an inner war, unsure of who to side with; my father or me. I knew why she always chose him, or so I thought.

I thought she chose him over and over again because a divorce would mean she failed. In the eyes of our family, *her* family, she'd be a disgrace, she'd get shamed. I thought she chose my father because if she got shamed, Moon, Sun, and I would've gotten looked down on by our family as well. I thought she didn't know how to care for us the way my father's money allowed it.

But I didn't think he was being physically violent with her.

"Sun didn't come home because she had problems at school, did she?" There are tons of other questions I should ask first. Or maybe not. All I should be doing is to be there for my mother when she clearly needs me right now.

"No."

Of course not. With the last of my parents' children gone, my father could do anything with my mother without either of us ever finding out. I wouldn't have come back home, my mother knew that. I would've made her come to me, but never in my life would I have moved back into this house, under one roof with my father.

Moon is the least reliable of us. He is almost ninety percent our father, so I don't think he would've cared much.

Hence why it had to be Sun.

"Come to New York with me," I say. I don't know where my mom thinks she can stay now, but it sure as fuck won't be this house anymore. She'll always have a place with me. I have a spare bedroom, and I'm barely at home anyway. So until she found something… "We can look for apartments there, Mom. I don't want you here with Dad, or anywhere near him."

"I can't. Sun is—"

"She can move, too. She's done with college. I'll get her an apartment somewhere close by, but until then, I bet she can stay with Emory and Miles." I look up to see where Luan's at, only to find him leaning against one of the walls, looking at my mom and me. When he notices me looking, he smiles a little, then winks. "I'll get you a hotel room for tonight."

"They can stay with us, you know? I have a spare bedroom," Luan says, now receiving a *very* confused frown from me. He laughs. "You really thought Doro, Sarah, and I didn't have one? I lied."

Of course he did. "Doesn't surprise me anymore." Luan from two years ago did *everything* to get me close to him, even lying about a spare bedroom, apparently.

"Well, would you have slept in my bed had I told you I had one?" Luan pushes himself off the wall at the same time as my mother pulls herself out of my embrace.

Mom sniffles and before she could excuse herself, Luan pulls out a tissue from his pocket and hands it to my mother with a smile.

"You are such an inspiration, Eun," he says. "I'm telling you, if your son ever does me wrong, I will come to you so you can break up with him for me."

My mother laughs through her tears. "If my son ever does you wrong, I will first have to find out what kind of alien he's gotten exchanged for because Grey would never intentionally hurt anyone like that."

Luan hums, slowly bobbing his head. "Nah, do you know what he did?" He sighs dramatically, then lays a hand over my mother's shoulders as we back away from my father's office. "The first time we met, Grey refused to tell me his name. I was *heartbroken*, let me tell you. Because there he was in all his glory, sitting by that beach, reading a porn book—"

I slap my hand to the back of his head. "It wasn't a *porn* book."

"Oh, no, no, Eun, it was. Don't believe Grey. He was reading straight up porn. Anyway…"

Chapter 5

"we are a secret, can't be exposed"—Uncover by Zara Larsson

Iwan

September 2026

"YOU'RE HERE," Grey says with a hint of surprise in his voice. Actually, he's all icy as ever when anyone else is around, but I can hear the surprise.

"I am," I confirm, smiling at my boyfriend as he slowly and cautiously closes the space between us. "It's your first game as captain, baby. I know how important this is for you. Of course I am here." It may only be a charity game tonight, but a game is a game, right? And it's his birthday soooo…

Grey looks around us, probably to check if it's alright if he either hugs or kisses me now, I am praying for both. He still hasn't made our relationship public, which I'm not sure is good or bad.

There's a good part; privacy and Grey not getting attacked for being now the captain of the New York Rangers and queer. Apparently if some jock is anything but straight and plays for the pros, it's a crime.

But then there's the downside, too. Sneaking around, pretending that we're not madly in love. He won't even hug me in public. I can live with not holding my boyfriend's hand when we walk down a street, but the fact that being seen with him stirs up rumors is annoying, especially when I haven't seen Grey in weeks and all I get as a greeting is a nod from afar like at the Stanley Cup finals back in June.

I flew out to Tampa to be there for my boyfriend, but I didn't get to *speak* to him until he was in his hotel room, and I *snuck* in.

He's mainly keeping our relationship on the downlow because of his father. His parents' divorce trial has just recently been closed. It's bad enough the divorce went public, and although nobody technically knows Grey is their son, he didn't want any more *negative* headlines for his family, and didn't want to put more eyes on them as they already had.

There's one good thing though, Grey says—I think it's a bad thing—the public didn't find out the real reason for the divorce. All they know is that Eun and Ji-Hoon decided to go separate ways due to difficulties in their relationship. If I had any say in this, I would've told the whole truth about the divorce and make that man pay, but it wasn't my decision to make.

Grey reaches for my hands, takes them in his. *So I guess that's a no for both hugging and kissing.* "How long are you staying?"

I shrug. "How long do you want me to stay?" I've got time. Just a few days ago, I announced to my soccer teams that I will no longer be their coach by the end of the year as I am moving across the country to be with my boyfriend. It was painful as fuck, but I am excited to move in with Grey next January.

"The season starts tomorrow…"

"I know." I googled it. Okay, I could've asked my boyfriend when exactly their first *actual* season-related game is, but I was a little embarrassed to be honest. Sometimes I feel like I know nothing at all about what Grey's passionate about. Granted, I really don't, and it doesn't interest me at all, but I *am* interested in my boyfriend and what he loves, so I want to know about it. And maybe I want to impress him a little with knowing more than what he tells me.

"I won't be home a lot."

"If this is your way of telling me I should leave tonight, Grey Davis, then just say it." I know he has a lot going on recently, especially with his parents' divorce. Sun and their mother are still looking for separate apartments in New York. They moved into one together, but it's neither very great nor ideal as Sun also wants her privacy. Apparently trying to find a place to live in New York City that's affordable and in good shape is pretty difficult. I do know Grey offered to pay for their apartments, but both his mother and Sun declined his offer.

So he's a little stressed about that.

Grey surprises me when his eyes soften and fill with something painful. "That's not it... I want you to stay, Luan." Then, like he doesn't care about someone possibly seeing us, Grey pulls me into his embrace. He plants a kiss to the side of my head, and holds me a little tighter. "I love you, okay? Getting rid of you is the last thing I want."

I clutch my hands around his jersey. "You're not gone for too long. You have like three games. One of which is right here. The other two games steal you away for maybe two days each time. It's not like you'd leave me all by myself for weeks."

And even if he did that, I'm used to it, aren't I? Sure, I'm usually at home with my friends and my family, but it'll change in a few months anyway, won't it? Might as well start getting used to it.

"Miles is there, isn't he? I can get to know your friend and his wife a bit better while you're gone."

"It's Brooke's birthday in two days," he tells me like this is supposed to be some kind of invitation. It's not, we all know that. I wouldn't need an invitation to be there because Grey would bring me either way.

"Is it?"

He nods. "She's turning nine."

Nine?! It feels like an eternity since I've met her for the first time. I guess it's only been four years, though technically this is the fifth year with Grey Davis in my life.

I pull away from our hug, now looking at Grey with knitted eyebrows. His voice is deeper, a little sadder, but why?

"And that's a bad thing? She's growing up like any other kid."

Grey nods, though absently. He isn't looking at me. "She wasn't even one year old when I first met her. It's a little… crazy."

I don't see how. He was twenty-one when we met, now he's twenty-six and you don't see me complain about that.

"At least now she can have an actual conversation with you," I try to cheer him up, it doesn't work. What's wrong with him?

Grey looks over my shoulder, then takes a huge step back. "I'll see you later, okay?"

My eyebrows dip with concern and confusion. "Yeah, sure."

He turns around, ready to walk away but I grasp his wrist before he can run off. The second he turns toward me, Grey rips his hand out of my grasp, taking yet another step back.

"Is everything okay?" I ask, ignoring the pinch in my heart his rejection caused.

"Just… nerves. I'll see you at home." With that, he leaves.

What just happened?

He'll see me at *home*. Not after the game, at *home*.

I'd like to correct my statement from a few years ago; being kept a secret is *not* fine with me at all. It sucks.

Grey hasn't shut me out like this in a long time, not when we were together in private. He didn't even shut me out like this when we were in public together before what happened back in February. Now, as it seems, every time we're together or *could be* together, he's pretending he doesn't know me.

Last March, Grey was in L.A. for a game, and he didn't come see me. I wasn't mad because I thought his schedule was just really tight, or he didn't want to be so close to his father yet, and he apologized like a million times. It was okay with me, I ended up going to his hotel, but even there he told me to try and leave the hotel without anyone seeing me.

It's… weird. Having to sneak around, not being able to love him out in the open, not being allowed to be seen with him.

—

I don't sit with Miles in the VIP area, figured a little moment to myself after the encounter with my boyfriend is much needed.

After a couple of years of forcing myself to watch every single one of Grey's games, I finally picked up on some of the rules of the game. I am no longer as clueless as I was when I watched my first game, but Miles could've at least told me when I missed something, like when the fans of the team I am rooting for are yelling with frustration when I don't see anything wrong.

The NYR are winning it seems, so why are they upset?

As always, there's someone lying on the ice or getting pushed up against the boards, so nothing new there either.

It is until I finally realize *who* is pushing someone up against one of those walls.

Well, that would definitely be a red card if this was soccer.

Why don't ice hockey games have red cards. Surely they have something similar because I know the players can get sent to the penalty box for some time, which might as well be the equivalent to a yellow card. Though, I'm not sure if they can get suspended for the entirety of the game. I don't care either.

What I do care about, however, is why the fuck my boyfriend is now throwing his *fists* at one of the opponents, not stopping even when the referee tries to get between them.

"It's always the quiet ones," I hear someone mutter under their breath from behind me. I would love to open my mouth and argue with that dude, but then I see that guy Grey's fighting take a swing and launch his gloved fist right into Grey's face. Thank god for that helmet, but still, what the fuck?!

Chapter 6

"but we know this, we got a love that is hopeless"—
Secret Love Song by Little Mix, Jason Derulo

Grey

September 2026

My first game as the team captain and I couldn't be more excited, at least on the inside. I doubt anyone really notices my nerves, but that's alright because I don't want them to either.

All my earlier worries leave my brain the second the referee drops the puck. The world's tuned out, all that matters is winning this game. Imagine if we lost, that'd look bad for me.

Unfortunately, I didn't reach the puck first. Fortunately, I'm good at stealing pucks from others, so it only takes two seconds before the puck is in my possession. Quickly, I shoot the puck over to my left toward Aaron. He brings the puck forward until three of the opponents circle him, that's when he shoots it back to me, and I pass it over to our right defenseman, who then secures us the first goal.

It only takes seconds to get the puck into the opponents net, if executed flawlessly. This goal counts as one of those.

First goal of this season since the season officially starts tomorrow, and I got to assist. Being the one to have shot the goal would've been better, but I can accept an assist. It's a *team* sport after all.

Minutes pass and it has got to be *moments* before halftime. Although the Islanders scored a few goals, my team's still leading by one point.

The first goal after halftime is executed by me, coast to coast. I start off by our goal, skate down the entire left side toward the opponents'. A few players try to get in my way, cut me off, and steal the puck from me but with a sidestep to my right, I manage to keep the puck in my possession. Then I shoot, and hit the net.

It's a great day for the hockey gods to be on my side.

We're winning, though that is easily changed in the blink of an eye. That is until I find myself snatching the puck from Saxon, the Islanders' center player, and that guy almost loses it.

Just when I pass the puck to one of my teammates, Saxon skates up right in front of me. His eyes lock with mine, angry, but that's nothing new on the ice. When I think he's about to bump his shoulder against mine when passing me, I'm quite literally surprised when instead he reverts back to insults.

A classic.

"Asshole," he mutters, which I don't even react to because this is mostly the game talking. It's the heat of the moment, both teams want to win and so yes, words like *asshole* get thrown around a lot. But what leaves his mouth next *does* earn him a reaction. "Gays like you shouldn't even be allowed to play sports."

I snort and shake my head, giving him more of a reaction than anyone *ever* gets from me. Guys like Saxon get insulted by people like me. They feel threatened because a queer person beat them, and that shouldn't be possible, right?

Over the years, I've learned that no matter what I do, there are always going to be people out there hating me for who I am, for loving who I choose to love, and that's okay. It's okay because at least it's me who chooses to love someone, and as long as I'm happy with my decisions, nobody gets to tell me who the fuck I can and cannot love.

But what *really* gets me is what follows.

"That guy you're dating, Chinese boy, I bet you're paying him to date you." My blood runs cold, the temperature inside of this arena dropping, I'm sure. "He looks like a gay male escort with his brown skin and stripper abs."

My head whips around, my eyes now filling with something so dangerous, it makes the guy who reverted to homophobia back off. His face immediately pales when he looks at me, and I don't even have to do anything until he slowly backs into the boards behind him.

This alone should get the referees attention, but nothing is happening, which is a bad thing because I don't know what I'm about to do next.

When Saxon's back is pressed against the glass, his eyes wide with fear, I snap.

"Say that again, I dare you." I get closer to his face, my voice lowering. "Come on, Saxon, try insulting my boyfriend again, see what happens."

He opens his mouth, but I don't wait for anything to leave it because I take off one of my gloves in a nanosecond before my fist collides with his half-helmeted face.

In seconds I have him pushed up against the boards, boxing into his body with every other word that leaves his mouth, always some stupid insult. The more he insults me or Luan, the harder I box him.

I only get three more punches in before both of the referees are beside us, trying to pull me away from Saxon. It doesn't work.

Though, when I finally give in, ready to flee the scene and go to the locker rooms to have Coach yell at me, Saxon gets a punch in, hitting me right on the side of my face.

"I hope your little male escort dies from his gayness, like you!"

Screw it. I pull my arm back, then with a great force and all of my strength, I let another fist collide with his face.

Saxon yelps and topples over, now lying on the ice. Some of his blood drips onto the ice, not nearly enough though. While his teammates come to gather around him, trying to see if their beloved center still has all of his body parts intact, mine come to check on me and I just skate right past all of them and off the ice.

The game's over for me anyway, so I might as well leave. There's no way I'm allowed back on the ice today.

So much for wanting my first game as captain to be a good one.

"Davis! What the hell was that?!" Coach snaps when I leave the ice, but I ignore him, making my way to the locker room.

As the doors close behind me, I finally allow myself to take a deep breath.

What the fuck just happened?

Not once in my life have I gotten genuinely violent with someone, not even during puberty. I always found reasons to stay calm, to be unshakable. So why did I snap? Why could I listen to my own father disrespect me for years and never once raise my voice, but some random guy says one bad thing about Luan, and suddenly I use my hands to *talk*.

I throw my gloves onto the bench in front of my cubby. The helmet comes off next. I seat myself across from my cubby, my head dropped between my shoulders as I stare down to the floor.

When I think I can finally have a short moment to myself, I hear the doors open. It has got to be one of the medical staff to see whether I am okay or if I need to go to the hospital or anything alike.

Only that the voice that speaks is too familiar to be one of the medical staff.

"Are you injured?" He comes closer, and without waiting for an answer, Luan lifts my face to his. His eyes travel over my face, but he must see something bad because there's a hint of sadness in his green ones.

"Is it that bad?" I feel blood running down from somewhere around my eyebrow, maybe, but I don't think it's that bad. Injuries happen, especially when someone hits you right in the face.

"Not bad enough to get doctors involved." That's good. "You

won't even need stitches."

Luan pulls the sleeve of his sweater over his hand then brings it to my wound to wipe off some of the blood. I don't think it's doing much, but it's a kind gesture anyway.

"How do you know?"

Luan smiles down at me, then winks. My heart fucking stops at that. "I work with kids from age four to eighteen, baby. I've seen my fair share of injuries caused by fights or simple lacerations, so deciding whether one might need stitches or if letting your blood cells build clots and scab will suffice, I can do that in my sleep."

I guess that makes sense. He's still not a doctor, but I trust him.

"Are you okay?" His voice is filled with sympathy.

I lay my hands on the back of Luan's thighs to pull him right between my legs. "No."

His eyebrows dip. "Do you want to talk about it?"

I shake my head. I barely know what happened, there's no way I will be able to tell Luan about it. "I want to go home."

"I don't think you're allowed to leave yet."

Neither do I. There will be interviews, even if it's just a charity game. These are still televised, reporters are here, and now they're even more eager to see the end of this game, so they have a chance to get all the details on the fight.

"Grey, can I ask you something?"

I slightly cock my head sideways. "Anything. You know that."

"Yeah, but I think you'll get offended, and I really don't mean anything bad by this question."

Asking if he could ask me something won't change the outcome then either way, I suppose. "Just ask."

"Do you want to break up?"

Oh.

I am not offended, but I do wonder what I did for him to think *that*?

"What?"

Luan swipes his thumb along my bottom lip, but I don't think there's anything he wants to wipe off. "You've just been so weird with me today. And like, yes, you were probably nervous earlier, and we were in plain sight, but even if you didn't want anyone to see us *act* like we're together, nobody could hear us talk. You still talked to me the way you did when we first met, and you haven't done that in a while. So, I just want to know if you want to break up because if you do, that's okay. Well, it's not okay because I will quite literally start to cry this instant, but it's still okay, you know? I'd respect your decision, not that I'd have any other choice anyway. But I need to know because if you don't want me around, Grey Davis, then please tell me so I can leave before I get even more attached."

I smile at him, to which Luan's eyes widen a tiny bit. Startled Luan might be one of my favorites. "I don't," I say, simple but effective, I hope. To strengthen my answer, I add, "I love you, Luan."

Luan blows out some air, the tension leaving his body. "Good, because, man, I was seriously about to cry. Imagine how awful that would be, too, with today being your birthday. Breakups already suck as it is, but a breakup on your birthday? These are *personal*. Well, it's not my birthday, so I would've been fi—"

"Shut up, Luan." I chuckle and lean my head a little farther back in my neck until Luan gets the hint. He smiles, leans down, and *finally* closes that stupid gap between our lips.

With my lips attached to his, I pull Luan down to sit on my lap like making out in the locker room with my boyfriend is a normality to me.

Luan grinds his hips against mine, a groan leaving me immediately. I couldn't have even stopped it from escaping me if I wanted to.

He kisses me with need, so fierce that it makes my head spin with a need for oxygen. He kisses me so deep and long that my lungs are begging me to set an end to this otherwise they might collapse. But you know what? Collapsed lungs sound great to me in this case.

Even when we finally part for a moment, I still can't seem to catch my breath, and that's also on my boyfriend. I love looking at him.

"What do you call celebratory sex when the game went well but the captain got a penalty for the rest of the game?" he asks. My eyebrows draw together, now wondering the same thing. "I want to fuck you."

I cough at the shock, choking on my breath.

We've been dating for over a year now, and even though we don't see each other all too often, we do get a whole lot of sex in when we manage to meet up. Not once has he asked to try it out, and I'm not going to lie, I thought he'd never even want to.

"Not here," I say when I finally manage to shake off the shock of his *very* random-timed wish.

"Obviously." Luan rolls his eyes, but he keeps a smile on his face, as he does so very often. "But maybe later, if you're up for it."

If *I* am up for it? Hell yes I am. However… "Miles is planning a birthday party for me, so I don't know when we'll be back in my apartment. Shouldn't be too late considering that I have a game tomorrow, that is if I am still allowed to participate." Also, Emory is pregnant, so I don't know how long Miles plans tonight to go because his wife definitely will need some rest sooner rather than later.

"That's alright, we have a lifetime left to try."

That we do. "I can tell him I'm not up to celebrate." It wouldn't even be a lie, after what happened out there, all I really want to do is spend the whole night in bed with my boyfriend. Not for sex, which might as well be a miracle for me. I just want to lie there and hold Luan in my arms, enjoy his company. "It's just another stupid birthday anyway."

"Twenty-six is a big number. You've officially passed half-time from twenty to thirty."

I groan. "Don't remind me." I don't really care about my age, what I do care about, however, is ice hockey. Turning twenty-six means I have about two to four years left before I will retire. At least twenty-eight to thirty is about the average most players retire because their bodies are now protesting. So what happens after I retire in let's say four years, if I'm lucky in five?

What am I supposed to do with my life? Sure, I have enough money to last me a lifetime, and an amazing boyfriend who'll move in with me in a few months. But that's all I'm going to have for the next fifty years until I die, that is if I die by the age of eighty. Well, I do have my friends too, and their kids, as well as my sister and hopefully for another long time my mother, but even so, their presence won't stop me from getting bored.

I am feeling great though, so maybe I can make it to forty, doubtful, but it is possible.

"Do you still want—"

"Davis?!" Someone interrupts me as he comes barging through the doors. "Oh, sorry. I didn't mean to interrupt."

"You didn't," Luan says all kindly before he climbs off me. "We were just talking."

I get up and turn toward Aaron, sighing because I know he's going to ask questions. "What can I do for you?"

"What the hell was that!?" Aaron lets the doors fall shut, but a second later they fly back open and Colin marches inside with the same stern look on his face as Aaron.

"Since when are you *beating* people on the ice?!"

I open my mouth to speak, but Aaron cuts me off. "You do know that this is going to have consequences, right?! I can already see the headlines; *Grey Davis turns violent with his new Captain title: how long will he last until the NHL kicks him out.*"

I snort, shaking my head. "You forgot to put *gay* in there somewhere." It's all the tabloids like to talk about these days. Actually, it has been all they ever talk about me for years. I thought they'd stop eventually, but nope. At least it died down a little bit, I guess.

Colin agrees, humming as he thinks of a way to rephrase the hypothetical headline. "*New presumably Gay Captain of the NYR throws fists at opponent because....*" He looks at me expectedly. "Because?"

"Because Saxon Grace is a homophobic bastard." Could've phrased this more nicely, but why would I when it's the truth? "Need any more details?"

Taking in my best friend's stunned expressions, I highly doubt they want to know more.

"I do." Luan turns my head around to face him. When I look at him, there's nothing left of the joyful guy I know. Every ounce of happiness is replaced with anger, with something vicious.

Chapter 7

"how much you wanna risk?"—*Something Just Like This by The Chainsmokers, Coldplay*

Ivan

September 2026

HE'S NOT SUPPOSED to answer questions, at least none that are related to the fight on the ice. His PR team advised Grey to keep it down, to deal with the matter in private and not drag out an unnecessary fight.

As the team captain, he already has a whole lot of cameras aimed at him anyway, but right now, if I had to guess, there are about a million more pointing at him, so it makes sense Grey's team wants him to keep quiet, withhold an answer to every question these bloodthirsty reporters throw at him.

But ever since Grey realized he is living his *own* life, that nobody can tell him what to do and what not, he prefers his own ways. That includes making sure Saxon Grace's name will be dragged through dirt.

It scares me a little because this right there is something I would've done a couple of years ago, before I decided I didn't want to be *that* guy anymore. Wanting revenge, not caring about what happens to people that don't have much value in your life, it's a very frightening territory to enter.

There is something funny about Grey sitting there in front of tons of cameras shoved in his face though, especially because his expression is so blunt, he doesn't show any emotions at all. But then he has this apple in his hand just munching on it while stupid reporters throw questions at him.

"Are you planning to make this season a better one than last year's?" one reporter asks.

Grey takes a bite of his apple, shaking his head. "Wait, we're supposed to actually *win* a game? Jesus, why'd no one ever tell me?"

God, I love this man.

"Now that you're the captain, do you think the team will be stronger than before?"

Once again, Grey takes a bite of his apple before answering. "We aim to win fights. With our fists."

"Does losing the Stanley Cup of 2026 by *one* point evoke more spirit to win in 2027?"

A muscle in his jaw twitches at the reminder. It was pretty painful to watch them lose by *one* goal, even to me. "2026's loss was solely to prove we're not some witches. Don't want the NHL burning us alive, do we?"

"Who started the fight, Mr. Davis?" a younger looking reporter asks.

From afar, I can see Grey take a deep breath before he lifts his head to the young woman. His eyes are darker than usual, nothing but hate in them, pain. He's been quiet about *that* the past ten minutes, ignored every question, every attempt of getting information about said fight, and now he's looking up. That's not good.

"Grace did," Grey answers, his voice coming through strong and low.

I keep telling my kids that you don't point fingers at anyone, that fights start on both sides. It takes two, always.

Except that this is bullshit.

It's true that it takes two sides to even get to a fight, but it only takes one to initiate it.

No person out there who gets bullied does *anything* to receive that hatred, and saying it takes both sides for it to escalade is stupid because no, it doesn't. The person who gets bullied doesn't ask to get bullied, they exist and that's enough of a reason for some people to be cruel.

Same goes for the Queer community. We exist, and there'll always be people hating us for that very reason. We don't ask for anyone's opinion, we don't ask to be hated on because we're not part of the norm. We *don't* start the fight, society does.

So to everyone out there who says it takes two, fuck you, because it doesn't.

"Mr. Davis!" another reporter calls for his attention, "Would you say Saxon deserved the punch?"

"He did. He deserves even worse."

Oh, Grey…

"What did Saxon Grace do to provoke you?"

I watch as two of Grey's teammates try to talk him out of answering, but I know that once Grey has set his mind on something, he'll follow through with it.

So, ignoring his teammates and the headshakes from his PR team from somewhere across the room, Grey says, "Saxon Grace doesn't know how to keep his preferences out of the arena. When he gets frustrated, he retreats back to insulting, which is fine, if his insults weren't aimed at my *boy*friend and me, and the fact that neither of us are straight white men." Grey leans back in this seat, seemingly relaxed while half of this room breaks out into gasps and shocked wheezes. His eyes find mine in the crowd, and when his lips slightly pull up into the softest of smiles that's invisible to everyone but me, I know he made the right decision.

No more hiding in the shadows.

"Maybe if Saxon didn't retreat back to insulting Luan and I's race and sexual orientation, I wouldn't have reacted the way I did. But unfortunately, he did, so yes, he deserved that punch and even worse. Any more questions?" The reporters keep surprisingly quiet when this would be *their* moment to shine. "That's what I thought."

Grey gets up, walks around the table, and comes over to me.

Once he reaches me, he presses his lips to mine then intertwines our hands and leads me out of that conference room.

As we walk down the hallways of this arena, both of us not saying a single word, the realization of what just happened starts to settle.

Grey made our relationship public.

Grey called out another NHL player for being racist and homophobic; surely the NHL has got to do something about it now, which again means he's no longer hiding what's happening behind the closed doors of professional sports. If Saxon Grace doesn't face *any* consequences, there will be a whole lot shit coming the NHL's way, especially the Islander team owner's way.

We're no longer living in the nineteen hundreds, professional sports are trying to be more inclusive that includes different races and sexual orientations, they're no longer excluded from their teams. Which means if *nothing* happens, it's a negative on their part.

I don't think there has ever been one moment I've been prouder of Grey. Except maybe when he stood up to his father.

Grey decided to postpone his birthday. Apparently it's Emory's birthday next week, so they'll just celebrate together. As much as I would've loved for Grey to spend the evening of his birthday with his friends, celebrating his arrival to this world at least a little bit, I understand why he's not up for any kind of celebration tonight.

We've been lying all cuddled up on his couch for the past few hours, watching *Jumanji*. I'm not really paying any attention to the movie as I seem to be far more focused on Grey's hand slowly stroking up and down my back with the most sensual and softest touch ever.

He's always so gentle with me, and I have no idea where

that's coming from. Looking at Grey, you'd think he's one of those guys who never smiles, and although that has *some* truth to it, he *does* smile a lot. He smiles when he's with me or his friends. Grey seems like the type of guy who'd fuck you over, but he'd never do that. He's so sweet and loving, I'm embarrassed to admit that I used to think he was an asshole.

Then again, he *was* an asshole to me once upon a time, but years later I finally know why that was. He never meant to ignore me, he just didn't have any other choice, so he thought.

I am glad we turned out the way we did though because I can honestly say that without Grey Davis in my life, I wouldn't be who I am now.

I probably would've fallen back to manipulating people as I wouldn't have had anything or anyone to hold on to. There's even a high chance I would've picked that bottle back up to drink all of my pain away, even if there hasn't been a lot of that ever since I met Grey. Only the occasional pain that hurts right in my heart when I'm separated from my boyfriend for weeks.

For a moment, I close my eyes and listen to Grey's heart beating inside of his chest, being more thankful than ever for it. It's such a little thing, yet when I think about that one day this very heart might stop beating, I can feel a lump build in my throat and tears swell in my eyes.

There has only ever been one other person who pulled that reaction from me… and then he died.

Maybe it's time I finally give Grey the whole story.

"Charlie died in a car accident," I say, being aware that this is completely random and uncalled for. Grey never really asked about Charlie except for that one time, which I still think was only to figure out whether I had a boyfriend or not. However, I'm sure he knows whatever happened to him made me turn into the guy I used to be before I met Grey. He tends to figure that shit out quite quickly. "I was in that car as well."

Grey's hand stops moving for a second, then he continues to caress my back. He doesn't say it, but I know he wants me to keep on talking, so I do.

"His parents picked us up from soccer practice, on our way to their house we stopped to get some take-out. Everything was alright until we rounded the corner to their house and some car came out of nowhere, crashing right into us." I look up at Grey, but his eyes remain on the TV. "I don't really remember what happened next in detail, but I do remember waking up with some firefighter trying to cut me out of that car. I was upside down, so I figured the car must've turned over. I couldn't move, not even turn my head to see where Charlie was at, if he was alright. I did see his parents though, and from the looks of it, they weren't alive anymore. Nobody tried helping them, I guess that was what truly confirmed their death to me. I blacked out again and the next time I woke up, I was hooked up to some machines in the hospital."

A tear slips down my face. "My parents told me Charlie died, so did his parents. I don't know why I survived, and even though I was angry that I did, I was angrier at two whole other things. The universe took my best friend from me as well as his parents. At least *they* were together, right? But Charlie has a sister, she wasn't in the car with us."

Even though Grey tries to keep the gasp as quiet as possible, I can still hear it leave him.

"My parents took Doro in after the accident." I blow out some air, trying to ease the tension that's building inside of my chest. "Although I technically now had a sister and wasn't alone, I felt lonelier than ever. And to ease the pain of losing my best friend, I turned to alcohol at the age of twelve. It made me numb, careless. I didn't care whether I was hurting someone, unless that someone was beneficial to me, then I made sure to *not* hurt them until they were of no use anymore. I *willingly* turned into a narcissist because it kept me from feeling, kept me from having to deal with emotions."

"Then why did you decide to change it?" His voice comes out choked, empathic.

Six Years

I think about it for a second. There is more than one reason to it, but I think there's only *one* that truly sticks out.

"Because all those years, even when I was being a complete asshole to everyone, Doro stuck with me. Even after she turned eighteen and could've left, she stuck with me. She was the only person—apart from my parents—who loved me no matter what. But that same year we met, on my birthday, she told me she couldn't do this anymore. She said she couldn't watch me die any longer or manipulate people into liking me because I had no idea how to make friends otherwise. I hurt her, and she was done letting me hurt her, which was good because she shouldn't have ever allowed me to do that in the first place. It was when I realized that this isn't who I want to be. I don't want to be someone who intentionally hurts people, especially not the ones I love. And so eleven years after the accident, I finally wanted to get sober, get a fresh start in life." I sigh to hopefully ease the pain in my chest as the memories start to flood my brain, at least the ones I have recollection of. "One of the therapists at rehab asked me a question that really stuck with me. He asked if I could see myself becoming a new person without losing myself. I didn't have a real answer at that time because, well, you know me, I said I'd always be me because why would I *not* want to be me? I just wanted to get rid of my alcohol problem and being a manipulator, but other than that, why would I want to change?"

When Grey thinks I am cocky now, he should've met me four months earlier. I'm glad he didn't because if he did, we wouldn't be where we are right now.

He turns his head, our eyes meeting. "Do you have an answer now?"

I nod. "I didn't want to become a *new* person, I just wanted to be who I was *meant* to be. I wanted to be the guy I was *before* I ruined myself. Sure, a little more mature and not that goofy twelve-year-old, but…"

"Well I mean—"

I lay my hand over his mouth, shutting Grey up before he gets the chance to finish his sentence. He was about to say I haven't matured at all, and I know that even without him having to say it. But these days I know he's just teasing me, cracking jokes like normal people do, and I am so glad I finally understand the differences between mocking and teasing.

"This is my moment to talk, Grey Davis," I say. "So, if you don't mind keeping that pretty, naughty mouth of yours shut."

I can feel him grin against my hand, which might as well be the only reason why I pull my hand away. His smile still brings my whole world to a halt every time I see it.

"Noted, you may proceed."

"My point is, I never had to become a new person, never wanted to become one, so there was never a chance that I could've lost myself trying to become *me* again. I've always been who I wanted to be. I just lost track of the right path, decided to take a quick detour through the ocean before I could find my way back to the guy I knew."

"I'm pretty sure you had an amazing guardian angel watching over you." He closes his arms around my body and presses the softest kiss to the top of my head.

I sure hope I did.

"I came back from rehab that day we met," I admit. "I had been there for four months, so when I say you're the first person I ever tried not being the old-me with, I never lied, Grey. You were literally the first person I even talked to after I came back. And I do admit, after you ignored me, I so badly wanted to *make* you like me, but I promised myself I wouldn't. So I decided to be patient."

"Especially since you knew I was in love with you right away."

I smile up at my boyfriend, then roll over to lie completely on top of him. "Exactly. There was never an actual reason why I should've tricked you into liking me because I am pretty awesome, and you fell for me the second you laid your eyes on me."

"I think your abs did it for me." *Right, because I was shirtless when we met.*

I gasp out loud, my jaw dropping. "I knew it! You're just here for my body."

"Obviously." He rolls his eyes, then slaps a hand to my ass. Hard. "Also the cute dimples and the perfect smile. Plus, you kind of always said if I was in love with you, I should just say it, and I'm always up for a good challenge."

Maybe a few years ago this would've confused me, made me believe that Grey only loves me because it was a challenge to him. But these days I know he doesn't mean it that way. Grey never only kept seeking me out because he saw me as a challenge, but because he knew that somewhere deep down in his heart, there has always been a thread that connected him to me.

"Well." I grin at him widely. "If you're in love with me, Grey Davis, you definitely should just say it. Though it might have consequences."

His eyebrows quip up, an interested smirk creeping onto his lips. "What consequences?"

With my lips brushing his, I say, "Like that you're going to have to propose to me in a year or two because I will not let you go ever again. And that we're going to have to adopt at least two kids and name them Sage and Ash. Or maybe we can get a surrogate, though adopting seems good too. I don't know yet, but we'll figure it out."

I'm not going to lie, I'm a little afraid to open my eyes and look at my boyfriend, especially because he's neither agreeing nor disagreeing with me. He's not saying anything.

But when I finally open my eyes, meeting his dark ones, his expression doesn't look half as frightening as I'd imagined.

"I am so fucking deeply in love with you, Luan Hayes."

My smile widens even more, if it does any further, there's a high chance the corners of my mouth might rip.

When he smiles back at me, earth might as well lose all its

gravity and fall right out of our solar system. That's how deep I'm falling.

"Of course you are." I shrug nonchalantly. "You'd be crazy if you weren't." I press a kiss to his mouth, then say, "But, Grey Davis, I am even more in love with you."

"I don't think you are."

"I think I am, because I love you more than apple juice, baby."

"And I love you way more than ice hockey."

I gasp, and I swear the only thing keeping me from falling off this stupid couch right now is Grey's arms being tightly wrapped around me.

"You take that back, Grey Davis! Right fucking now."

He chuckles. "Why? Does that scare you?"

I nod. "You're practically *begging* for three kids and a dog with this!"

Grey shudders. "Fine, I'll take it back. I don't love you more than hockey. I also won't be able to handle more than two kids."

Yeah, that's what I thought.

Chapter 8

"never thought we would get this far"—Higher by Shawn Mendes

Grey

September 2026

"Move," Luan begs and pushes his ass against me, urging me, pushing me deeper inside him.

"You're so bossy." I squeeze his ass cheeks with my hands, then slide them up to his hips as I pull out of him then slam back inside. "And mighty lazy for someone who coaches soccer."

Upon Luan's request from two days back, I suggested he top this morning, but he said it's far too early for him to even have enough energy to do *any*thing. I think he's chickening out, but that's okay.

Though I'm not quite sure what he's so afraid of, and maybe I wouldn't understand even if he tried to explain it to me. So he broke his dick once, big deal. But I am happy to wait for him to be ready. If it turns out he still doesn't like being on top, or he never even wants to try it after all, that's also fine with me.

"Not lazy, but it's *early*, Grey Davis," he argues, looking over his shoulder to meet my eyes. I wink at my boyfriend, then thrust into him a little harder, only to hear him gasp. "Not everyone can—" He moans when I tease his prostate.

"Not everyone can what?" I ask, trying to sound as unbothered as ever, but that's really fucking difficult when you're buried to the hilt inside of your boyfriend and your balls are pulsing with the need to come.

"I don't—" He falls forward and presses his face into the pillow when I reach an arm around his hips and wrap my hand around his dick, giving him a long and slow stroke. "*Fuck*."

I still inside of him, leaning forward until my chest is pressing against his back. Bringing my mouth to his ear, I whisper, "I love you."

Luan shudders at my words to which I smile but he's too busy burying his face in the pillow to see. Sucks for him.

"Just so you know, I'm smiling," I tell him. Luan gasps and immediately tries to turn his head, and because I know looking at me from this angle will do *nothing* for him, I pull out of him and turn Luan on his back, hovering my face right over his.

Luan reaches his hands up to cup my face, sliding his thumbs over my lips. "I love you, and your smile, baby, but…"

I connect our lips, not being able to not kiss him for another second. How could I ever think I'd be able to resist this guy? Screw twenty-one-year-old me, he was far too stupid.

"But?" I grasp my dick in my hand and nudge my cockhead against his hole, not yet reentering him.

"Make me come, man."

Bucking forward, I thrust inside him all at once, but that's okay because he's already stretched enough.

We both moan out loud, gasping with need with every other thrust.

Luan closes his arms around my neck, pulling me down for a kiss so deep, I almost forget to fuck him *again*. Thank fuck for my cock yelling at me to finish, otherwise I definitely would stop moving because that's just what Luan's kisses do to me. They let me forget everything and everyone around us.

I bring my hand between us, grasp his cock, and slide my thumb over his pulsing head, swiping away the little beads of precum.

I stroke his dick with the same rhythm as I thrust in and out of him, swallowing up every sound that leaves his swollen lips.

"Fuck, Grey, I'm—" He doesn't get to finish his sentence before hot cum spurts out of him and right onto his stomach, some drops hit mine as well. He's a mess, taking deep and shallow breaths, his eyes are closed, and his mouth stands half open at the orgasmic shock, but his arms never leave my neck.

Now that that's out of the way, I chase my own orgasm. I kiss his lips, his jaw, and when I drop my head beside his, I can feel my balls tighten as I come inside of my boyfriend.

My breath comes out hard and ragged, my body going slack.

We lie here for a hot minute, not moving, not talking, just lying here, chest-to-chest, trying to calm ourselves down when I hear the door to my apartment open.

"Shit," I mutter, lifting my head to look at Luan.

Luan's eyes widen with horror when he hears the door close, then looks down to where our bodies are *still* joined. "That's not like… one of the kids, right?"

I shake my head. "They should be at school and daycare." The second those words leave my mouth, the door to my bedroom opens. Thank god for that ridiculously long hallway between the door and the actual room.

Technically, I could just pull out of Luan, and we could pretend like nothing happened, but that's one of the last things on my mind right now.

"Okay, hear me out," Miles begins, but I am quick to shut him down.

"Leave. We're busy."

I can hear when he stops walking, and when he turns around to walk out again.

I love Miles, and maybe college-me wouldn't have cared if my best friend walked in on me fucking some random person, but twenty-six-year-old me *does* mind my best friend walking in on me and my *boyfriend*. And I know Luan minds it.

"I give you five minutes. Then you both better get your asses out here because I need to fucking rant and—"

"Yes, yes, now go!"

The door closes and Luan instantly lets out a breath of relief.

I stare into his eyes, an apology being on the tip of my tongue, but he smiles at me before pressing his lips back to mine. "Just go," he chuckles. "I'm going to take a shower."

Pulling out of Luan, I still don't move off of him. "You're not," I say.

"I'm not?"

I shake my head. "Not without me."

"But *we* don't take five-minute showers."

True. We always get... distracted. I mean, his lips are just so there in front of me, so I cannot *not* kiss him, and make out a little. It's impossible. And then we kiss and forget we're showering so minutes pass, and some more time passes until one of us gets cold and we finish up our shower.

"He's just here to talk about how sad he is that Brooke's turning nine today."

"So be a good best friend and listen to him whine about it, Grey Davis." Luan pushes me off him. Before I get the chance to roll back on top of him, he stands and makes his way over to the bathroom.

"But I'll whine with him because how dare she?" I want to cry just thinking about Brooke growing up, and she's not even *my* kid.

Luan chuckles. "See, one more reason to be there for Miles. Cry together."

"I hate you, just so you know," I say when he walks into the bathroom.

Luan turns around to look at me with raised eyebrows, keeping that sexy as fuck smile on his face. As always. "Hm, I remember you saying something else just a few minutes ago."

My eyes fall to his cum on his stomach, and I can feel myself slowly starting to harden again at the sight of it. "Must've heard wrong."

"Apparently so." He disappears into the room, leaving me behind.

I get up, then follow my boyfriend into the bathroom, not to get into the shower with him, although I want to, but to at least have the decency to wipe off Luan's cum on my torso before putting on some boxers to go see Miles.

—

"She set a flipping *plastic* bowl onto a *hot* stove, Grey!" Miles complains, being near damn tears. "I love Emory, really, but sometimes…"

Turns out, his much-needed rant isn't about Brooke after all.

"It was an accident, I know, but I love my stove." *That he does*.

"Remember when you 'accidentally' punched Emory's newest painting that she was freakishly proud of?" I ask. "She probably felt the very same as you do right now."

Miles groans because he knows I'm right, then leans his head against my shoulder. "I should've given you ten minutes. You smell like—Anyway…." Miles straightens his back again, pulls up his legs onto my sofa and turns to face me. "Brooke said I'm being mean."

"You are," I confirm without even knowing why she said it. If my little Brooke says Miles is being mean, he is. I'll *always* side with that kid.

"Shut up and hear me out."

"Fine." Only because I'm curious.

"Remember those chores 'gift cards' she made for me for my birthday last year?" I nod. "Yeah, well, this morning after I woke her up for school, I handed her one of them and said I'll be cashing it in today. And so she called me mean because, apparently, I was supposed to forget they existed."

She's not wrong. "It's her birthday, love. Cashing one in today is rude."

"IT WAS THE HUG ONE!" He leans back on my sofa, looking up at the ceiling. "I just wanted a hug from my daughter."

"You get those all the time anyway. Brooke loves you. It's a miracle when she's *not* hugging you." It's not as bad anymore as it was when she was four or five, but Brooke is still very fixated on Miles. A pretty unhealthy amount of fixated if you asked me. Then again, she only just turned nine years old today, and I have absolutely no idea how much is too much. Maybe it's a normal amount of being clingy, I wouldn't know. It's not like Brooke doesn't stay away from Miles, because she does. She goes to school like every normal kid does, she plays ice hockey and takes ballet and figure skating lessons, and she has occasional sleepovers with her friends and me every other time I'm back home. However, whenever she is at home, Brooke rarely occupies herself. She's mostly wherever Miles is, helping him cook or clean, or they're playing games, cuddle.

"I know, but since I can't cash them in with Eden, I thought a hug on her birthday won't hurt. Turns out, it will."

"Did you try asking Eden for a hug?" That kid hugs me all the time, I don't know where Miles's problem is with him. Though, to be fair, Eden loves his father, he simply prefers his mother.

"Did I try—" He laughs, sitting up again. "You know, I tried kissing my *wife* yesterday, and he won't even let me do that. Now imagine me asking him for a hug. That kid is the devil in person, I am telling you."

"He looks pretty adorable to me, love. And it's not like he ignores your existence. He loves you… every time he's hungry or wants a new toy."

Once again, Miles groans. "That little kid is lucky I love him, otherwise I would not tolerate his behavior."

"You would, because he's four."

"Don't remind me!" Miles slides both of his hands down his face ever so dramatically. "Anyway, tonight's going to go a *whole* lot differently than planned."

Already figured as much. Just yesterday Colin and Aaron both dropped that huge bomb on us that Sofia and Lily are pregnant, which now makes *every* single woman in our friend group pregnant. Emory's about five months along though, I think? Sofia and Lily aren't.

Anyway, with now three out of eight of us pregnant, there will be a whole lot less drinking once the kids are in bed. Lily usually stays sober anyway because the alcohol doesn't mix well with her antidepressants. She's the one to take care of Brooke and Eden whenever everyone is wasted.

And since Lily, Sofia, and Emory can't drink, neither will Colin, Aaron, and Miles. Luan can't drink either because, well, he's an addict that only leaves me, and I don't drink by myself.

But I don't think this is what Miles was hinting at, at least his face doesn't look like it was.

"What else changed?" I ask.

He sighs deeply. "There was a little incident at Brooke's school this morning." Oh, no…

"What does *a little incident* mean, exactly?"

"Two older guys from her school found out that Colin is Reece's brother, they didn't even bother to connect Reece to his own father, but alright, and since Brooke and Reece are really close, they're calling her a gold digger. I didn't even know fifth graders knew what that is, but I shouldn't be surprised, to be honest. Brooke asked me what that means though, and after I explained it to her because, as always, she wouldn't let me brush it off as *nothing*, she asked if they'd get even meaner should they find out where we live and that she calls all three of you her uncles."

"Did you say no?" Because knowing Miles, he probably did. He tries to be as transparent with his kids as possible, but he also does his best in depicting the world as a pink fluffy cloud to them.

"I said nothing, which was more than enough. It was also Brooke's invite to run after those guys and tell them that should they ever decide to be mean to her, she *will* have the entire NYR team come for their asses because they're her friends. I've never been prouder of that kid, but at the same time…"

I nod, already knowing where he's going with this. He's scared for her; that it'll get worse, that she'll eventually be frightened to go to school because she might get bullied, that she won't be able to trust anyone because she will think everyone is trying to use her.

"The *entire* team?"

"Yup."

"It'll only take Brooke to scare those little beasts away though."

Miles agrees. Brooke doesn't let anyone tell her what to do, apart from Miles and Emory, obviously, or when she's with either of us, actually. Strangers though, Brooke has a big mouth and even sticks up for those at her school who do face some mean kids. She's going places someday, I'm telling you.

"So, anyway, now Brooke uninvited all of her friends except for Reece, because she thinks they'll call her a gold digger when they find out about you, Colin, and Aaron, which is bullshit because those girls are more ballet girls than interested in hockey, so I don't think either of them even knows who the fuck you guys are. And when I was about to tell her that her frien—"

I hold up my hand to stop him. "You do *not* get to disagree with my little princess, okay?"

Miles snorts a laugh. "You spoil her too much."

I always did. "Well, I'm probably never going to have kids, so I only have yours to spoil."

He cocks his head, his eyes moving over my shoulder toward my bedroom door before they're back on me. "You don't want any?"

Sighing, I lean back on the sofa. "I don't know," I answer in all honesty. "Luan wants two, but I'm not even sure he's being serious about that. If he still wants them in a few years, I wouldn't be opposed to adopting, but as of now, I couldn't imagine having a child. I don't know how Aaron and Colin plan to do this, with being gone so often, you know? And I mean, yes, there are *tons* of hockey players out there with kids and they manage it just fine, but personally, I couldn't imagine leaving my child at home with my partner for most of the year, being gone from them all the time. You should understand because you, too, choose your family over hockey, but I'm not ready to do that just yet."

Miles bobs his head. "I also had my restaurants to retreat back to."

"Exactly, and I have *nothing* else. Sure, I have my degree, but the fuck if I know what to do with that? It's a little too late to go back to school and become a psychologist."

He puts his hand on my shoulder, grinning a little. "Well, if you ever need a job in the future, love, I'm happy to employ you as a host. Anything else, I'd fear you'd burn down the entire building."

I'm a little useless like that, I'm not going to lie. But I'm still learning. It only took me seven years of living away from home, but I can now boil pasta and heat it up with premade sauce, and I can make scrambled eggs, Brooke taught me. So, I'm doing pretty well, I'd say.

Also, I know how to make Kimchi because my mother thought it was a crime that I didn't know how to before.

Chapter 9

"you so fucking precious when you smile"—Mine by Bazzi

Grey

September 2026

"UNCLE GREY, LOOK!!" Eden comes running toward me the same second I have the door open to the apartment. He stops in front of Luan and I, holding up both of his hands. "HANDS!"

I pick him up from the floor, plant a quick kiss to the side of his head before giving myself in to his newest discovery. "Oh, you have hands?"

"YES!" Eden looks at Luan, then with a gasp holds his hands up into Luan's direction. "Look, Uncle Grey's friend!"

Eden has met Luan, but they never interacted. Brooke knows we're together, but I don't think Eden has *any* real idea who Luan is to me.

"Wow, when did you grow them?" Luan asks, chuckling. I look at my boyfriend just to catch that adorable smile of his. I rarely appreciate the fact that he smiles so much, but I should definitely start to do that more often. I love his smile.

Eden shrugs. "I waked up, then—" He gasps again and looks at his own hands, turning them over like this is the first time he sees them. "—Boom! Hands."

"Must've been quite the surprise waking up to having hands, huh?" I brush his wavy blond hair back, making sure the strands won't get in his eyes. Eden wants to keep his hair a little longer like Miles, it's kind of adorable. Especially when one takes into consideration that Eden is more of a mommy's-boy.

"Yes. And I tell Mommy, and Mommy says that she's proud and then I went to tell Brookie, but she say that my hands always been there, but I know she just speaking the lie-language."

Ah, yes... the lie-language. "You definitely grew them over night," I say, "Brooke's just being silly."

Eden agrees. "I didn't tell Daddy."

"Why not?"

"Because Daddy always steal Mommy from me, so he don't deserve to know."

I shoot Miles a disapproving look from right here, making sure to look extra grumpy for once. Miles laughs at that, though I'm pretty sure he has no idea what my expression is all about. On second thought, he probably heard Eden talk because that kid doesn't know what an inside-voice is.

"How dare he?"

"RIGHT!" he shrieks, then turns to Luan again. "Do you know he sleeps in Mommy's bed, too? But when he sleep there, then where I sleep, Uncle Grey's friend?"

In his own bed, I'm pretty sure.

Luan shrugs. "I don't know, on the floor?"

Eden nods, though I know that's not true. "On the floor," he confirms. "Always on floor." Miles would *never* let Eden sleep on the floor when there's more than enough space in his bed.

"Do you want me to get mad with your daddy?" I ask, tickling his cute little stomach. "I can tell him to sleep on the floor next time."

Luan next to me chuckles.

Eden shakes his head, then leans into me a little bit as though he's about to tell me a secret. "I think Daddy can't sleep without Mommy, like me when I not have Mini Froggo."

Ah, yes... Mini Froggo. Miles *dreads* the frog, we all do. He's creepy as fuck and the only reason Eden even has that thing in the first place is because Colin thought it was hilarious. Since

Lily loves frogs and Colin has to live with creepy little frog statues and stuffed animals all around his apartment, Colin gifted Eden a frog about a week after he was born. It was his revenge on Miles for constantly making fun of him for the whole frog thing at his apartment.

Colin also named the frog, clearly.

I live for it, but I do *not* want that frog anywhere near me.

"Why'd you think that?" I mean, it is the truth. I honestly believe Miles is incapable of sleeping alone ever since he has Emory.

Eden leans in even closer, whispering, "He never sleep when Mommy away with auntie Sofia."

"LUAN!" a sweet little high-pitched voice screams, running up to my boyfriend instantly.

When I look at him, he's just as shocked as I am. How dare *my* little Brooke say hello to my boyfriend first?

Brooke jumps into his arms, fully trusting him to catch her. He does, obviously.

"You came!" She giggles and wraps her arms around his neck like she's known Luan all her life. Theoretically speaking, she's known him for years. Technically speaking, Brooke has only met Luan a handful of times, so that doesn't really count as *years*.

"Well, yes, of course I did. I wouldn't have missed your birthday for anything." He didn't even know it was her birthday today until I told him two days ago.

"What's my present?" She takes a step back, her eyes gleaming with eagerness.

"Brooke," I say in a warning tone. It even surprises me.

Brooke sighs. "I know, I know"—she rolls her eyes—"I can't open my presents before dinner. But why do I have to wait *so* long?!"

I don't know, but Miles told us not to give her any presents *before* dinner.

"I heard you uninvited all of your friends last-minute, huh?" I set Eden down, then sit down on the floor myself just because.

"What's that all about?" Yes, yes, I know why she did it, but I want to hear it from her.

Brooke takes a seat on the floor with me, her smile turning upside down. "I think they're going to be mean to me, but that's okay. I only need Reece anyway."

"Well, if they're ever mean to you, they're not your friends."

While I talk to Brooke, Eden drags Luan away. I'm guessing to show Luan his truly awesome bedroom. The entire room is Lego themed because he loves Lego's, even though he's not allowed to play with them unless Miles or Emory are watching. Or any adult, really. Miles and Emory are afraid he'll try to swallow the tiny pieces.

His walls are hand-painted by Emory to make it look like they built an entire wall out of Lego's. It took her several days to paint, but the result was totally worth it. His bed also looks like it was built using bigger Lego's, and any decoration he might have, they're all built from Lego's. He even has *pillows* in the shapes of Lego pieces.

"Daddy said that, too," she tells me. "Oh, Uncle Grey, do you think Sofia's baby will be a girl?"

I shrug. "I don't know that." As far as I know, neither Sofia nor Lily are even far long enough to find out the gender yet.

"And Lily?"

"… I know Emory's having another boy." And a girl, but Em and Miles refuse to tell Brooke just yet.

Brooke rolls her eyes, again. She's sick of only having boys in her life, but I get that. If Lily's and Sofia's kids turn out to be boys as well… Brooke's going to go feral.

"Really? I thought I'm getting a sister."

"You already wanted Eden to be a girl. Maybe you should start wishing for a boy, then they might turn out to be girls."

"Alright. So when Luan and you have a baby, it better be a… *girl*. Uncle Grey, *please*. I want a sister."

Sighing, I say, "She wouldn't be your sister though. More like an unofficial cousin."

Brooke shakes her head. "But she'd be like a sister to me someday. And when she's a little older, I can dress her in my old princess dresses and teach her how to annoy Daddy, and you, and Luan, and Eden. She better annoy Eden a lot because he annoys me a lot."

The pleasure of having siblings. Siblings are the definition of hating someone and loving them at the same time. One would give them a kidney but draw the line when it comes to sharing something like food.

I'd give my life for Sun, but if she were to steal my food…

Chapter 10

"I'd walk through fire for you / just let me adore you"—
***Adore You** by Harry Styles*

Iuan

September 2026

AT FIRST I WAS A little confused as to why nobody was allowed to give Brooke her gifts yet, but when a few hours later, Miles and Colin came back from "a short walk" with a karaoke machine,… actually, no, I still don't understand.

But it's safe to say Brooke enjoyed her new karaoke machine a whole lot more than any of the other presents she got.

According to Miles, the karaoke machine is only allowed to be used on one day of the year, and that'd be Brooke's birthday, but from what I've gathered about Grey's friend group, Sofia and Colin will definitely make sure to use that machine a lot more often.

And if I am judging the past two hours correctly, all of them had fun. I, for my part, really enjoyed it when Brooke begged Grey to sing a Barbie song with her and he knew the lyrics. It was mediocre singing on Grey's part, but karaoke isn't about it sounding good anyway. Karaoke is for fun, it's laughter, and enjoying the time you spend with your friends, not some song contest. Although Brooke and Reece, as well as Eden, gave everyone points and there was a clear winner of tonight's karaoke marathon.

It was Emory. Emory won, and Miles believes she only won

because Eden always gave her ten out of ten possible points because he's "the mini devil in training". I think she deserved first place because unlike everyone else, she has a good voice. Then again, it's not about the singing.

Overall, today has been a fun day. I do, however, feel like I could never be an active part of this friend group. They're already so close and I'm just now showing up more regularly. Sure, they all try to include me, and I really appreciate it, but I worry that they're only doing this for Grey, not because they truly want me around. Maybe in a few years I'll think differently... I hope.

Brooke fell asleep ten minutes ago, so Miles went to tuck her in. Reece seems to be wide awake still, even though it's late already.

"You know what time it is, Gumball?" Colin taps his brother's nose, to which Reece swats Colin's hand away. Colin laughs.

"I'm older now, *Gigante*. Mamá says I can stay up until ten."

"She also said you're not allowed to eat any more sugar after six, and did I listen? No. I still gave you a piece of cake. Besides, it's already ten-thirty."

It's not. In fact, it's not even nine yet.

"I don't believe you," Reece retorts and narrows his eyes at his brother. "*Besides*," he mocks, "you're not my dad."

Colin pulls Reece onto his lap, hugging him tightly. "Be glad I'm not, otherwise your bedtime would be five PM, even on the weekend."

Suddenly a hand lays down onto my thigh, causing me to flinch. My head whips around, only to find my boyfriend frown at me.

"Are you okay?"

"Yeah, just in my head." Or rather focused on a sibling-relationship I never got to experience.

As an only child, I sure was happy growing up, especially because I got everything I've asked for, but it was lonely. It *is* lonely.

Six Years

Seeing all those people with siblings fascinates me. Sometimes they're all up in each other's faces, screaming, shouting, hating each other, and the next second they act as though nothing ever happened. It's a kind of bond to someone I will never understand, which I envy a lot, because I *want* to understand it.

Also, siblings will never have to grieve alone because they'll always have someone else to experience the same pain. I, on the other hand, only have me, myself, and I. And Doro, I guess, but she's not technically my sister.

I smile at Grey then bring both of my hands to his face only to push the corners of his mouth up. His frown deepens which makes me smile even more.

"Ever tried smiling more?" I ask.

"Did you ever try frowning more?"

I haven't, actually. So I do now. I draw my eyebrows together and turn my smile upside down. I can't hold the frown very long because I can feel Grey start to smile. Quickly, I pull my hands away from his face and watch his eyes light up, his lips turning upward though I know he's trying to fight it.

"Is that a genuine smile on Grey's face?" Lily whispers, probably to her husband.

Just like that, Grey's smile falters.

"You know, you are allowed to show your friends that you aren't all *that* bad." I wink at my boyfriend. Turning to his friends, I say, "Did you know that he can *laugh*?"

All of them gasp, but of course they already knew it. It's just that Grey's smile and laughter is so rare that even though we've all witnessed it before, it's still a surprise seeing or hearing it.

"Nah, must be the other Grey, because our Grey doesn't know how to experience *joy*," Miles says to which Grey flips him off. Miles blows him a kiss in response.

"You guys think you're so funny, don't you?" my boyfriend asks, not wanting an answer.

I answer anyway. "Actually, I know I am, Grey Davis. I am

the funniest guy you have ever met."

"I beg to differ."

"And I beg to get—"

He covers my mouth with his hand. "I don't trust you and your mouth. God knows what leaves it."

"Anyway," Aaron chuckles. "Now that the kids are sleeping…"

I guess Reece went to bed after all. I didn't even notice.

"We're heading home?" Colin finishes, to which Aaron's face falls.

"Of course not." He turns away from Colin, now looking at Grey like he's the only person who'll potentially disagree with whatever he is about to suggest. Knowing my boyfriend, he will. "How about we play Mario Party?"

"We're eight people," Grey states, "Mario Party is a game for four."

"So?"

I lean my head onto my boyfriend's shoulder, he leans his head against mine in return. "We could do teams," I suggest.

"Exactly!" Emory chimes.

"Oh, my God. We can do *couple*-teams. Let's see which couple is the superior one." Miles lays an arm around Emory's shoulders, then plants a kiss to the side of her head.

"Or, and now hear me out—"

Now it's my time to cover Grey's mouth with my hand. "Let's do it. I don't hear anyone veto, do you?"

"You're my new favorite person, Luan," Miles says and beams a smile at me before flipping Grey off once more. "Your boyfriend is a whole lot better than you."

I remove my hand from my boyfriend's mouth to let him respond.

"You're just saying that because, from this day forth, you'll use him to get me to do whatever *you* want, love."

Miles doesn't try to deny it.

—

SIX YEARS

Thirty minutes into the game and Grey and I are in the lead. We already have three stars, Sofia and Aaron, as well as Lily and Colin have one star, and Emory and Miles have zero, but that's because Grey stole one from them.

Most of the mini games, Grey and I won, and I have a theory as to why that is. The other *teams* switch every other round; meaning one round let's say Colin plays one of the games, and the next Lily does. Grey and I, however, we play the games we think we'll win. Once the little preview on *how to play* finishes, we discuss who'd have more chances in winning, and then the person who is more confident plays. As it turns out, we're not doing such a bad job.

I love winning.

"You cannot be fucking serious!" Aaron mutters under his breath. "Neither of us has a chance of winning this round! It's like this one was made for Grey and Luan."

Grey looks at me and I smirk while reading the instructions to this mini game one more time.

"We're all trained in this, Aaron," Colin corrects. "Even the women."

"Can you stop making everything sexual?" Miles groans. "It's just a game."

"A mini game that's called *candy shakedown*. And we're literally jerking off the air."

"You're holding a controller..."

Aaron drops the controller into Sofia's lap. "Fuck this. I'm not doing that."

"Don't mind if I do." Sofia giggles and eagerly takes the controller. "But, seriously, Nix, you need to grow up."

"Yeah, I'm going to sit this one out," Lily adds, clearly siding with her brother. "Have fun *jerking off* the air, babe."

Emory gives her controller to her husband as well.

Now that everyone has decided who will play, they're staring at Grey and me, waiting.

I lock my eyes with Grey's, silently asking him who's going

to do it. "You should," I say, Grey shakes his head, disagreeing. "You have more experience."

Not even a hint of a smile crosses his face. It's the same frown from the first day we met; my favorite frown.

"I don't. I've never played this game before," he argues. "And since I don't think this game resembles jerking off, your excuse doesn't count." He lowers his voice so only I can hear and adds, "Actually, no, if we're going by that theory, *you* have more experience."

"Fine." I cover his hand with mine. "We'll do it together."

"That won't work."

"It will, Grey Davis. As you should know, I always get what I want. And since I want to win, there's no way we won't."

Grey shakes his head. "You're so full of yourself."

I grin. "Jesus, you're saying that like you're in—" My grin turns into a smirk when I realize "You know, if you're in love with me, Grey Davis, you can just say it."

Grey presses a kiss to my lips. "I'd rather die than respond to that very sentence." Bringing his mouth to my ear, he whispers, "But if we win this game, I might know a way to celebrate."

"How?"

"Instead of fucking the air, how about I fuck you instead?"

I should've known this was coming. "We better win then."

Spoiler: we won.

Chapter 11

"'cause nobody ever loved me like you do"—pov by Ariana Grande

Grey

December 2026

"I CAN'T BELIEVE you've never met my dad before." Luan finishes buttoning his dress shirt, then walks over to one of the million moving boxes to find a pair of shoes good enough to wear with a suit, to his father's company Christmas party.

Surprisingly, I'm free this weekend, so I thought why not be my boyfriend's date to this party. Parents don't like me, so maybe that would be a reason why I should've stayed in New York. Especially if we remember the part where I'm supposed to be the son of Luan's father's rival. I'm not in touch with my dad, but he doesn't know that. And Mr. Hayes is yet to find out I'm said rival's son in the first place.

All while Luan's supposed to move in with me in three weeks, right on New Year's Eve. Officially, anyway. Luan's going back to New York with me in two days, then he'll stay until Christmas, fly back home for a day or two to officially say goodbye to everyone and celebrate Christmas with his family, too, before he's back with me a day or two before New Year's Eve.

"I can't believe I'm meeting him today," I mutter, plopping down on the only standing furniture; his bed.

"He'll love you," Luan says. "My dad has a big heart. He's more likely to adopt you than ever say anything bad about you.

Trust me. There was this one time in fourth grade when I brought home a homeless guy because I thought he could use a shower, and instead of getting mad, my dad agreed. He fed him, gave him some money and new clothes, then told him to show up at our house again if he ever needed anything. So, yeah, you'll be fine."

That's nice… but it doesn't help.

"Grey, seriously. Even if he doesn't like you—which won't be the case—it won't change anything." Luan takes both of my hands in his, pulling me up to sit. "I'm an adult, almost thirty. I can date whoever I want, even if my parents don't approve of the relationship. Besides, you know very well how fond my mother is of you. And my dad asks about you a lot as well, so seriously, stop worrying about it."

"Twenty-seven isn't *almost* thirty. It's… twenty-seven."

"I turn twenty-eight in less than two months, so it *is* almost thirty."

I don't want him to say that. If he's almost thirty, that means *I'm* almost thirty, which pushes me closer to retirement with every passing second. Before I know it, I'll be spending my days trapped in my apartment with my future husband, Luan, doing nothing all day. Maybe we'll go on a million trips a year because what else are we supposed to do?

Though, there is a high chance Luan will find a coaching job in New York, so perhaps traveling as much isn't going to happen either, which then means I will be spending most of my days hanging around at my friend's apartments to pass time. That shouldn't sound too bad, given that I do exactly that now whenever I'm at home.

Luan lays his hands on my jaw, sighing. "I love you, Grey Davis, but your negativity is driving me nuts today."

"Sorry." I place my hands onto his ass, pushing him a little closer to me until he gets the hint and sits down on top of me.

"It's okay, I don't know you any other way."

That's a lie. Luan knows more sides to me than anyone else. "You promise everything will be okay?"

Luan nods. "Of course, baby. What should go wrong?"

I don't know, but I feel like something bad is about to happen.

"Dad, this is—"

Mr. Hayes swings an arm around my shoulders before Luan even gets to finish introducing me. "Was about time you showed up here, boy."

"I'm glad to finally meet you," I say, though judging by the adrenaline that's rushing through my body, I don't think I mean it. Well, I do, I guess, but I would've preferred meeting Luan's father somewhere more private. A rather public event like this means other people are there to hear our conversations, and I'd have preferred it if private information about me didn't come out into the world for everyone to find with a quick google search.

"Likewise." Mr. Hayes clears his throat and steps back from me, now paying his own son some attention. Knowing Luan, he didn't exactly like being greeted by his own father last, but he's also getting so much better at accepting that not everything is always about him. Though to be fair, I, too, would be upset if my mother chose to greet Luan before me.

"Luan's been talking our ears off about you for years, and all Amira and I ever get to see of you are your interviews or brutality on the ice. Now tell me, why ice hockey? I'm sure Luan would've rather you played soccer instead, but this isn't about him so forget I said that."

I can already tell Luan gets the talking from his father.

"You do *not* have to answer that," Luan tells me, sending a warning look into his father's direction. He interlocks our hands, ready to drag me elsewhere to end a conversation we both know I'd rather not have.

I love talking about ice hockey, so that's not the problem. However, ice hockey will quickly drift over to another direction, more personal, and I loathe those conversations.

"It's alright, really."

"Luan, honey, stop trying to hide your fine boyfriend from us." Luan's mother lays a hand on her husband's shoulder, smiling up at me the same way she did when we first met. "How have you been, Grey?"

"Uhm…" Well, now that's a question I haven't been asked in a while.

How have I been?

So, I cut all the ties to my father because he is a homophobic asshole who'd rather not have a son than have an unlabeled one.

My parents divorced and my father is trying to sue my mother for money that she doesn't have for no reason other than dragging their divorce process out publicly for her own safety.

All of my friends are married and have kids or are about to pop some out which results in me feeling as though I'm not doing this whole being alive thing the right way, which I know is bullshit because everyone goes about their life at a different pace. But it sucks seeing all three of my best friend's growing their families while my boyfriend is just about to move in.

I haven't seen my boyfriend in person in weeks, and now that we're finally together again, I'm not even sure we'll make it through tonight okay.

Also, I've been dying to rip off that tux of Luan's ever since he put it on, but I probably shouldn't say this to his parents. Actually, I shouldn't say *any* of this to them.

"I've been great," I answer.

Luan gasps and holds the hand that's still holding mine over his heart. "How dare you give my parents more answers than you did me when we first met?"

I shrug. "Well, I didn't like you when we first met."

His jaw drops. "You *loved* me. I am a great person, Grey Davis."

"Maybe in your dreams you are." I smile at him, to which Luan's expression instantly softens.

I'm so proud of Luan for being able to know when I am joking and when I'm being serious. It may be a rather normal thing for anyone else to see the difference between those two, but only a little while ago, Luan would've thought I was being serious.

Just when I started to think that maybe meeting Luan's parents, or well, his father, isn't going that bad, Luan looks around us to see who's already present. When his eyes are back on his father, they fill with guilt, and I know what's about to leave him.

Honestly, I wish I could confidently say that his parents freaking out on us and telling Luan he can't date me that our relationship would survive. And as much as I want that too, I could never make Luan choose me over his family.

The only reason why I chose him over mine is because I didn't choose *him*, I chose my freedom, and he happened to be that freedom. Luan happened to be the one to show me that I could never be myself if I don't cut the ties to the only person who was holding me back.

His family isn't like mine, and I guess their support through all the years of Luan doing more shit to other's than he should've, them staying when he needed them the most even when he's already majorly fucked up, proved that.

Taking that away is something I could *never* live with. So, yes, if it does come down to him having to decide, I won't give him a chance to choose because that's cruel. He'll find love again, but he won't find a second family like the one he already has.

"Mom, Dad," Luan begins. He blows out a heavy breath and squeezes my hand like he's trying to reassure me. "There's something we should probably tell you."

"We?" Amira's eyebrows quip up in surprise. She looks from me to her son, and although she should be scared hearing those words, she just smiles. "Oh, my... Honey, you're not getting married, are you? I mean, woah, I'd be so happy for you two, and I'd throw you the *biggest* wedding in the whole wide world, but you didn't even officially move in together yet."

Luan chuckles, but I can't seem to find that same humor inside of me.

"Not yet, Ma. But uh… Actually, this is more about Grey and *his* family. I don't think you'll—"

"My dad's Li Ji-Hoon," I blurt out before Luan could. "As in the CEO of Li Co. That guy."

Amira sucks in a sharp breath, but honestly, it's not her I am terrified of. It's Luan's dad who frightens me.

Mr. Hayes nods slowly as he's trying to process what I've said. Instead of getting upset with me like I expect him to, he snorts a laugh. "Quite the father you've got there. Very… *supportive*."

"Can't choose my parents, can I?"

Amira now looks at me with sympathy. "Oh, I am so sorry, dear." She steps forward, and much to my surprise, takes both of my hands in hers. "I heard about your parents' divorce, please don't tell me this happened because your, uh, father didn't… you know… accept you. You've been in the media a lot lately and I doubt he didn't hear the news about you and Luan together yet."

That's quite up-front.

"Ma," Luan sort of groans.

"Oh." Amira lets go of my hands and brings one of hers up to cover her mouth. "I didn't mean to be rude, I apologize."

"It's alright, really." I exhale a little heavily. "They didn't get a divorce because of me, though me telling my father about Luan and I did somewhat finalize it." There's no use trying to pretend my father didn't treat me like crap, or that he'd ever accept my relationship. And truthfully, I am so sick of making excuses for that man.

If he can't accept me, so be it. I'll no longer paint him to be great either. He doesn't deserve it.

Even if he decided to accept me now, he fucked up. He may gladly walk all over me for the rest of my life, but he doesn't get to touch my mother again. Not e*ver* again. It might've taken me years to draw the line when it comes to my own life, but I am *very* quick to draw a million lines when it comes to the woman who raised me.

"At least we don't have to see him at your wedding, am I right? Or the holidays." Mr. Hayes shudders with disgust at the thought of spending even one hour in a room with my father. I get it though, it disgusts me as well.

"No, he won't be there. My father is no longer a part of my life."

Luan leans his head against mine, sighing softly. "But the good thing is, Grey Davis"—he sneaks his hand back into mine—"you will now receive tons of calls from *my* father asking if you're okay, if you need anything and such."

Will he though?

When I look at Mr. Hayes with a questioning look, he laughs. "Luan's not wrong. I can narrow my calls down to twice a week, but that's really cutting it, son."

Son.

What is happening?

"Ah, you didn't think Amira and I would, what? Disapprove of you now?" He tsks. "You said it yourself, you can't choose your parents. It's not your fault your father happens to be a shitshow of a person. But just because he is an awful human doesn't mean you are, Grey. And I know you've been making Luan very happy so for that alone I'd be *begging* you to stay in his life"

Oh, well, alright. I guess that means I get to keep my boyfriend after all. And thank fuck for that because I have absolutely no idea how I am supposed to live without that little stupid ray of sunshine in my life. My little curly-headed monster.

Chapter 12

"it's almost over, it's just begun"—All Eyes On Me (Song Only) by Bo Burnham

Juan

December 2026

"I JUST LANDED," Grey's voice comes through the phone a little sleepily. It makes me smile.

"Figured, otherwise you wouldn't have called, Grey Davis." It's New Year's Eve tomorrow, but Grey has a game in L.A. *tonight*. Their flight yesterday got canceled so they have a *really* tight schedule for today, but I love that he's still calling me to let me know they landed, even though I am sure the team is currently rushing to their bus to get to the arena in time.

Their flight back home is around one in the morning Pacific Standard Time, so when I said tight, I meant *tight*. It's currently six PM, their game starts at eight. Let's say the game doesn't run as smoothly, then it ends around ten, maybe. That gives them barely any time for interviews, let alone freshening up, before they have to head back to the airport. I do worry about the stress this puts them under, but I guess that comes with the job.

"I didn't want you to worry," he says.

Yep, those are butterflies making themselves comfortable in the pit of my stomach right now.

I know Grey cares about me. I mean, he should, given that I am officially moving in with him in less than a week, well, technically I moved in a day ago. It still baffles me when he says that he doesn't want me to worry about anything because it means he truly takes my feelings into consideration, and nobody has ever really done that before. Not like he does.

"My parents will be there to watch you," I tell him. My mom recently informed me about it. She was really excited to watch a game of Grey's in person, even though she gives maybe minus ten fucks about ice hockey.

Both of my parents have practically adopted Grey now. I swear, my father calls him more often than me, and if Dad does call me, he only ever asks about Grey. I love and hate it at the very same time.

Grey chuckles. "So your mom told me."

Of course she did. "If you get the chance to, hug her for me, okay?"

"Will do." Knowing Grey, he will do it even if he doesn't want to. "Listen, baby, I have to hang up. We're on our way to the arena now, I'll text you when I get there."

"You'll call, won't you?" I'm grinning, knowing he will, even if he has to put me on speaker because he's rushing to get geared-up.

"Probably."

"I'll be waiting for it."

"Of course. I love you."

Before I can reply, I hear a gag in the background which makes me laugh. I bet it came from either Colin or Aaron because they do this all the time when they're around us. Apparently seeing Grey in love is as rare to them as finding a potato growing on a tree. And they love to make fun of him a little. Maybe I'd find it weird if I didn't know all four of them do this to each other.

"I love you, too," I finally say with a hint of a chuckle in my voice. A second later, Grey hangs up the phone.

As I grab the remote to turn on the TV to catch the beginning of the game, even if that's still two hours away, I hear the door to Grey and I's apartment open.

Grey and *I's* apartment. It still sounds surreal to me.

Six Years

I turn around on the sofa in time to catch blond hair running inside. "Wuan!" Eden shrieks and comes to a halt right in front of me. "Daddy made food and he tell me to tell you if you, uh, if you want to… eat too? And we watch the hockey game together after, uh… we eat the food Daddy made."

Since I've been technically living here for two weeks already—minus the couple of days I went home for one last Christmas with my family—I realized something; when your boyfriend's best friend is a chef, you will eat a whole lot more than what you're used to. And you suddenly become a lab rat. Anything new Miles tries, he makes all of us try it and give our opinions.

The worst bit, I don't think this guy ever made a single dish that wasn't good enough to be served up in heaven.

I get up onto my feet. "Free food and ice hockey, of course I'm in, little guy."

Grey hasn't called yet, and the game was supposed to start five minutes ago.

The moderators said there will be a delay for the game and that it's possible it will start around 8:30 because the bus hasn't arrived yet.

Why the fuck hasn't the bus arrived yet?!

They had *two* hours to get from the airport to the arena, and the arena is fifty minutes away by car. Let's say an hour-thirty with heavy traffic, but definitely not two hours.

Lily, Sofia, and I are sitting on Miles and Emory's sofa with our phones in our hands, all of us waiting for a stupid phone call. Even a message will do.

"What if they've died?" Lily mumbles, and from the corner of my eye I can see that she's dialing Colin's number for the tenth time in two minutes.

The call goes straight to voicemail.

"They probably just have their phones turned off," Miles tries to comfort Lily, but it doesn't work. When he realizes that it doesn't work, Miles lays both of his hands on her shoulders. "Lily, you need to calm down. I know this seems impossible right now, but you *really* have to. Stress isn't good for the baby."

Fuck, right. Lily's pregnant. So are Sofia and Emory. I don't know how I forgot about that.

The worst part about this, while everyone here is scared about their friends and partner, Lily has it a million times worse. If the worst-case scenario happened—praying to everything holy that's not the case—that they've gotten into an accident and the entire team died, Lily wouldn't just lose her husband and *friends*, she would lose her husband, friend, and twin brother. Oh, and her father-in-law.

My hands are trembling, my eyes glued onto my phone screen, waiting. Waiting for what I don't think is going to come anymore.

I am a very optimistic person, but right now, even I can't think of any other reason as to why the game had been delayed by half an hour.

"We are so sorry to announce that tonight's game will be canceled. At this moment, we are unable to give you a reas—" Miles switches the channel, turning on the News, but there's nothing yet.

Canceled.

They canceled the game.

Those bastards know something's wrong, so why the fuck aren't they saying anything?

The whole room is quiet. Nobody has said anything because all of us know this isn't good, all of us know that whoever of us is going to be contacted first, the news won't be good at all.

"Daddy?" I hear Brooke say in a soft tone, her voice choked with tears. "Are they okay?"

I don't know what Miles answers or if he answers at all, because I tune out everyone around me.

Please don't let him be dead.

Please don't let him be dead.

Please don't let him be dead.

Our lives were just about to begin. I just moved in with him. We had no time together at all, this can't be happening.

One phone rings, and I am so stuck in my head that I don't even realize it until someone shakes me so hard, it might as well give me a concussion.

Lily picks up her phone though she doesn't manage to utter words. So I take the phone from her.

"Colin?"

"Shit, Luan? Uhm... *Fuck*." It sounds like Colin tries to cover the speaker but he doesn't succeed, which allows me to hear his next words. "How the fuck am I supposed to tell Luan that Grey is—"

The line goes dead.

Chapter 13

"can you hear me screaming? please don't leave me"—
Hold On by Chord Overstreet

Juan

December 2026

WE WON'T KNOW if he'll ever be able to play again until he wakes up.

Grey has a broken shoulder and one of the bones in his forearm is broken as well, but I can't really remember which one. When I got to L.A. and they told me about Grey's injuries, I only half-listened.

He also has a sprained ankle, but it's the least bad injury.

As of now, Grey is in a, I believe, medically induced coma. If I understood the doctor correctly, Grey's injuries are worse enough that he'd be in a lot of pain if he were to be awake right now, so they did him a favor with this. I don't know why this would be a favor and why they couldn't just put him on a whole shit ton of morphine, but I guess they know what they're doing.

Oh, wait never mind. It's not a medically induced coma, they want to put him in one should he wake up before his brain swells down.

God, I don't know. I have no idea how medicine works, I just know he's not awake and I'm too afraid to ask one of the nurses or doctors to explain it to me again. I probably wouldn't listen anyway.

As far as I know, there are two other guys on Grey's team

who are in a coma, but I'm not sure if their conditions are worse or better. I didn't ask.

Colin and Aaron are okay. They don't even have a broken bone, I think. Again, I didn't really ask, but Miles filled me in on them this morning.

It took us two seconds to book the next flight to L.A., and while Miles keeps switching rooms to visit all of his friends, I am practically tied to Grey's bed, even when the nurses keep telling me that I can't spend the night here.

There is nothing that could get me out of this room until my boyfriend wakes up and I know that he is okay.

I think the nurses hate me because of it, but I can live with that.

My head leans against the free mattress space on one side of my boyfriend while I hold his hand. I can't look at Grey because every time I take in those machines he's hooked on, it brings back flashbacks I don't want.

They're mostly me sitting by my *dead* best friend's hospital bed while I wait until the OR is ready and doctors would come in to steal all of his organs to give them to other kids who needed them.

So every time I look up and see that stupid ventilator Grey's hooked on to, I can't help but think some doctor is about to march in here and tell me it's time to say goodbye because they're now taking his organs out.

I already lost my best friend this way, I can't lose the love of my life like this as well.

I press my lips to Grey's hand. "Please come back to me," I beg, even though I'm not sure he can hear me.

I wait for a reaction that doesn't come, a reaction I don't think will come any time soon either.

Chapter 1

"but nothing ever stops you leaving"—when the party's over by Billie Eilish

Ivan

January 2027

"HONEY, YOU SHOULD go home and take a shower." My mother covers me up with a blanket.

"No, I'm good." This hospital is a little over an hour away from where I *used* to live, there's no way I'd get into a car to go 'home' just to take a stupid shower. Anything could happen in an hour. Besides, I'd be gone for more than an hour because I'd have to drive back to my parents' or my old house first, take a lightning-speed shower, and drive another hour back here. Nope. Not going to happen.

"Then at least take one here. It's been a week, honey, and excuse me for saying this, but you taking a shower is of *everyone's* interest."

I ignore my mother and go back to telling Grey all about his precious ice hockey. Someone's got to keep him updated.

Out of solidarity, the whole team decided to step back from playing any more games this season, though I'm not even sure that's allowed. They have enough players who somehow got away from the accident with a few bruises and nothing more. Only one of them had broken something and another three are still in the hospital, though everyone but Grey are already conscious again, the rest are good to play. Except for that one guy who's now paralyzed…

A few of them stick around though. They pop in to check on Grey a couple of times a day, and truthfully, it annoys me a little bit because it makes me wonder why they don't go back home like the others did. They must have someone waiting for them, I'm sure. Or maybe they don't. Maybe this team is their family and that's why they can't seem to go back home without knowing everyone is alright.

Grey's mother and sister stopped by yesterday. I thought maybe their presence would bring up the vibe a little, especially with Sun being mostly like me, but even she was quiet.

I don't know how much time passes, but the next time I take in my surroundings it's already dark outside.

Assuming that nobody would come visit anymore today, I lie my head back down, though this time onto Grey's body, looking up at him. A week after the accident and I'm now able to look at him without thinking about Charlie.

Wait, never mind, I just did.

I hate this. God, I hate all of this so fucking much.

I miss Grey. I miss his voice, his eyes. I miss seeing his frowns and the rare smiles. I miss just having him around even when we don't talk. I even miss being on the opposite side of the country, desperately waiting for his nightly phone calls. I just miss *him*.

What if he doesn't make it—No, I cannot think like this. Grey will survive.

But what if he won't? What am I supposed to do without him in my life? How am I expected to just keep on living when I would've lost the man I thought I'd marry in a few years?

Grey's the reason the world keeps spinning. If he's not there, the whole sky might as well collapse.

To every single person out there, we might not make sense, and maybe we are polar opposites, but he's who I can't live without. If he goes down, I go down. If he's upset, I'm upset. If he hates someone, I hate them, too.

SIX YEARS

If he dies, I die.

Then suddenly the door to Grey's room opens, but I don't bother to look up because there's only a few people who'd show up at this hour. Only that the presence in this room now feels heavy.

"What are you doing here?" the deep voice asks, something spiteful in it.

I ignore him. If there's one thing I am not willing to do right now, it's argue with a shithead of a father. *Grey's* father.

The question isn't what I am doing here, it's what *he's* doing here.

While this man is totally okay with hating his own son for a stupid sexual preference, I know I will marry Grey one day. I know that I want to spend the rest of my life by Grey's side, and I pray to everything holy that he feels the same way about me.

So I guess that gives me the right to be by my boyfriend's side at every hour of the day, hold his hand, be there for him even if I'm not sure he knows I'm here.

His father, on the contrary, has no right to be here.

"Could you step outside, I'd like to spend some time with my son without you here."

"He's not your son." I keep holding Grey's hand, still not bothering to look up. "I don't think he's been your son for a long while, has he? Not ever since Grey kissed that first guy."

"When my son's in a coma, his... questionable lifestyle doesn't matter."

"Well, it took you a whole week to get here, so I'm not sure that's believable."

"I was busy."

"And I was on the opposite side of the country, so that's not an excuse. When you love someone, you're never too busy to be there for them." I finally sit up and turn to face Mr. Li. Only when I do, I don't see the same man I did last year. The man who had his whole life together.

I see a guy who looks like *he* was in an accident. His hair is tousled, and he has a faint bruise on his cheek. He wears sweatpants and a baggy shirt, and I could swear he smells a little too much like a hospital, as though he's been here for a while.

Even if he had been in an accident, why would he be in *this* hospital? Li Ji-Hoon lives in Malibu, an hour away from this hospital. There are plenty of hospitals around where he lives, where his office is, so what would he be doing *here*?

Then my eyes fall on his broken arm. Sure, he could've gotten that one today, but the bruises on his face are at least a few days old… if not a *week* old.

"What happened to you?" I ask, not caring that there's a high chance I won't even receive an answer.

To my surprise, I do.

"Car crash."

I narrow my eyes at him. Jokingly, I say, "Drove into a bus, huh?"

My mother told me that the police believe the "accident" wasn't so accidental, that it was targeted. According to witnesses, there were a few cars on the road, though not enough to cause three cars to crash into the bus out of nowhere. There were no traffic lights, no intersections that would allow a car to reach the sides of the bus.

Unless someone *planned* for this to happen.

When Mr. Li doesn't react, I almost gasp. *Almost*.

Instead of reacting to the news with shock, I chuckle. "Wow, so you hate queer people so much that you willingly risk your own life just to hopefully take out your son's?" Not even I would ever think to sink that low. "I hope you're aware that you weren't just playing with Grey's life and your own, but you also could've killed a bunch of other guys who were on that bus. Some of them are married, have kids, some whose partners are expecting."

I point toward the door. "There is a five-year-old little girl just down the hall, praying for her father to wake up." *He already woke up two days ago.* I drop my arm again. "And another one-year-old boy whose father has broken both of his legs and suffered injuries on his spine. He is paralyzed. He's never going to play a single game ever again. He's only *twenty-one*."

Grey's father swallows thickly, loud enough for me to hear. His eyes fill with what seems to be remorse, but from my own experience, I know he's faking that guilt. I know he doesn't give a shit about any of what I've just told him.

"If I left this room, what would you've done?" I hold Grey's hand tighter. "Suffocated Grey? Turned off the machines that are keeping him alive?"

"No one's going to believe you if you go to the police." He smirks at me, his eyes shining in victory. "Nobody would believe *I* would ever try to harm my son, that I would go to these lengths."

I don't know if he's right, that even if I report this, nobody will believe me. Chances are, they won't.

For once, Li Ji-Hoon might be right. Why would anyone believe me?

No one would because in a perfect world, no father would ever try to murder his own son because of a sexual orientation. I'll assume nobody *saw* this man on the scene, and if they did, he could always make it out to have been there because he was on his way to the arena himself, about to watch his son's game. Make it out that it all happened so fast right in front of him, and he was no longer able to stop the car before he crashed right into the bus as well.

And I am sure whoever he *hired* to drive into that bus with him, they would never dare open their mouths to admit this was planned.

No matter what I could say, this man will *always* be able to have his words against mine.

Even if I do decide to fight this, fight him in the name of everyone who was inside of that bus, I'll lose. It'd only take one look into my records, and I'll be titled as someone who's unreliable, someone nobody could trust, which then automatically makes me the liar.

"I can give you one piece of advice," Mr. Li says as he makes his way back to the door, about to leave since I clearly don't plan on exiting this room ever again. "Leave Grey and he will stay alive."

Chapter 2

"call me when it's over, 'cause I'm dying inside"—Sober by Demi Lovato

Ivan

January 2027

WHEN I STEP INSIDE my mostly empty bedroom, the first thing I do is look around. My eyes fall to the boxes on my floor, my empty bed, the empty walls. I took everything down already because I was supposed to be fully moved in with my boyfriend a week ago. I *did* move in with him. Grey and I wanted to come back yesterday to pick up the rest of my stuff.

We never got to do it.

I carefully lay the brown paper bag onto my bed before I drop down beside it. A breath so deep and pain-filled that it makes me cry leaves me in one go. Even if I tried to force these tears to stay inside of me, I don't think I would win.

It's moments like these that make me wish I still didn't know how to feel. Moments like these that make me want to go back in time, somewhere where I could drink away my feelings, drown them in liquor, or well, not feel them in the first place because I was numb to *feeling*.

But I feel this.

I feel my heart breaking into more and more pieces with every single second I'm not inside of Grey's hospital room. I feel it tearing apart at the seams with every moment that the reality of my decision sinks in, finding a cozy spot on one of the broken heart pieces.

It's kicking me in my guts, to the point where I choke on my own tears, feeling as though I can't breathe. There's a rope tied around my neck, and it tightens with every breath I draw in, or so it feels.

I stare up at the ceiling, though I can't see anything but a blurry mess. I can't find a spot to focus on, a spot to stare at and calm myself down because there is *nothing*. Nothing for me to see, nothing for me to keep my head occupied with, nothing that could fix me.

Then I turn my head, my eyes find the head of a bottle that's peeking out of the paper bag.

I don't know why I bought it.

I'm so stupid.

So stupid.

So fucking stupid.

Reaching for the bag, I pull out the bottle then sit up. I stare at the logo, trying to find one sentence that would keep me from opening it.

There is none, but why would "think about what opening this bottle would do to you and your relationships" be written on a bottle of whiskey?

What relationships anyway?

My family will still be there even when I'm a drunk again because they love me. They'll want to fix me again.

Doro won't actually leave me behind either, I don't think.

And Grey? He'll be so much better without me. He'll *live* without me.

But this isn't going to be forever anyway, right? Because once I found a way to make this right…

I open the bottle, turn to look out of my window, then toast the Li mansion like it was another person drinking with me before I take a huge sip. Or three.

Or down the whole bottle.

Chapter 3

"swept in the thoughts of you and me"—10 by Elouiz

Grey

January 2027

I STARE ABSENTLY INTO the distance while one of the doctors keeps talking about my stats, what happened that had me end up here, and what they did in surgery.

Apparently I've been in a coma for two whole ass weeks and woke up about two hours ago.

It's not the shock of having been in a coma for a while that's making me detach from the world, though I wish it was. It's Luan not being here.

I get it.

I was in a car crash, and he lost his best friend in one. *He* was in one before. Luan's traumatized and I think he couldn't go through this again. He couldn't watch someone else he loves leave him because the last time this happened, Luan turned into someone he couldn't recognize.

Which is precisely what's got me worried.

Colin said he's trying to reach him, but Luan just won't pick up his phone. And yes, he might be asleep given that it's four in the morning, I think, but some part of me worries that he is in some bar, drinking again.

He wouldn't do that. Luan's sober, and he knows what he's got to lose if he ever starts drinking again.

It still sucks that he isn't picking up his phone, or that he's not here in the first place, but since I know why, I don't take it badly.

"I take it he's still not picking up?" Miles asks as Colin throws his phone onto the armchair beside him, looking defeated.

"It went straight to voicemail this time."

Lily cocks her head at her husband. "Really?"

Colin nods.

"That's so strange," Aaron notes. He wraps his arms around Sofia's neck and rests his chin on the top of her head. "First he doesn't leave this room for a whole week and now it's like he—"

"What?" I interject, feeling my eyebrows furrow. Or maybe that's my imagination. At this point, I am not even sure I can *move* my face at all. I'm pumped with morphine to reduce the pain in my body, and I'm actually waiting to be high as a kite so I can stop worrying about my boyfriend and my hockey career, but I think whatever Aaron just said sobered me up real good.

"Yeah, Luan's been sitting by your side all day and night for like nine days, only to disappear. I swear, he barely even wanted to get up to use the toilet. Sun had to force him to eat and drink. Before he left, he demanded either one of us should *always* be with you because he fears you might not wake up again should you ever be alone," Miles tells me. "He left, and I thought he finally decided to take a shower, but he never returned."

Luan was here.

And then he wasn't anymore.

That doesn't sound like him, does it? Well, it does in some ways, but then it doesn't anymore.

The Luan I know wouldn't just run off like that.

Or maybe that's exactly what he'd do.

"And neither of you thought to look for him at his house?!"

When I woke up and I found all of my friends—excluding Emory because she's eight or nine months pregnant now—, Brooke and Eden, and my mom and sister standing inside of a way too white room, staring at me, I thought this was my end. I thought I had died.

Six Years

I didn't remember what happened, but those memories *slowly* made it back to me. At least to a certain point. The last thing I remember is me getting onto a plane to L.A.

So when they told me that I am in a hospital in L.A., my first thought was we had a plane crash that I somehow survived, but nope, apparently three cars crashed into our bus on our way to the arena.

Then talking about a hockey arena, I had to suit up because the following news would ruin my life.

My mom told me that I was out for the entire season, but that would be okay because the whole team wasn't going to play anymore to honor those of us who didn't make it out of the accident without any bad injuries. That would be five of us, though only three of those five were in a coma—me included, apparently.

It's speculated that the accident wasn't an accident, or so my *friends* believe. The police never gave a statement on it, let alone bothered to investigate the matter.

Anyway, my shoulder is broken as is one other bone in my arm. If I am lucky, the fractures will heal perfectly, and I will be good to play again. If I am unlucky, I will need months of rehab and tons of practice to even regain the ability to *move* my arm. If that's the case, my career ended with this accident.

After that whole shock wore off—which also didn't really last long—I started to look around for my boyfriend. He was the first person I wanted to see when I woke up… but he wasn't there.

As it seems, I woke up too late.

"In case you forgot, which I wouldn't put past you right now," Sun starts, "We have no idea where he lives, Grey."

I look at my sister. "You can see our house from his bedroom window. It's, uh…" Jesus, think, Grey. You know how to describe a house. "It's a white house, gray roof, and it has a red front door. They're missing a few tiles on the stairs to the porch because they're too lazy to have them fixed. And, uh, it's basically straight ahead if you looked out of my bedroom window."

"Grey…" My mother sighs.

Sun and Mom are the only ones who would ever be able to find that house according to my description, but I'd never ask either of them to go back near my dad's house to look for Luan.

All of my friends grew up around New York, well Miles excluded. He sort of grew up in Malibu, but I'm pretty sure he lived on the other side of Malibu.

Or maybe he didn't. When he came to visit a couple of years ago, Miles walked around El Matador Beach like he knew every inch of that place.

It doesn't matter because even if Miles knew the whole country like the back of his hand, if something bad happened to Luan, or if he started to drink again, Miles would never be able to do anything about it.

Besides, the faster he can go home the better. Emory could give birth any day now.

"Did you contact Doro?" I ask, remembering that Luan's most definitely with her.

"Who?" comes from almost everyone inside of this room.

"Luan's best friend?" Shit, yeah, they don't know that. "Where's my phone?" I try to get up but I'm basically being—nicely—tackled down the moment I hint to move. "Woah there, friends, I have a broken arm, not a broken head."

Neither of them laughs.

Too early?

I swear, you try to joke *once* and suddenly nobody finds you funny anymore. Luan would've laughed.

"You can't go anywhere, Grey," my mother says, putting on her new-found strict tone. "You were in a *coma*, you'll be here for at least another week without seeing the outside world," she adds in Korean.

"Because that's such a punishment for him." Sun laughs. "Grey loves being indoors."

"This isn't a punishment. Grey almost *died*," Mom says to my sister. "I am not putting his health behind finding his boyfriend, who's most likely asleep at this hour. I bet Luan's just as worried as we all were, and he will show up once one of us reaches him. We all had our struggles taking in the sight of Grey lying there all reckless, this wasn't any less difficult for Luan. All of us have other breaking points, and his probably just snapped and he couldn't sit around here any longer, thinking the guy he loves might never wake up again."

"Or he's drunk off his ass," I mutter under my breath, but thankfully no one hears. "So, my phone?"

I have to call Doro, she's the only one who'd know where he's at.

Aaron lets out a deep sigh, one I most definitely don't like. "Most of the phones were useless after the accident, yours included. You can try turning it on, if you can find your screen, or the other parts to your phone."

Great. This is just great.

"I need *one* phone then," I say, but even I can hear that I sound desperate at this point.

Sun opens her purse, pulls out her phone and then hands it to me. "Do you know her number by heart?"

I shake my head, but regret doing so immediately. Shit, why'd no one ever tell me waking up from a coma does all sorts of things to your brain? "No, but I can google Luan's father's business number. He owns Hayesland, so with a little luck, I will reach him, and he can give me her number if Mike doesn't know where his son's at."

"Hayesland?!" Sun covers her mouth up with her hand. "Dad's going to murder you when he finds out!"

"Well," I chuckle, "it's not like he was very fond of me before, so what does it matter?"

All of my friends know what actually went down, so I'm not surprised when the whole room quiets down and the only sounds being heard are the *beep beeps* from whatever machines I am still hooked on to.

Using that silence to my advantage, I type *Mike Hayes* into the google search bar, and lo and behold, his contact information is one of the first information about him that shows up. I know the phone number standing there isn't his private one, but this might allow me to talk to an assistant, and they might be able to transfer me. Hopefully.

Instantly I click onto the call button. Surprisingly, it doesn't take very long until someone picks up. Before whoever picked up could even introduce themselves, I'm already talking.

"Hi, this is Grey Davis, could you possibly transfer me to Mike Hayes?" I don't think they will, not without any further explanations.

"I'm sorry, Mr. Davis, but I can't do that. If I transferred every call to Mr. Hayes, he'd be booked for more hours of the day than possible."

Guessed that much. I've been living with my father for long enough to understand at least a little bit of their whole business. Or how they deal with it, rather. "I am his son's boyfriend, and this is really urgent. Look, I know you still won't transfer the call because I could be anyone, I could be lying. But I *really* need you to trust me on this one. This is about life and death"—a little dramatic but tell me I'm wrong—"Luan could be lying in a dark, abandoned alley, dying. My phone is wrecked because of an accident I was in, apparently, I don't remember much because I was in a coma for like weeks, and... could you just get me through to Mike, *please*?"

I watch as Colin leans into Aaron, faintly hearing him ask, "He can talk that much in one go?"

"Maybe they exchanged him for a new one while he was in a coma ," Aaron whispers back, to which Sofia is kind enough to slap him for me.

On the other end of the line, I hear the woman sigh heavily. "I really hope you're not lying to me because I will lose my job if you're tricking me."

"Promise, I'm not."

A second later, the line goes seemingly dead, and when I check whether she hung up or not, someone speaks. "Hayes."

"Mike? This is..." Shit, why am I dizzy? I clear my throat and blink a few times, hoping that'll fix it. It doesn't. "This is… uh…"

"Grey? You woke up!"

"I, er, yes. Uhm..."

"Grey, are you okay?" Mom takes my face in her hands, forcing me to look at her.

I attempt to nod but stop myself before the room could spin any more than it already does. "Yeah, good. Little, uh, dizzy."

Sun takes her phone away from me, and maybe if my brain was working at a normal speed, I would fight it, but I just let her take it.

Brooke comes walking up to my bed. She takes my hand in hers, and with tears in her eyes, she says, "I'll find Luan for you, Uncle Grey. Don't worry about it, okay?"

Did I ever mention that I love this kid?

Once again, I try to nod but the movement makes me even feel like I'm about to empty out whatever substances are inside of my stomach right now.

"You sleep, Uncle Grey." Eden comes up next to his sister, giving me a stern look. His eyes are narrowed at me as though if I don't fall asleep this instant, he's going to haunt me for the rest of my life.

I think I'm moments away from drifting off to sleep—not because Eden demands I do, but because I can't quite seem to keep myself awake any longer—when I faintly hear my sister mutter something. Despite my interest in finding out what she's pressed about, I don't have the strength to reopen my eyes and ask, so all I can do is listen while I try to keep myself awake for a little while longer.

"What do you mean they thought he was still here?" Miles, I believe, asks.

"Nobody's seen him…"

Chapter 4

"is your love from before still strong?"—Broken by Isak Danielson

Grey

January 2027

After another torturously long week in the hospital, I finally got to go home. Only that instead of staying back at my hotel to rest some more before I can get on a plane to actually go home, I snuck out.

Yes, I *snuck* out at the age of twenty-six. My mother tries her very best to make sure I don't overwork myself, and while that's nice, the second I was allowed to leave the hospital, all I wanted to do was get my ass over to Malibu to look for my boyfriend since nobody has seen him in two *weeks*.

Doro said he wasn't home, but something tells me she's lying, so naturally I have to go there to check.

My friends are convinced Luan ghosted me and this whole thing is his way of breaking up with me, but I don't believe that. If Luan wanted to break up, which is already very unlikely, he would've waited until I woke up. Although I don't doubt he would've done this very thing before we met, before he wanted to get better. Luan has changed. He is a better version of himself, and he wouldn't just ghost me anymore because he's "done" with me.

I knock at the door of their house over and over again, but nobody ever opens it. I think I've been standing here for five

minutes already, just hammering against the wood and ringing the doorbell. Just when I'm about to give up, someone *finally* opens the door.

"What do you want?" Doro snaps as her eyes lay on mine. She looks in distress, worried, and exhausted.

I contemplate on arguing with her. What am I doing here? Looking for my boyfriend, perhaps? But I decide to ignore it all and storm past her instead, making my way straight toward Luan's bedroom.

"He doesn't want to see you!" Ah, so he *is* here after all. Somehow, knowing this makes me feel worse. "He's not in the right… state to have a conversation."

"I don't give a shit." I barge into Luan's room, shutting the door right in Doro's face because as much as I know Luan might want her around, I don't, not right now anyway. I lock the door and then turn around only to find Luan lying on the floor, staring up at the ceiling with an empty bottle of whisky in his arms.

The very moment I realize what he's done, my entire soul breaks for him. He's going to hate himself more than ever when he's sobered up again, when he has a clear head and can think straight again.

But I'll be there to catch him when he falls.

"Did you get the new bottle?" He slurps on his words. My heart breaks all over again just seeing him in this state. Getting drunk is fine for everyone who's not fighting an addiction, but for Luan, getting drunk means relapsing, a setback. Relapsing is part of recovery, but I hate it anyway. And I'm not so sure if that still applies after years.

I don't respond, just walk over to him. He lies between my legs while I stand over him, looking down. Luan's eyes are closed, and I'm kind of relieved they are because I don't know what will come out of his mouth when he sees me.

His face is as beautiful as ever, though the bags underneath his eyes tell me all about how awful his past weeks must've been.

His clothes are covered in what I assume is a healthy mixture of alcohol and old food. Luan's hair is a mess as well.

Oh, Luan…

I look around his room yet again finding nothing but a pure mess. There are tons of bottles all over the floor and his shelves, telling me that he hasn't been drinking starting today. It must've been day*s*. He has moving boxes all over as well, and it hurts in my heart to know why they're here.

We were supposed to get them over to New York like two weeks ago.

After a short moment of looking at him and his room, I shake off my nerves, bend over, and grip the neck of the bottle in his arms, ripping it away from him.

"HEY!" Luan's eyes rip open. He's ready to reach for the bottle when his eyes set on mine instead, his arms drop immediately.

"Get up," I say and take a step back so he can sit up. I don't think he'll be able to sit up on his own, at least he doesn't look like he could.

I'm just praying I have enough strength in my one functioning arm to help him up.

"Hello, Grey Davis." He smiles or tries to. Luan blinks a little weirdly, slowly, and like he's trying to focus his eyes. Must be nice seeing two of me.

"Sit up, Luan."

Luan shakes his head. "Nah. I'm good down here."

Fine. I throw the empty bottle onto his bed then take a seat on the floor. Grasping Luan's wrist, I pull him up to sit, forcing him to face me. He swings slightly back and forth, not quite being able to keep himself steady.

I guess working out a couple of times a week does come in handy eventually.

"D'you miss me?" he asks, grinning or at least some form of it. I don't answer. "Aw, Grey Davis, I think you did."

"Why? Did you miss me?" I can't really do much except look out for him until he's sobered up. There's no magic spell to remove alcohol from his body right now, and even if I made him throw up, there'd still be alcohol in his bloodstream, we'd only get rid of some excess inside of his stomach that hasn't been absorbed yet. So until he's sober, I can't do anything but sit here with him and wait, listening to his drunken babbling. The good thing is, I can say whatever I want because he will not remember a single word tomorrow.

I did think he'd put up more of a fight though. I thought he'd scream at me, demand I let him drink, but he's surprisingly quiet.

Luan shakes his head. "No, I never loved you anyway so…"

Okay, ouch. Still, I don't believe him. "I'm going to ask you again, and this time you'll say the truth, okay?"

"I will?"

"Yes. So, did you miss me?"

He nods. "I should've never broken up with you."

Now that's something we both agree on, I guess. Especially since I'm only now finding out he broke up with me.

I shouldn't ask because right now, whatever he says, his words may be true words, but he can't really control what he lets out. And still… "Then why did you?"

Luan blows out some air, then rubs the back of his hand over his nose like he's wiping it. "Because of your dad."

Huh? My dad? I haven't talked to him since I cut him off.

"Because he was all, *Luan, if you don't break up with my son, I will… I will do this and that.* And because I didn't want that to happen, I had to break my own heart. Do you know that I love you, Grey Davis? Like, wow, I didn't think I could ever love you so much but then I broke up with you and I felt like dying. Like, when I came home that evening, I fell into my bed and then I could feel my heart break more with every passing second." He rolls his eyes with a heavy breath leaving him. "And I was just like *well, shit, I did that*. I pushed the only good person in my life away because his stupid ass homophobic father was all like, *If you don't break up with my son, I will kill him myself.* And like, honestly, what kind of fucked up father threatens to have his own son murdered only because he isn't straight? That's like, sick. But I didn't want you dead because if you were dead, then I could only ever love you in or on your grave, anyway I'd rather not have you at all than love a ghost. Because like, I love you so much more than apple juice, for sure. And when I went to the cops, they laughed and said Ji-Hoon Li, no Li Ji-your dad, he would never do that because he's a man of honor. He's not. I know that. You know that. We all know that. Why don't they know that?"

I blink. Yeah, that's all I can really do right now. And swallow, *hard*. Maybe I should wait until he's no longer drunk off his ass to get the whole story because *this* does not sound like something that makes sense in my brain. To me this sounds like Luan broke up with me because my own father threatened to have me killed if we stayed together, and that would be ridiculous.

Me. Killed. What the fuck?

I know I was just recently in an accident and that I must've hit my head hard enough to end up in a coma for two weeks, but I didn't think I hit my head hard enough to hear Luan say my own father wants to kill me.

"And, you know, I wanted to break up to stop you from getting murdered, and then go to the police and tell them that Ji-Li-Hoon said he—that he would kill my perfect and pretty and handsome boyfriend with the perfect dick size only because he sticks his dick in my ass and not some woman's pussy. Like can you believe that? And then when I got your dad in jail, I would've told you about all of this and then I would've prayed that you still loved me and that we could get back together and finally get married but no… they *laughed*. And, God, Grey Davis, did you know that this sucks because I love you and I will always love you, but I can't be with you because if I am, you'll die, and I'd rather not be with—"

"I got it, baby. You'd rather not be with me than see me dead." And I guess I will now have to spend all night wondering how much of Luan's story is true and which parts are fiction.

My dad is an asshole, but he wouldn't have me murdered, I don't think.

"I try to not act in my own favor once and suddenly I have a million shattered mini heart pieces instead of one whole heart that's beating just for you." He closes his eyes like he's about to fall asleep, but when they open up again, I notice he didn't close them because he's tired but because he's crying. "Are you mad?" Luan asks, falling right into my arms. I barely have a second to even catch him.

I close my arms—or one and a half—around his body and pull him on my lap. "No, baby." I guess I should be, but I just… can't.

It isn't often that Luan genuinely tries to do something good for anyone but himself, and yes, he might've gotten a whole lot better at it the past years, but it's still rare. His thinking might've been awful, too complicated because if he only talked to me before he decided on anything, we could've found a solution. Then again, Luan can barely even tell when he's giving *into* his narcissistic tendencies, so how would he know when he's overdoing *kindness*?

He meant well, and I appreciate it, even though I wish he would've waited and talked to me.

"Good," he sighs. "Because I love you, Grey Davis. And my life is so bad without you. I couldn't even—" Luan hiccups, though I'm not sure if that's because he's crying or simply from all the alcohol in his bloodstream. "—I couldn't even sleep or eat or breathe. Everything hurts, Grey Davis. My throat, my eyes, my stomach, my head, and my fucking heart. It all hurts. And I didn't know how to stop it."

I hold him a little tighter, squeezing my eyes shut as I listen. With every word that leaves him, you'd think the pain in my heart would lessen, finding out he didn't want this breakup, that I didn't even know happened either, but it only ever gets worse.

"Then I drank, Grey Davis. And I couldn't stop. And I'm so stupid, you know that? Because I feel great now, but then when I wake up you'll be gone because I'm pretty sure I'm only hallucinating right now, and then I'll feel bad again, and I'll drink again. And I don't know how to make it stop, Grey Davis. I love you. And I miss you. And I just want… I just want *you*. Here. Actually here with me. Not just… Wow. I wanted to move in with you, you know? I still do, but now you probably hate me."

"I don't hate you, Luan." How could I? Every inch of my body is screaming for him. Every nerve, every blood cell, every *atom* of mine is useless without him.

He's the other half of me, and without him I don't work.

Hating him would be like hating myself.

"Grey Davis?"

"Yes?"

Luan clutches his fingers around the fabric of my jacket. "Someday, when we get back together… even if we're like a hundred years old, do you think we'll get married?"

"How about we talk about this tomorrow when you've sobered up?" I don't want to talk about a possible marriage with him when he's drunk. Chances are still great that he won't remember any of this, but I will, and I'd rather not remember hearing him talk about our potential wedding when it might never even happen.

I can feel Luan nod, then he lets out a groan. "I think… I think I have to puke."

"Now?"

Again, he nods, and so I pull his arms away from around me, get up, and somehow pull him up with me before hooking his arm over my shoulder to get him into his bathroom.

Chapter 5

"you kiss away the pain of all the hell I'm in"—
Medicine by James Arthur

Iuan

January 2027

MY HEAD IS THROBBING, my muscles ache, and I feel like I'm sucked completely dry. There's not an ounce of water inside of me.

But that's alright.

I reach my hand to my nightstand drawer, trying to find whatever liquor bottle I know I put there last night for exactly this moment in the morning. It's what I've always done before I went to rehab. I always had an extra bottle on my nightstand for the next morning. Can't be hungover if you don't stop drinking.

But to my horror, there's nothing.

My eyes jump open and my head snaps toward my nightstand to make sure my hand is feeling the right things. It's empty. Completely empty. Not even my lamp is still standing there.

What the fuck?

Ah, right… never mind. My lamp is in a moving box. No, it is not. I only packed my clothes and important documents as well as other important things. But no lamps.

"The fuck?" I mutter when I look around my room only to find it completely… clean. Did I drunkenly tidy up? No, I'd never do that. Drunk-me is lazy, except when he thinks he can conquer the world and then falls off a chair or something. But the point is, drunk-me doesn't clean.

My room door opens, but I don't bother looking because it's just Doro or Sarah checking whether I'm still alive or if I finally died of alcohol poisoning. Only that the voice speaking isn't either one of theirs.

"Do you want coffee?"

It sounds like… My head snaps into the other direction, my mouth opens with shock when I find Grey standing in the doorway, dressed in nothing but boxers and the cast on his entire arm. *My* boxers, mind you.

Did I die?

"Am I dead?" I voice out loud, then look down at myself. I, too, don't wear anything but my boxers. Interesting.

Shit, didn't he just recently wake up from his coma? I think Doro told me.

Fuck, he looks so good, even with that stupid cast on. And he is so handsome, so…, I need a drink because I cannot fucking do this.

"No, but you did throw up what felt like your entire soul."

Funny, because it feels like it, too.

Hold on. Hold the fuck on.

Grey is here. As in, he is *here* in my house. And I am hungover. And he witnessed me throw-up. Fuckfuckfuck.

"Oh, God." I lean over, pressing the tips of my fingers to my temples. I am so fucked.

I hear Grey close the door, then walk toward me. But even when my mattress dips beside me and he lays a hand on my thigh, I continue to stare at my blanket.

"Luan…"

"Did you sleep in the bed with me?" I ask.

"It's not like we haven't done that before." He lays a bottle of apple juice down in front of me, then takes my hand and drops an Advil into my palm. "Take it."

"Grey, we're broken up. You can't—You shouldn't be here." Does his dad know he's here?

"You're supposed to give a two weeks' notice before quitting."

What is that even supposed to mean? "You do realize our relationship isn't a job, right?"

"Yeah, but you can't quit a job without telling your employer, and you can't end a relationship without telling your partner either. I was in a coma when you apparently broke up with me, Luan. I couldn't talk back, let alone hear you tell me we're breaking up. Yesterday evening was the first time I even heard about said breakup."

He might have a point there, but I couldn't wait and say it to his face, it would've broken me more than it already has anyway.

"Do you want to know what I did when I woke up?" Not really because, chances are, I will cry. "I asked for you the second I opened my eyes, Luan. I made excuses as to why you didn't stay around the hospital because I figured it must've been too hard on you given your past, and that was okay with me. I didn't take that badly, I wasn't mad or anything. I only got worried when nobody could reach you, and when your parents told me they haven't seen or heard from you in days."

He called my parents?

"So, if you actually wanted to break up with me that badly, you could've at least had the decency to do it *after* I woke up, or you should've done it before we already brought most of your shit into our apartment."

When I don't look up, Grey lifts my head for our eyes to meet. He looks mad, but I suppose that's to be expected. "Our breakup isn't very valid given that I had no say in it whatsoever. Also, I think you were just getting cold feet before officially moving in."

Cold feet? I was ready to marry him right on the goddamn spot... then his father happened. "It is valid. I don't have feelings for you anymore, Grey."

Ah, shit, saying this out loud hurts more than I ever thought it could. And truthfully, I'm not even sure I have any pieces of my heart left that would be able to break.

But this is the right thing to do.

He chuckles. *Why is this funny to him?* "I think you do."

"I don't."

Grey crosses his arms over his chest as much as he can with the cast on, a smirk tugs on his lips. "Doro couldn't make you stop drinking in days, baby. I showed up here, and you didn't even argue with me when I took that bottle away from you. You've been drinking for days, and I might not know shit about addictions, but I highly doubt it'd be that easy to take drinks away from an alcoholic once they relapse. I think you were waiting for me to come save you."

I guess it depends. I've never relapsed, which is a surprise to me as well, but I also never had a reason to before. Sure, I was craving a drink every once in a while, but I always texted Grey to distract me, even when I knew he wouldn't respond. And after a while, I never thought about alcohol anymore.

I'm hoping I don't go through the horror that I faced when I went to rehab once again. The aggressiveness when I wanted a drink and couldn't have it? No, thank you, I don't want that.

I now know how great life can be without being drunk ninety percent of the day, and I really don't want to fall back to where I once was. Though I'm sure losing Grey is worse than becoming an active addict again, it shouldn't be, but to me it is.

"I was done drinking for the day." Unless I passed out a second later, I definitely wasn't done yet. Anyway, I pop the Advil into my mouth and then down it with some apple juice. "Where'd you get the apple juice?" I know for a fact we didn't have any here.

"Went out to buy it after waking up."

I lift my eyebrows. "You bought them for me?"

He nods. "Now, can we stop talking bullshit here, Luan? Could you just tell me the truth about why you're trying to break up with me?"

"Because I don't love you anymore." I don't think I'll ever not love this guy.

"Yeah, no, you do. You told me like six times last night."

"I was drunk, so that doesn't count." I take another sip from my apple juice, internally smiling because apple juice makes me feel better. Then I look at the bottle to find out what brand he bought because I don't like all of them, but I also never told Grey which ones I like and which ones I don't.

He bought my favorite one.

"It counts, Luan." Grey takes my hand in his, and I know I should pull mine away and keep on insisting that I don't love him, but that's costing me so much energy. I do love him, and I want to hold his hand because I know this is going to be the last time he will do so. "Do you remember anything from last night?"

I shake my head, but still try to find some things inside of my head. It's like a bomb went off when suddenly all of the events from last night come crashing into my brain. Every *I love you* I uttered, every *I miss you*, every stupid word that left my mouth like I had nothing to lose.

The mention of his father.

I told him. Of course I did. I'm so stupid. I was never good at keeping secrets, especially from Grey.

I don't know what Grey sees on my face right now, but it's horrifying enough for him to nod and press his lips into a thin line. "He really said he'd have me murdered?"

There *is* a way for me to deny it. If I blamed it on the alcohol, I could say I must've mixed up reality and some movie I watched... but some part of me is incapable of continuing to lie to him. And so I nod. Faintly, but it's there. "I... You're going to think I'm lying if I tell you what I know."

Grey cocks his head. "When have I ever not believed what came out of your mouth?"

Good point, once again. But this is different. None of what I have ever told him weighed as much as *this* does. "He came to visit you," I say, then clarify, "your dad, I mean."

"Figured he did, otherwise you wouldn't have run off."

Right.

"If I hadn't been in that room, I don't know what he would've done, but…" I swallow thickly at the thought of it. "He hinted at wanting to, uh, get rid of you. But before you say anything, that wasn't what made me leave. It was him admitting that he was behind the accident, and that this very accident was supposed to murder you already. That didn't work and thank God it didn't. But he won't stop trying unless I'm gone. The worst bit, I can't even report it because nobody believes me. He admitted all that to me and I don't have any proof. So I decided to leave because otherwise who knows how long you'd have left to live?"

He nods once, slowly. "You do realize that even if I'd accept your attempt in breaking us up, he'd still want me dead, right? Because, Luan, as much as I know you don't want this to be true, I'll just be with another guy eventually. It doesn't matter if it's for a quick fuck or a relationship. As long as I don't marry a woman, my father will always want to get rid of me."

"I wasn't going to let it get that far," I mutter.

"So, you wanted to go to the police and have him arrested before you told me?"

Well, if he says it like that, of course it sounds stupid. "I thought, if we broke up, at least your life would be safe and then I could figure out the rest, somehow get rid of your father. And when I managed that, I would've told you what happened, and I would've prayed you'd understand."

"But they didn't believe you," he states, though his voice hides a hint of a question.

"Why would they? I showed up at the police station *drunk*, then told them your father threatened to have you murdered. Mind you, the father who nobody even knows *is* your father. So basically, I accused a man of wanting to murder you and they brushed it off as a drunk man from a rival company wanting revenge."

I showed up *drunk*... I haven't had a single drop of alcohol in years, but apparently, breaking up with the love of my life made me lose every functioning brain cell.

"Well, I believe you," he says.

Somewhat of a smile creeps up onto my face, but it's not the same as it used to be. "That's not enough, Grey."

"It's Grey Davis to you."

I tilt my head up to the ceiling, blowing out some air like it would somehow push out all of the bad things in my life. When my eyes settle on him again, I find myself smiling a bit more. "Is that so, Grey Davis?"

Grey slowly gets closer to me. Not by a lot, but it still feels like even that inch broke down whole galaxies between us. "That is very much so."

My eyes move down to his lips but jump back up instantly. *I cannot go there.* "I'm sorry you had to come here and take care of me."

Grey looks at me, his eyes soft and far from mad. "I didn't *have* to be here, I *wanted* to be here, Luan. You broke your sobriety, baby... I wasn't going to allow you to fall back into that hole you won't come out of again. In addition to that, I don't let people break up with me."

A soft smirk pulls on my mouth when I say, "If you're in love with me, Grey Davis, you can just say it."

Grey chuckles, then lays his okay hand on the back of my neck and pulls me right to him until his lips touch mine.

My heart explodes at the contact. Every bad thing from the past weeks just leaves me like nothing ever happened. This one kiss, one stupid kiss makes me feel like I'm on cloud nine again.

"I still don't answer to that, Luan Hayes," he whispers and leans his forehead against mine. "We'll find a way to make this right. I just don't know how yet."

"I love—"

"We need proof of some sort, otherwise nobody would ever believe us. And you're right, me believing you isn't enough, but it's a start." Oh, well, glad to know he likes to hear me out first.

Grey straightens his back, allowing me to continue to hold his hand. I play with his fingers while I let him think.

"What *exactly* did he say to you?"

"Uh…" I'm good at memorizing things, I just need a second to remember. *"Nobody would believe I would ever try to harm my son, that I'd go to these lengths. And leave Grey and he'll stay alive."*

Grey turns his head to look out of my window, and I know the second his eyes lay on the mansion he grew up in because his dark eyes go completely black with anger. "The police don't know I'm his son."

Well, they did laugh and say the public would know if Li Ji-Hoon's son was a world-wide known ice hockey player. "Nope."

Grey's head bobs. "So, if I throw out a statement, make my association with Li Co. and its CEO public… Internet users will already draw their conclusions as soon as they dig deeper. My father's homophobic interviews are easily found, and knowing his very own son is dating a man—"

"Baby, that's a start, but it won't do much," I interrupt. "Random internet users and hockey fans won't be able to convince the police that the man who raised you now wants to murder you." There's nothing we can do. "Unless you know someone with the ability to get whatever they want, make everything possible, nothing's going to change."

Grey snaps his fingers. "Storm."

"What?" I'm pretty sure it's sunny outside, but I check anyway. I look out of the window and nope, not a single cloud in the sky.

"Not the weather." He jumps off the bed and walks out of my bedroom, I run after him. "Atlas Storm," he says like I'm supposed to know who that is.

Six Years

Grey grabs his phone—oh, I see he got a new one—from the coffee table in the living room, scrolling through it.

"And who is this man?"

"His daughter is dating my cousin. He was a huge investor in Li Co.—"

"The guy who cut ties with the company after your parents' divorce was announced?" I didn't read any of the articles, but I know my father was *very* happy about that.

"Yeah," Grey confirms. "He witnessed my dad yell at me on his birthday the year we met. Knowing that man, he has the security footage of it just in case it might come in handy one day."

"Why would he—"

"Because Atlas Storm doesn't do things half-assed. He has plans for *everything*. Triple backup plans for a backup plan. I don't think he does sketchy shit, but if he has to, I wouldn't put it past him. When I was fourteen and we were in Seattle and I first met him, I told him about my dad because Phoenix told him about it. Atlas said if I ever needed his help someday, I can be sure he'll be the one to help me out of *anything*. He's been in a million meetings with my father, and I bet most of those were taped as well. There has got to be *something* useful."

Why don't I know people like that Atlas Storm guy? My life would be so much easier.

Before he presses the call button, Grey looks at me with worry in his eyes. He lays his hand on the back of my neck and pulls me a bit closer to him, then leans his forehead against mine. "Are you going to be okay?"

"As long as you are, yes."

"Luan…" His voice is soft, and he drags my name out.

I know he's talking about the whole alcohol thing, but that's one of the less important concerns of mine. Perhaps I should be more worried, fear that the past weeks catapulted me right back to where I started several years ago, if not even farther back. Somehow, I'm not worried about that at all.

Okay, maybe a little bit.

"I guess I'll just be miserable for a bit, but I'll be okay."

"I'll be there for you no matter what."

I know he will.

Grey lifts the phone to his ear, waiting until Atlas Storm picks up.

Chapter 6

***"did you think we'd be fine?"*—Bad Blood by Taylor Swift**

Grey

January 2027

"I WAS WAITING FOR your call," Atlas says when he picks up. I didn't even know he had my phone number to be honest. "Your parents got divorced months ago."

"I'm not calling because of that." But I bet he already knew that.

"It's because of your dad."

"It is," I confirm. Can I just tell him? I barely know the man. Sure, I know his kids but the man himself not so much. "Do you remember how you said if I ever needed your help—"

"I do."

Great. "I was in an accident a few weeks ago, and as it seems, my father purposefully caused that accident to kill me," I blurt out.

"I know."

HE KNOWS?! "What do you mean 'you know'?" How the fuck would he know? Like, that man is good, so I've heard from his daughters, but he's not God.

"There was an outgoing phone call on December twenty-sixth, 2026, at 4:29 p.m. One of the Li Co. company phones was used. They're all powered by an extra system from a security company I, well, now my daughter invests in, and those phones track everything that's being done with it, even record phone calls. Your father knew, but it seems he had forgotten about it." He speaks in a low, professional tone like all this is *nothing* to him. Like this happens on the regular. "My people listen to those recordings and report back to me, or again, now that my daughter owns my company, they report back to her. Grey, I've heard the calls, knew what he was planning, and I take it you're calling because you want me to do something about your father."

I'm like ninety-nine percent sure this whole thing is mainly used for sketchy shit that happens behind the scenes of companies, but whoever invented this technology, right now, I'm really thankful to them.

"If you knew, why didn't you... I don't know, do something before I almost died?!"

"Because I only looked into it after I heard about the accident." He clears his throat. "I hope you're aware that your name will be all over the news should you really want my help."

Figured as much, but that's better than any of the alternatives, I guess.

"Allie's team will publish the recordings, but your name was never mentioned in them. Ji-Hoon only ever refers to you as 'his son', so I am asking you, before the recordings are out in the open, to give an interview about the whole accident. I'm sure you have a lot of requests for them anyway. Speaking about it, you will subtly mention that your father has not visited you in the hospital once and do say his name, also talk about your parents' divorce, and yes, you will have to name the reason for it. People have to be able to associate you with him directly and be given reason to sympathize with you to really care, but don't make it obnoxious. You're going to have to pretend as though you believe it was an *accident*, not a targeted attack to murder you, otherwise the recordings will sound unbelievable. The police will *have* to investigate, especially with the pressure from the public wanting to see your father go down in flames for what he has done."

He's going to jail.

Li Co. will die, I'm pretty sure about that.

And there will be more eyes on me than ever before.

"Do I have to mention Luan?" I ask carefully. I don't want to drag him into all this mess.

"That's up to you, but they'll talk about him either way."

I spend another ten minutes on the phone with Storm, listening to him tell me in detail what's likely going to happen, not forgetting to explain the best and also worst-case scenario.

For a moment I want to say fuck it and forget it, not do this because I'm not sure the worst-case scenario is worth the fight, but I have to stop hiding in the shadows. I have to stop letting him walk all over me and finally start to fight back. Cutting him off was only the beginning, it was me claiming my freedom, but I will never be free of him unless he's behind bars and has no chances of disrupting my peace.

And on top of that, getting justice for my mother also makes this whole thing a lot more worth it.

Chapter 7

"but you've been telling your side / so I'll be telling mine"—Skin by Sabrina Carpenter

Ivan

February 2027

"BUT WHAT IF THEY cut the entire interview to make me the bad guy?" Grey keeps on nervously bobbing his leg and up and down. At this point, he might as well have run an entire marathon with that movement alone.

It isn't often that Grey Davis is nervous, but when he is, oh boy…

I get it though. His entire life is about to be exposed to the public, every aspect, how he grew up, what happened when he was twelve because, apparently, if you mention having a bad relationship with your parents, those reporters abandon the actual reason you came in and dig deeper.

It was what Grey wanted, or Atlas Storm, whoever's the operator for this ordeal, but it doesn't make Grey worry any less about what's to come.

His whole privacy will be thrown right out of the window, so will mine because I am sort of the reason why all of this even happened, and people will dig into it to figure it out. He puts his entire career in jeopardy with this, even though he talked to his management, PR, and more people about the whole situation. Even his team is informed about what Grey is about to do, though they don't know most of the details of his past. While some of them were skeptical about Mr. Li having been the cause of all of them ending up in the hospital for at least a day or two and believe they should just get over it, the majority of Grey's teammates fully support his approach to take down his father. They want redemption for what happened after all.

This isn't just about Grey, this is about the entire team who will keep on having to fear that something will happen to them at any moment for as long as Grey is on that team. Sure, they could kick him off to ensure the team's safety, but there is a reason why Grey is their captain.

"Baby, you have the entire uncut interview to publish if that's the case," I remind him.

"Right." Grey blows out some air, then shakes out his okay hand. He's still wearing a cast, but they'll take it off in a week.

I scoot a bit away from my boyfriend—yes, yes, we're still boyfriends, we also officially moved in together like nothing ever happened. Some of my belongings are still in Malibu, but they're not so important.

Anyway, I scoot a bit away from my boyfriend then pull him down so his head rests on my lap. I push my fingers into his hair, playing with his strands while we both stare at the TV and wait for his interview to come up.

Yes, Grey made sure it's a televised interview because that shows his reactions better than a written interview ever could. It doesn't really matter with Grey because the only expressions he ever shows to the public are grumpy and grumpier, and his voice barely gives anything away either. It still makes more sense this way, I guess?

"I hate this," he mutters under his breath.

"What exactly?"

"The waiting." He sighs. "I hate my own voice, too, so I'm not even sure I'll be able to sit through this."

"I love your voice. And I love it when you talk, especially when you say more than two words at once. But the quiet Grey Davis is also good because he allows me to talk on and on without any interruptions, and in case you haven't noticed, I like talking."

Grey chuckles. "Really? I had no idea."

———

I turn off the TV the second the interview is over, bracing myself to comfort my boyfriend because, well, most of his trauma is now out there. He's quiet though. Grey still has his head lying on my lap, staring at the now black TV.

"Are you okay?" I know this is a dumb thing to ask.

"Mm-hmm." He sighs. "If I think this is bad, I can't wait to find out how much worse it'll be once Storm publishes the recordings in a few days."

"Look on the bright side; you'll be able to live in peace again. Genuine peace. No more fucked up father who will come for you. And, yes, okay, it might destroy Li Co., but getting justice for what your dad has done to you and your mother is far more important than that company."

My dad will be thrilled because sales for Hayesland will shoot through the roof, but this isn't about *my* dad right now.

"I know. It's just… weird, you know? For as long as I can remember, I did my best to hide my past, and now it's *there*. In a few moments you'll be able to read about it everywhere online. There'll be tons of websites talking about it, and some will question whether I've been lying. My life shouldn't be that big of a deal." Grey turns onto his back, looking up at me. "You won't run away again, will you?"

"Maybe in June. I don't know, depends on our engagement rings." I shrug, trying to seem serious but the grin on my face says anything but.

"June, huh?"

"Yup. I think five years is long enough for you to propose to me."

"You do realize that we've only *known* each other for five years. We haven't been together for that long."

I take his face into one hand, slightly squeeze his cheeks

together. "I want to be married by thirty, Grey Davis. So, unless you can manipulate time, we'll have to get engaged this year."

"Or next year. You won't turn thirty for another two years. So we could get engaged next year and get married the year after that in January."

I lean back on the sofa, letting out a heavy sigh. "No, no, this year is better. It has a better vibe to it. Get engaged this June, then get married… the year after also in June because that seems to be the only month you're off work."

"The Stanley Cup is in June."

"You know, sometimes, I wish you'd still ignore me because at least then I wouldn't get answers like *these*."

Chapter 8

"no one ever got me high like this"—Like This by Jake Scott

Grey

April 2027

MOST OF THE TEAM has been hiding inside of their houses, condos, or apartments for the past two months, all because they're trying to avoid the paparazzi that might as well be ready to commit a crime just to talk to any of us.

Much to my surprise, I received a lot more support after the recordings were released than I thought I'd get. Random people slid up into my DMs to let me know that they're feeling for me or just let me know that they're sorry for what happened. Even old business partners of my father's tried to reach out to me, a lot of them even put out statements about shit I had no idea even happened. Like that my very own father *constantly* talked badly about me at work. You know, the very place where my name didn't belong at all because I had absolutely nothing to do with Li Co.

The more people that spoke up about my father, the more pressured the authorities were to do something about it. And thank fuck for that because my father is currently in jail, though they're still discussing what he'll be charged with and how long he'll have to stay in prison. At least there's one thing I know for sure, he'll be off my family's ass now that he knows what I am capable of.

It was long overdue anyway. Someone was bound to show him that he doesn't get to walk all over everyone without consequences. It was time someone did something about him. And although even a few months ago I still thought he would never be able to do worse things than hate me for a sexual orientation, I'm sad to know he is, in fact, ready to commit murder just because things don't go his way.

People like Li Ji-Hoon would never show remorse and they do belong behind bars, locked away from everyone.

Anyway, ever since my last interview, tons of magazines, news sites, and blogs, etcetera have been trying to get me to speak about it again. Even if my lawyers suggested I didn't because it might get me in trouble, I wouldn't agree to any interviews either way. All I wanted was to feel safe again, to finally get at least some justice for what my father has done to my mother, sister, and I. Even to Moon, though he hasn't tried to contact me at all, which is fine with me.

Now that I don't respond to requests, reporters are trying to get ahold of me out on the streets, but since that doesn't happen as I've been spending the past two months locked up in Luan and I's apartment with only rare visits to my lawyers and courthouses, they're now targeting my teammates. But once again, these guys go out of their way to be as disrespectful as humanly possible until these people finally realize that there won't be any more interviews coming, especially not when they're trying to force one onto me.

"Grey Davis." Luan snaps his fingers against my forehead to which I instantly narrow my eyes at him. He laughs. "You have an exercise to finish."

Right. In order to regain my mobility in my arm the way it was before, I have a couple more months of physical therapy ahead of me. At least the doctors are positive that I'll regain all of my strength, or enough to spend a few more years on the ice.

"I don't like this one." Pectoralis stretches are annoying. Not a lot of work, but I just don't like them. They make me feel incompetent, especially on those days when even these stupid stretches seem too much for me to do.

Today is one of them.

"I know, baby." Luan presses his lips to mine. "But think about how grateful little Sage and Ash will be when you can carry them around and *not* complain about having a dead arm."

I sigh. "You really do have our entire life planned out, don't you?"

He nods. "I am open to discuss the names, but I am pretty sure that whatever you will suggest won't be nearly as good as Sage and Ash."

"I think we should go with Blue and Peach." I don't really think that, but Luan's reaction makes saying this worth it.

Luan scrunches his face up with what seems to be him trying not to look disgusted. "Really?" I nod. "Might as well go for Kid A and Kid B then."

"Kid A and Kid B has a nice ring to it."

"Oh, you think you're so funny, huh, Grey Davis?" He steps closer to me, laying his hands on my hips.

"The funniest," I answer.

Luan's face comes even closer to mine, to the point where I can feel his hot breath roll over my skin. "Maybe in another universe."

I lean forward to kiss my boyfriend, but that guy *swerves* me. "Do your exercise, and you'll get a kiss." He presses his lips to my cheek and takes two steps back.

"Rewards for a good job, I see."

"If you ever start to take your physical therapy seriously, maybe you'd actually do a good job someday. But as of now, it'll be a kiss to reward your participation."

Harsh, much. "I am injured, you're supposed to be nice to me." I wish I could cross my arms right now. Well, I can, in some ways, but it won't have the same effect when it looks wobbly and uncomfortable.

So instead, I sigh and lift my arm to a ninety-degree angle, my palm against the doorframe, ready to feel the pain that I know is about to flood my whole body.

"I'll be nice when you deserve nice. Now, twist your body."

I do. I twist my body to the outside, increasing the stretch until I can feel that stupid pain.

Apparently Luan can see the pain on my face because he slightly turns me back around then lowers my arm a bit. "Stop overdoing it. This isn't supposed to hurt."

See, it has its advantage that my boyfriend did sports medicine in college to become a PTA, so he knows his fair share of what I'm supposed to do and what not. It allows me to do physical therapy at home and only check in with my DPT every once in a while. It's also a lot more fun than having a stranger tell me what to do. However, I thought Luan wouldn't take all of this too seriously.

He does.

"I know you want to get this whole process over with but going too far too soon is only worsening your injuries." Luan lays the softest fucking kiss known to mankind to my lips, then steps back. "I know something else that might keep you motivated though."

"I can only be bribed with kisses or sex." I miss sex, okay, sue me. It's not like we're not having any, but let's just say my arm that seems to be completely useless doesn't make things very easy. Especially when Luan hates to be on top in *any* way, so we're very limited to things my arm allows us to do. But the good thing is, I broke my left arm. I am right-handed.

Luan winks, then turns around and walks toward the exit of the gym.

"Where do you think you're going?"

"I just need a little helping tool."

Oh?

"You know, when you said a *helping tool*, I thought of lube."

Luan snickers. "I know, that's why I said it."

The second I feel a pinch of pain in my arm, I drop the ball that I am supposed to press up against the wall, internally cussing myself out.

I feel so… weak. Holding up a stupid soccer ball is *nothing*, and yet it's too much for me. I hate this.

When I am about to hit my head against the wall, my boyfriend turns me around and presses another of his stupid praising stickers onto my sweaty torso, then kisses me.

I'll gladly take more of the kisses, the stickers not so much.

"Why do you even have these stickers?" I don't try peeling them off because I know if I do, Luan is going to make me do that Shoulder Pectoralis Stretch again, and I'd rather be covered in praising stickers than feel like a failure again just because I can't even hold my hand to a door frame without wincing in pain.

"Because the little kids I used to coach loved them, and I am hoping my new kids will too. Besides, praising is great for someone's mentality. It makes them feel better about themselves, even when they've done a seemingly bad job."

"I didn't know you had a praise kink." I lay both of my hands onto his hips to pull him against my body. I lower my voice. "Do you want me to call you a good boy next time I get the chance to?" I brush my lips along his jaw.

"Don't—"

"Or tell you just how *good* you're taking me?"

A quiet whimper leaves him when I push my hips into his and he can feel my growing erection. "Grey," he chokes out. "I don't know why I *always* have to remind you, but this gym has security cameras."

Although I can feel the chuckle bubbling up, I keep my face as unbothered as always. I then look up, directly into one of the cameras and wave.

Luan lets his forehead fall against my shoulder, groaning. "You're so embarrassing."

"Well, I wasn't the one to stick *good job*, *Wow!*, and *great job* stickers all over my torso."

"I have a sticker roll that says all kinds of kinky stuff. Like *Hot*, *Fuck Yes,* and *Nice Cock*. They're star shaped."

This should surprise me, I think, but somehow this makes a lot of sense. And I honestly think there's nothing Luan could ever tell me that *would* genuinely surprise me. "Please tell me you didn't accidentally buy them and hand them out before."

He laughs, lifting his head again. "No, but I did buy them when I was nineteen and drunk and… you know, maybe this is the point where I should stop myself from telling you everything for once in my life."

Nineteen. That's almost a whole decade ago, and he still has them, apparently.

When Luan tries to escape to terminate this conversation, I stop him and pull him right back into my body. "I want to know what you did with them so I can laugh about you."

"I know, that's why I refuse to tell you."

"Look on the bright side," I begin and lay both of my hands onto my boyfriend's ass, "you'll hear me laugh."

"Tempting."

"Aw, come on, baby. Be a *good boy* and tell me." Luan sighs *really* heavily as he closes his eyes, still refusing to tell me. "As your future husband, I am entitled to know. Who else would know these kinds of things about you? No one. So,… tell me."

"Wow, you really had to go there, huh?" He smirks, but despite how much he's trying not to let the *future husband* part affect him, there's still a faint blush on his cheeks.

"Sure did."

"Fine. I stuck them to myself, fell asleep, and the next morning, because, again, I was still drunk or drunk again, whatever you prefer, I forgot I had them on me and got ready for my classes. When I got to my first class that day, I was wondering why people kept staring at me, but I didn't care much either. At least until Doro found me in the hallways and asked me why I have a bunch of stickers on my neck and arms. If they had been *normal* stickers, it wouldn't have been half as bad. For the rest of my college path, people thought one of the soccer guys I—presumably—hooked up with was weirdly into stickers and praises."

I don't know what I was expecting, but it wasn't that. "But you were the guy who did it."

"Yeah, but that was honestly the least bad thing I did. I took a picture of my cock with the *Nice Cock* sticker on it and sent it to my then crush—the soccer guy, who sent the picture to his friends, who made sure to send them all around campus. But the good thing was, the picture looked like someone else took it because I had my phone upside down. Don't ask me how I managed to do that, I have no idea. So anyway, the guy's friends thought *he* put them on me and that we hooked up, mind you, he was straight as a ruler. And according to that guy, we drunkenly fucked, which I know we never did. In hindsight, I don't think he was as straight as he claimed to be because, like I said, *he* told people we hooked up when we never did. Anyway, I was hurt over his rejection, well not hurt but… you know, he didn't serve any purpose for me anymore after that, so whenever someone asked me about it, I would just say, 'Oh, yeah, Travis or whatever his name was, he was a really weird and bad lay' and people would believe me because, I don't know if you knew, but I used to be a *real* and brutally honest asshole."

I stand corrected, maybe Luan can still surprise me after all.

"I think you just traumatized me a little there."

"And I think you're full of shit, Grey Davis."

"Still you love me."

His smile widens. "Only because I feel bad for you. I mean, you fell in love with me the second you saw me. Your whole grumpy play-pretend was pretty obvious right from the start, but I figured I could do you a solid and go with it. For your own sake, of course."

I roll my eyes and step away from him to get my gym bag.

"Do you have a brother I could date instead?" *He doesn't.* "Maybe he's less… like you."

"You'd be bored out of your mind without me, Grey Davis."

Chapter 9

"lovin' you now, a little more tomorrow"—Intentions by Justin Bieber

Luan

June 2027

"PLEASE TELL ME you didn't just put the eggs into *oil*."

When Grey and all of his friends told me he didn't know how to cook, I thought they meant he was bad at it, not that he legitimately didn't know *how* to cook.

"Is that not how you boil an egg?"

"IN WATER!" I fish the eggs out of the oil with a spoon and throw them right into the trash. Sure, I could put them into a fresh pot of water, but God knows what happened inside of these eggs while they were *frying* in oil with its shell on.

"I told you we should eat the leftover Kimchi."

"I love you, baby, but I think I've had enough Kimchi in the past two days to last me a lifetime." All thanks to Miles and Emory being on vacation with the kids. I could've cooked—because I actually know how to fucking do that. Maybe not Miles-level-cooking, but I know at least the bare minimum—or, we could've ordered in, but Grey insisted we do neither.

"Fine, we can go out for breakfast." He turns off the stove and walks over to the living room. So before we accidentally burn down the entire building, I push the pot over onto a stove plate that wasn't used to let the oil cool. At least he turned off the stove, I guess.

"Maybe you should take a cooking class. Or five. Or a hundred."

"Why would I?" He grabs one of his black cargo pants from the drying rack and puts them on.

"Because you shouldn't forever rely on your best friend. He has *four* kids and a wife to feed, and sometime in the future, when we, too, have kids, that'll be *ten* people he'd cook for at least three times a day."

"Fair point. But, if I have to take stupid classes, so do you."

I smile, as always. "There's nothing I'd rather do than take cooking classes with my boyfriend."

"What about taking cooking classes with your fiancé?"

My eyebrows rise without me even noticing at first. "Fiancé?" I snort. "What happened to 'Before you get your hopes up, I will *not* propose to you this June because I know you're expecting it. *If*, and only *if* I ever propose, I'll do it when you least expect it'?"

Trust me, I've been secretly murdering him piece by piece in his sleep ever since he said this two weeks ago.

"Well did you expect it right now?" His face stays unreadable, as always. Well, not always. Sometimes his eyes show more emotion than any facial expression ever could. But right now even his eyes are… blank.

"That wasn't a proposal." I cross my arms over my chest, now pissed that Grey thinks playing with me like this is funny.

Grey reaches a hand into his sweater pocket. "Then why do I have a ring in here?" He pulls it out and just holds it up.

Before I let him laugh at me because I, once again, believed an obvious lie, I force myself to stay calm. Grey wears rings on the daily, so this one in his hand might as well just be one of the ones he already owned.

"Because you've decided April fools is now on June 30th." The corners of his mouth tug up ever so slightly. "Oh, no. You're smiling. So you *are* fucking with me."

"Not currently, but we could." He steps closer, but I instantly take a step back for no reason other than to maintain the space between us. I love Grey, I really fucking do, but joking about this is…

This is not him.

Grey wouldn't joke about *that*, he barely even jokes in the first place. Sure, he smiles more than whenever we met five years ago. Or is it six?

If we counted the years we've known each other *in*, it'd be six, but the *year* itself says five. It doesn't even matter because whether it's been five or six years that I've known the love of my life; it doesn't change the fact that Grey only ever smiles around people he trusts and loves, and even that doesn't happen often.

"If this is truly your way of proposing to me, Grey Davis, you're doing a really bad job."

Grey stands before me, eyes holding mine. "We've never done anything in an *actual* romantic way."

We haven't?

No, he's right, we haven't. Our meet-cute was fun but not romantic in any way. Our first date was rather lazy and, yes it was adorable and cute, and maybe a little romantic, but we've never been out on an actual date, which I blame on his profession.

We've spent more time apart than together, and yet somehow we're right *here*.

However, I refuse to tell my family Grey proposed to me in the least romantic way possible, so if I have to give him instructions to do it right, I will. And if that doesn't work, I might have to pretend he didn't propose by saying, *What about taking cooking classes with your fiancé?*

With my arms still crossed over my chest, I say, "I want you on your knees."

Grey narrows his eyes at me with suspicion, that is until he manages to push every sexual thought—and I know they're running through his mind—away and he realizes what I am saying.

"I don't get on my knees for anyone."

"You get on your knees for me all the time."

He sighs, and I could swear he mutters something under his breath before he actually does go down on one knee.

I smile at him so widely, that even I fear I might rip my face into two. Grey, however, looks back at me more annoyed than ever.

Finally uncrossing my arms, I gesture for him to go ahead.

Without cracking a smile, and a lowered, *bored* voice, he asks, "Luan, will you marry me?"

"I was expecting more of a speech, if I am being—"

Grey wraps a hand around my wrist and pulls me down to the floor. "I didn't even have to ask you because I know that in every universe, every scenario possible, you would always say yes. So be happy I asked and didn't just drag you down that aisle in two hours. Though, I wouldn't have to drag you because you've been ready to be my husband for months." He slides the ring onto my finger without ever receiving my approval. "Congratulations, Luan, you're now engaged. Any complaints?"

I shake my head and immediately press my lips to my *fiancé's*. It's fierce and I swear I feel this kiss in my guts. I almost shed happy tears. "If you're in love with me, Grey Davis, you can just say it."

Grey rolls his eyes, but he's now smiling. "I am in love with you, Luan Hayes."

The gasp that leaves me might as well be audible in Malibu. Instantly, I fall into Grey's arms, toppling him over. "You actually responded to it."

"I thought you might deserve that now."

"And I think we can skip breakfast, *you* deserve *that* now."

Grey presses his lips to mine but not nearly long enough for this to lead anywhere. "Or we fetch some breakfast and when we come back here, we put on a movie and spend all day in bed."

"We do that every day."

He nods once. "Not for long anymore. The season starts back up in September, though practice starts a little earlier than that."

"Your doctors cleared you?"

"Yeah, but they advised me to take it slow. No hardcore exercises, and I should limit brutality on the ice to once a game at most."

I snort a laughter. "We both know that won't be happening."

"Right?! I told them there's a higher chance that I'll break my arm again than *limiting* me pushing someone against the boards or being pushed against them."

"You know, you could assist me. My kids would love you."

Grey shudders with disgust. "No thank you, I'll stick to ice hockey."

"Saying you hate soccer is like saying you hate *me*!" He didn't *say* it, but the shudder of disgust implied it, besides, I know Grey isn't much of a soccer fan. That man tried talking me into coaching hockey instead. I still can't skate.

"Well, I do hate you."

The old Luan would've stood up from the floor and ran away, or tried fighting Grey, put him down, but now I just smirk. "So much that you want to spend the rest of your life with me."

"I guess even someone like me could use a little sunshine every now and then. I mean, I could technically go outside for sun, but that seems dangerous. The sun could burn off my entire skin."

If I told anyone that Grey Davis is anything but the stern-looking bad guy he pretends to be, nobody would believe me. But that's alright because at least that way I get to have one side of Grey that nobody else sees. Sure his friends know this side of him, but they're more like family, and I always liked sharing secrets with family.

"Now, get off me. We're getting married in two hours."

"WHAT?!" I'm back up on my feet in seconds, but not because Grey told me to get up. I stare at him with huge eyes, telling myself that he's joking. Surely he is.

I watch Grey get off the floor, taking his sweet time before he even attempts to give me an explanation. "If you don't want to, that's fine, but I figured we should elope *today*, obviously without telling anyone. You'll still get a wedding in a few months or a year, I don't know how long planning a wedding to your expectations takes, but since you want to get married *before* turning thirty, we won't have to rush anything that way."

I think I just fell even more in love with my fiancé, or apparently very soon-to-be husband.

Clearing my throat and shaking off *some* of my nerves, I say with as much calmness as I can offer—so barely any calmness at all, "Alright, let's get married then."

Chapter 10

"I'm in love now"—Kiss Me by Ed Sheeran

Grey

November 2028

WHEN LUAN SAID he wanted a not-all-that-typical wedding, I didn't think he meant making one of my best friends a flower girl.

I suggested having two of the kids do it, so basically Brooke and Eden because Kieran, Colin and Lily's son, and Jamie, Aaron and Sofia's son, are too young. The twins Miles and Emory had at the beginning of last year are too young as well, and they're a few months older than Kieran and Jamie.

Eden didn't want to do it because he's afraid of crowds, but Brooke agreed immediately, *if* Reece got to do it with her.

We had two flower girls, or one flower girl and one flower boy, but either way, we had two. Until Luan decided that Colin should most definitely be the third to do the job. I know my husband has a thing for all things coming in threes, but my best friend, seriously? Of course Colin agreed in less than a heartbeat, said he even had an amazing idea how to do it. He was also the only one who would've ever thought to agree without any complaints.

Brooke and Reece went first, *she* did an amazing job spreading rose petals, and she looked cute doing it. Then again, Brooke's my little princess, so whatever she does, no matter how bad of a job it might ever be, she'll excel in my eyes.

Reece was okay, too, I guess.

Anyway, now that Brooke and Reece are done, it's Colin's time to shine, and shine he does.

Colin comes *jumping* through that door like a little girl—mind you, we're on a soccer field and he demanded we put up an arch with some sort of door for this very moment—, wearing a white tank top paired with a white tutu. And fairy costume wings. I almost choke on the air when the image of twenty-one-year-old Colin in that very same outfit flashes back into my memory like a shooting star. At least now he's not wearing skates and a helmet, however he's wearing ballerina shoes and a crown, so I don't know which one is better.

He dances down that aisle like he has no care in the world, like he's not embarrassed by any of this at all, throwing rose petals around like he was born to do it.

All of Luan and I's guests are cheering Colin on, laughing, whistling as though they're at a live striptease show. The music he chose isn't helping the situation either.

Had I known my 'official' wedding day would turn into this, perhaps I would've tried talking my husband out of it. I mean, we've already been married for a little over a year anyway.

When Colin's finally done with his show, he walks up to me even though he wasn't technically supposed to do that, I think.

"Aren't you cold?" It's snowing and we're outside—why am I even asking? He spends most of his days in an ice hockey arena, on the ice. We're all used to the cold.

Colin shrugs. "I thought you were, so I brought some heat." *Of course.* "I have not seen you smile even once today. Shouldn't you be happy?"

"I am happy," I say, my voice monotonous.

"Really? Because you look like you're about to run away. Well, either that or you have to pee really badly."

"I'm about to run away from *you*."

"Fair enough." He laughs, then slaps me on the back before he turns around to stand by his wife. I would've loved to have him as one of my groomsmen, but since he already had a job, I refused to give him another. Not even Miles got two titles, he's my best man and that's it.

Then Luan comes walking toward me, though he gets distracted by the snow for a hot second. I still can't believe that last year was the first time he's seen snow. He looks at me, stopping in his tracks, then slowly lifts his arm only to end up flipping me off.

It's moments like these that I wonder why I ever married him in the first place, but then I think about what my life would be like without that weird guy in my life and suddenly, getting flipped off every other second, or having been forced to put up yellow decorations in our apartment doesn't seem half as bad anymore. I still think black interiors and yellow decorations don't fit all that well, but then again, people would say the same about my relationship, and we make it work anyway.

Nope, I cannot compare interior design with my relationship, that's as wrong as saying soccer is better than ice hockey.

When Luan finally stands before me, I feel a little relieved because I know this whole thing will be over soon. I really don't like the attention, having everyone stare at me. I wouldn't say we have a small number of guests because our whole circle is bigger than what I ever thought my social circle would be, but at least there aren't any truly unnecessary people here. Well, apart from my sister's boyfriend.

Luan leans into me, not to kiss me I realize. "Congratulations, Grey Davis, you get to marry me a second time. There aren't a lot of people who are awesome enough to marry me even once."

"So, how many husbands do you have?"

I expect everything to come out of Luan's mouth. A number somewhere between one to a million, but what comes instead leaves me speechless. "Two. You and Miles. I get the feeling I married him the second I married you."

I don't get to agree or disagree because the officiant gets impatient. "Shall we?"

I turn to look at him like he just ruined my whole day with that stupid question. I mean, we're paying that guy to be here, so he might as well be patient enough and let me and my husband have a private conversation before we get started.

"Just so you know, I didn't prepare any vows because I refuse to offer my friends free ammo to make fun of me," I tell my husband, then nod for the officiant to go ahead.

Luan chuckles, then pulls out a piece of paper from his sweatpants.

Oh, did I mention that we're not even wearing a suit? Luan insisted we wear something comfortable, something that's unusual for a wedding, so we're wearing our matching hoodies, his yellow, mine dark gray. He's wearing white sweatpants while I wear black cargo pants.

When for most weddings the guests aren't allowed to wear white, we made the rule that nobody is allowed to wear black or yellow.

Luan unfolds the paper. "Good thing I found your vows this morning. I'll just read them out for you." He taps a finger to the first line and clears his throat. "I vow—"

"We didn't even start the ceremony yet," the officiant interrupts.

Luan drops his arms, laughing. "Right. You may proceed. Or start. Wait, should I walk down that aisle again? Should we just start over from like the *very* beginning? Brooke and Eden could—"

I press my lips to Luan's, shutting him up.

As usual, we're doing everything with a little extra confusion on top, even getting married.

Epilogue

"and I'm not scared to say those words, with you, I'm safe"—Falling Like The Stars by James Arthur

Grey

January 2034

"BUT LIKE, DON'T TELL Mom, okay, Uncle Grey?" Eden jumps off the couch, ready to go give his "girlfriend" a visit at nine p.m. If he thought I'd let that happen, he thought wrong. Eden's only twelve. Correction, he's still eleven, turning twelve this September.

Honestly, I'm not even sure Miles or Emory know Eden's having somewhat of a crush on this girl in his English class. Unlike Brooke, Eden tells neither of his parents anything. Although Brooke is turning seventeen this year—yes, *seventeen*—she tells Miles every single detail about her life. She doesn't know how to keep her mouth shut.

The good side to that is, Miles not once had to worry about her because he always knows where she's going. But I don't think he wants to know about everything his daughter does. I mean, Brooke even tells him about her bathroom breaks at school, or how Reece and her snuck out of class just to make out in the hallway.

It's a miracle Miles didn't pull Brooke out of school and far away from Reece the second he learned that Brooke's now dating him, though I suppose we all knew it was coming anyway.

But Miles isn't me, so I can imagine he somewhat likes

knowing most about his daughter's life. I, on the other hand, when I picture Sage coming up to me in twelve years only to tell me she skipped one class to make out with her partner, I'd most definitely throw that person and her into jail myself. Don't know what for, but I'll find something.

My husband would probably cheer her on though.

Oh, Sage.

Luan and I were *extremely* lucky when we finally chose to have kids. Although we planned to adopt, we decided to try a surrogate first. Okay, it was only because Luan desperately wanted either a son or daughter that looked like me, God knows why, but I said if he gets a mini me, I want a mini him. And so here we are.

We wanted them to have the same biological mother, so we decided the first baby should be biologically Luan's since he's older than me. Only by a year but who cares?

He initially wanted a boy first, but Sage definitely didn't give a fuck about that. After her, we had to pray to everything holy to get a boy next only so we could make use of the names Luan gave them both ages ago. We wouldn't have cared either way, but I am glad we have a girl and a boy now.

Sage turned four today, and Ash is turning three in May.

"Henry will tell your parents when he sees you leave the building at this hour," Luan reminds Eden the second he's by our front door, about to leave. Henry's one of the people by the front desk who has been asked to report back to Emory and Miles should they ever spot Eden leaving the building sometime after six.

I have the slight feeling that Kieran and Jamie will be just like Eden, simply because these two love everything Eden does. If they could, they'd put up his picture on a shrine. Also, Eden keeps teaching his two younger siblings how to *not* listen to what their parents have to say, and Elliot and Nova do their best to teach Kieran and Jamie.

Sage and Ash won't be like that, I don't think. They're scarily like Luan and me. Sage *talks* so awfully much, ever since she knew how to. I never thought there could ever be someone who talks more than Luan, but I was wrong because our daughter sure can.

Ash is quiet. He observes a lot, doesn't speak much. To be fair, he's only two and most of what he says is unintelligible babbling, but I do think he's way too quiet for a two-year-old.

"You are supposed to be the cool uncles, so help me sneak out, please."

I shake my head, as does Luan.

"You're eleven, Eden," I remind him. "Now, go back home and ask Brooke if she would like to take you to the ice cream parlor. I doubt she'll say no to ice cream, and that way you'll get outside at this hour."

Luan slaps me, tsking disapprovingly. "Don't find stupid loopholes for him, Grey Davis."

Eden rolls his eyes. "Reece is here, he stays the night, which means she will say no."

It still surprises me every time Miles allows Reece to spend the night. As far as I know, Colin dedicated *hours* to telling his brother the dos and don'ts for his new relationship the second Brooke announced they were trying out the "being a couple thing" about two years ago. Ever since that day, the number of sleepovers was cut in half and Miles keeps giving Reece a heavy dose of side-eye whenever he's around.

"It's not a loophole," I tell my husband, then lean into him and lower my voice so Eden would hear. "But Sage and Ash are *finally* asleep, and we deserve some alone-time."

"Alone-time," he repeats back to me, amusement in his voice.

"You can tell me when you want me to go home because you'd rather watch TV by yourselves," Eden chimes in. Ah, I guess kids really do hear everything they shouldn't hear. "Mom and Dad do this *all* the time. They're always like *Go to your room, Eden! You can't just throw your Lego's from the balcony and then—* Wait, never mind, wrong scenario. The point is,

Uncle Grey, I prefer to watch TV on my own as well. At least then I don't have to watch those princess shows Brookie always watches, or the kids channel. I'm a big boy now, I no longer even watch Paw Patrol."

Without giving either Luan or me the chance to speak, Eden's out the door, saluting us goodbye before he closes the door and disappears.

"I bet twenty bucks he watches Paw Patrol whenever he has the TV to himself."

I chuckle and wrap my arms around Luan's neck, pulling him in for a kiss. "I'm not taking that bet."

"Why not?" His eyebrows fall with disappointment.

"Because you'd win."

A victorious grin pulls on the corners of his lips. "I always win."

"I beg to differ."

"No, it's true," he vetoes. "I hit the jackpot in life."

Inch by inch, I nudge Luan to lay back on the couch. "How so?"

My husband drags out a sigh. "Because I made you fall in love with me. And now we're married and have two kids. There's no way you could ever run from me again."

"Maybe I made you fall in love with me."

Luan wraps his arms around my torso, humming a no. "Nobody likes rude ice hockey guys who barely smile."

"You do."

He grins. "I could potentially think of *one* guy I might like a *liittllee* bit. But I'd really have to dig deep in my brain to even find his name."

"I can help you with that." I press my lips to his cheek. "I believe his name starts with a G."

"Oh?"

"It might even end with a Y." I kiss down his neck. "First name should be Grey."

"Sounds familiar." His voice comes out as a whisper, shaking.

"Does it?"

"A tiny bit, yes."

"Last name Davis. Ring any bells?" Before I let him answer, I plant a kiss on his lips.

"Oh! He's the guy who has way too many expectations for our house. Like a garden that can't be too big but not too small either. Or a spare bedroom that must be cool enough for guests, but also kids because God forbid Sage and Ash's future friends spend the night in their bedrooms."

I lay my head down on his chest. "Speaking of the house, Aaron said he'll have all four plans ready by the end of the week."

Aaron decided he wanted to build a house for his family as they needed more space. At first, we were all a little bummed out because Aaron and Sofia will move away from us, but then Colin had this brilliant idea.

There were six houses for Sale on one street, so all four of us bought one and had them torn down so we could build ourselves new ones to our liking. Aaron is putting his college degree in use and promised to make the plans himself, so we'll get everything we want. If possible, that is.

Luan and I decided on something on the modern side, black exterior with huge windows and a flat roof. It won't be too big because that'd be a waste of space and money. We only need three bedrooms as there won't be any more kids for us, but we decided on four bedrooms anyway just in case we might have a guest over to spend the night.

It'll still take a little while until we can move in there, but I'm excited for it.

I had one request. I want a pond in our backyard because I hope it'll freeze over thick enough that we can skate on it. To be completely honest, my first suggestion was a small ice rink, but my husband said no, so I'm settling on a pond.

"Hopefully Sage and Ash will like their new bedroom," Luan says.

"I love it, Papa!"

I don't have enough time to see where Sage is hiding because a second after she made herself known, she's throwing herself on top of me, giggling.

"Aren't you supposed to be asleep, Peach?" I ask, only for my daughter to fake snore in response.

"She's fast asleep," my husband lies, and I'm pretty sure he just winked at her as he does very often when they're teaming up against me.

"Are you asleep, Sage?"

She giggles again. "Yes, Daddy."

"You sure? Because if you were, you wouldn't be talking."

Sage snores once more. "I asleep-talking, Daddy." Ah, yes, of course. So very stupid of me to assume she was awake. "But can I sleep in your bed?"

Sage slides off me, and I sit back up and pull that little curly headed monster junior into my lap. I cock my head at her, internally sighing at the sight of her tousled hair.

Luan said it's for the best if she doesn't sleep with her hair down, so he always puts it up in some cute bun or braids, I think. Tonight, I got her ready for bed because Luan was at work, but honestly, I still don't really know how to handle her hair, which is why Luan usually does it. And clearly, I've done an awful job because her hair is down… and *very* fluffy. I'm learning though.

"You brushed her hair, didn't you?" Luan chuckles as he sits up.

"Yup, Papa. Daddy brush my hair and I say, 'No, Daddy. Papa says never brush my hair when I sleep' but he didn't listen and brush my hair anyway." She shrugs.

Sage hasn't reminded me of that even once. Sometimes I just forget about what happens to curly hair when you brush it, and yes, I could've stopped brushing it after I realized, but then I thought it'd look weird if Sage had *one* brushed strand of hair and the rest of her head is all tight curls.

Maybe in a year or two I'll have it down. Hopefully.

Six Years

Either way, I frown at my daughter for ratting me out to Luan without having a reason to do so, but she starts to laugh, then frowns right back at me.

Luan sighs extra heavily. "Let's go fix your hair, Peach." He holds his arms open, and Sage instantly climbs over me and right to Luan. When he stands, he glares at me as madly as he can and walks away.

Especially at moments like these, I am more than thankful that I chose myself over family for once in my life, that I fought and took my own happiness into my own hands. And although I might've lost a really shitty father, one sibling, and a few other family members along the way, I now have a way better family. A family who loves me for who I am, including not smiling all that often and making it a joke more times than they take my expressions seriously.

If someone had told me twelve years ago that I'd be living maybe a tad too close to my best friends who are more family than *friends* by now, and all of us are happily married with kids, I wouldn't have doubted it. But if they told me I'd be married to Luan, someone who was never supposed to happen, someone who couldn't be more unlike me, that I would've questioned.

There is something I've learned along the way though, even when I always thought I knew everything about life already.

You'll never truly live until you live for yourself. If you let others dictate who you are, make choices for you, you'll never be happy. There's always going to be people talking about you, not liking what you do, who you are, trying to drag you down, so you might as well say fuck you and provoke them a little more by loving yourself and being *you*.

People will love you, and the ones who don't aren't worth your time anyway.

The End

Acknowledgements

To my mom—Thank you for doing everything in your power to make sure my brothers and I felt more loved than anything. Thank you for making sure we never had to hide any side to us, because we knew you'd accept us no matter what or who we become. Thank you for your support even when you knew right away that it would be a mistake, but you'd rather watch us learn from them than keep us from the experience.

Also, I know I'm your favourite child, so you can stop saying you love my brothers as much as you do me. As your only daughter and middle child, I have the right to be the favourite.

To Dorothy-Jane Hausmann—You're welcome for naming a character after you (not like I had much of a choice). On a serious note, thank you for your friendship. It's still kind of crazy how a school change and a chemistry lesson can form a friendship like ours. We may not speak a lot or even see each other that often since we graduated, but I know I can always count on you to be there when I need someone.

To Laura—Go read my books. (Written in 2023 just so you know because you'll probably read this in like 2033)

To my Beta Readers—Thank you for your honest feedback and making this book the best it could've been with your advice.

To everyone out there stuck in the closet—Keep going at your own pace! And if times get tough, know there's always going to be at least one person who will welcome you with open arms.

To Joel Böhm—Once again, thank you for helping me with some of the ice hockey aspects. Truthfully, I only understood half of what you told me, but I appreciate it.

To certain family members of mine—go to therapy, please.

Printed in Great Britain
by Amazon